REIGN OF FOUR

BOOKS 1 & II

JAKE BIBLE

A PERMUTED PRESS BOOK

ISBN: 978-1-61868-537-7

REIGN OF FOUR
Book I and Book II

Cover art by Dean Samed, Conzpiracy Digital Arts

Permuted Press, LLC
275 Madison Avenue, 14th Floor
New York, NY 10016
permutedpress.com

REIGN OF FOUR

BOOK I

Act I

A Young Master Rises

"While it is the current trend to think back on the early days of our civilization as barbaric and primitive, considering the propulsion drive hadn't even been rediscovered yet, I cannot stress enough that we wouldn't be the Unified Stations if we did not have the groundwork laid out for us by such luminary monarchs as Alexis I and Alexis III of Station Aelon.

Without them the concept of passenger freedom would still be a punchline to the jokes told by stewards and stewardesses in parlors and banquet halls."

—Dr. D. Reven, Eighty-Third Archivist of The Way

"For Evil is not hidden, but staring us in the face. To hide from it is to shame oneself and our Dear Parent Helios. We must look straight at Evil and declare to ourselves, and the System, that only Helios can sway us. And when swayed, it is for Good alone."

—Book of the System 9:14, The Ledger

"Family. That is who we can and must trust. But what defines family? Blood? Lineage? Close quarters? Are we not all family on a station? Perhaps trust comes first, then family sorts itself out."

—Journals of Alexis III, Mistress of Station Aelon and its primes

Chapter One

Turquoise.

That is all the Minor of Aelon Station, Alexis Teirmont, could see as he stared up at the sky above him. His eyes were dazzled by the cloudless sky that only appeared above The Way Prime, while the rest of the planet was covered in Vape clouds so thick that barely anything besides breen crops could grow.

Helios.

A planet ripped apart by the Cataclysm, sending its inhabitants fleeing to orbiting stations, artificial planets in of themselves, so many millennia before.

A planet that leaked Vape—a gas that fueled everything from the shuttles that launched from The Way Prime to the very rotational drives that kept the stations spinning with artificial gravity.

The planet had once been covered by a pristine ocean with one central continent, but after the Cataclysm became a world of boiling, poisonous seas and fractured land masses known as the primes.

Helios.

A star. *The* Star.

Helios.

A solar system. *The* System.

Helios.

A god. *The* God.

Everything Alexis had learned through his young life on Station Aelon, and occasionally down on Aelon Prime, whirled through his head as he stared at that impossible turquoise. That color held him, spoke to him, taunted him. It was a color he had fought for, but in the end realized it was too much and had to give in, just as the other stations gave in when The Way finally triumphed and ordered a truce.

A truce he would have to sign despite his feelings about corruption of The Way's High Guardian and gatekeepers. Those men and women may have controlled the only way on and off the planet, and used that control, along with the power of Helios, to maintain a religious hold on the stations, but they could not use it to control the essence and spirit of each individual.

Alexis had fought for that spirit; fought with men around him, men he led, men that looked to him as their minor, the heir to the crown of Station Aelon; fought and watched those men die by the hundreds and hundreds as The Way's Burdened mowed them down with superiorly fueled vehicles and weapons.

In the end, it was The Way's mastery of Vape that decided the outcome of the war, not their mastery of the people they purported to represent spiritually in this life and the next.

Alexis flinched as he felt his fingernails dig into his palms, the fire and anger still so fresh.

"Your highness?" a voice spoke softly behind him. "I apologize for interrupting."

Alexis turned and beheld the diminutive figure of Gatekeeper Clegg and smiled. He shoved all thoughts of aggression away and looked on a man who had known him almost all his life.

"Clegg," Alexis greeted the holy man of The Way. "What a treat. I wasn't expecting you to be here on the surface."

Clegg, a man twenty years Alexis's elder, smiled softly and nodded to the young minor and heir. He drew back the dark grey hood of the obligatory robe all gatekeepers of The Way wore and stood tall, which still put him a good foot shorter than Alexis's nearly seven foot height.

"Greetings, your highness," Clegg said. "It has been a long time since I have set foot down on The Way Prime. I must admit I enjoy the station life much more. The gravity on the planet can feel so oppressive."

"Yet it builds one's strength, don't you think?" Alexis grinned, puffing out his chest. "Once I return to the artificial gravity of the station I'll feel like a god. My muscles won't know what to do with the slightly lesser weight of space."

"Yes," Clegg nodded. "I see your point. Although it borders on blasphemy."

The gatekeeper looked into Alexis's eyes for a long few seconds, making the minor a tad uncomfortable. It was not polite to stare at an heir to a station's mastership. Nor was it prudent to stare at a Teirmont, many of which had been known throughout history for their volatile tempers.

"You have something on your mind, Clegg." Alexis frowned. "Unburden yourself, old friend. You know we can always speak as equals when alone. You helped raise me almost as much as Father did."

"Yes, your father was a great parent as well as master of station," Clegg replied. "He will be forever loved."

"I think you exaggerate about his role as master of station," Alexis laughed. "While it is true he has been a loyal and loving parent, his leadership as Master of Station Aelon has left a lot to be desired." Alexis spread his arms. "Otherwise I would not be down here signing the Treaty of the Primes. But, again to my father's credit, he does know how to delegate. It has given some too much power on Station Aelon, but it has also allowed me to learn the duties of master well before I am forced into the role."

Gatekeeper Clegg did not respond, but only frowned deeper. He swallowed hard, looked about the sparse quarters The Way had assigned to Minor Alexis, found the water pitcher, and quickly hurried over to pour a glass. Alexis watched him with amusement, well used to the gatekeeper's penchant for melodrama. The older man gulped at the water as if he hadn't had a drop in ages and Alexis had to cover a condescending grin with his hand.

"Speak your mind, Clegg," Alexis said. "Unless it is to tell me that the High Guardian has negated the truce and Aelon is at war once again. But who will we fight this time? Not The Way, since your burdened handed us our helmets. Station Thraen? Haven't they played us against each other enough? Talks have been solid regarding our lease holdings on their prime, so I do not think it is them. What, gatekeeper? What is the trouble?"

"Your highness," Clegg began then stopped as he poured another glass.

Alexis strode to the holy man and gripped him gently by the wrist.

"Out with it, Clegg, now," Alexis said. "I think you have primed the pump enough. And Helios knows that once primed, that pump needs no more encouragement."

"True indeed," Clegg smiled weakly. "I have been known to prattle on once I get going."

"Then prattle," Alexis prodded. "Spill what it is you must say."

The gatekeeper motioned for Alexis to sit on one of the few luxuries in the quarters, a high-backed chair, fully upholstered in breen fabric and stuffed with spun breen fiber. It was not adorned with patterns such as the furnishings on Aelon Station, but it did allow Alexis the illusion of the small comforts of home.

Once seated, Gatekeeper Clegg continued to stall, his eyes roaming the quarters, taking in the plain grey metal walls, the skylight above, the less than simple furnishings. He looked at the dark grey metal chest of clothing the minor had brought down to the planet. It held trousers and thick tunics, undershirts, and socks, several pairs of heavy breen gloves and an assortment of caps. To the side were the minor's weapons—a long blade, two short blades, and a handheld sling with packets of sharp flechettes stacked next to it.

Alexis sighed loudly and sat back in his chair, crossing his long, muscular legs that gave him the nickname the entire Station Aelon knew him by—Longshanks. Alexis was not a fan of the name.

"Clegg," Alexis barked, his patience gone. "I said out with it and I mean out with it."

The gatekeeper turned his attention back to the young royal and sighed.

"Your father has died, your highness," Clegg said quickly. "You are being recalled for your coronation as the new Master of Station Aelon. The master is dead, long live the master."

Clegg took a knee and lowered his head, showing the shaved X on top of his scalp. Alexis's eyes focused on the shorn pattern of the X as a million thoughts ran through his head.

"That's why you addressed me as 'your highness,'" Alexis said finally. "I caught the mistake, but didn't say anything as I know you get your titles mixed up at times. I was just happy you hadn't said it in front of Father, as you know how he gets so angry at the misuse of titles."

Gatekeeper Clegg looked up and furrowed his brow.

"I am sorry for your loss, your highness," Clegg said. "It must come as a shocking blow."

"It does and it doesn't," Alexis said. "How did he pass? No, let me guess. He was crushed by a beam as he insisted on helping one of his construction crews rebuild yet another deck."

"He passed in his sleep, your highness," Clegg replied. "A peaceful way was his end."

"Ha," Alexis laughed. "I know that must have sent his ghost into such a rage!"

Clegg tried to smile, but couldn't, his mind not understanding the young minor's, and suddenly master's, reaction. Alexis saw the look on the gatekeeper's face and dropped the smile, his hand reaching out and patting the holy man on the shoulder.

"Forgive me, Clegg," Alexis says. "Helios must think I am a monster to react such a way to the news of my father's passing."

"Helios does not judge those that are pure of heart," Clegg responded. "Judgment is for the wicked and evil of intention."

"I thank you for that reminder," Alexis said. "And as explanation, I knew Father wasn't going to be long for this system. His servants have been keeping me informed of his failing health for many months now."

"They have sent you word? Even down here on the planet?" Clegg asked, surprised by the information. "What else have they told you, your highness?"

"Nothing of station importance," Alexis replied. "Those secrets of station are not for my ears. Although, I guess they are now." Alexis waved his hand. "But never mind about the servants. They only told me of my family's health, especially my father's and Eliza's. I shall be adding another heir to the Teirmont line soon. Or, Eliza shall be, since I have already done my part."

"Yes, your highness, congratulations," Clegg said and stood. He glanced back at the chest of clothes and stack of weapons. "Will you need assistance with packing?"

"Assistance?" Alexis said. "Not yet, no. Once the Treaty of Primes is signed and business is concluded then I'll be ready to depart. Thank you for being the one to tell me, Clegg. I do appreciate that."

Alexis stood and clasped the gatekeeper on the shoulders then brought him in for a strong embrace, pressing the older man's cheek into his chest. He slapped the man's back twice then pushed him away, nodding at him in gratitude.

The gatekeeper frowned deeply and his brow furrowed even more until it looked as if the holy man's face would split in two.

"I am sorry, your highness, but you do not understand," Clegg said. "You are to return to Station Aelon today while the planetary rotation is in synch. To delay would mean a full rotation before you could leave the planet. I can assist you with the packing, but we must depart the Way Prime within the hour."

Alexis took a step back and watched the old gatekeeper. The minor's generally easy, affable nature was quickly replaced by a look that those close to the Teirmonts knew all too well.

"I have to sign the treaty first, Clegg," Alexis said. "Otherwise so many hundreds of loyal Aelons will have died for nothing. This treaty establishes the first hard and fast rules of trade between the stations, their primes, as well as the planetary regulating nature of The Way beyond spiritual guidance and shuttle launches."

"But, your highness, your father has died," Clegg said. "Surely that is of greater importance than—"

"If I am to be the new Master of Station Aelon then I cannot let my personal grief overpower my duty," Alexis said. "I will mourn my father, and prepare for my coronation, as soon as the treaty is signed and I know the future of all Aelish people is secured."

A twitch at the corner of Clegg's left eye caught Alexis's attention, but he said nothing.

"Your highness, I must protest—" Clegg began.

"Protest away, gatekeeper," Alexis interrupted. "But it will not change my mind. I sign the treaty with the other delegates and then I return to Station Aelon. I know it means another week here on the planet, but that will give me time to return to Aelon Prime and see the homeland before I return to the station and my blood duty. Once I am master, Helios knows when I can return to the planet and Aelon Prime again. The delay before rotational synch couldn't be more perfect."

"Yes...of course, your highness," Clegg replied, bowing slightly as he backed towards the door. "As you see fit."

"Oh, knock it off, Clegg," Alexis grimaced. "No need to kowtow to me. You've seen me standing in a station passageway with my trousers soiled with my own urine after my uncle nearly shot me with a sling. You were even the one to clean me up. And not just on that occasion."

The gatekeeper winced as if the memory caused him physical pain.

"But those days have passed, your highness," Clegg responded. "Whatever history we have shared is no more. You will be crowned Master of Station Aelon and Gatekeeper Lewis will be the new representative from The Way." He sighed and reached back, grasping the metal handle of the door. His fingers curled tightly around the pocked and pitted surface of the metal loop. "I will inform the delegation that there will be no delay despite the unfortunate circumstances. The signing will remain on schedule as planned."

"Yes, it will," Alexis nodded. "I will be there at seventeen-hundred with everyone else and will conduct business just like everyone else. Please inform Gatekeeper Lewis of my intentions and to spread the word that I expect the treaty to be signed before any ceremonies of condolence commence. Can you do that for me, Clegg?"

"Gladly," Clegg replied as he pulled the door open and stepped into the passageway. "Until then, your highness."

The holy man bowed once more and backed from the quarters, shutting the door in his wake.

Alexis waited for several minutes before turning his eyes back to the skylight and the sky beyond. He watched the clearness and shook his head back and forth, stunned by its beauty. He knew once he left The Way Prime to travel to Aelon Prime for a last look at the ancestral lands, he would see only Vape clouds and murky oceans. He knew he had to enjoy the wonder above him while he had the chance. His whole world had changed in the blink of an eye.

As if in answer to that thought, he suddenly had to struggle to blink back tears that filled his eyes. The large, heavy drops could not be stopped and they rolled down his ruddy cheeks to his chin where they hesitated, then fell so many feet to the hammered metal floor of his quarters.

*

"You're standing on the hem of my dress," the girl snapped, her brown eyes glaring daggers up at Alexis. "Move it."

"Sorry about that," Alexis laughed, taking an exaggerated jump to the side. "Being as tall as I am, I sometimes forget to look down at where I'm walking."

"Being as old as you are, you'd think you'd have learned by now," the girl responded.

"Ha!" Alexis laughed again and knelt by the girl. "I'm only twenty-three, you know. Still young."

"I'm eight," the girl smirked. "And you are going to die way before me, so that makes you old."

"Meredith!" a woman screeched as she wove and diplomatically shoved her way through the throng of envoys, representatives, royalty, and nobility representing the six stations of Helios and their planetary primes. "There you are! I have warned you about letting go of my hand while on the planet!"

"Your hand is sweaty and stinks of breen oil," the girl, Meredith, barked. "I don't need a nurse anymore. I'm eight." She looked over at Alexis and turned up her nose. "But you can get rid of this old geezer. He's bothering me and was rude."

"Sir!" the nurse exclaimed as she came upon the two. "Do you know who you are addressing? This is Meredith Herlect, third daughter of the Master of Station Thraen, Paul the Third."

"That's a lot of thirds," Alexis said as he stood up, instantly towering over the woman. "My father is...was a third, as well. But I guess I'll be a first once I return home."

The nurse stared at Alexis for a split second then immediately dropped to a knee, her eyes cast down, her voice trembling as she said, "My apologies, your highness. I was not aware it was you. Please forgive me for not realizing it instantly, Master Alexis."

"Get up, nurse," Alexis laughed. "There are so many pompous faces around here, mine included. I would expect them to all start being a blur. You've done no offense. In fact, you and your ward here have reminded me just what a puffed up show this all is."

He glanced over at a group of stewards from Station Ploerv. They stood in a tight knit circle, their eyes narrowed and lips curled up at those not from their Station. Alexis looked down at the Minoress Meredith.

"Looks like they are trying to figure out which one farted," he said, giving the girl a wink.

No matter the intention of her demeanor, an eight year old girl was an eight year old girl, and Meredith couldn't help but giggle at the word "fart."

"My lady, it is time for business to start," the nurse said, hiding her own smile. "I'll take you to your quarters now."

"I want to stay," Meredith snapped.

"And one day you will," Alexis responded. "Just not today. I had to wait my turn when I was your age. Waiting is not fun." He leaned down and put his hand to his mouth in exaggerated conspiracy. "And neither are these things, really. I'd rather be out on a cutter, racing towards my prime than stuck in a meeting hall like this."

"I as well," a man said, coming up behind Alexis. "Perhaps after the signing I can invite you onto my personal cutter? We are taking a tour of the west coast of Thraen Prime."

"Minor Paul." Alexis nodded. "Good to see you. And I will take you up on that offer since I'm missing my rotational synch launch and cannot return to Station Aelon for another week."

"Why would you return so soon?" asked Minor Paul Herlect, first son and heir of Paul III, Master of Station Thraen. "I'm never in a hurry to return to those floating cans. Even with the Vape ready to cook your insides, I much prefer planetary life on the prime than station life. The day I am forced to stay up there in space will be a sad day indeed."

"Then enjoy the days you have," Alexis said, grasping Paul by the shoulder. "They disappear faster than you think."

"More reason to join me on my cutter," Paul said.

"So true," Alexis replied. "But only if your spirited sister will be there."

"Watch me try to hold her back," Paul laughed as a bell rang out, signaling the start of the treaty signing. "But, first, duty calls."

"As it always does," Alexis smiled as the minor bowed slightly and walked to his delegation's table.

"I hope to see you later, minoress," Alexis said, then looked to the nurse. "How is it you know of my father's passing, and my becoming a master, but his highness does not? Or I assume he does not. If he does then that conversation was more than weird."

"News travels fast with passengers, your highness," the nurse responded. "We have less to talk and worry about than the royalty."

"Well, I'm not so sure about that," Alexis laughed. "But maybe news means more to passengers since the slightest shift in power can upset a passenger's life, while the royalty insists on finishing lunch first before being bothered with anything."

Again the nurse had to hide her smile. She curtsied low and then took Meredith's hand before making her way from the grand hall.

"My lord? I, uh, mean, your highness? Shall we take our seats?" a short, well-fed man asked, his hands clasped across his stout belly.

The man waved his hand towards a row of chairs where the Aelon delegation waited, standing at attention until their monarch was seated.

"Of course, Alasdair," Alexis nodded.

"Your highness, it would be more appropriate to address me as Steward de Morlan," de Morlan said as he directed the new master to his seat. "The familiar can upset some of our more formal cousins."

"Almost everything upsets many of our more formal cousins here." Alexis frowned as he took his seat.

The Aelish delegation immediately sat down once the master's chair had been pushed to the table. Alexis looked left then right and nodded and smiled as expected despite his misgivings about most of the other members of the delegation.

Being the new master meant he could clean house and reassign some key posts. He knew he'd have to discuss it all with Eliza once he returned. As long as she was up to the task and not too exhausted from her pregnancy.

Alexis leaned over to de Morlan and whispered, "You have informed the gatekeepers that I want no mention of my father's death until after the treaty is signed, correct?"

"I did, your highness," de Morlan replied. "I was assured that the High Guardian would be told of your wishes."

"Good. Thank you, Alasdair," Alexis nodded, ignoring the man's eye roll at his use of the familiar name once again.

Chimes sounded and Alexis found himself back on his feet as High Guardian of The Way, Benedict XI, walked into the room, followed by a train of gatekeepers that looked as if it would never stop. The pontiff limped his way to his chair, which was more ornate and larger than any of the other seats in the room, stood for a moment then almost collapsed into the breen cushions.

He waved a hand and everyone took their seats once again.

"Welcome," Benedict said. "All thank Helios for the grace of life and gift of our souls."

"All thank Helios," the room intoned.

BOOK I

The High Guardian took a deep breath and then began his speech, one he had said a thousand times before many an official occasion.

"Helios—the One True System," he began. "Planet, Star, System, Deity. Helios is all. Helios is our God and Protector. The Dear Parent who watches over us, watches over our primes, watches over our very souls. Helios, giver of the Vape and grower of breen. Helios—the One True System. May we praise the Dear Parent and all that Helios provides."

"Praise to the Dear Parent and all that Helios provides," the room repeated.

"So long ago, our ancestors believed in many gods and goddesses," Benedict recited from memory. Half the room had to bite their tongues to keep from groaning. "Their belief in those false gods was what led to the Cataclysm; an event so violent that it ripped a continent apart into the primes, sent vast amounts of gas that would be known as Vape into the atmosphere, and forced all of humanity to flee to the safety of the stations and their orbits about the planet."

He nodded his head six times and everyone in the room did the same.

"Almost all of the knowledge of those first peoples has been lost, but we fear not because Helios provided us with a better understanding of the universe," Benedict said. "The Dear Parent gave us The Way."

"The Way," the room replied.

"Ordaining the gatekeepers as the moral and spiritual guides of all, Helios proved his intentions by allowing The Way Prime to have a clear path on and off the planet. It is the holy miracle that parts the Vape clouds only over this piece of land that shows all the ordained nature of The Way and the gatekeepers. Praise be to the men and women that keep you from sliding into evil and dying in the atmosphere."

"Praise be to the gatekeepers," the room droned.

"Helios," Benedict said quickly, ignoring the lack of enthusiasm. He raised his arms above his head and let his long sleeves slide down to his bony and age-spotted elbows. "By your mercy we live."

"Helios," the room said. "By your mercy we live."

A low noise was heard as everyone present finished the prayer by humming the deepest note they could. The sound was discordant and slightly off putting due to the differences in range, but no one cared as they knew it meant the end of the invocation.

"Thank you. I know we have important business, but first we must all bow our heads in silence for the passing of one of Helios's chosen," Benedict sighed. "Henry III, Master of Station Aelon, is no longer with us on this plane and has moved on to travel the System, his corporeal being of no use to him any longer."

Fists clenched, Alexis kept his anger under control, making sure his face was passive and open as the entire room looked to him. He gave perfunctory nods to those of stations that were once only hours before close to his rank as minor then lowered his head in silence as a set of bells rang six times. There was a long pause and then a final ring to symbolize the singularity of The Way in the eyes of Helios.

"Although you have not been crowned as of yet, Master Alexis," Benedict said once the last tones of the bells faded away. "I believe, as the only master amongst us, you should open these proceedings with some words of encouragement and wisdom."

A couple of muffled snickers could be heard, but Alexis couldn't find the sources. Again, he kept his anger in check and looked about the room.

"Thank you, your holiness," Alexis said. "I do not have any words planned, and the news of my father's passing has only reached my ears this hour, so I will keep it brief."

He took a deep breath and gathered his thoughts for a moment.

"As many of you know firsthand, my father was not a leader of any extraordinary measure," Alexis said. More muffled snickers. "He was brash, fiscally irresponsible, and aloof to many of the basic needs of being a master. His passion was for architecture and engineering, not leadership of an entire station and people."

"Helios praise his soul," de Morlan said.

"Yes, Helios praise his soul," Alexis nodded. "He will be traveling the System, I'm sure, looking for new ways to combine the molecules that bind us all."

There was some genuine laughter and Alexis smiled.

"May I propose we postpone the signing?" Minor Paul said, standing from his seat across the room from Alexis. "Your grief must be overwhelming and we would not want you to sign out of duty or duress. You were instructed as to what the parameters of the treaty must be by your father, but now you are master and can make your own decisions."

The room was silent at the interruption; all eyes moved back and forth from Alexis to Paul.

"While I thank the minor for his sentiments," Alexis said, nodding to Paul. "I do not believe any delay is needed. Despite my admissions to my father's failings, his wishes as to the future of the primes match mine in almost every way. I will gladly sign the treaty we have agreed upon, as former minor and as newly risen Master of Station Aelon. Having the prime lands on this planet secured and trade agreements in place would be the highest honor I could give my father's memory."

He waited for a response from Paul, but the minor merely bowed and took his seat.

"High Guardian?" Alexis said. "May we proceed with the signing?"

"We may," Benedict nodded, motioning for the gatekeepers in the room to move forward and provide copies of the treaty to each of the head delegates. "Please take your time to read the documents before you. Make sure the wording is as was agreed upon. If it is to your satisfaction then please adorn them with your signature and pass your document to the right. Once all copies are signed then this meeting will be adjourned and we can welcome in a new age to relations between the stations and their primes, as well as between the monarchies and The Way."

The delegates settled into their seats and began to read the many-paged documents before them.

It would be a long evening.

*

"Ahhh, free!" Paul cheered, raising his arms into the air as the royal cutter sped across the steaming ocean of Helios.

Mist rose and curled into streaks, running across the thick glass and polybreen dome that kept the occupants of the cutter from being suffocated and blistered by the planet's inhospitable atmosphere. The cutter was close to twenty feet long, with a hull that began narrow in the bow and spread into wide, arching wings that glided across the surface of the water towards the stern.

"Relax, Master Alexis," Paul said, motioning towards an empty cushioned bench across from his own. He glanced over at the small group of Aelish royal guards that stood uncomfortably across from the large contingent of Thraenish royal guards. "And tell your men to relax, as well. They make me nervous. Enjoy the sight of the Vape at night, Alexis. It is a wonder to behold." He clapped his hands together. "Tell the pilot to cut the ship's lights. We cannot enjoy the night if all we see are reflections."

"But, my lord, we would be sailing blind," a man said from off to Paul's side. "It would not be safe."

"We are in the middle of a vast ocean," Paul snapped. "What could we possibly run into? Tell the pilot now!"

"No need to put us at risk or give the pilot added stress," Alexis said as he sat down and gave a quick, reassuring nod to his guards. "I'm enjoying the ride as it is."

"You're enjoying nothing," Paul said. "Look at you. I've seen passengers with the weeping sickness have more fun than you do now."

"My father did just pass," Alexis said, taking a glass of brown liquor from a tray offered to him by one of the ever present servants. "Thank you."

Paul frowned and waved the servant away then leaned forward, his forearms resting on his knees. Dressed in a tunic of blue breen material tucked into a pair of dark green breen trousers, Paul tried to give the air of a casual commoner and not the next in line for the mastership of Station Thraen. He would have pulled it off if not for the amount of jewelry and precious metals he wore about his neck, wrists, and fingers.

"My apologies, Master Alexis," Paul said. "I forget myself when I am out on the water. I've always believed that open water is the great equalizer. It doesn't matter what our place is in the hierarchy of the stations, the waters of Helios could give a shit. If this cutter were to capsize, then we'd all boil and die in seconds, just like the servants around us. Crowned or not, we are flesh and bone."

There was a sharp hiss and then intake of breath from the corner of the dome and Alexis smiled as he saw the figure of Gatekeeper Clegg tense up. Paul heard it as well and turned to follow Alexis's gaze.

"Have I offended your sensibilities, gatekeeper? Was my use of such crude language too much for your sheltered ears?" Paul laughed.

"The gatekeeper has heard worse, trust me," Alexis said. "I believe his less than subtle objection was to your lumping royalty with commoners."

"Yes, your highness," Gatekeeper Clegg said quietly. "The hierarchy is important to the stability of the stations. Saying anything less puts the royalty, the nobility, as well as those of us of The Way, at risk for rebellion."

Paul grimaced in exaggeration and waved his hands about. "Well, we can't have that, can we?" He laughed heartily and rolled his eyes. "Not that the passengers or any denizens of our Lower Decks will ever rise up against the status quo. They'd have to learn to think first."

"You underestimate your people, minor," Alexis replied. "Societal class hardly dictates a person's intelligence. I highly doubt I am the smartest person on Station Aelon, and I am almost certain there are passengers living below the station's surface that could outthink the majority of the stewards, sector wardens, and deck bosses that cling to their supremacy."

"Ha! Alexis! You surprise me, sir. Do I detect the hint of a revolutionary hiding behind a regal facade?"

"No, Paul, you do not," Alexis replied. "I don't believe revolution will help anyone. Helios knows democracy was tried millennia ago and all it did was lead to corruption and slaughter of innocents. No, the monarchy works and it should stay in place." Alexis leaned forward, matching Paul's pose. "But maybe we should take advantage of the assets we have in our stations, and down here on the primes, and allow passengers a seat at the table. The voice of the people should be heard, at least."

"Ah...a populist then."

"Perhaps," Alexis nodded.

Minor Paul watched the young master closely, his eyes revealing nothing of his thoughts.

"Yes...perhaps," Paul responded finally. "But I'll let you be the one to tread those waters first. Thraen is stable and happy as it is."

"Of course," Alexis nodded and took a sip of his drink. "So is Aelon. But for how long?"

"Forever," Paul replied. "Helios willing."

"Praise the Dear Parent," Clegg murmured.

"Praise the Dear Parent!" Paul echoed loudly.

Alexis turned his attention to the gatekeeper then looked about the dome at the Thraenish servants, guards and dignitaries.

"No gatekeeper of your own?" Alexis asked. "It is my understanding that all ships that traverse the ocean must have a gatekeeper to bless their way."

"What? Oh, no, not this trip," Paul said. "I hate traveling with the robes. All that hissing and murmuring." He turned and smiled at Clegg. "I joke, gatekeeper. No disrespect meant. No, the truth is Gatekeeper Schoul was under the weather. A touch of the planetary trots, if you catch my drift. Your gatekeeper was kind enough to volunteer to accompany us. Although I suspect it was more to keep an eye on you than as a kind gesture to Thraen."

"Is that so?" Alexis smiled. "How nice of Gatekeeper Clegg."

The master and the holy man locked eyes for a brief second before their attention was turned to a porter ringing a bell by one of the dome entrances.

"We are approaching Thraen Prime," the porter announced. "We will be docking shortly. Please prepare to depart on the hallowed grounds of Thraen Prime. Praise the Dear Parent."

"Praise the Dear Parent," everyone present repeated.

"Hallowed grounds," Paul snorted as he stood and stretched. "My father would abandon the prime in a heartbeat if it stopped producing Vape and breen. He hates the planet that much. A station man through and through is Paul III. I, of course, love it here. No intrigue, no politics, no worthless society balls and banquets. Just Vape mining and breen harvesting. Jobs to be done and work to complete, that's what matters on the prime."

"I'd almost agree with you there," Alexis said, "if Station Aelon didn't house my family which includes my wife, children, and unborn child."

"That's right!" Paul exclaimed. "You're about to have another heir! Congratulations!"

"Thank you."

"Boy or girl? Do you know?"

"A boy," Alexis smiled.

"Your first?"

"Second," Alexis replied.

"Very good," Paul nodded. "Get that succession lined up and secured straight off. I feel sorry for Master Franz of Station Ploerv. All daughters. His brothers are circling the crown like swamp sharks, hoping to put one of their sons into the mastership when the old man finally kicks the bucket."

"You forget yourself, Minor Paul!" Clegg snapped. "The Mistress Eliza is one of Ploerv's daughters! You not only insult the Station Ploerv, but you insult the Station Aelon which she married into!"

"Calm down, Clegg," Alexis laughed. "Minor Paul didn't mean offense. He was just stating what everyone thinks."

"It's a talent of mine," Paul smiled then stumbled as the cutter lurched to the side. "What was that?"

"Felt like a rough docking," Alexis said.

The porter quickly returned to the dome, his face red with anxiety and embarrassment.

"I must apologize, my lords and ladies, but there has been a mishap," he gulped. "The dock appears to have been damaged by the latest Vape storm. We are not able to be pulled into the hangar properly. The pilot insists that we will need to don our environmental suits and walk the distance to the Thraen Prime castle."

The dignitaries protested and grumbled their dissatisfaction at the indignity of donning the polybreen environmental suits like common prime workers and being forced to risk exposure to the toxic air of the planet. Paul silenced the protests quickly with a wave of his hand.

"Excellent," he said. "I haven't had a walk outside the castle in ages. It'll do us all good to remember the power Helios has over us. Don't you think, gatekeeper?"

Clegg's eyes were focused on the sight through the dome of the castle lights far off in the distance. Paul snapped his fingers, bringing the holy man's attention to him immediately.

"My apologies, my lord, you were saying?" Clegg responded.

"It doesn't matter," Paul said. "Maybe you could broadcast a sermon in our helmets while we walk to the castle?"

"I would be honored to—"

"I was joking, of course," Paul interrupted instantly. "No one wants to be preached at while they worry about whether or not their environmental suit was inspected properly and they could be seconds away from a gruesome death, now do they?"

"No, I suppose not," Clegg replied, his voice ice and barbed wire.

"I think I have upset your gatekeeper," Paul whispered as he walked to Alexis and took his elbow. "Now, help me fetch my sister from the bridge, will you? She has always been fascinated by ships and refuses to ride anywhere but up front."

"I'd be glad to," Alexis smiled, looking over his shoulder at the fuming gatekeeper. "Lead the way."

*

"I know how to fasten it properly!" Meredith scowled as the nurse fumbled at the clasp seals around her boots. "Get off!"

"Here, let me help," Alexis said as he knelt down before the minoress. "I have a daughter about your age and I do this for her all the time."

"I said I can do it!" Meredith snapped. "You're as bad as my brother. Never letting me do things myself."

"That's what my daughter tells me," Alexis laughed and stood up. He nodded at her boots and smiled as he grabbed his gloves from his belt. "Go ahead. Show me you can do it."

Meredith scowled even harder and struggled with the clasps. Finally, after having to chastise the nurse again, she got the clasps sealed properly and an audible hiss of compression could be heard from her suit.

"See?" she sneered. "Done."

"Not quite," Alexis said, already dressed in his own suit. He grabbed a small helmet from a shelf and handed it to her. "You still have to get that settled."

Meredith looked at the bulky helmet then up at Alexis. The master tried not to smile, but he couldn't help it as he watched realization dawn on the girl's face.

"Want help with that?" he asked.

"No," she said quickly.

"Ready?" Paul asked as he came up to the two, his own helmet tucked under one arm. "Ahh, right. The helmet stage."

"You're a jerk," Meredith growled.

"A jerk that can put his own helmet on," Paul grinned. "Come on, Master Alexis; let us leave her care to the nurse. We need to chat about the lease holdings on the coast of Thraen prime."

"You mean the lease holdings that are now part of the treaty we just signed a couple hours ago?" Alexis asked.

"Yes, those," Paul said, stepping to the airlock that was surrounded by Thraenish guards. He pulled his helmet on and snapped it into place. A hiss was heard then a small internal light came on, signaling a full seal. "Ready?"

"Yes, of course," Alexis said as he situated his own helmet and spoke through the communications system.

The two royals stood by the airlock as they waited for the guards to make sure the external chamber was clear of any danger. After a couple of seconds they were ushered into the secondary chamber, but not before a quarter of the delegation, along with Minoress Meredith, joined them. Paul rolled his eyes at Alexis and turned a dial on his wrist. He tapped at the dial and indicated for Alexis to follow.

"Can you hear me?" Paul asked.

"I can," Alexis replied. "I assume this is your personal channel?"

"It is," Paul replied. "And if anyone dared to eavesdrop they would be stripped and left to the Vape without a moment's hesitation."

Alexis looked about at the group, wondering if anyone was eavesdropping, but he saw no change in conversations, reactions, or body language. Yet he didn't kid himself that their conversation was completely private. Nothing in royal life was completely private. Ever.

Claxons rang out and the outer door slid aside. Guards moved out quickly and established a secure lane for the party to walk along as they made their way across the scrim grass and gas puddles that covered the barren shoreline. They'd gone several yards before Paul spoke again.

"My father never wanted the treaty signed," Paul admitted. "He thought we were conceding too much by leasing Station Aelon mining rights to the coast of our prime."

"And what do you think?" Alexis asked. "Are you in agreement with your father?"

"Of course," Paul nodded. "A dutiful son always agrees with his father. Especially when that father is master of station."

"I didn't always agree with my father," Alexis said.

"And did you ever admit that while he was alive?" Paul asked then backtracked immediately. "My apologies. That was rude."

"But apt," Alexis replied. "The answer is no. I never publicly disagreed with him."

"Then you know my answer," Paul smiled behind his helmet's mist coated visor.

"So...why tell me this?"

"Because I want you to be prepared when the Thraen Ambassador calls on you next month," Paul responded. "He's been dispatched to Station Aelon for your father's funeral and is waiting for the official mourning period to end. I can bet he's already on the top of the diplomatic audience list. Get used to it, the man is persistent."

"That still doesn't answer why you are telling me this," Alexis said. "What do you want?"

"I want the income those leases will produce," Paul said. "Your father nearly emptied the treasury with all of his remodeling of your station, while mine has spent it on bribes and liquor. Sometimes both at the same time. At least you have a remodeled station to show for it."

"And Thraen doesn't have indebted connections with those bribes?"

"Of course, of course, but for how long? The problem with using bribes as a tactic is that anyone you bribe is dishonest enough to be bought by your enemies as well," Paul laughed. "You are buying deceit, not trust."

"I'll keep that in mind once I am crowned," Alexis said.

"Is that all you talk about? Boring stuff?" Meredith asked from only a couple feet behind them.

"Is she to be stripped and left to the Vape for eavesdropping?" Alexis smiled.

"Unfortunately, no," Paul responded. "That is out of my power." He turned quickly and grabbed his sister by the arms. "When father hears you were listening in on official business, he is going to be more than just a little cross with you."

"Father's always cross with me," Meredith replied. "That's why he sent me here with you. He didn't want me on Station Thraen mucking it all up."

"You're how old?" Alexis laughed. "What could you possibly muck up?"

"You'd be surprised," Paul snorted. "Now, get off this channel and leave us alone, little girl."

"Fine," Meredith growled. "You two are boring anyway."

Paul and Alexis watched as the girl turned and stalked back to her nurse, her suit crinkling in the night air, sending sparks here and there from the static electricity the scrim grass and Vape created.

"Where were we?" Paul asked.

"The leases," Alexis said. "I do have to bring up that Station Thraen benefits just as much from the trade agreement we have set with the Flaenish and their breen processing factories. The payments for those mine leases are not just in credits, but in tons of finished breen as well."

"Oh, I know, I know," Paul said. "And that is the only reason my father didn't outright balk at the deal." He spread his hands. "Thraen Prime is rich with Vape mines, but unlike your prime, we do not have enough good soil to grow the breen we need. It's a shame since if we could accomplish that we wouldn't need any of the other stations at all."

"But then we couldn't go on cutter rides together," Alexis grinned.

"Very true," Paul nodded. "But, let's move on from—"

He stopped talking and grabbed Alexis by the arm as two of the guards in front of them collapsed to the ground. Alexis instantly went to draw his long sword, but realized it was back at The Way Prime in his quarters with his other weapons. He could have kicked himself for the mistake.

"Down!" Alexis yelled as he tackled Paul to the ground.

A slight *tink* sounded and he realized a flechette had hit his helmet's visor. Someone was shooting a sling at them!

"Are you hit?" Alexis asked.

"No. You?" Paul replied.

"No, I'm fine," Alexis said.

Then a scream filled their ears and Alexis looked over to see Meredith crumple to the dirt.

"My lord, you have to come with us now!" a Thraen guard shouted at Paul as half a dozen men surrounded him.

"My sister! The minoress!" Paul yelled, but he was swept away by his security detail.

Others in the delegation began to panic and stampede towards the waiting airlock of Thraen Prime Castle, ignoring the collapsed royal at their feet.

"I have her!" Alexis yelled and sprinted towards the fallen girl.

He raced to Meredith, fighting against the flow of the frightened crowd. Alexis fell to his knees and tried to find where she had been hit. He quickly saw the oxygen flowing out of a hole in her suit near her shoulder. He could already see the small sparks of combustion from the mixture of oxygen and Vape and knew he didn't have long to get her to safety before her environmental suit filled with flames.

"Move!" Alexis yelled as he lifted the girl up in his arms. But the crowd was deaf, hearing only their own fear and self preservation.

He was jostled from side to side, shoved this way and that, no one caring about the Aelish royal seal emblazoned on his suit. But the crowd's disregard for his status was what saved him as he was knocked to one knee just as a long blade came towards the place his head had been a split second before.

Alexis looked up in time to see the second strike come at him and he rolled to the side, his body protecting the young minoress, from the long blade that imbedded itself in the scrim grass by his head. The new master didn't recognize the cut of the breen suit the attacker wore, but did recognize the style of the blade.

The Burdened.

The elite guard of The Way and only members of the religious order sanctified to kill without fear of eternal damnation at the center of the Helios sun.

Alexis barely had time to register that revelation before the blade came at him again. He lashed out with a hard kick to the man's knee and the blade missed its mark once more as the assassin fell to the grass. Very aware of the minoress's distress, Alexis leapt onto the man and dug his fingers up under the clasps sealing the helmet to the suit. With one tremendous yank, Alexis ripped the helmet off, exposing the man to the atmosphere of Helios and the deadly Vape.

The face he saw bubbling and blistering before him was not one he recognized and gave Alexis no clue as to who might have ordered the attack.

"Who sent you?" Alexis yelled, but the dying man couldn't hear him without the communication system in his helmet. "Tell me who ordered this!"

The man struggled under Alexis's grip and clawed at the master's hands that held him to the scrim grass. Scrim grass that was quickly covered with the liquefied skin and muscle that sloughed off the assassin. Bright purple sparks flitted around the man's eyes, mouth and nostrils as the oxygen in the blood that leaked out was ignited by Vape.

Hands grabbed at Alexis as his personal contingent of guards were finally able to fight through the crowd to get to him. They pulled him to his feet as the assassin took his last breath and his chest cavity burst open, spewing tissue and blood across the ground. Alexis raised a boot and let it fall hard on the man's skull, crushing the bone into the grass.

"The minoress!" Alexis yelled at his men. "Take her and hurry!"

"Your safety comes first, your highness!" a guard named Corbin Breach shouted.

"To Helios with my safety!" Alexis yelled. "She's dying!"

Corbin nodded and quickly lifted the girl up. "Cover him the whole way!" he ordered the other guards then took off running towards the airlock.

The Aelish Royal Guard looked at each other then at the master and closed ranks, making sure no one could get through to their monarch. They moved forward quickly, eyes cast about the area, ready for the next strike.

The night was a haze of Vape fog and mist rising from the scrim grass at their feet, making it almost impossible to discern shapes smaller than the castle ahead of them. The guards pushed the master along, never letting him slow even as he stumbled over clumps of grass and dirt. They held him by his arms and kept him on his feet, but soon half of them were no longer on theirs.

Guards fell left and right as their suits were ripped open by a flurry of flechettes. Alexis watched in horror as his men died horrible, Vape deaths. Flames filled suits as the Vape seeped in and mixed with the oxygen. The men's screams were soon nothing but gurgles from charred and roasted throats.

Two shapes came at Alexis from the fog and he reached down and picked up a dropped long blade and then a short blade. He raised the long blade just as one of the shapes rushed him, meeting his metal with more metal. The hollow clang of the blades colliding could be heard even through Alexis's helmet. He felt the impact up his arm, but didn't let the jarring pain slow him.

With one fluid movement, Alexis ducked low and jammed the short blade into the attacker's gut. The man shuddered as blood gushed and sparked from the wound. Alexis pulled the blade free then shoved the man to the side as he brought down his long blade. The helmet, with head still inside, flew from the man's shoulders and tumbled through the air.

The second attacker paused, seeing what had befallen his comrade. That was pause was his undoing as Alexis flipped his short blade in his hand, gripped it blade first, and threw. The weapon flew end over end at the second man and pierced the man's visor before he could think of sidestepping.

Alexis didn't wait for the man to fall to the ground before he took off towards the castle. He could see Corbin's shrouded back several yards ahead, but could also see shadows off to each side closing in on him. Long blade still in hand, Alexis dug deep and pushed himself as he sprinted towards his guard and the wounded minoress.

"*Down*!" Alexis roared.

Corbin hesitated, but then saw he was penned in and quickly skidded to a halt, dropping to both knees while keeping the minoress secure in his arms. Alexis reached the man just as the attackers from each side did. They turned to face the master, but neither was fast enough as Alexis lashed out, severing two heads with one swipe of his long blade.

"Get up," Alexis cried as he pulled at Corbin's upper arm. "We're almost there."

Corbin didn't say a word, too stunned to have been rescued by the man he was sworn to protect. Alexis yanked him to his feet and shoved him towards the airlock.

"Open up!" Alexis shouted as he looked about, ready for the next attack. His hand was at the small of Corbin's back and he pushed the guard on, urging him to run faster. "Open the airlock now!"

They reached the castle wall and a face appeared in the thick glass porthole of the airlock door. Gatekeeper Clegg.

"Thank Helios!" Alexis yelled as the airlock opened and they rushed inside.

Or Corbin and Meredith rushed inside. Alexis's path was blocked by the gatekeeper.

"Clegg? Move," Alexis said then saw what the holy man held.

"I am truly sorry, your highness," Clegg said as he thrust the blade into Alexis's belly. "But I know you. You will change things in ways we cannot allow."

Alexis fell to his knees, taking the blade with him. He looked up into the helmeted face of his former teacher and childhood mentor.

"Clegg..." he whispered.

"Hush now, young master," Clegg said. "Let Helios take you. It will all be over so—"

The inside of his helmet's visor was splattered with blood as Corbin shoved a blade through the back of the gatekeeper's head. The guard shoved the traitor aside and dropped to the wounded master.

"Your highness? Oh, Helios, no," Corbin said as he took Alexis in his arms. "No, this can't be. I failed you."

"Is she still alive?" Alexis grunted. "The minoress? Is she still alive?"

"Yes, your highness," Corbin nodded. "But barely."

"Make sure she doesn't die and you will have not failed me," Alexis said. "She has such a rich life to lead. Tell her that for me, will you?"

"Yes, your highness," Corbin said, his eyes looking at the blade that protruded from his monarch's belly. Then he looked at the bleeding man's helmet and gasped at the glazed eyes. "Master Alexis? Master Alexis!"

CHAPTER TWO

The long, sleek shuttle cut through the vacuum of space as it made its approach to the slowly spinning Station Aelon. Over four hundred feet long with a diameter of one hundred feet, the Thraenish shuttle adjusted its trajectory by firing Vape thrusters from coordinated jets so the nose pointed directly at the large shuttle dock port on the east side of the station.

"Prepare braking jets," the captain said as he made several adjustments from his seat in the fore cockpit.

When the time came for the shuttle to leave the station the flight crew would take their places in an exact copy of the cockpit, but in the aft end of the shuttle since the massive vehicle was perfectly symmetrical. Unlike the shuttles that transported people, goods, and equipment from station to planet, the shuttles that travelled from station to station only needed simple thrusters and could be shaped as perfect cylinders, letting them dock and depart with ease.

"Approach trajectory locked," the co-pilot announced. "Braking jets firing in three, two, one."

Vape gas erupted in small bursts from the front of the shuttle, slowing its speed until it barely coasted towards the docking port that quickly irised open. The flight crew kept all eyes on the instruments, making sure no last second adjustments needed to be made the synchronized docking protocol. But, as was the case with the dozens of shuttles that came and went from station to station, not a problem was detected and the shuttle easily locked into place inside Station Aelon.

The captain looked over his shoulder at the grim faced guard that sat in one of the jump seats.

"Your master has been delivered home," the captain said. "You are free to depart when he is ready. Will you need any of the crew's assistance?"

"No, thank you," Corbin said as he unbuckled and stood up from the seat. "I have this well in hand. Please let your crew know we appreciate their accommodating us, as I am sure you are not used to having royalty travel aboard the vessel."

"Our pleasure," the captain nodded. "Breaks up the monotony."

Corbin didn't respond, just nodded and left the cockpit to take his place as protector of the new Master of Station Aelon.

"Pleasant chap," the co-pilot smirked. "He should be more serious about his job."

"Couldn't pay me to work directly with the royalty," the captain replied. "Now, how about we shut down and go find a bar? I could use a bottle or two of gelberry wine."

"Praise Helios to that," the co-pilot laughed.

*

"Calm yourself, mistress," Stewardess Lesha de Morlan said to the pacing Mistress Eliza. "The master will be fine. In your condition you cannot let yourself get upset."

"But you saw him, Lesha," Eliza frowned. "In the transmissions. He looked so pale and sickly."

"That's the transmissions, not the master," Lesha sighed. "Everyone looks pale and sickly in those grainy pictures."

"Well, you would think someone would fix that!" Eliza snapped. "We live in space, but we can't communicate without static and interference? We are barbarians compared to our ancestors."

"So much knowledge was lost when humanity was forced from the planet, mistress," Lesha said. "We should be thankful to Helios that we survived as a people. Feel lucky the techs got the transmission to come through at all."

"Survival is not life, Lesha," Eliza frowned. "It is the postponement of death. I vow from this day forward that I will not be a survivor, but a liver."

"A liver, your highness?" Lesha smiled. "Shall I fetch you a robe of caramelized onions?"

"Oh, shut up," Eliza grinned. "You know what I mean."

She winced and grabbed at her swollen belly, grunting as a sharp pain forced her to take a seat on her bed.

"Mistress? Eliza?" Lesha said, her worry pushing away all formality. "What is it? Is the baby alright?"

"Gas," Eliza said. "That's all. A gas pain. I haven't voided in two days. It's a wonder my pores aren't seeping shit."

"Mistress," Lesha laughed. "As distressful as that sounds, you still have to keep your composure as mistress of the station. Pores seeping shit, is not something you want to share."

"I'll share every last shit seeping detail," Eliza snapped. "I have the heir to the crown sitting on my bladder and kicking me in the lungs every five seconds. The station can kiss my backed up ass with their composure."

Lesha sat next to the woman that was twenty years her junior and took her in her arms. "It will be over soon, your highness. The physicians will make you comfortable during labor and then you can cradle your newborn son in your arms and forget all about troubled bowels."

"I'll probably drop a crap as heavy as my son when the birthing starts," Eliza said. "There's no way one is coming out without the other."

Lesha laughed heartily and kissed the young mistress on the forehead. "I do love you, your highness."

"I love you too, Lesha," Eliza said. "Now help me back up so I can be standing when my love walks through that door."

No sooner had the mistress been helped to her feet than there was a chime at the entry door to the royal quarters. Even being four times the size of any other quarters within Castle Quent—the master's and mistress's main residence on the surface of station Aelon—it only took a brief few steps to reach the door. Station Aelon had still not caught up with the other stations' trend of updating the surface castles and keeps into sumptuous manor houses and estate mansions.

It was something Alexis had promised his wife he would begin to correct upon his return from Helios, but that promise was delayed by months as the master convalesced on Station Thraen. Eliza wondered if her husband would have the strength to lead his people, let alone tackle something as superficial as the renovations of their various residences across the Surface of Station Aelon.

"Breathe, your highness," Lesha whispered into her mistress's ear. "He will be just as you remember him."

The door to the quarters slid open and several royal guards stepped into the quarters, their eyes taking in every detail of the room.

"Are we safe, my lady?" Corbin asked as he took one step forward and addressed Stewardess de Morlan.

"We are safe, Mr. Breach," Lesha replied.

"Your highness," Corbin said to Eliza as he bowed low. "I am pleased to present your husband, Master of Station Aelon, Alexis the First."

"Oh, move it, will you?" Eliza said as she hurried forward and shoved the head of the royal guard out of the way, patting her belly at the same time. "You don't have to introduce me to the man that did this to my body. We are well acquainted, I assure you."

"Of course, your highness," Corbin said as he stumbled and was helped from falling by a steady hand from Stewardess de Morlan.

"Hello, my love," Alexis said as he strode past the guards and took his wife into his arms. "Miss me?"

"Yes, I bloody well missed you, you stupid, heroic idiot!" Eliza cried, letting herself be wrapped inside the embrace of a man that stood almost two feet taller than she. They kissed long and hard before Eliza finally let their lips part and pressed her cheek to his chest. "I never feel whole without my Longshanks about."

"Ugh," Alexis groaned. "I hate that name."

"Well, I love it," Eliza said, her face buried in his chest. "My Longshanks. He stands above us all, but can never be apart."

"Where did that come from?" Alexis frowned. "Is there already poetry about me?"

"My husband wrote it as part of the welcoming campaign," Lesha said. "The people have been nervous with you gone and the coronation happening on a foreign station. There has been grumbling that you have forgotten the Aelish and become a supporter of Thraen."

"A man gets stabbed in the belly by a traitor and this is the thanks I get?" Alexis laughed. "The people never cease to amaze me."

"It is a small faction, your highness," Corbin said. "The vast majority would never think such a thing."

"But all it takes is a small faction to foment talks of rebellion," Lesha countered. "Thus my husband's plan to rebrand you as Longshanks, Alexis the First, Master of Station Aelon."

"And not son of Henry III," Alexis replied. "Which I think is Alasdair's true goal. My father was a great man, but not a great master. I'm sure my supporters are looking for any way to distance me from the previous reign."

"Well, they can't distance you from your current brother," Minor Derrick Teirmont laughed as he stood behind the row of guards blocking the door. "Even if I was your brother during the previous reign as well." He looked at the guards then in at his brother. "Do you mind?"

"Please clear the way for my brother," Alexis ordered. "And never block him from me again."

"My apologies, your highness," Corbin said, bowing his head. "I gave my men strict orders that no one was to be trusted no matter how close they are to you personally. I believe recent events have proven that to be a wise course of security."

"I'll have to make a list of exceptions," Alexis nodded. "I can't have my family barred from me every time I move to a new room."

"Yes, your highness," Corbin said. He looked at the faces of the royals then at his master. "I will leave you to your reunion. Guards will be posted outside your quarters, if you need them. I am only a call away, as always."

"Thank you, Corbin," Alexis said. "Go have your own reunion. Two days leave, and no argument, for those that were forced to stay with me on Station Thraen. You should all see your loved ones and get some rest."

"None of us were forced, your highness," Corbin replied. "It was our honor and duty."

"Get," Alexis said, waving the man off. "Now."

Corbin bowed low and then turned and strode from the royal quarters, his men following in step.

"So, let's see the scar," Derrick smiled. "Can't have a war wound and not show it off."

"That would be my cue to leave," Lesha said. She looked at the mistress who was still tightly wrapped about her husband. "You need to rest as well. Please take a nap as soon as you can." Her eyes shifted to Alexis. "I trust you will see to that, your highness."

"Yes, mum," Alexis smiled.

"Don't be cheeky," Lesha smiled back. "I changed your diapers more than once."

"As you have reminded me my entire life, Lesha," Alexis nodded. "Please tell Alasdair I will come see him as soon as I can."

"I will, your highness," Lesha replied as she started to leave then paused. "It is good to have you back...Longshanks."

"Go," Alexis growled.

Lesha left with a chuckle, leaving Derrick to stand there and wait.

"What?" Alexis asked.

"The scar!" Derrick said. "Let's see it!"

"Leave him alone, Rick," Eliza snapped. "He's just gotten home and you're already pestering him."

"Knock it off, you two," Alexis said. "I'll show you the scar, but then you leave me with my wife, alright?"

"Sure, kicking me out already," Derrick grinned, clasping his brother on the shoulder. "It is good to see you home. I'd prefer not to be regent again. Can we have our dear sister, Melinda, do it next time? She is older than us both."

"If the stewards won't accept a woman as ruler of the station then they certainly won't let her be regent," Alexis said. "As much as I disagree with the notion." He looked about the quarters and realized something was missing. "Where are the children?"

"With Melinda right now," Eliza said. "She thought we'd want some time alone."

"I get it, I get it," Derrick replied, his hands up in surrender. "I'll go."

"Hold on," Alexis said and gently removed himself from his wife. "Take a look at this."

He pulled his tunic from his trousers and lifted it up over his abdomen. He peeled back the long, and soiled, bandage that was pasted just below his ribs. Both his wife and brother gasped involuntarily at the sight of the several inch long gash across his side and belly.

"Is it infected? It looks infected," Eliza worried.

"It's still draining," Alexis said. "The physician said it could be weeks, maybe even months, before it stops doing that. I'm looking at a year of keeping it clean in order for it to heal up properly."

"A year? Why so long?" Eliza asked.

"The Vape," Derrick frowned. "Once that gets in there it's near impossible to get clean air to the wound."

"Exactly," Alexis responded. "It's why wars on the planet are so deadly. You know the saying—"

"You don't have to kill 'em, just wound 'em," Derrick finished.

"I know what you are thinking," Alexis said, seeing the look on his wife's face. "And not even the ones that came before us could heal this any faster. It's why they left the planet to settle in space. The Vape always wins."

"Well, I've had my gore for the day," Derrick said, embracing his brother. "Get well, Al. Want me to have Melinda bring the kids?"

"No, we'll fetch them," Alexis said. "I think I'm going to clean up and have a nap. They'll be fine until then."

"Rest up, brother," Derrick said then bowed low. "Or, I should say, rest up, my liege."

"Kiss my ass," Alexis said and feigned a kick at his brother.

"My mistress," Derrick said to Eliza then slid the door open and left.

Once the door was closed again, Alexis took his wife up in his arms. "Longshanks? Really? Is that truly catching on?"

"It's always been there," Eliza laughed as she was carried to the bed and set down softly on the breen comforter. "You know that. Even before we met I had heard of the tall young man called Longshanks."

"Helios, have they been calling me that since then?" Alexis laughed. "We met when we were ten and wed at thirteen. I wasn't that tall yet!"

"Yes, you were," Eliza said as she slid her hands up under her maternity dress, coming away with her underpants. "You have always been my handsome, tall minor. Now my master."

"And now you are my mistress," Alexis smiled at her then looked at her belly. "What about the baby?"

"He can't see us," Eliza grinned, lust in her eyes. "And the midwife says it's good for me. Helps prepare for an easier birth."

"Well, if the midwife says so," Alexis replied as he pulled his tunic off and quickly shimmied out of his trousers. He climbed onto the bed and his hands slid up her legs to the insides of her thighs. "Oh, how I have missed you."

"Well, if you'd just stay here you wouldn't have to miss me," Eliza said as Alexis's hands moved up higher. "Promise me we won't part again."

"You know I can't make that promise," Alexis said, his mouth going to her neck.

Eliza's hand traced the outline of his abdomen, careful to avoid the bandage, and then trailed down to below. She gripped him hard and fast.

"Promise me," she sneered.

"E! Ow!" he cried out.

There was instantly a knock at the door. "Are you alright, your highness?"

Eliza started to giggle, but didn't let go. "Are you, my master?"

"Yes!" he called out. "I'm fine!"

"Yes, you are," Eliza said as she rolled to her side and wrapped Alexis's arms about her then pulled her dress all the way up. "Now make *me* fine, Master of Station Aelon. That's your first official duty."

"If it's my duty then it's my duty," he laughed.

*

"Father!" a small girl of four shouted as the door slid open and in walked Alexis and Eliza, arm in arm. "You're back!"

"I am, my little Bora," Alexis said. "And I missed you."

Two more children, a boy of three and girl of six, both blonde like their father, came running at him and he had to brace his legs to keep from being bowled over.

"I hope I get these types of greetings every time you see me," Alexis said.

"Do you also hope to get stabbed every time you leave?" the six year old asked, her eyes locking with her father's.

"Esther," Eliza snapped. "Knock it off."

"I don't know where she gets a tongue like that so young," a tall woman, red haired and fair, said as she strode forward, a breen shawl around her shoulders that hung down over her bright blue tunic and down to the waist of her deep red trousers. "It's not like the two of you are mouthy at all."

"Helios, I miss trousers," Eliza said as she eased her bulk into a chair. "I can't stand the draft that's constantly blowing up this maternity dress. I feel like my cooch is just hanging free most of the time."

"And my point is made," Minoress Melinda Teirmont said as she casually pushed the children aside and hugged her brother. "Welcome back, Al."

"Master Al," Alexis smirked

"Yeah, that's not going to fly with me, son," Melinda laughed. "I changed your diapers."

"Why does everyone insist on bringing that up? A man becomes master of station and every woman around him has to point out how they've wiped my ass when I was a baby."

"We don't want power going to your head," Melinda said, rapping her knuckles on his forehead. "We all know how that turns out."

"Grandfather," Esther said.

"Not your grandfather," Melinda corrected, looking at her brother. "Our grandfather. The man nearly lost the station because of his ego."

"He was more mean than egotistical," Alexis said. "I don't think he actually cared about the slights he punished people for, he just wanted to punish."

"But you are not your grandfather or your father," Eliza said.

"No, I'm not," Alexis said then looked down at the boy that had moved to hover by his mother's chair. "And how is the future master of station? Last time I saw you, you were getting over another cold."

"I threw up," the boy, Thomas, said. "Aunty Melmel got mad."

"I did not, you little bugger," Melinda said then shrugged. "Well, maybe a little mad. But he got sick all over my new rug. I just had it imported from Station Flaen. Six months I waited for it to arrive because of all the havoc your damn Prime Treaty caused. Gummed up trade forever."

"And now that trade is flowing free," Alexis said, taking a bow. "Thanks very much to your little brother."

"Oh, I'm sure others played a part," Melinda scowled. "Careful of that master ego."

"I was only a minor when I was on the planet," Alexis said.

"But a master when you signed the treaty," Melinda countered. "My warning still stands."

"You two," Eliza sighed. "Exhausting."

Melinda frowned at her sister-in-law. "How are you feeling? How's the baby?"

"Still inside me," Eliza grumbled. "I'd give my left tit if you'd take it out for me."

"Mother!" Esther snapped. "The little ones!"

"Says the six year old," Eliza said, holding out her arms. Esther came to her and was wrapped up instantly. "You talk like an old woman sometimes. Relax, little girl. You'll grow up too fast for your mother's heart."

Alexis sighed and closed his eyes for a second.

"Al? Are you alright?" Eliza asked.

"Sit," Melinda responded.

"No, I'm fine. Just tired," Alexis replied. "Let's gather these little ones and get back to our quarters. I think I could rest for a bit. Tomorrow's a big day."

"Tomorrow?" Melinda asked.

"I've called a meeting of stewards," Alexis replied.

"Aren't all meetings of the stewards?" Melinda smiled.

"Not for long," Alexis smiled back. "This master plans on making some changes."

Melinda narrowed her eyes and then looked at Eliza. "What is he up to?"

"I don't have a clue," Eliza said. "But I'll find out and let you know."

"I'm standing right here," Alexis said as he ushered his children towards the door. "At least conspire when I'm out of earshot."

"Shall I call a nurse for the children so you two can rest?" Melinda asked. "Or they could just stay here like I've offered a hundred times. I really don't mind."

"No, we won't need a nurse," Alexis replied. "This isn't Thraen."

*

"A toast to our new master! May Helios bless him with a long reign and many heirs!" de Morlan said as he stood and lifted a glass of gelberry wine.

The men seated at the long table all stood and lifted their glasses.

"May Helios bless him!" they toasted.

A sip was taken by each and they quickly sat back down, all eyes cast to the young master at the head of the table.

"Thank you," Alexis nodded as he stood and raised his glass. He winced slightly and his free hand involuntarily went to his wound. "I wish I could truly enjoy this, but I'm afraid the physicians have me on water and lemon tea for the next few weeks. Apparently a pint of gelberry wine is too much for me in my delicate state."

The table laughed and glasses were raised once more.

"I thought the mistress was the one in the delicate state!" someone shouted.

"Are you expecting as well, your highness?" another added.

"Ha, funny," Alexis said. "And, while on the subject of my wife's condition, I have been told by the midwife to expect my new son in the next day or two. Another heir will be added to the line of succession, assuring the people that the reign of Family Teirmont will continue for at least another generation."

More raised glasses, laughter, and applause.

"But, until I am called away to attend to that splendid occasion, I am here at the stewards' disposal," Alexis said as he sat down. "I know there have been issues that my father shoved to the side while on his campaign of rebuilding Station Aelon. I think it only fair that I give each of you time to discuss those issues and air any grievances you may have."

The table of stewards all looked at him, surprised by his request.

"Your highness, surely you would rather have these types of discussions in private," de Morlan suggested. He was seated to Alexis's left while Derrick was seated across the table to the master's right. De Morlan looked down the table at the confused faces then back to the master. "Some subjects may be of a sensitive nature."

"Oh, I am well aware of sensitive subjects," Alexis said. "I have had to tiptoe around dozens of gatekeepers and even the High Guardian himself these past months. Which is exactly why I believe we need to have all meetings open. At least when amongst the stewards. We have to show an example to the passengers."

There was a tense and confused silence.

"Uh, the passengers, your highness?" another man asked, Steward Emeric Hume. "Our posts as stewards are example enough to the commoners."

"If only that were true, Hume," Alexis said. "But we all know that it is not."

"I do not mean to disagree, your highness—"

"Then don't," Alexis grinned. "Especially when you have no idea what you are disagreeing with."

Steward Hume nodded and went quiet.

"Perhaps you'd like to illuminate us with what it is we should be disagreeing about," a young man said as he walked into the great hall. "My apologies for being late, your highness. My skid broke down on my way from Sector Kirke. I was forced to walk the last bit of the way. I took the liberty of showering in my guest quarters here at court before joining you. Wouldn't do to have the steward of Sectors Kirke, Shem, Maelphy and Bueke smelling like the lower decks."

The man, average height with dark hair and deep set brown eyes, took his chair next to Derrick. He nodded to the master and then tapped a glass and looked to the wall of the great hall.

"No gelberry wine for me?" he grinned, leaning forward and peering into the master's glass. "Maybe I should indulge in some water like your highness. It could be a trend of sobriety that the station could follow."

"I believe life is hard enough as it is, Cousin Stolt," Alexis said. "I wouldn't dare condemn my people to that."

"Nor I," Stolt said as a servant filled his glass with the deep pink liquid. He lifted his glass to Alexis. "A long and interesting life."

"That toast could be considered a curse, Cousin," Alexis said.

"It was not meant as such," Stolt responded after taking a long drink. "And I thank you for always acknowledging our blood ties."

"Yes, of course," Alexis smiled. "Oh, and congratulations on your recent marriage! I am sorry my convalescence prevented me from attending. You must be proud to add Sectors Maelphy and Bueke to your holdings."

"More proud to have such a lovely woman as my wife," Stolt said. "While I do have plenty of children to carry on my name, Gloria is still of childbearing age and will produce fine offspring."

"Just in case," Alexis replied.

"Just in case, indeed," Stolt laughed.

"You speak of your wife as if she were a common shaow heifer just waiting to be milked," Derrick snapped. "You know that Gloria is also our cousin on our mother's side, don't you, Cousin? She may not be Family Teirmont, but she is family to me and my brother."

"Rick," Alexis said quietly. "Cousin Stolt was just expressing his happiness at the new marriage in the context as steward. We all must look to our lineage. You never know when a plague could hit the station and take those we most love away from us."

"Helios forbid," Stolt said and clenched a fist then made an X across his chest.

"Helios forbid," the rest of the table said and all X'ed themselves as well.

"So, what is this about the passengers that has Steward Hume so worked up?" Stolt asked after finishing half his glass in one swallow.

"I am not worked up, sir," Hume grumbled.

"No, I quite expected some to get worked up," Alexis said. "What I propose will upset a great many of you."

The room was deathly silent and not a steward dared move as they waited for the master to explain.

"You all know why I was sent down to Helios," Alexis began. "It was a crusade to wrest control of The Way Prime from the gatekeepers and the High Guardian. Which was my idea and not my father's."

There were chuckles as well as grumbles from the assembly.

"Not the most popular campaign, I know," Alexis laughed. "But one I felt passionate about. The Way Prime is the only land on all of Helios with sky clear enough, and stable enough, to allow station transports to land and launch. Without The Way Prime we cannot get men and supplies down to the planet for our own prime, nor can we bring the canisters of Vape we mine back to Station Aelon. The Way controls all trade and movement on and off the Helios planet."

"But you didn't secure control, did you, your highness?" Stolt asked, his face nothing but innocence and inquiry.

"No, I did not," Alexis admitted. "I expected, and was assured, the support of the other stations, but one by one they withdrew that support, Thraen being the last, and I was left to make a hard decision." He looked down the table, making eye contact with each and every steward. "I could keep fighting, and most likely lose Aelon Prime, or I could sit down with the The Way and work out a more agreeable compact between them and the stations. The latter was the prudent choice."

"And the only choice," de Morlan added.

"How many men did we lose before that choice was made?" Stolt asked. "I know of four hundred alone from my sectors that did not return."

"We lost over three thousand men," Alexis said. "Good men. Loyal men. Men I wish I could resurrect and bring back to their families right this second."

"Resurrection is The Way's purview," Stolt laughed. "You should have added that to the negotiations."

"Careful, Cousin," Derrick growled. "You overstep."

"It's alright, Rick," Alexis said. "If I believed they could be brought back then I would have negotiated those terms as well. But they cannot be brought back. What can be done is their memories are honored, and the memories of all that have fallen in campaigns for Station Aelon, by establishing a new meeting. The meeting of passengers."

Alexis sat back and watched that news set in. He looked at his brother, whose eyes were wide with surprise, then looked at de Morlan who looked like he was suffering a case of serious indigestion. The table erupted into excited and angry chatter. Only Steward Stolt seemed nonplussed by the news.

The man emptied his glass then held it out for a servant to fill once more. He raised the full glass towards Alexis and winked.

"All the luck in the System with this one, your highness," Stolt grinned.

"No luck needed," Alexis said. "It is within my power to create new legislative bodies for the governance of the station. I am doing just that."

"But, your highness," an obese man at the far end of the table exclaimed. "Passengers? Passengers are to be ruled, not consulted on how to rule!"

"They won't be consulted at all," Alexis responded to Steward Nele Gervès. "That is not the point. They will rule alongside the meeting of stewards. An equal body in all senses and powers."

"Oh, Helios," Derrick said, hanging his head in his hands as the great hall erupted into shouts and protests, the stewards completely throwing off all decorum. "What have you done, Brother?"

"I have kept a promise," Alexis said. "That is something I plan on always doing as master."

"Do you have any idea how naïve that sounds?" Derrick asked, lifting his face from his hands to look at his brother. "Being master means breaking promises constantly. You do what you have to for the good of the station." He waved a hand down the table. "Does this look like it will do good for the station?"

"I believe it will," Alexis said. "Once the stewards calm down."

"Quiet!" de Morlan shouted, standing and pounding his hands on the table. "Be quiet! All of you!"

It was another couple minutes before the stewards settled down enough for Alexis to continue. When the master spoke again, he was addressing a very hostile audience.

"To appease you all, I will say that members of the meeting of passengers will be appointed by the stewards from the sector wardens and deck bosses," Alexis said.

"That will limit the chaos and pool to choose from," Stolt said. "I like that rule."

"But," Alexis said, looking at the steward. "You men will need to choose wisely who you appoint. A provision will be in place for the passengers to recall their representatives and choose one of their own if the members are found to be favoring the interests of the stewards and not the passengers. The entire point of this is to allow the people a voice and hand in their own governance."

"This sounds dangerously like democracy, your highness," Steward Jacon Oweyn stated. A man of advanced age, he was the elder of all stewards. "History has shown that democracy does not work on the stations. That is why the monarchy and stewardships were created millennia ago. The people cannot be trusted to rule; they do not have the stomach for it."

"The people will not rule," Alexis said. "Just like the stewards do not rule. The only ruler on Station Aelon is the master. Or have you forgotten this fact, Steward Oweyn?"

"I meant no insult, your highness," Oweyn said then nodded to those around him. "I just wanted to make an observation regarding your proposal."

"It is not a proposal," Alexis said. "It's a ruling." He snapped his fingers and porters waiting by the walls stepped forward with papers in hand. "Because that is what rulers do, *they rule.*"

The papers were set in front of each steward and soon all eyes were cast down at the table and the writs handed them.

"To take effect immediately?" Steward Horach Gylis asked. "But we have not had time to decide who will be the members of this meeting!"

"You will have three days to return to your sectors and interview your candidates," Alexis said, standing up to indicate the meeting was over. "I plan on touring each sector myself starting in four days. This way I can gauge the mood of the people as well as meet your chosen candidates. Once my tour is completed I will make the candidates' posts official and the first meeting of passengers will be called. As well as another meeting of stewards, marking the first annual conjoined meeting."

The stewards all stared at their master until de Morlan stood up and gave a small bow towards the head of the table.

"Of course, your highness," de Morlan said. "I would welcome a royal tour of my sector, as I am sure my colleagues would as well."

Slowly, one by one, the rest of the stewards stood and bowed to Alexis. Stolt was the last to stand and his eyes never left Alexis's when he bowed.

"Read your papers," Alexis said. "I believe you will find that my ruling is not as horrendous as you think it may be. With another legislative body, the blame when things go wrong can be spread about."

Some at the table chuckled, but most stayed silent in their anger.

"Rick? Walk with me," Alexis said as he left the table. "My lords, I thank you all."

Alexis strode from the great hall, his long legs covering the distance quickly.

Once out in the passageway, and safely out of sight and earshot, Alexis reached out for his brother. Derrick was at his side instantly as the master stumbled and winced.

"You will push yourself to an early grave," Derrick said. "How bad is it?"

Alexis looked down at his tunic and was glad he chose dark blue since it hid the spreading stain across his midsection.

"You need a physician," Derrick scolded. "You're oozing life everywhere."

"Your highness!" a porter shouted from the far end of the passageway. "Your highness! The physicians need you at once!"

"Ask and you shall receive," Alexis chuckled.

"The master was on his way there now," Derrick said. "Please hurry back and inform them the master will need his wound attended to."

"His wound? No, my lord, it is the mistress!" the porter nearly shouted. "That is why the physicians need you! They say there are complications with the birth and the midwife will not let them take control!"

"Oh, dear Helios!" Alexis exclaimed. "Rick! Help me there now!"

*

"Master Alexis?"

Silence.

"Master Alexis? We must take him now."

The nurse stood to the side of the monarch, her eyes watching carefully as the man held the body of his stillborn infant boy.

"Did he suffer, do you think?" Alexis asked as he slowly took a deep breath and handed the body to the nurse. "Did he feel it when he died?"

"I...I don't know, your highness," the nurse replied as she took the swaddled corpse from his hands.

"He did not suffer," the midwife said as she came from the bedchamber and into the main area of the royal quarters. She quickly walked to a sink and began to scrub her hands of the blood and afterbirth that coated her skin. "The umbilical cord became wrapped about his throat. He died peacefully from a lack of oxygen to the brain. It was as if he went to sleep."

"But he never had a chance to be born and awake!" Alexis roared. He stood and stormed over to the woman, his frame towering over her. "How can he have gone to sleep if he never woke up to begin with?"

"It was like sleep, but not sleep itself," the midwife replied, not intimidated by the brutally tall monarch who quaked before her with grief driven rage. "But your question was whether he suffered, and I can swear on Helios that he did not."

"To shit with Helios!" Alexis shouted. "The Planet, the Star, the System and the God himself! The Dear Parent abandoned me this day so I will abandon him!"

The nurse gasped and the midwife turned a cold gaze to her. The woman quickly left the quarters, ready to deliver the small body to the station's gatekeepers for ointment before burial. Once the nurse was gone, the midwife looked up into the mad eyes of her master.

"Would you like to see your wife?" she asked, a hand going to the master's arm.

Two royal guards moved from the wall and stepped towards her, but hesitated the second she looked at them.

"I have stopped the bleeding and she is resting, but I believe the comfort of her husband will be the best medicine right now," the midwife said. "For her body as well as her soul."

"Yes...yes, of course," Alexis said, the anger leaving him as quickly as it came. He looked towards the bedchamber, feeling lost and adrift.

"Here, let me help you," the woman said as she gripped his arm and led the man towards the door. "Comfort her, share her grief, be with her now. Be *for* her now. She has lost a part of herself and will need your love to replace that."

"Right..." Alexis said as he opened the door. He stopped before entering and looked down at the midwife. "None of this will be easy for you. The physicians will try to convince me this is your fault."

The midwife studied the master's face and nodded.

"And do you believe it is?" she asked.

"No, I do not," Alexis said. "Children die all the time in this station with physicians present. Yet their abilities are never questioned. I will not question yours if you can assure me you did everything within your power."

"I assure you I did," the midwife said, pushing him forward into the room. "The health of the child always comes first, then the mother's." She nodded towards the woman covered in blankets and comforters in the bed before her and the master. "I will remain outside for the rest of the night in case she starts bleeding again. Call me for any reason. I am here for you as well."

Alexis nodded and stumbled forward as the midwife quietly closed the door behind him.

"Al?" Eliza's weak voice called from the bed. "My love?"

"It's me," Alexis said as he made his way to the bed and climbed in next to her.

His hands hovered above her form, afraid to touch her and cause her any distress. Eliza reached back and wrapped him around her, moaning in pain as his forearm brushed her abdomen.

"I'm hurting you," Alexis said.

"No, you could never hurt me," Eliza whispered. "Never."

Alexis buried his face in her hair and held back his tears.

"Was he beautiful?" Eliza asked. "Like you?"

"No," Alexis replied, the tears refusing to obey as they slide down his cheeks. "He was beautiful like you. Even the Dear Parent pales in his beauty."

"Hush," Eliza said. "Don't blaspheme."

"It is a day of blasphemy when our son does not get to live," Alexis said, his chest hitching with sobs. "I cannot say or do anything worse than what has already been done."

"Then say or do nothing at all," Eliza said. "Just hold me and warm me."

The two parents lay there, souls battered by grief, bodies entwined in order to cling to some small comfort of life.

*

"This is not a good idea," Derrick said, standing at his brother's side as the lift slowly took them down through Sector Kirke's main levels to the first of the subterranean decks. "You're still grieving, still healing, and should be home with your family, not on a tour to drum up support for something you've already decreed is happening. What do you hope to accomplish?"

"The passengers need to know I'm not just the monarch of the stewards," Alexis said. "They have to know I'm for the people as well. No one will trust or believe in the meeting of passengers if I don't do this. When was the last time Father toured the decks other than to figure out how to tear them apart and rebuild them?"

"He could have cared less about the passengers," Derrick replied. "I see your point."

"But will the *passengers* see your point?" Stolt asked, standing behind the two royals. "They are used to hearing opinions, not being asked for theirs."

"Then I'll be the first," Alexis said. "As my great grandfather did when he signed the Bill of Meeting, giving the stewards a say in the overall governance of Station Aelon, so I will give the passengers a say by including them in that Bill."

"Don't misunderstand me, your highness," Stolt said. "I know why you are doing it, and you are about to explain that why to the people themselves, but my question is will they see the point of it? Will they care, is what I am getting at."

"I'd be surprised if they don't," Alexis responded. "What man or woman doesn't care about their voice being heard?"

"Men and women that have never been asked before," Stolt replied. "Ask a man who has never experienced planetary gravity which he prefers and he will always say station gravity. But we all know that no matter how well the rotational drive does in creating artificial gravity for each station, there is nothing like the feel of gravity on Helios. It is solid and better for our bodies. But the station bound passenger does not know that."

"That's your metaphor?" Derrick laughed. "Gravity?"

"I thought it fitting," Stolt smiled. "Considering the gravity of this endeavor."

Alexis grinned at the pun, but shook his head.

"This tour may be so the stewards see the point as much as the passengers," Alexis said. "We all have a lot to learn from each other."

"Then why do you wear your blades?" Stolt asked. "Long and short. What exactly do you expect to learn if you need those?"

"I insisted, my lord," Corbin said from the front of the lift, his body blocking the doors, ready to take point with the security detail when they reached the deck. "There has been some unrest on the decks due to the high casualties passengers suffered during the planetary conflict."

"The people don't want to die for us," Stolt said. "So why would they want to lead with us?"

"Because they will have the choice to for once," Alexis said. "And because I plan on apologizing to them for the unnecessary loss of the lives of their loved ones. In the end, it was discussion and compromise that won out. So it will with the meetings."

"Apologize?" Derrick said. "Has a master ever apologized to his people before? The master of station's word is supreme, second only to Helios. He never has to apologize."

"I'm a monarch of many firsts then," Alexis said.

He looked about the lift and frowned. It was nothing but a metal cage with thin sheet metal sides over the heavy duty safety mesh. The lighting was dim and made his head hurt while the ride itself could be considered nothing but jarring.

"One of my other firsts will be to upgrade the lift systems in the station," Alexis said. "There are how many lifts and sub-lifts?"

"Not counting the ones within the stewards' estates? Close to a hundred," Derrick said. "Father had looked at redesigning them but decided he'd start with the decks themselves."

"Sound thinking," Alexis said. "No point in upgrading something that's going to get beat to all Helios transporting supplies and construction crews."

"Or only serves to move passengers from one deck to the next," Stolt said. "I rarely use a deck lift at all. I make sure my subjects come to me above. As it should be."

Alexis looked about and found the lift operator sitting silently in the corner, his hand poised near the brake and throttle controls.

"Excuse me, what is your name?" Alexis asked, pushing past Derrick and the royal guards to stand next to the operator.

The man looked as if he would faint and die right then. His eyes grew wide and he instantly got off the stool to kneel before the master. Alexis shook his head and grabbed the operator by the shoulders which elicited a small squeak from the man.

"Relax," Alexis laughed. "I just want your opinion and expertise regarding the lift."

"Yes, your highness," the man stammered. "Anything you need, your highness."

"The lift is powered by the main Vape generators like the rest of the station, correct?" Alexis asked.

"He's an operator, your highness," Stolt smirked. "Not an engineer. He makes it go up and down. He doesn't know why or how it does it."

The operator's eyes moved to Steward Stolt and he nodded, but Alexis could see the hint of disagreement in the man's face.

"You do know how the lifts work, don't you?" Alexis asked. "It's alright to disagree with a steward when the master is present. In fact, I'd prefer that you did."

The man turned his full attention on Alexis and smiled. "Yes, your highness, I know how the lifts work. There's been a lift operator in my family going back twenty generations now," the man said. "I'm very familiar with their engineering as well as operation."

"So they are powered by the Vape generators then?" Alexis asked.

"Yes and no, your majesty," the operator said. "While their main power source is the electricity generated by the combustion of Vape gas within the station's power plant, there are also auxiliary canisters embedded within the floor that connect to backup generators should the main power fail and anyone finds themselves trapped in a lift."

"I didn't know that," Derrick said. "But I've never been trapped in a lift."

"That's interesting," Alexis said, glancing sideways at Steward Stolt. "Backup generators in the lifts. They must have to be inspected because of disuse. I can't remember the last time there was a station wide power outage."

The man smiled, but Alexis could see the insincerity.

"Am I wrong?"

"No, your highness, never," the operator said looking like he wished for nothing more than to sit on his stool and become invisible once again.

"I am, I can see it in your eyes," Alexis said. "When was the last power outage?"

"Just a couple of days ago, your highness," the man nearly whispered.

"There was?" Alexis asked, puzzled. He looked to his brother. "Did you know about it?"

"Power never wavered in Quent," Derrick said. He turned to Stolt. "Any issues here in Sector Kirke?"

The steward glared hard at the lift operator then looked at Alexis. "There has had to be rationing of power throughout the sectors. Until we know for sure that The Way will honor the Prime Treaty, the stewards decided that rolling blackouts from the lower decks up was wise. Of course, now that our master is safely back in the station, and has assured us of the strength of the Prime Treaty, there won't be any need of the rationing."

"When in Helios did the stewards decide that?" Derrick snapped. "I was acting regent and not one word of this reached my ears."

"It was a sector by sector decision," Stolt replied. "It did not need regency approval. It just happened that all stewards decided the same course."

"Are you bloody kidding me?" Alexis barked. "I'm going on a tour of the sectors to garner the support and goodwill of the passengers and you didn't think I should know that there have been periodic blackouts for the decks? It'll be a wonder they don't string us up the second we step off this lift!"

"I will make sure they don't get within an inch of you, your highness," Corbin said. "I'll die before I let them string you up."

"You may well die if they string you up first, Corbin," Alexis growled. "Cousin Stolt, this will not stand. Any other decisions the stewards have made that I should know about?"

"Not that I can think of," Stolt replied.

"Well, perhaps you should think harder, steward," Alexis responded, his voice cold and deadly.

"I'll do my best, your highness," Stolt nodded, bowing slightly. "And you have my humble apologies. I will make sure the word is spread to the other stewards that rationing power is no longer the will of nobility."

Alexis struggled to regain his composure and it took all of his strength not to lash out at the smug steward. By the time the lift slowed and then stopped, Alexis had gotten the rage under control and took a deep breath as the doors slid to the side and Corbin and his men stepped out to secure the immediate area.

"Clear, your highness," Corbin said. "If you will follow me."

"Thank you, Corbin," Alexis said. "But I will be fine. Which deck are we on?"

"Middle Deck Twenty, sire," Corbin replied. "I believe the deck boss's name is Gornish Wyaerrn."

Stolt snorted from behind the master.

"Something you'd like to share?" Alexis asked.

"You'll see, your highness," Stolt smiled. "Mr. Wyaerrn is quite the individual, as you will find out soon enough."

"Intriguing," Alexis said. "I look forward to meeting him."

"This way, sire," Corbin said as he led the master and his entourage from the lift corridor and out into the main atrium of Middle Deck Twenty.

The space was enormous. A massive cavern of metal and polybreen plastics, the atrium had three levels to it, each level jammed with people, all bargaining and haggling in front of merchant carts over food and other wares. Most of the surfaces of the atrium were coated with the same drab grey paint as the rest of Station Aelon, but the banisters at the edges of the levels and stairways were painted in the deep blue and dark red of the Teirmont crest.

Slowly, on a wave of gossip, word spread that the master was on deck and the atrium began to quiet down. Faces turned away from the haggling and looked down at the master, showing a mixture of fear and awe, support and contempt.

"All kneel for Master of Station Aelon, Alexis the First!" Corbin announced.

As one the people took a knee, but their eyes never left the master's.

"Please rise," Alexis called out. "While I thank you for your courtesy, I am not here to interrupt your lives, but only to observe them and speak with your deck boss. Please carry on with your day."

No one moved.

"The master said to carry on!" Corbin shouted.

"Corbin, be nice," Alexis said. "I doubt many of these folks have seen their own steward, let alone master of station."

Stolt caught the barb, but did not react to it.

A portly man hurried towards the group, a long box in his hands, trailed by six women that seemed to be talking to the man all at once.

"Yes, I know, I know!" the man snapped. "Let it be!"

The man skidded to a stop, almost toppling against the barrier of Corbin and his guards. He looked past the armed men and smiled at the master.

"It is an honor, your highness," the man said. "To have a master visit our humble deck is nothing short of a miracle." The women behind him hissed. "I mean, not that it takes a miracle for the master of station to visit amongst his people. I was never implying that—"

"The honor is mine, sir," Alexis interrupted. "And you are...?"

"Gornish Wyerrn, your highness," Gornish said as he bowed so low that he had to be helped back upright by two of the women. "Deck boss of Middle Deck Twenty, at your service."

"I see you have something there, Gornish. Is it a gift?" Alexis asked.

"Yes, it is, sire!" Gornish exclaimed and tried to move forward, but was stopped by Corbin.

"Let him through," Alexis ordered. "I'd like the deck boss to present the, well, present to me himself."

"Thank you, sire!" Gornish said as he squeezed through the ranks of the reluctant guards. "This is something I know you will find marvelous! I have been trying to get it before Steward Stolt, but he—"

"Just open the box, man," Stolt snapped. "The master doesn't have all day."

Alexis frowned at the steward, but let it go and nodded to the deck boss.

"Please. I'm dying to see what it is," Alexis said.

Gornish knelt and set the long box on the ground. He opened it quickly and pulled out what was inside, holding it out to the master with both hands.

"What is this?" Alexis asked as he took the gift. "Is this a sling of some sort?"

"Yes!" Gornish cried out. "It is called a longsling and can hit a man from a thousand feet away!"

"Preposterous," Stolt grumbled.

"A thousand feet?" Derrick asked. "You must be joking. No sling has ever had that kind of range."

"This does," Gornish said, grunting loudly as he stood back up. "The longer barrel of the sling means the flechette will achieve better distance and accuracy. But it's not just the barrel that allows the flechettes to fly so far." He held out his hands. "If I may, sire?"

"Of course," Alexis said and handed the longsling back.

"The key is combustion of the Vape within the firing chamber," Gornish explained. "Instead of shooting a projectile using compressed Vape only, this design actually sparks the Vape, creating a small explosion which propels the flechette at a speed and distance that couldn't have been achieved before."

"Seriously?" Alexis asked, his eyes wide and skeptical. "You combust Vape in this small chamber? How do you not blow your hands off?"

"The metal is tempered over one hundred times, your highness," Gornish replied, looking very satisfied with himself. "It is a technique used for many other applications, but I was the first to think of how it would work with a longsling."

"Quite brilliant," Alexis said. "I'll have to have you give a demonstration one—"

"*Death to the hierarchy*!" a voice bellowed from the top level of the atrium. "*Equality for the people of the lower decks*!"

The royal party looked up to see a man dressed all in black pull his arm back and throw something down towards them.

"Grenade!" Corbin yelled as he tried to get back to the master.

But before he could, Gornish pulled a metal box from his pocket, slapped it into the bottom of the longsling, put the weapon to his shoulder, turned up and fired. The grenade exploded above them as Gornish drew back a bolt on the longsling and then fired again.

The man above screamed in a spray of blood then fell back away from the railing.

The entire atrium began to scream and panic as they fled the huge space, all looking for safety elsewhere. There was shouting and yelling around Alexis and several hands began to pull at him, but his feet were rooted in place as he looked from Gornish to the longsling and back.

"Spectacular," he grinned, clapping the deck boss on the shoulder. "Simply spectacular."

Chapter Three

The council sat at the table, all eyes on Alexis as he read the report in front of him.

"This makes the tenth attack this month," Alexis said. "Do we know anymore about this group? Or are they allowed to just run free terrorizing innocent people."

"We have yet to capture any of the attackers alive, your highness," de Morlan replied. He looked over at Derrick. "But there is a name that has started to circulate amongst the passengers."

Alexis looked from de Morlan to Derrick. "Is the name a secret or are you going to tell me?"

"Lucas Langley," Derrick answered. "After each attack someone paints the name on a wall of the affected deck."

"That's just insurgent propaganda!" Stolt cried from his seat next to Derrick. Other than de Morlan, he was the highest ranking steward on the council, because of his sector holdings. "We need to send a regiment down to the lower decks and stop this at the source!"

"Insurgents?" Alexis mused. "How can there be insurgents on Aelon when everyone here is born and raised? An insurgency implies an outside force. Do you believe an outside force is pushing these attacks?"

"No, sire, I do not," de Morlan said quickly. He glared at Stolt and shook his head. "This is completely homegrown, your highness. Langley is part of a long line of engineers from the lower decks. As you know, under your father's rule, the lower decks were constantly mined for cheap labor to help with the rebuilds. Unfortunately, if anyone objected to their new position they were tossed into the Vape chamber in the rotational drive." The steward cleared his throat. "Your father called it, uh..."

"Gravitational justice," Alexis nodded. "Yes, I'm aware of my father's proclivities towards creative forms of punishment."

"Execution, not punishment," Steward Joff Klemshir said from a seat towards the end of the table. "The lower decks see every one of those deaths as an unjustified execution and have called for an eye for an eye. Can't blame them."

"Steward Klemshir!" de Morlan exclaimed. "That is dangerously close to treason!"

"No, it's close to honesty," Klemshir replied. "I didn't say I agreed with them, I said I didn't blame them. Can you? If one of us was yanked from this room and thrown out of an airlock for no reason other than we refused to vote on a measure, how would the remainder of us feel? Pretty damn pissed off, is how."

"Point taken, Steward Klemshir," Alexis said. "And yet another reason I insist we go forward with the meeting of passengers."

"That cannot be allowed, your highness," de Morlan said. "The main reason being that security has blocked all access to the surface of the station until the unrest can be put down. Even if we had the full support of the stewards, which we do not, we cannot risk allowing an extremist onto the surface, let alone into Castle Quent!"

"Then we meet below," Alexis said. "We don't have the meeting of passengers on the surface in Quent or in any of the stewards' manor houses. We take the meeting to the very people it is meant to represent."

"People that already have representation by their stewards," Stolt said. "Which has been enough for millennia. You are upsetting a boat that does not need to be upset."

"Your protestations have been heard and noted," Alexis sighed. "Countless times. How about you skip your next protest and help decide where we should hold the meeting of passengers."

The council looked about at each other, none wanting to offer up space within their sectors. Alexis waited patiently, making sure to meet the eye of each person seated at the table. When no suggestions came forth, he stood up and brought himself to his full, impressive height. The Teirmont fire burned in his eyes.

"I know my succession was sudden and happened during a huge amount of conflict and turmoil with Station Aelon and Aelon Prime," Alexis began. "But it still does not change the fact that I am master. I have been master for several months now, yet all I see are condescending faces and conniving smirks." Derrick started to argue, but Alexis held up his hand. "With various exceptions, of course."

"Of course," Stolt said.

"Do not count yourself amongst those exceptions, cousin," Alexis growled. "In fact, I would put you at the top of the agitator list."

"Your highness!" Stolt exclaimed, jumping to his feet. "You must be kidding? I have been nothing but loyal to the crown!"

"You were loyal to my father because he was easily manipulated with flattery and gifts," Alexis said. "Which explains why your sectors have the most improvements done to them." Alexis smiled, but it did not reach his eyes. "Come to think of it, wasn't the Middle Deck Twenty-Six atrium in Sector Bueke widened and restructured to allow more people to gather there during the Last Meal festival?"

"Your highness, Last Meal is a high holy day," Stolt replied. "You cannot compare this farce of a meeting to the celebration of Helios devouring the false gods. That borders on blasphemy."

"And your argument borders on sedition!" Alexis roared. "We will hold the meeting of passengers in your Sector Bueke in the Middle Deck Twenty-Six atrium! I do not want to hear any other response out of your mouth other than 'Yes, sire!'"

The room was silent and still as all eyes turned to Steward Stolt. The man's struggle with his emotions was plainly visible on his face. But after a few seconds he regained himself and took his seat.

"Yes, sire," he said quietly. "My apologies."

"I'll forgive you for the extra two words, Cousin," Alexis grinned. The fire still remained in his eyes, but it was tempered by satisfaction. "Let's adjourn the council for today. You all have much to prepare for. I expect you to pick, notify, and assist those from your sectors that you deem fit for the meeting without further delay. Have your choices to me by the end of the week. We will call the meeting to order in one month's time."

Alexis looked to Corbin as the man stood at attention off to the side.

"I expect you to coordinate the security needed with Steward Stolt's men," Alexis said, his eyes flitting to Stolt and back. "Tell them they are to do as you order as if it was my words they are hearing directly from my lips. You will report to my brother on all matters and he will report to me if there is a problem. Understood?"

"Yes, your highness," Corbin nodded. "I will not fail you."

"I expect not," Alexis grinned. "Gentlemen? Good day."

*

"No!" Alexis shouted. "Preposterous!"

"Preposterous?" Eliza frowned, her arms folded across her chest. "Please tell me you did not just use that word with me."

"I will not, *cannot*, allow you to accompany me below the Surface!" Alexis yelled. "You are with child again!"

"I am," Eliza said, keeping her voice even and cool, the direct opposite of her husband's booming tone. "But only a month and a half along. The midwife suggests I get out and stop hiding within Castle Quent." She looked about the sparse royal quarters. "Which I think is a fine idea. If I stare at these stupid tapestries for another day I will go mad. Is that what you want, husband? For your mistress to go mad while carrying your child?"

"But what about the other children? The ones that have already been born? Will you abandon them?" Alexis grumbled as he slumped into a less than plush chair. His fingers picked at the breen upholstery as he looked at his wife. "They need their mother."

"They need their father also," Eliza replied. "But you are continually leaving the castle while I remain behind. The children have nurses and they have an adoring aunt. They will be staying with Melinda at Castle Helble. Her late husband may have been an awful boor, but he did leave her with an amazing home."

"One she never uses because she is always in her quarters here at court," Alexis responded. He thought for a second then sighed. "I guess it will get her out of here as well. She should tend to her estate now and again."

"There will be other children there ours can play with," Eliza said. "Melinda has an open invitation for the sector wardens', and even deck bosses', children to come to the Surface and play on the estate when they want. The place is more of a park than a working farm."

"Yes, the stewards keep reminding me that Sector Helble does not make its quota of resources ever," Alexis said. "Maybe we should set up the area as a children's refuge and have that be her contribution?"

"I doubt she'd object," Eliza smiled. "And if the royal children endorse it then you know the stewards, and their wives, will jump on immediately. If for nothing else than pure sycophancy."

Alexis rolled his head on his neck and then nodded. "Fine. You can come with me."

"Oh, thank you, my lord," Eliza replied with an exaggerated curtsey. "You honor me with your permission."

"Come here," he smiled in spite of himself.

"Who? Me?" Eliza said, walking slowly towards him, her hands on her ocean green tunic. "Why, your highness? Do you need something?"

"Yes," Alexis said as he reached for her. "I need you."

His arms took her in and she fell onto his lap. Hands moved quickly and the ocean green tunic, as well as Alexis's bright blue one, fell to the foot of the chair. Trousers followed and soon the chair was forgotten as the royal couple moved to the floor.

*

The massive atrium was filled to bursting with long tables, banquets to the side, men, women, and even some children, as the meeting of passengers was about to start. Alexis, seated at the head of the longest table that split the atrium down the middle, looked up at the five levels of balconies above him. All he could see were people jammed together shoulder to shoulder, their expectant faces watching the last minute preparations for a historical event the likes their generation had never witnessed before.

"They seem scared," Eliza said, leaning close to her husband's ear so she could be heard. Despite more than a few grumblings from some of the stewards in attendance, Eliza's seat had been placed to Alexis's right. De Morlan had happily given up the spot to please the mistress. "Why do they seem so scared? I would think they'd be elated considering their voices will truly be heard for the first time."

"I think they are afraid for many reasons," Alexis replied, taking his wife's hand and kissing the soft skin. "Mostly they are afraid their representatives will not be up to the task and the meeting will fail. Many of these men taking their seats have been nothing but subservient to stewards their entire lives. Sure, they lead as sector wardens and deck bosses, but that's not the same as actually making decisions that not only affect their people, but all passengers on Station Aelon."

"Yes, it must be very hard for all these *men*," Eliza said, her sarcasm not concealed in the least.

"Patience, my dear love," Alexis said. "One day women will join these tables. But it must be one step at a time. Making sure the meeting of passengers is a success will be key to ushering changes for the fairer sex."

A hand gripped him under the table. Hard.

"Fairer?" Eliza mocked, squeezing even harder. Alexis grunted, but tried to keep his face passive so as not to alarm anyone. "What's that about fairer?"

He gently removed her hand and placed it on her belly.

"You know what I mean," he said, his own hand rubbing at her midsection that was just starting to protrude. "And you know how I feel."

"And you know how I feel," Eliza said. "Thomas may be your male heir, but Esther is who should truly take the crown when, Helios forbid, you pass. I love my boy dearly, but he does not have the temperament for ruling like you do. Esther was born to be a mistress, and not because she marries into the position."

"I know," Alexis said as he watched a portly man make his way through the crowd and to Corbin who stood a few paces away. "I know that man. Where have I met him?"

Eliza looked over and shook her head. "Not a clue."

"Ah! I know," Alexis exclaimed and stood up quickly. "Deck Boss Wyerrn! Come, meet my wife!"

Corbin looked over his shoulder at the royal couple then turned back to Gornish and gestured for him to proceed.

"Your highness, thank you so much for granting me an audience," Gornish said, bowing low. "I know you have many more important people to attend to than a lowly deck boss such as myself."

"Not true, not true," Alexis said. "A man of your ingenuity should always be in favor of a master's attention."

Gornish let out a little squeak at the compliment and his face turned bright red. Eliza chuckled at the sight and stood up to offer her hand.

"So you are the man that created the longsling and the, uh, what do you call them?" Eliza grinned as Gornish clumsily took her hand and nearly fell over as he tried to bow and kiss the hand at the same time. "The new flechettes?"

"Particle barb flechettes, your highness," Gornish replied. "Thicker and heavier than normal flechettes because they are designed to splinter and shred upon contact. I have been testing a new version and finally perfected one that can cut through even the toughest of polybreen armor."

"Cut through polybreen armor?" Eliza replied. "I didn't know that was possible except for the sharpest long blade."

"It is now, my mistress," Gornish responded. "I was hoping to gain an audience with the royal armorer, but he will not see me."

Alexis furrowed his brow. "He won't? I gave strict orders to accommodate your needs in bringing the longslings, and ammunition, into full production."

"I appreciate that, your highness," Gornish nodded. "I wouldn't trouble you with it, but..."

"Out with it," Alexis said. "You are speaking to someone that was raised to appreciate innovations of engineering and construction. Don't hesitate in being honest."

"It's that I have sunk my entire life's fortune, as well as my wife's, into the design of the longsling and particle barbs. If I can't get them into production soon then I will lose everything," Gornish said shyly. "And now my appointment to the meeting of passengers, which is a true honor, will take up more of my time. Time I should be using to shore up my holdings. I am not a young man such as yourself, your highness. I have limited days to provide a legacy for my daughters."

"Then I'll do what I can to help with that legacy, Gornish, my man," Alexis grinned, clapping the man on the shoulder. "Corbin!"

"Yes, sire?" Corbin asked, his eyes turning reluctantly from the task of scanning the crowds.

"Will you take Deck Boss Wyerrn to find my brother? If you accompany him he'll be seen right away," Alexis said. "I know Derrick is about here somewhere." The master turned to Gornish. "Tell my brother that he is, by royal decree, to expedite the production of longslings and the flechettes.

He's a long time drinking buddy of the royal armorer. Derrick will know how to get things moving."

"Thank you, your grace!" Gornish exclaimed. "I mean, your highness! Your aren't High Guardian, I don't know why I called you your grace. My apologies—"

"It's fine," Eliza interrupted. "He can be very graceful."

"Corbin? Please," Alexis said as the deck boss started to stammer more gratitudes. "Hurry before the proceedings begin."

Corbin tugged at Gornish's elbow and led the thankful man away through the milling groups of passengers and stewards. Alexis watched them go with a bemused smile.

"I like that man," Alexis said.

"I like it when you say 'royal decree,'" Eliza grinned. "Maybe you can say it to me over and over later this evening?"

"If the day doesn't tire us both out," Alexis said.

There is a commotion towards one of the side tables and soon shouting could be heard. Then there was the crash of glassware and the shouts rose in volume until the atrium was filled with a roar of angry voices.

"Steward Thierri's party," de Morlan said as he hurried over to Alexis's side. "His choice of passenger representative was seated two chairs down from the one that represents Sector Glebe."

"Steward Alote's sector," Alexis said.

"Precisely," de Morlan nodded.

"Helios," Alexis sighed as he rubbed his face. "This meeting is about the passengers and not about petty feuds between stewards."

"The passenger delegates represent their sectors," de Morlan shrugged. "Which means they bring their stewards' grudges with them to the tables."

"Shaowshit," Alexis said and pushed past the steward. "I'll teach them what this day is supposed to be about."

"Your highness!" de Morlan called out. "Sire, no!"

He tried to follow the angry master, but the taller man's stride was too much and he soon lost him in the crowd. As soon as people saw who was walking amongst them they parted and the master could move even faster. De Morlan was held back even further as the crowd closed in behind the striding Alexis.

"Don't try to catch him," Eliza said from de Morlan's side. "Just get there in time to minimize the damage."

"My mistress," de Morlan said with surprise. "You should not be here! Please, your highness, return to your table!" He looked about for Corbin, but couldn't find the head guard. "Here, I will escort you."

"Like Helios you will," Eliza snapped, yanking her arm away from the steward as he took it to steer her back. "I saw the look in Alexis's eyes. His patience is thin and he's ready to make an example. He has too much of his grandfather in him."

De Morlan looked from the mistress to the crowd that was gathering and following the master to the side of the atrium.

"You need to go control this situation," Eliza insisted. "Now."

"Fine, your highness," de Morlan said. "But you do not leave my side, understood?"

"Did you just talk to me as if I was a child, Steward de Morlan?" Eliza grinned. "Can I have candy if I'm a good girl?"

De Morlan's jaw dropped in confusion and embarrassment.

"Close that trap, Alasdair," Eliza said as she took the lead. "You'll attract honey wasps."

Eliza pushed through the crowd to reach her husband just as he was pulling two men off of each other. She shook her head and stopped at the edge of the fight, watching her husband tower over the much older and much shorter passengers.

"Is this how you want to legislate?" Alexis shouted. "With grudges and fists? How is this behavior any better than just letting the stewards decide your fate? You two should be ashamed of yourselves and think long and hard on whether you are the right men to represent your sectors!"

He gripped a skinny, freckled man by the back of the neck and shook him.

"What is your name, sir?" Alexis barked.

"Deck Boss Bothe Teg, your highness," the man winced.

"And you?" Alexis asked the other, equally pained man.

"Sector Warden Montieth Wyatt," the other man replied, his mouth a rictus of pain as the master's grip increased.

"Well, Sector Warden Montieth Wyatt and Deck Boss Bothe Teg," Alexis smiled, violence shining from his white teeth. "Shake hands now and call your stupid bickering over and done with. Extend those hands or I will cut them off, do you hear me?"

The two men stared up at the master, their eyes wide with fear and confusion. Then slowly they extended their hands and shook.

"Good," Alexis said, letting them go and shoving them away. "Now if you don't mind, I would like to start this meeting so we can make history."

Deck Boss Teg stumbled as he stepped away from the master and his feet went out from under him. He tried to break his fall by grabbing one of the tables, but his hand slipped and instead his head smacked a corner. The man crumpled to the ground and there was an audible gasp.

"Father? Father!" a younger man shouted as he shoved people out of the way to get to the fallen deck boss. "Oh, Helios! Father!"

Blood pooled around Teg's head and the younger man fell to his knees and lifted him into his lap. The older man's eyes were blank and glazed, showing his soul had already fled the flesh.

"No! *No*!" the younger man screamed. Then he looked up at a stunned Alexis. "You killed him! You killed my father! He was a good man! *He was good*!"

"Oh, Helios..." Alexis whispered.

"Alexis? Come along," Eliza said as she moved forward and took his hand. "We need to leave."

There were harsh whispers and grumbles started to move through the crowd as Eliza looked about, suddenly fearful for her and her husband's safety for the first time that day.

"Alexis," she hissed.

"I'm sorry," Alexis said, gently moving away from his wife and crouching before the grief stricken man and his dead father. "It was an accident, I assure you. I'll compensate—"

"Compensate?" the man yelled. "Compensate me how? With a new father? You can't get a new father when one dies! It's not like you and your stillborn brood! One dies and you can fuck the Ploervian whore you married and make another one! I'd fuck that slut too if it would bring my father back! But it won't, so take the whore cunt away from here!"

The whispering crowd went silent at the man's words. Alexis didn't move or say anything for a long while. Then he abruptly stood up, walked over to de Morlan, removed the man's long blade, spun about and jammed it through the eye socket of the grieving son.

Blood spurted out around the blade as Alexis leaned into it, kneeling as he pushed it through the man's skull up to the hilt. The master's face was one of shaking fury and he moved in close to the second dead man.

"See who you can fuck in Helios, asshole," Alexis snarled.

Then he stood up and yanked the blade free, whipping the blood from the metal in one shake of his hand. He turned to look at the crowd and was about to speak when several roars were heard and six men shoved through, all running at the master with blades drawn.

"Alexis!" Eliza screamed.

The master spun about and ducked low just as the first blade swiped empty air where his head had been. Alexis slid his long blade easily into the attacker's soft guts and pulled to the side, sending intestines spilling out onto the floor.

"*Corbin*!" Eliza screamed, the only voice in a stunned crowd. "*Corbin*!"

Even the other royal guards stood silent and still, their minds confused by what they were seeing.

A second attacker brought his blade down with both hands, but Alexis raised his blade in time to block the blow. He stood up, his long legs like unstoppable pistons, and shoved the man back with one hand while he reached out and snagged the man's short blade from his belt. Before the attacker could regain his balance he found his own short blade sticking out of his chest.

Alexis strode forward and pulled out the short blade, then spun and threw it at a third man that came at him. He smiled as the blade slid into the man's forehead like a knife through butter. On some level he wondered what the man had used to sharpen the blade.

"Sire!" Corbin yelled as he finally reached the fight. "What are you men doing? Stop this!"

The head of the royal guard hurried at the master and grabbed him by both arms just as another attacker was about to meet Helios in person.

"Sire! Stop!" Corbin shouted up at Alexis's ear. "Stop now!"

Alexis threw off his protector and whirled on him, long blade ready for battle. Corbin parried and knocked the master's blade to the side, but didn't unhand it.

"Corbin," Alexis said, his voice calm and even, not matching the wild look in his eyes or the way his chest hitched up and down with the exertion and adrenaline. "About time you showed your face."

Corbin shook his head and frowned as he stood back from the master. "Sire, I was—"

"No matter," Alexis said, waving his hand as he tossed the long blade to the ground. "All of these men? Have them brought to their knees and lined up."

"All men of Sector Glebe and Sector Gwalter will step forward!" Corbin shouted. "Do so now!"

Almost two dozen men reluctantly separated from the crowd as guards hurried forward and shoved them to their knees. They looked up at the master, many with nothing but rage in their eyes, but most with terror and sadness.

"You hold a grudge against each others' sectors for what reason?" Alexis snarled. "Because your stewards say so? Cowards. All of you. I bring you here to be able to speak and think for yourselves and all you do is pick other men's fights. You don't deserve a voice. None of you do."

He stood up and walked slowly away from the line of men, his eyes focused on Corbin's.

"Cut out their tongues," Alexis said. "And if a single one makes a sound while you do it then execute them all."

Corbin watched his master for a second then moved in close, his voice barely above a whisper.

"Please, sire, do not ask me to do this," Corbin pleaded. "This was all a mistake."

"Are you saying the Master of Station Aelon made a mistake?" Alexis grinned. "Please, *guard*, say what you just said again."

Corbin closed his mouth and swallowed hard then shook his head.

"That's what I thought," Alexis said. "Now. Cut. Out. Their. Tongues."

"No, Corbin, do not," Eliza said as she moved forward and pushed the miserable head guard out of the way. "Because my husband is about to rescind that order and turn and apologize to these people. Do you hear me, Alexis Teirmont? There will be no tongue cutting, no executions, and no more violence today. Turn and show these men mercy and show your people the humility I know you possess."

"You are shaming me in front of passengers," Alexis said. "De Morlan? Take my wife away from here. This is no place for a—"

The slap came so fast and hard that Alexis didn't have a chance to brace for it. Even at the awkward angle of the blow, his head still nearly whipped all the way about. He raised his own hand in retaliation, but then his whole body went cold and numb with the awareness of what he was about to do.

"Show them," Eliza said, not flinching an inch from the raised hand above her. "Show them now."

"My love," Alexis whispered, his hand falling slowly to his side. "Forgive me."

"I already have," Eliza replied. "It is their forgiveness you need."

Eliza reached up and stroked her husband's cheeks, wiping the single tear away that escaped the corner of one eye. She gently pulled his face towards her and then kissed the quivering lips once they were close enough.

"You are not a monster like your grandfather," Eliza said. "Nor a fool, like your father. You are Alexis the First and a man unto yourself. You wanted to make history today. Now is your chance."

She kissed him again then placed both hands on his chest and pushed him away from her. Alexis looked at her for a long minute, his eyes going over every detail of her beautiful face. He saw everything he loved about her in that moment and knew this day would be lodged in his heart for the rest of his life.

"People of Station Aelon," Alexis said strongly as he turned and addressed the crowds, both on the ground and up on the four levels. "I speak to you not as master of station, or as his highness or sire or whatever names we royals were given so many hundreds and hundreds of years ago. No, I speak to you as a man; a man just like you."

He smiled at an older woman who stared at him in fear.

"Well, maybe not just like all of you. I don't exactly have the anatomy for it. But I do have the same heart and that is from where my words usher forth."

Eliza smiled and put her hands to her mouth, knowing the feared Teirmont storm had passed. She just hoped another wasn't on the horizon.

"I called this meeting of passengers to show the people of Station Aelon that it is time to recognize who you are and how none of this would be possible without every single person's effort," Alexis said. "I witnessed that on Helios as I led regiments of men to their death. At the Battle of Aelon Prime, I watched as wave after wave of brave young men fell under the flechettes and blades of the Burdened. Those masters of warfare fought and killed blindly for the Way, not once thinking of sparing a life instead of taking it. They had no emotion in their eyes. Not like the Aelish. No, the Aelish, even in death, showed who they were. Men of courage, bravery, fear, regret, love, loss, and humanity."

Alexis looked up towards the very top level and pointed at a woman by the railing.

"You. Ma'am, what's your name?"

The woman looked about then replied, "Helen, your highness." Her voice echoed about the quiet atrium.

"Helen," Alexis nodded. "Did you lose anyone in the conflict?"

"I did, your highness," she said with a shaky voice. "I lost my cousin."

"Did you love him?"

"I did, sire."

"Do you miss him?"

"Not as much as my aunt does, your highness," Helen responded then gasped at her own impertinence. "I mean that—"

"Where is your aunt?"

"I am here, sire," a woman responded, moving next to her niece. "I lost my son as well as a younger brother."

"And I want you to know I am truly sorry for that," Alexis said, bringing murmurs of surprise from the crowd. "I am sorry to all of you for the rash actions I took when I proposed sending fighters down to the planet with the rest of the stations. It was a fool's errand and here I stand before you all, a fool."

Voices cried out, "No" and "You are not!". Alexis smiled and held up his hands.

"No, it's true," he replied and walked over to the corpses of the men he had just slain. "Here is proof of my foolishness. My continuing rashness." He looked over his shoulder at de Morlan. "Make sure their families are taken care of for life, steward. Pay them directly from my personal accounts."

De Morlan started to protest, but Eliza's hand on his arm quieted him.

"I wish I could pay all of those that lost loved ones under my leadership on the planet," Alexis announced. "But I cannot. Instead, I can offer you a chance to stop me, or any master from here on out, from acting like a fool. By creating a meeting of passengers, I am creating a legislative body that can keep the monarchy, as well as the meeting of stewards, in check. If any other leader decides he will use the people of this station like pawns, he will have to ask the people's permission directly. That is my payment and my penance for my sins."

He turned about in a circle, making sure to look at the entire atrium, making sure they saw the sincerity on his face.

"Thank you for being here today," Alexis said. "And I hope you can forgive me for what I have done and will have presence of mind to keep me from repeating it."

The atrium was silent for several seconds then voices were lifted as one in a riotous cheer. Arms were pumped into the air, scarves and hats tossed about, women and men turned and kissed passionately as everyone was swept up in the moment.

One of the kissed was Alexis as Eliza hurried to him and nearly leapt into his arms.

"That is the master I love and the man I married," she cried just before her mouth found his.

De Morlan stood there, happy to see the sway his master had over the people, but saddened by the blood that still pooled upon the ground and the corpses that were being gently lifted up and carried away. He watched one body being taken through the crowd when he saw Steward Stolt staring at him. The man smiled then nodded and slipped back into the still cheering throng.

The steward was not comforted by Stolt's smile.

"Your highness," Corbin said roughly. "I would feel much more comfortable if I could show you back to your table. There is still much tension here."

"Yes, of course, Corbin," Alexis replied as he lifted his wife up into his arms.

The crowd quickly parted for the master and mistress, and many hands reached out to touch the passing royals. It took them some time to get to their seats as every steward in their path insisted on saying words and congratulating the master on such a fine speech and such honest sentiments.

By the time Alexis was seated again, his arms felt like wilted scrim grass and he was sweating heavily. Eliza laughed at a joke a steward told and glanced over at her husband to see how he liked it, when she saw the look on his face.

"Oh, for Helios's sake," she whispered as she moved her chair closer. "You've hurt yourself, haven't you?"

"I'm fine," he snapped. She raised her eyebrows quickly and he closed his eyes. "Yes. My wound is on fire."

"Corbin," Eliza ordered and the man came forward.

"Yes, your highness?"

"Can you provide us with some privacy, please?"

"Certainly," he replied and snapped his fingers.

Several guards came forward and cleared the area around the master's seat, creating a human wall of privacy.

"Let's see what we have here," Eliza said as she untucked her husband's tunic and pulled the shirt up over his head. "Helios..."

The wound was puffy and an angry red. Black lines spread out form the oozing gash and Eliza's fingers traced them, measuring each one. She narrowed her eyes and patted her husband's cheek.

"How long have these lines been here?" she asked, her tone telling Alexis that anything less than the truth would not be accepted.

"Since yesterday," he admitted.

"You worked hard to make sure I didn't notice," she responded. "While I applaud your effort, I condemn your deceit. I should make you stand up and give a speech on that."

"I'm all speeched out." Alexis grimaced as Eliza pressed her fingers to the wound.

"We need to get you to the physicians," she replied.

"No," Alexis said, his voice strong and unwavering. "I stay here. If I leave then this all falls apart. The meeting of passengers is more important than one wounded master of station."

"Not to me," Eliza snapped.

"Yes, even to you," Alexis said and kissed her before she could argue. "Because it will be important to our children and our children's children. This is my legacy, not a failed war on the planet."

Eliza took a deep breath then let it out slowly.

"Fine," she said. "But the second it is politically prudent for you to leave then you leave. No arguments."

"No arguments," Alexis nodded and kissed her again.

"Good," she said as she pulled away and helped him settle his tunic. "Then call this meeting to order and let's see what the people of Station Aelon have in store for us."

*

From a far corner of the very top level railing, a man stood, a mess of wild, curly red hair tucked into the hood of a breen cloak. His hands were lifted in front of his eyes and stayed there for a long while. When they were finally dropped they revealed a set of binoculars clutched in his gloved fingers.

"Not quite the outcome we had hoped for," a voice said from back in the shadows.

The hooded man turned to face the voice and peered into the gloom.

"For a moment there I thought the master would do my work for me," the hooded man said. "He almost lost the station in one fit of homicidal rage."

"You'd be surprised how many times that scenario has played out through the ages with the Teirmont family," the shadowed man replied.

The man in the hood looked about and stepped towards the shadows, gesturing to a barely visible door set into the metal wall.

"Follow me," the hooded man said. "We can talk in private."

"I only have a couple of minutes before I'll be missed," the shadowed man replied.

"It will only take a couple of minutes," the hooded man said as he opened the door and slipped inside.

The man in the shadows looked about the platform, but no one paid him any notice. They were all too engrossed in the proceedings below. He followed quickly and found himself in a tight corridor. The man in the hood was already several yards away, waiting by another door.

"For a man who is short on time, you sure are taking yours," the hooded man laughed. "Get a sense of urgency, steward."

"Quiet," the shadowed man hissed as his face was illuminated by the dim lighting that flickered above. Steward Girard Stolt. "If anyone over hears you it will be both of our heads."

"No, it will be your head," the hood man replied. "I'm the outlaw and not exactly easy to catch."

"I could call my guards right now and have you arrested," Stolt responded. "I'd be an instant hero."

"To the gentry, yes," the other man said. "But not to anyone on the decks. And especially not to the lower decks. You'd become Target Number One like that." He snapped his fingers then pointed to the door. "In."

Stolt strode to the door and entered the small room, his muscles tense and eyes wary. It would be a perfect trap and the lower decks would make a killing if they ransomed him. At least that's what Stolt wanted to believe. Deep inside he wondered if Master Alexis would even pay a single credit for his hide. Despite being cousins, their alliance was shaky at best.

"Sit," the hooded man said. "There."

"In the chair?" Stolt sneered. "What an amazing idea. And who would have thought the leader of the lower decks rebellion could be so creative."

"Sarcasm is not your strong suit, steward," the man replied as he removed his hood to reveal a handsome, youthful face. A mass of red hair poofed out from his head and he smoothed it down as best he could with his hands. "Stick with the threats, they sound more authentic."

"You called me here," Stolt glared. "Now what do you want?"

"More funds," the man replied. "And weapons. I hear there's a new sling being talked about on the surface. Tell me about it."

"It's nothing," Stolt said. "Some idiot deck boss from one of my sectors believes he has created the best thing since our ancestors realized they could throw rocks to kill each other."

"Never underestimate the power of a good rock," the man laughed. "I learned that on Aelon Prime."

"Right, you were a Vape miner once, weren't you?" Stolt said. "Any nasty scars to show for it?"

"More than you have time to see," the man said. "Tell me about the weapon."

"It's nothing, I tell you," Stolt insisted. "And besides, I've made sure my agents squashed any chance of its production. The monarchy will not have access to any other weapons than you do."

"That's the problem, steward," the man said. "We don't have access to weapons. Unless you count monkey wrenches and bolt hammers. My men need blades. We need slings and flechettes. We need real arms if we are going to be able to truly fight."

The man started to pace the room, his eyes never leaving Stolt's.

"Do you have access to a weaponsmith?" the man asked.

"I do, of course," Stolt replied. "I have a stable of them in each sector. When the station goes to war, the monarchy looks to me to outfit them."

"You mean the monarchy looked to your father," the man said. "You have yet to prove yourself with anything."

"Then I'll prove myself by getting you what you need," Stolt said. "With a price, of course."

"We can pay," the man said. "There are others in places of power that have the same goals as the lower decks. Well, they think they do. You're the only one that really knows our aim."

"Complete independence," Stolt sighed. "I know your pipe dream."

"It's not a dream," the man said cooly. "You would be wise to believe that."

He pulled a long roll of paper from his cloak and handed it to the steward.

"I need a hundred of those as soon as possible," the man stated. "Plus regular long blades, short blades, slings and mounds of flechette cartridges. If this is going to be a war then I need war supplies."

Stolt unrolled the paper and looked at the schematics before him. He shook his head and his eyes went wide.

"Do you know how much a blade like this will weigh?" he asked, shocked at the listed specs on the paper. "How can someone wield this? It would take two hands and even then I doubt it would be effective."

"How heavy do you think a rotational torque wrench is? Or a span driver?" the man laughed. "That in your hands is nothing. Just like the real blades that will come from those plans will weigh nothing to us. We've been preparing for this for centuries. Now it is our time."

"You mean it is *your* time," Stolt said as he rolled up the paper. "But this isn't just about you, is it? This is about you regaining some lost glory you believe your family possessed generations ago."

Stolt stood and tucked the roll inside his own cloak he had wrapped about his tunic. He shook his head as he walked to the door.

"Be careful, Lucas Langley," Stolt said at the door. "Most of the time staying in the shadows is better than being in the light."

"Says the man that lives on the Surface," Lucas Langley replied. "I'm sick of the shadows."

Act II

A Rebellion Halted

"The reign of Alexis I of Station Aelon has been studied for centuries. The vision, the fortitude, the eventual decline, and most of all, the black mark that was the lower decks rebellion. It could have been a reign that surpassed all others before it, but in the end, it comes down to a hurt and angry monarch versus the voice of a people. A sad tale told many times over."

—Dr. D. Reven, Eighty-Third Archivist of The Way

"I don't know what they talk about up on the surface of Station Aelon, but down here, in the lower decks, we talk about being equal. We talk about getting a better life for our children and grandchildren. We talk about being more than just cogs in the nobility's machine. We talk about everything. And that talk is what frightens them the most."

—Lucas Langley, Liberty Tapes (unabridged)

"When your enemy comes to you, do not hesitate. They are not there for you; they are not there to support your position. Strike first, strike hard, and let Helios know you will not waver in righteousness."

—Book of the Lesson 21:4, The Ledger

"He was a stupid gnat that had to be crushed. My father did what was right and what was just. You can't have blights like that on Station Aelon. That blight spreads and then all that is beautiful is ruined. I abhor the ruination of beauty."

—Journals of Alexis II, Master of Aelon Station

CHAPTER FOUR

"My whole damn life is babies!" Esther shouted as she set her infant brother down on the bed, a fresh diaper over her shoulder and a soiled one waiting for her. "I'll never marry and have children! Why would I need to?"

"Hush now," Eliza scolded as she hurried around the royal quarters, looking for a shoe here, an errant sock there, all in order to get the family prepared for the day's festivities. "You're scaring Alexis."

"Oh, I am not," Esther grumbled. "Look at the little turd. He's the happiest baby I've ever seen."

"You said turd," James laughed, his four year old finger up his four year old nose.

"Stop that!" Bora scolded, her hand slapping her little brother's finger right from his nostril. "Haley! Why aren't you watching James?"

"She's using the bathroom," Eliza sighed. "Let her pee in peace."

"She's not using the bathroom," Thomas said. "She's in the closet reading."

"She's what?" Eliza snapped. "We are going to be late for the procession and she's reading?"

"Better than changing diapers," Esther responded. "I'm serious, Mother. I am not getting married and I am not having children."

"You say that now, but give it a couple of years and you'll change your mind," Eliza said.

"You were already married when you were my age, Mother," Esther replied.

"I had just gotten married at thirteen," Eliza said.

"Then had me four years later," Esther said. "You want me to start having babies at seventeen? Is that what you mean by give it a couple of years?"

"No, Esther Teirmont, I do not want you to start having babies at seventeen," Eliza replied. "I want you to live your life and be happy, any way you want. But right now? Your life is mine and that means changing Alexis's diaper."

"Why does he get to be Alexis?" Thomas asked. "I was the first born son, why didn't I get named after Father?"

"Because you were named after your great, great, great grandfather," Eliza said. "He was a Master of Station Aelon like no other. His wife, Mistress Imelda, was known as the Lady of the Breen because of her father's holdings she brought with her."

"Those were the Thraen holdings Father went to fight for when I was little, right?" Thomas asked. "That led to the Treaty of the Primes."

"It was much more complicated than that," Eliza said, finding a half eaten sandwich behind a throw pillow on one of the couches. "Really?"

"I leave it there in case I get hungry," James said, running forward to take the sandwich from his mother. "It's my four o'clock sandwich."

"Sweet Helios," Eliza sighed. "What I wouldn't give for a nurse or two right now."

"We'd have one if Father could defeat that nasty lowdecker," Esther smirked. "But even a good job isn't enough to fight Lucas Langley's song of liberty. Ha!"

"Don't mock your people, Esther," Eliza scolded. "Whether they disagree with you, refuse to work for you, foment rebellion against you, or talk of murdering you, they are still your people. You learn to understand them, and if possible, forgive them."

"For raising arms against the nobility and royalty?" Esther laughed. "They should all be ejected into space so they can float towards Helios and burn up as they plummet to the planet."

Eliza shook her head and frowned at her eldest child.

"I'm glad I get to rule Station Aelon next and not her," Thomas said. "She'd throw me into space for just going into her room without asking."

"Then don't go into my room without asking!" Esther shouted. "You little snot!"

The baby on the bed began to whimper then cry at Esther's outburst.

"Esther, please," Eliza groaned. "Can't you try to be agreeable today? Just one day and then you can go back to your moody self."

"I'm moody? Father's the moody one," Esther replied as she was pushed out of the way by her mother.

"That's because he has been fighting a rebellion for seven years now," Eliza replied as she double checked her daughter's work then picked up her swaddled infant son. "Try ruling a station when a quarter of the passengers want to secede from your rule. See how your mood is then."

"I'd love to see that," Esther grinned. "But I'm a woman and can't rule."

"You're a girl and can't rule," Minoress Melinda said as she came into the room. "And a good thing since I haven't heard once of a successful reign by a spoiled brat."

Esther stood there, her mouth open, and just gaped at her aunt.

"What?" Melinda asked, looking over at Eliza and giving her a wink. "You think you aren't a spoiled brat? Try visiting the lower decks. Then you'll see just how good you have it. And trust me, from one that watched her younger brother take the crown, ruling isn't all it's cracked up to be. Better Alexis than me any day. I certainly don't need white hair at the age of thirty."

"Do you mind?" Eliza asked as she held out Alexis to her sister-in-law. "I have to pee again."

"You aren't pregnant, are you?" Melinda smirked.

"Helios no!" Eliza exclaimed. "Just under the weather. Can't stop peeing and my back hurts."

"Uh-oh," Melinda frowned. "Sounds like a urinary tract infection. Better have a physician check you over. If it gets into your kidneys then you could be in trouble." She shooed the mistress away. "Go pee, woman. We have to be leaving soon."

"Yuck," Esther grimaced. "I don't need to hear this."

"It's because of the rotational gravity drive slowing down," Thomas said. "My friend, Bibby, says that the lowdeckers have slowed down the station's spin and now people are getting sick and going mad."

"The station's rotational gravity has not been changed," Melinda said. "That's just fearmongering. Your friend Bibby is an idiot and you shouldn't listen to him."

"Her," Thomas replied.

"You shouldn't listen to her then," Melinda said. "Open a book, child. You'll see that the rotational gravity drive has two settings: working and not working. If it stopped working then we'd all be floating on the ceiling. Are we floating?"

"No," Thomas said. "But that would be fun."

"Yeah," James nodded, his finger back in his nose. "That would be fun."

Melinda rocked Alexis back and forth in her arms and cooed at him then looked over at her niece.

"What's up your gully?" Melinda asked.

"Auntie!" Esther blushed at the slang term for her privates. "Not around the little ones!"

"Like they haven't heard worse from your father or your mother," Melinda laughed. "Or from you, either, minoress. I've heard you curse like a Vape miner plenty of times."

"Ahhh, better," Eliza smiled as she came back from the bathroom then looked at her second youngest son. "That finger is going to get stuck in there, you know. Think of all the horrible names the people will call you then."

James's eyes went wide and he yanked his finger out of his nose. "I don't want to be called names."

"Then act like you are supposed to," Eliza said. She looked about the main room of the royal quarters and frowned. "Is Haley still in the closet? Haley!"

"I'm here," Haley said, walking from her bedchamber, book in hand. "Can I bring this to the procession?"

"No, you may not," Eliza said. "You won't have any time to read. We'll be shaking hands and curtseying to the nobility as well as the delegates from the lower decks."

"I'm not curtseying, I'm bowing," Thomas said.

"Not with a girl face like that," Esther said and smacked him on the back of the head.

"Knock it off!" Eliza roared and everyone in the room froze in place. "Be good! Just for today, you need to be good!"

A loud chime sounded and Melinda handed the baby Alexis to Eliza. "Here. This one hasn't spoiled yet. I'll make sure the brood is herded along behind you. You just keep eyes forward, head up, back straight, and look like the great mistress that you are."

Alexis burped and a wad of curdled milk spewed across Eliza's formal tunic and shawl.

"Oh, for Helios's sake," Eliza said, her eyes filling with tears. "I pray today is the end of this conflict. I need a nurse back so badly."

"We all need our servants back," Melinda said, taking the baby from Eliza once again as the mistress stripped off her tunic and hurried into her bedchamber. "Won't stop this one from puking though."

"No, but he'd puke on a nurse and not me!" Eliza called from the bedchamber.

*

"Seven years of conflict," Alexis said from the head of the long table. "That is a long time to hold out against an entire station."

The master's blond hair hung down to his shoulders, his blue eyes staring daggers at the man at the far end of the table from him. They were the only two seated, their advisors standing directly behind them, eyes locked on their counterparts at the other ends.

Alexis lifted a glass of gelberry wine and sipped at it, his eyes never leaving his adversary's. A dribble of the pinkish liquid dripped from his lip and onto his neatly trimmed beard; a beard that was streaked with white and covered a long scar that crisscrossed his chin.

"I am not holding out against an entire station, Alexis," Lucas Langley replied, taking a flask from the pocket of his worn and tattered cloak. He uncorked it and swigged liberally, smacking his lips when he was done. "I have only had to hold out against the royalty, nobility, and gentry. The passengers have been very accommodating. It's almost as if they want change as well."

"They have gotten change," Alexis replied, setting his glass down a little too hard.

Gelberry wine splashed onto his hand and he stared at it for a second, watching the drops slide down his hand over skin that was cracked and dry from wearing thick, breen gloves under battle gauntlets for so long. He finally looked back up and grinned wide. No one standing by the table, or standing at attention along the wall of the great hall, had any illusions of mirth from that smile.

"The meeting of passengers was created to address every concern you have had," Alexis said. "But you never gave it a chance. You started this war before I could do what was needed to equalize the balance of power on Station Aelon. All the blood that has been shed these last few years is on your hands, Lucas. Not mine."

"I can accept some of that blame," Langley replied. "But not all. You made choices, or better yet, your stewards made choices that were beyond ruthless. I have lists of innocents slaughtered at the hands of your men. Slaughtered by everything from your fancy longslings to basic fire axes. Not just adults, but children. Entire passageways wiped out. That is on you."

Alexis felt the weight of the words and wanted to acknowledge them, but he had been advised not to concede a single point. De Morlan and Stolt, in a rare moment of agreement, both told Alexis that even if Langley said that his breen trousers were blue, he would have to argue that they were red.

It was not advice Alexis found helpful or comforting.

"I have wanted nothing but peace," Alexis said. "Despite what you think. I have reached out to you through the years with treaties and offers of asylum. You have rejected every single one with the murder of my messengers, sending their severed heads back as your answer."

"Yet you still sent them," Langley laughed. "How many messenger volunteers do you have left? My blade has been lonely these past few months. I almost killed the last one, but decided I would hear the poor wretch out. Thus I am here." He took another pull from his flask them placed it back in his cloak. "Explain your terms so I can reject them and we can get back to work, Alexis."

"Sire, I cannot allow this disrespect!" de Morlan cried from just behind Alexis and to the right, his hand on the hilt of his long blade. "He will address you properly or I'll cut out his tongue!"

"Stay yourself, steward," Stolt said from the other side of the master's chair. "He is less than a passenger and was raised poorly, just like all the lowdeckers."

"You see, Alexis," Langley smiled, brushing a lock of his wild, curly red hair from his face. Just like Alexis's beard, Langley's hair was streaked with white. Smugness was not defense enough against the stress and trials of war. "Lowdeckers. Not even considered good enough to be passengers. We are, and always have been, the castoffs. We are like the untouchables of the old fables. How could your meeting of passengers represent us? We aren't even worthy of that title."

"Yet you have quite a bit of passenger support," Alexis said. "So don't act as if you are a race of your own. No one believes that. Stewards and wardens, even deck bosses, may talk as if you are, but under the eyes of the crown, and the charter of the station, lowdeckers are passengers. Always have been and always will be. Your refusal to accept or see that is your own issue. That, my friend, is on you."

"Tit for tat," Langley laughed. "Tit for tat. That is the story of the last seven years. You tit, I tat. I tit, you tat. Back and forth, over and over, again and again."

"Which is why we are here," Alexis said. "So you can stop your idiocy and rejoin the station proper. I am willing to make concessions to the charter and adjust the scope of the meeting of passengers. I bring that to this table. What do you bring?"

"The willingness to never stop fighting," Langley said as his laughter ended abruptly. "That has always been my offer unless you surrender the station to the people and end monarchial rule."

Half the room erupted into shouting while the other half replied in kind. The two leaders ignored the mayhem, their eyes never leaving the others'. Eye to eye they waited, their ears taking in the insults and calls to fight that were thrown back and forth.

Finally, Alexis raised his hand and his side of the room quieted instantly. Langley's side laughed and jeered, slinging epithets and slurs about how the men were owned and not even real people. Langley let the words be hurled for an extra minute then cleared his throat and his side slowly quieted.

"I'd say you have a knack for monarchy," Alexis smirked. "They listen to you as if you were master."

"They listen to me out of respect, not out of fear, as your people do you," Langley replied. "I would gladly give up my seat here if I knew someone could do a better job."

"Your assumption is that I would not," Alexis said. "Let me tell you something: being master is not all feasts and evening balls. Life on the station is hard for us all."

"But harder for most," Langley sighed. "So stop comparing yourself to people you do not understand. If you want to experience how hard life is then toss off your shackled crown and end the rule of the masters once and for all."

"And do what?" Stolt cried. "Bring back democracy? Turn Station Aelon into a republic? Our ancestors, the ones that fled the planet when the Vape tore apart the lands, tried democracy on the stations. It did not work then and it would not work now. The establishment of the monarchies on this station and the others, is how we kept humanity from ripping itself apart. Each man with an equal vote? Ridiculous! Nothing would be accomplished!"

"Nothing is preferable to the something we have now," Langley replied.

"Anarchy!" someone yelled from the gallery of spectators.

"Perhaps," Langley shrugged. "Only way to know is to try it."

"Which will not happen," Alexis said. "I sympathize with your cause, despite your beliefs in me. I fought side by side with many of your people during my time on the primes." Alexis looked towards the men that stood behind Langley. "Moses. Moses Diggory. I see you standing there. You think I forgot our time in that trench, up to our asses in mud, as a flechette barrage rained over us like the air was made of metal? You think I don't recall how we charged the line that day and pushed the burdened until their backs were up against the ocean? I see you, Diggory. I know you, Moses. And you know me. Do you truly believe your man is right and Station Aelon should be ripped apart at the seams? Is that what we both watched men die for?"

"I fought with you and for you, your highness," replied Diggory, a short, muscular man in his late thirties. Like most of the lowdeckers, he had a shock of red hair, but his was cropped short to his scalp and not a wild halo framing his head. "I would have died for you. But that conflict is over. Now I will die for this one."

"Fair enough," Alexis said. "I understand your loyalty to your people and the lower decks. It was that loyalty that I admired in you all those years ago."

"Why are we here, Alexis?" Langley asked. "Tell me what you will so I can refuse and be done with your castle and all the wealth it represents."

Alexis furrowed his brow then slowly smiled as he looked about the great hall. Centuries old tapestries hung along the walls, depicting scenes from station history that many of the professors and teachers no longer understood. The grey metal walls that peeked out from behind the tapestries were stained with rust and pocked with corrosion. Alexis laughed at the idea of wealth, knowing that the conflict had nearly drained his coffers.

"You know nothing," Alexis said finally. "You have your head shoved so far up into your little world that you forget we aren't the only station in this system. You call this wealth? I call it decrepitude. Funds that should be going to badly needed repairs are instead going to pay for an internal war that we cannot keep fighting!"

The master stood up quickly, knocking his chair back and making the entire hall jump. Hands went to blades, slings were raised, eyes watched and waited for the signal to fight.

"Stop it," Alexis said quietly. "Release your arms."

He began to pace back and forth as he shook his head.

"The issues you have with the monarchy are from the reigns before mine," Alexis said, turning and pacing, turning and pacing. "I saw those issues, I felt them too. Not as you felt them since I was raised in this castle of wealth."

He laughed bitterly and stopped his pacing, slapping his hands on the table.

"From the moment I took the crown I set out to change what was wrong with Station Aelon. As did you. This conflict isn't about two sides fighting for their beliefs. It's about bad timing. You saw an opportunity to go after a young, new master. I saw an opportunity to use my youth and place to go after an old, weak nobility. We both wanted what was right for the station and its people. We just attacked it from two ends, not two sides."

"I think you have oversimplified what I fight for," Langley responded.

"No, I have not," Alexis said. "Because there is nothing simple about any of this. Do you have any idea the resistance I encountered when I proposed the meeting of passengers? The odds were very strong it would never have even seen more than the first session. But your attacks gave me the power to insist upon the meeting as a way to bring passengers into the fold and away from you. Your rebellion has strengthened the meeting of passengers, not weakened it. Now help me strengthen it even more."

Langley watched the impassioned master closely, looking for the deceit and lie he knew was just under the surface. But he couldn't find it and finally nodded.

"Strengthen how?" he asked.

"Lucas," Diggory hissed. "Don't even entertain the thought. The Lower—"

Langley held up his hand and the man fell silent. "I'll hear out the master about what he proposes."

Alexis smiled and then sat back down.

"Good," he said and snapped his fingers. A thick stack of papers was set before him as a porter hustled down to the other end of the table and set a copy of the papers before Langley. "We better get started. This will take a while."

*

"You can't be serious, sire!" Stolt almost yelled when the great hall had finally cleared and all that were left were Stolt, de Morlan, Derrick, and Eliza. The latter having been grudgingly accepted by the former two. "This is just one step closer to democracy! A form of governance that nearly brought our ancestors to their knees! The very people with the intelligence and knowledge to build the stations! Do you think you know more than they did about the dangers of popular rule?"

"Careful, Girard," Derrick said. "You are speaking to the master, remember."

"I know exactly to whom I speak!" Stolt snapped. "A fool that will give everything away that we fought so hard for!"

"That *I* fought so hard for," Alexis corrected. "Of the people in this room, I was the only one to take up arms and bleed for this station. The rest of you did no such thing. I don't begrudge that, Steward Stolt, as you were all needed here, but never attempt to speak as if you know what it is like to stand on a battlefield with your comrades' guts splattered across your polybreen armor."

Stolt started to speak, but stopped. He took a deep breath and then continued. "My apologies, sire. I would never presume to understand the horrors you experienced."

"Apology accepted, Cousin Stolt," Alexis responded. "And my apologies are also offered if I offended any of you. I know your roles on the station were of the utmost importance. Derrick, my brother, you reigned in my stead once father died."

"I reigned while he lived," Derrick replied. "He was not one to cross T's or dot I's."

"Very true," Alexis smiled. "And Alasdair, your years of service have made you invaluable to the Master of Station Aelon, no matter who that person may be."

"I thank you, sire," de Morlan said.

"And my wife," Alexis grinned. "I'm nothing without you. This family, and its legacy, would be nothing without you."

"But you plan to give part of that legacy away," Eliza said, surprising everyone except for Alexis. "I have some of the same worries as the stewards. But I know you and I trust you must do what your heart says."

"Thank you, my love," Alexis said. "There is no backing out of this now. I have signed the accord and the changes will be made to the charter and to the meeting of passengers. Elections will be held by season's end. I want this business behind us so we as a station can enjoy Last Meal with the rest of the System. By Helios, I am too tired and getting too old to keep fighting."

"You are thirty, Alexis," Eliza smirked. "That is hardly too old."

"It feels it though," Alexis sighed. "It's like I never left the battlefield. I was born there, I live there, I'll die there."

"Stop it," Eliza said. "You're being maudlin and morose."

"Aren't they the same thing?" Derrick asked.

"Are we playing crosswords now?" Eliza snapped.

Derrick shrank back and held up his hands. "Sorry. I was just playing."

"I believe my wife is as tired as I am," Alexis chuckled. "A new baby will do that."

"As will raising five other children with that new baby," Eliza said. "If we get one thing out of this, it will be to have all of our servants and nurses back. It's petty to say, I know, but I too feel like I have been at battle my whole life. I'm just battling diapers and tantrums instead of blades and flechettes."

"I know my dear Lesha could use some help in our manor house," de Morlan responded. "She has kept us to our chambers most nights in order to avoid looking at the squalor the place has fallen into."

"You see?" Alexis said. "This is why I have signed the accord. We are complaining about not having servants while the lowdeckers complain about not having rights. They get freedoms they didn't have before and we get clean toilet seats once again."

"Our toilet seats are plenty clean," Eliza said. "I do make the children earn their keep in some respects."

"Minors and minoresses cleaning toilets," Stolt huffed. "The lowdeckers should pay just for the indignity they have brought on the crown."

"Have you not been listening to me, Cousin?" Alexis asked.

"I have, I have," Stolt said. "But understanding and acceptance are two different things. As you will see once the meeting of stewards convenes next week. They have to ratify the accord, remember. This is not settled yet."

"Which is why I expect everyone in this room to be busy these next few days drumming up support," Alexis said as he stood. "We will get the votes, of that I have no doubt, but I want more than just a majority. I want a consensus. I want the nobility to be in agreement so we can truly move forward and make Aelon the station it was always meant to be."

"But first we sleep," Eliza laughed as she stood up and took her husband's hand. "The children are with your sister tonight. I have expressed enough milk for Alexis to eat until lunch tomorrow. We can fall into our bed and sleep as long as we want."

"I could sleep for eternity," Alexis said as he kissed his wife deeply. "So we don't exactly get to sleep as long as we want."

"I'll make sure the royal quarters are not disturbed," Derrick said. "Then starting tomorrow I will work on swaying support for the accord."

"As will I." de Morlan bowed.

All eyes looked to Stolt. He shook his head then shrugged.

"I will do everything in my power to see your vision through, your highness," Stolt said. "I may disagree, but only because I do not have the view that you do from your position. I'll get the support we need."

"Thank you, Cousin." Alexis smiled then yawned. "Now, if you'll excuse us, it has been a long day."

The three men bowed as Alexis and Eliza left the great hall, trailed closely behind by Corbin and a contingent of the royal guards. Once the echoes of the doors shutting faded away, the three men all took seats at the long table.

"Can it be done?" Derrick asked.

"Possibly," de Morlan replied.

"Highly unlikely," Stolt added. "But the master has already pushed us down this path. If we don't get the support he needs then he will look weak which means the entire station looks weak to the rest of the System. That is something we must stress when we present the accord to our fellow stewards."

"Then we better get to it," Derrick said as he stood up and stretched. "I'm done for the night. We'll check in with each other tomorrow?"

"Of course," de Morlan said.

"Certainly," Stolt responded.

The two stewards watched the minor leave then looked at each other across the table.

"Do I need to worry about you, Stolt?" de Morlan asked.

"Worry? About me? Whatever for?"

De Morlan studied the younger man for a second then shook his head. "You are good, Girard. Better than your father and better even than his father. The way you navigate politics is a sight to behold."

"I'm thinking that wasn't a compliment," Stolt smiled.

"You have more sectors than any other steward. Yet why do I have the feeling that you have higher ambitions than just steward?" de Morlan asked then stood up and held out his hands. "Don't bother answering. Whatever you say will be calculated and less than sincere. Just know that I have zero intention of letting the master's plans for Station Aelon fail. You have been warned."

"That I have," Stolt said, still smiling. "Good night, Alasdair."

"Good night, Girard."

Steward Stolt waited until he was alone in the great hall before he stood up as well.

"Fools," he whispered.

*

The sound of blades being drawn was like thunder in the close quarters of the passageway.

"You," Diggory sneered as Stolt walked out of the shadows, his hands raised. "In a million years I never would have thought it was you."

"That was the point," Stolt said. "If the lowdeckers would never suspect it then why would the stewards? Or the master?"

Diggory watched as the man before him removed his breen gloves and tucked them into his belt. One of those hands was extended and the lowdecker just stared, looking at the appendage as if it were covered in filth.

"I don't do business with those that refuse to at least be civil," Stolt said.

Diggory reluctantly shook the offered hand and then wiped his palm as if he'd been contaminated.

"How pleasant," Stolt said. "Your leader had more tact. Much more. Which doesn't put you in the greatest light since Langley's tact was almost nil."

"Why'd you reach out to me?" Diggory asked. "Why not one of the others?"

Stolt looked past the lowdecker to the group of armed men behind him.

"It looks like you brought them all with you anyway," Stolt said. "I believe you misunderstood my request for you to come alone."

"My need to live is stronger than any traitor's request," Diggory laughed. "But you needn't worry. These are all my men. Not one of them would dare speak a word of this meeting without knowing their privates will be taken from between their legs and stuffed into their mouths."

"Delightful," Stolt frowned. "Can't you just kill a man? Why does everything with you lowdeckers involve removing private parts and feeding them to your enemies?"

"Because it's fun," Diggory said. "Now what business do you have for me?"

"The same business I have had for Langley," Stolt said. "Weapons, of course. You will need them, and a lot of them, very soon. I can provide you with a fresh supply of those horrendous blades your people prefer as well as possibly getting you the plans to the longsling. If you were to have that in your arsenal then I believe you might actually win the next round of conflicts."

"Next round?" Diggory asked, his eyes narrowing. "There will be no next round with the accord being signed."

"The accord will not be signed," Stolt said. "I can guarantee that."

"How?"

"I have my ways," Stolt shrugged. "The accord will never finalized."

"You make no sense," Diggory replied. "You would undermine your position for what? Profit?"

"The only thing undermined is the monarchy," Stolt snapped. "My place will always be secure."

"Then why should I help you?" Diggory asked. "Why support another overseer?"

"Because the overseer you have now has caved in and given away your freedoms for the illusion of peace," Stolt said. "Have you read the accord?"

"I have," Diggory nodded.

"And was there anything in there about disbanding the monarchy?"

"No, not a thing."

"And isn't that the basic tenet of your entire rebellion? To take down the monarchy?"

"It was," Diggory replied. "But there has to be compromise somewhere."

Stolt started to laugh, but kept it under control as he saw the fire build in the man's eyes.

"I am sorry. Forgive me," Stolt said and bowed slightly. "But monarchs do not compromise. Langley has given up. He has left your people to trade one mantle for another. That is all. That is why I have come to you. Because I know deep in that lowdecker heart of yours, you think compromise is an abomination. Did Helios compromise when he devoured the other gods? Will the Dear Parent compromise when the Final Feast happens and he devours all of existence?"

"No," Diggory said and was echoed by his men behind him.

"No," Stolt smiled. "Then let's talk terms. I was a little harsh with Langley on the profit margin, but you, Diggory? I see good things with you and might be able to lower my price if you are willing to take a good quantity of blades."

"What about the longsling?" Diggory asked, already hooked and almost landed.

"Let's focus on those blades first," Stolt said. "Once you take control of the station then the longsling will come into play. Can you imagine what the other stations would pay for that design? Best to keep that in your back pocket."

"You have to think long term," Diggory nodded.

"I knew I liked you, my good man," Stolt replied. "You are a man with true vision, that is for sure."

*

"This is ridiculous," Dormin Sloughtor said as he stood next to Derrick in the lift. "The stewards each want their own copy of the accord? Signed? Why?"

"I don't know, Dormin," Derrick said. "But do shut up about it."

"Yes, sire," Dormin replied. "I apologize. It is not my place to criticize the nobility. I am here merely to serve you."

"That's right," Derrick said and gave the man's cheek a firm pat. "And the way you'll serve me best is by keeping your mouth shut once we get down to the lower decks. And also by lugging the copies of the accord for me."

Dormin looked at the handcart stacked with heavy boxes filled with copies of the accord. He sighed and said a few words of prayer for his poor back. He had been Master Henry III's valet at one time, but that was many years ago. Now he was relegated to be the minor's assistant in all matters. There were plenty of worse jobs for an aging servant, so he didn't complain. Much.

"We will be at your beck and call at all times, my lord," a guard said from the back of the lift. "And I would still like to stress that we should take point. Letting you walk from this lift unprotected is not a wise strategy."

"Nockmon, right?" Derrick asked.

"Yes, my lord," the guard nodded.

"Well, Nockmon, what do you think will happen if I let the royal guard lead the way? What would you do if heavily armed men came out of the lift at you?" Derrick asked. The man was silent. "Exactly. If I walk out of this lift first then it shows that the monarchy has faith in the accord. If you walk out first then it can be interpreted a million ways, one of which is as an attack. We'd be under siege before I could even get past you to explain."

"Of course, my lord," Nockmon nodded. "I was only thinking of your safety."

"And I'm thinking of the entire station's safety," Derrick replied. "That's why I'm a Teirmont and you are not."

"Yes, my lord," Nockmon replied. "As you wish, my lord."

"You bet your Vape ass it's as I wish," Derrick grumbled. "Shitty enough I have to do this duty. I sure as Helios don't need a guard questioning my moves."

"My lord! I was never questioning—"

"Oh, shut up," Derrick said. "I was talking to myself. I had a long night last night with some of the pleasure girls in Sector Forbine. You know how those women are trained, right? You get your credits' worth there, that's for sure."

"I've never had the opportunity, my lord," Nockman responded. "The pleasure girls in Forbine are strictly for the nobility."

Derrick kicked the boxes of accords. "Should have had that put into this thing," he laughed. "Although I would guess that in of itself would prevent the stewards from signing off! The nobility doesn't like to share whores with commoners. I could give a grendt's ass feathers who a whore screws as long as she washes up after. Right, Dormin?"

"If you say so, my lord," Dormin frowned.

Derrick was about to respond when the lift lurched to a halt and the doors slowly slid to the side. Everyone inside tensed as they faced the unexpected.

"Ah, good," a man said as he stepped forward to take the hand cart. "We were hoping it was you coming down. Langley is not happy about this and having to sign all of these copies will cut into the important business of his day."

"No one said it would be easy to wrap up a rebellion," Derrick said, looking the man square in the eye.

"You are addressing Minor Derrick Teirmont, lowdecker," Dormin snapped, slapping the man's hand away from the cart.

"I know who I'm addressing," the man said. "We've been expecting you." He reached out once more, but his hand was slapped again. "Stop doing that! I'm here to help wheel this into Langley's quarters for you!"

"I have been entrusted by the meeting of stewards to see that these copies of the accord are delivered directly to Lucas Langley," Dormin nearly shouted. "I just spent four hours on a lift to come down to this Helios forsaken place and I will not have an impertinent commoner like you take that duty from me!"

"Calm down, Dormin," Derrick said. "He's not taking it from you, just helping you wheel it to Langley. That is a good thing since it will get us there faster and get this job over and done with."

"Of course, my lord," Dormin said. "I spoke out of turn."

Derrick shook his head and looked at the lowdecker sent to greet them. "What's your name?"

"Sperry Langthon," the man replied. "I'm from one of the original engineering families of the lower decks." He nodded towards the lift. "My great grandfather ten generations back invented the servo in the lifts that allows it to maintain equilibrium even when getting closer to the rotational drive core. You think four hours is long? It used to take three days to get from the surface to this deck before that. Show a little respect, will ya?"

"My respect is earned, not shown," Dormin snapped.

"Dormin? Calm down," Derrick said. "Just push the cart and let's get done with this business."

"Yes, my lord," Dormin nodded then looked at Langthon. "Will you lead or should I guess where I am going?"

"Testy servant you got there," Langthon smiled. "We could use his scrap down here."

"I would never—"

"Dormin, shut up," Derrick growled. "No more talking. That's an order."

Dormin nodded and waited for Langthon to show the way.

"Come on," the lowdecker waved. "Langley is this way. We don't got no fancy great hall for you to see. You'll just have to make do with the mess hall like the rest of us."

Langthon and the rest of the lowdeckers turned and started walking briskly down the passageway. Not another soul was seen as they passed door after door, passageway intersection after passageway intersection, but the sound of whispers and hushed exclamations could be heard in their wake.

"We are being intentionally mislead, my lord," Nockmon said quietly from behind Derrick. "It does not take this long to get to the mess hall on this deck."

"It does if you have to go around all the fortifications we have in place," Langthon responded, making it known he could hear the man perfectly well. "Feel privileged you are being allowed this far into the heart of things. Just a couple days ago and you wouldn't have lived long enough to take five steps off that lift."

"Yes, we feel quite privileged," Derrick said. "The honor is overwhelming."

"I am sure it is," Langthon snorted. "You can express your gratitude directly to Langley. We're here."

Langthon stopped before a set of double doors. He pushed them wide with both hands until they locked into place then stepped aside for Dormin to wheel the cart of boxes into the dimly lit mess hall. Men and women that were busy chatting and eating all stopped and turned to look at the delegation from the surface.

"No weapons," Langthon said, stepping in front of the royal guards after Derrick and Dormin had already entered.

"My lord?" Nockmon said. "I cannot give up my blades to these men."

"Understood," Derrick said then looked about the mess hall at the many heavy blades set upon benches and on tops of the tables. "Then I would expect the same from your people. My guards will leave their weapons out in the passageway once your folks do the same."

All eyes instantly turned to Langthon. He licked his lips then sighed.

"Fine," Langthon said. "Keep them. But any moves toward those blades and this room will fall on you like a Vape storm."

"When have you seen a Vape storm?" Derrick asked. "Because I've seen more than my share on the planet. Have you even left this deck?"

Langthon moved quickly and was in Derrick's face before the guards could even twitch.

"I've been off this deck plenty, you spoiled royal brat," Langthon snarled. "I led the slaughter of two hundred of your men in Sector Gwalter. They thought they could hem us in on Lower Deck Forty-Seven. They thought wrong."

The mess hall let out a loud cheer then went quiet. Derrick looked once more at the faces that filled the hall and saw nothing but pure rage. And bloodlust. He had to wonder what in Helios his brother was thinking in agreeing to Steward Stolt's request and sending him down here with only his assistant and a small band of guards. They would all be ripped apart in seconds if it went sour.

"No offense meant, Langthon," Derrick said and gave a slight bow.

"Hey, Langthon!" someone shouted. "You just got a royal curtsey! Ain't you something special now?"

"Shut up!" Langthon yelled then nodded to Derrick. "Follow me."

The man led them to the far right corner of the mess hall where Langley was seated; busy eating a plate of porridge that looked like it had congealed several days before. He was the only one seated at his table, but the surrounding tables were filled with men, their hands gripping the hilts of their heavy blades.

"Minor," Langley smiled as Derrick walked up to him. "I am sorry you had to make the trip."

"What do you mean? Four hours in a metal box is exactly how I like to spend my day," Derrick chuckled.

"I am sure it is," Langley laughed then looked over at the cart of boxes. "Your meeting of stewards is more than a little paranoid, don't you think? Requiring my personal signature on each copy of the accord? Do they plan on signing each one as well?"

"They have," Derrick said. "It took forever. The signatures towards the end of the day ended up being nothing but drunken scrawls since more than a few barrels of gelberry wine were consumed." Derrick rubbed at his temples. "I may have participated in that, as well. So the sooner we can get done the sooner I can look forward to another four hour ride in a lift."

Langley pointed to an empty space by the far wall then looked at Langthon.

"Set the boxes there," Langley ordered. "Then clear this line of tables. Set out all the copies and I'll go down the line, one by one, and sign them. It'll be faster if we do this assembly line style."

"Yes, sir," Langthon nodded.

"Langthon and Langley?" Derrick asked. "Any relation?"

"No more than someone named Teirmont and someone named Peirpont," Langley said.

"Point taken," Derrick replied.

"Good," Langley said. "Let's get this over with."

"My sentiments exactly," Derrick grinned. "Dormin? Go set the boxes over there and oversee the laying out of the copies."

"Yes, my lord," Dormin bowed and pushed the cart towards the wall.

"May I sit?" Derrick asked, gesturing towards the empty bench across from Langley.

"If you must," Langley said.

"You'd rather I stand right here and hover over you?" Derrick glared.

"I'd rather you weren't here at all," Langley said as he looked over at Dormin as the assistant began to unpack the top boxes. "Your guards aren't going to help? It will take your man forever to get all of those out of the boxes."

"Then maybe have some of your men help," Derrick said as he took a seat across the table. "Neither of us want to deal with this so how about a little less attitude and a little more cooperation?"

"I have no desire to cooperate with royals," Langley said. "But the sight of you is ruining my appetite. The sooner you are gone the sooner I can eat in peace."

He shoved his bowl of porridge away and crossed his arms over his muscular chest. He studied Derrick for a minute then looked over at the table of lowdeckers closest to Dormin and the cart.

"Micho? Treal? Morgie? Help the old guy out," Langley ordered. "Now."

The three men looked at each other, glared at Langley, then glared even harder at Derrick before they stood up and started to help.

"What are you eating?" Derrick asked as he reached across and took the bowl into his hand. He sniffed at it and frowned. "Smells off."

"Fermented wheat berry porridge with myco-oil swirled in," Langley replied. "It doesn't taste as good as it sounds."

"It sounds disgusting," Derrick said. "No shaow bacon or cutlets? Grendt eggs?"

"This is the lower decks, Teirmont," Langley responded. "I haven't seen shaow bacon since I was a little kid and my father took me up to the surface for one of Henry III's random feasts."

"Right," Derrick laughed. "He would throw one anytime one of his architectural projects was completed. Sometimes me and Alexis would just sleep in the great hall between feasts. We'd wake up and grab a plate of something, steal some wine, then pass out in the corner again until the next one." The minor looked about at the bowls of mush that everyone was eating. "A far cry from this subsistence, I guess. I can almost see why you rebelled."

"Almost?" Langley asked. "What else do you need to see? The lack of physicians? The eight person families crammed into a closet? The missing limbs from rotational drive engineers because their safety harnesses haven't been updated since the last century?"

"Alright, alright, you can stop," Derrick sighed. "I've heard it all before. Trust me when I say that my brother understands all of this and truly wants to help."

"And you?"

"Me? Honestly?" Derrick mused. "I could give two shits. I've lived under the shadow of others my whole life. I let them make the hard choices and just worry about staying out of the way. I do as I am told and don't rock the boat."

"So you live as a coward," Langley stated.

"I live," Derrick replied. "Not always the easiest thing for a royal to do." He leaned forward and lowered his voice. "I used to set a timer to wake me up every fifteen minutes. That way no one could sneak into my room and kill me in my sleep."

"That's pretty paranoid," Langley said. "How do you sleep now?"

"Oh, I sleep fine now," Derrick said. "That was what I did when I was eight. That was the year Alexis came down with the weeping sickness and almost died. My sister told me if he died I would be next in line for the crown which meant there would be plenty of people wanting me dead."

"Nice sister," Langley chuckled.

"She's gotten better," Derrick smiled. "Now she scares my brother's kids instead."

"You have no children of your own?" Langley asked.

"No," Derrick said, shaking his head. "Never married."

"Marriage isn't how children are made," Langley winked. "I should know. I have three by my wife and probably more than a couple others running around the lower decks wondering who their daddy is."

"Some royals have a stable of bastards," Derrick shrugged. "I've always been careful."

"Why? Knock up a whore and so what?"

"Because if anyone found out who sired the bastard then that child would be dead in an instant," Derrick replied. "You forget I hear the secrets of other stations. Master Rutge of Station Klaerv sent three of his bastards down to Klaerv Prime to hide. Within the month they were returned to him, piece by piece, until he had their whole bodies. Then someone sent him an instruction pamphlet on how to sew them back together."

Langley stared at Derrick for a good long while before he shook his head.

"That story makes my case for why the monarchy should be abolished," Langley said. "And to think lowdeckers are considered the barbarians of this station."

"Please," Derrick laughed. "You understand brutality and violence, but we royals understand that and cruelty. You haven't met evil until you've looked royal ambition in the eye."

"What do you call that?" Langley asked, pointing at the stacks of paper being set on the table. "Looks like royal ambition to me."

"Hardly," Derrick responded. "My brother wanted nothing to do with this. It was all the meeting of the stewards' idea."

"I am willing to bet there was one steward in particular that wished for this to happen," Langley smiled.

"What does that mean?"

"Nothing," Langley shrugged. "It's business better left unsa—"

His voice was lost in the massive explosion that roared towards them in a split second. Langley and Derrick were both thrown from their seats and sent flying against the wall. Smoke filled the mess hall and body parts rained down on those still left alive. Bits of paper floated lazily to the ground.

Derrick struggled to open his eyes and blinked several times before he could focus on the carnage.

The dead were everywhere. Legs, arms, and torsos covered every inch of space. Small fires burned here and there and Derrick realized most were fueled by human remains. Of the several dozen lowdeckers that had been present, only a third seemed able enough to stagger about and try desperately to help their fallen friends.

Derrick tried to look for Dormin, or any of the royal guards, but the space where they had been, where the hand cart had been, was nothing but a smoking crater and massive hole in the wall. No one within a thirty foot radius could have survived the blast. Derrick quickly realized he was alone.

That wasn't his only realization: he could see all the panicked activity, but he couldn't hear any of it. He reached up and snapped his fingers by his ears, but there was nothing but a high-pitched ringing and the low thump-

thump of his pulse. He wiped at the skin just below his ears and his fingers came away bloody.

But his attention was quickly diverted from his new disability as hands grabbed him and yanked him to his feet. All were suddenly screaming at him, fingers jabbing Derrick in the chest. Bloody spittle flew onto Derrick's face, but he didn't care. All he had eyes for was the heavy blade one of Langley's men was pulling free from its scabbard.

"*Hey. Stop*!" Derrick shouted. "*I didn't do this*!"

His words were a far off buzz in his head. The minor started to thrash and fight against the men that held him, but a couple quick shots to his kidneys stopped that. He felt as if his back was on fire and he wondered what other injuries he had.

The men dragged him over to an overturned table and forced his neck against the edge. Derrick continued to fight, despite the constant battering he took, but his strength gave out quickly as he felt wetness run down the backs of his legs. He was bleeding and badly, he knew it.

Not that it mattered as a man stepped in front of him and showed him the razor sharp blade of impossible size. Then the blade was lost from sight as it was raised over his neck.

Derrick's last thoughts were how in Helios's name could anyone even lift a blade like that.

Then it was over.

*

The lift came to a stop and the guards turned to open the doors.

"Welcome back, your highn—" one of the guards said then stopped, his jaw dropping.

The other guard shoved him out of the way, stared at what was inside the lift, then turned and vomited.

Inside were piles of papers, most scorched and charred by fire, with each pile topped by a bloody body part or two. A couple of fingers on that pile, an ear on the other; a foot over there, a shoulder on that one.

In the middle of the grotesque scene was an almost pristine pile of paper. And on top of that was the severed head of Derrick Teirmont, Minor of Station Aelon.

CHAPTER FIVE

The blade cut so cleanly that the man's eyes widened with surprise and confusion in their last dying light after his head was severed from his body. It tumbled through the air and sent a spray of blood across the attacker's face. The man shoved the headless body aside, ignoring the geyser of blood that tried to drown him in one last ditch effort of violence.

"Press on!" Langley shouted, not bothering to wipe any of the red liquid from his eyes as he pushed forward, urging his men on, keeping them from retreating to the safety of the lift that led to the lower decks. "Take it to them!"

The lowdeckers snarled with rage and fought with a fury that only the ruthlessly oppressed could know. Nothing to lose and everything to gain was the fuel that stoked the flames of hatred and revenge. They tore their way through the royal guards with their heavy blades, sending men to death like a Vape wind parting wild scrim grass on a prime.

They were a force of nature that was bottled inside a station made by men. A trapped cyclone of strained muscles and sheer willpower, any that stood in their way were cut down without regard or mercy. The passageway was flooded with blood and offal. Lowdeckers stood ankle deep in the bodily fluids of the royal guards and regiments sent by the stewards to keep the wild ones from ascending any farther than the lower decks.

"I see you, Klemshir!" Langley roared as he spied the steward at the far end of the passageway holding the lift to the middle decks with a contingent of his men. "Run, if you like! But know you die if you stay!"

"End this, Langley!" Klemshir shouted back. "Go back to your world below and stop this idiocy! You can't win against the crown or the meeting of stewards! Save yourself!"

Langley hacked at a soldier that tried to spear him in the belly. He took the soldier's hands, as well as half the spear, with one swipe of his blade. The man collapsed to the ground, his spurting stumps held before his face. Another swipe and the stumps became new stumps and the soldier's head joined his body parts that lay about him.

Langley kicked the man to the floor and then fell back against the wall as a volley of flechettes ripped down the passageway. He turned to see three of his men double over and hit the ground, their thin breen armor no match for the power of the longsling projectiles. Another volley was fired and Langley barely had time to dive into the inches-thick gore and keep from being shredded by the metal rounds.

He lifted his face from the gore and looked towards Klemshir as a squad of longslingers poured from the lift and set themselves before the soldiers that held the way up. It took only a fraction of a second for them to get in place and begin firing once more.

Those of his men not fast enough to flatten themselves cried out as the flechette particle barbs split and split again, blossoming within their bodies over and over with every contact of flesh until the pieces were so minuscule they started to rip apart the very atoms the men were made of. Blood mist filled the air as men so muscled that their breen armor stretched to breaking were cut down by things smaller than gelberry pollen.

Langley saw what was happening and calculated how many men he had left versus how many longslingers kneeled in front of the soldiers that held the lift up. If it was his heavy blades against only the long blades and spears of the soldiers and guards then he would have pressed the attack; they had been that close.

But the longslingers hadn't lost a single man in their ranks and Langley knew the day was over. He waited for the next volley of death to fly over him before he shoved himself to his feet and retreated down the passageway.

"Back below!" he shouted. "We have wounded them and they won't soon forget it! We fight again another day!"

"Run, you lowdecker trash!" Steward Klemshir screeched. "Scum like you will never leave the lower decks!"

"Neither shall you!" Langley yelled as he kicked a spear up into the air with his foot.

He caught the shaft, cocked his arm back, and threw it as hard as he could. The look on Klemshir's face turned from smugness to fear. Then to pain. The life left him before his hands could even grip the spear that pierced his heart. His men gawked wide eyed, stunned that their steward's polybreen armor couldn't hold back a spear it was designed to repel. Langley laughed as the noble collapsed to the ground and the soldiers closed ranks around him.

"His soul will be damned with the rest of ours!" Langley shouted as he backed into the lift to below, his eyes watching the longslingers, ready for the next attack. "Helios will never let him ascend to the Surface again!"

With their leader slain, the soldiers' resolve began to fail and Langley honestly considered one more attack. But the longslingers were beholden to no steward, having sworn fealty to the crown only, and their eyes narrowed, their fingers tightened, and another volley of flechettes exploded towards the retreating lowdeckers.

The lift doors closed just as the particle barbs reached the end of the passageway. The lowdeckers stared in wonder as the metal began to bubble inward, pocked by the ever-splitting flechettes. Langley looked about and realized that a fifth of his men hadn't made it onto the lift. Their screams were cut short quickly as the particle barbs tore them up; then lost completely as the lift began to descend to the safety of the lower decks below.

"We need our own longslings," one of Langley's men said. "Then we wouldn't have to run like lasses."

"We will get them," Langley sighed.

"That's what you have said for a year now," another man stated. "But where are they?"

Langley turned on the man, his face stone cold. The man was easily six inches taller than Langley, but he quickly withered under the shorter man's cruel gaze.

"If any of you doubt my leadership then please bring it up with the others," Langley said. "I will gladly walk away from this fight and let those more capable than myself take over."

There was no response from the man, or any of the men, as Langley looked about the lift. He locked eyes with each and every one of them until they were all forced to turn away. They knew the rebellion was nothing without him. It was an unfortunate truth, but a truth nonetheless.

"Exactly," Langley said. "I have gotten us this far and I will take us further until we all stand on the Surface of Station Aelon as equals amongst the stewards."

There was no response and the lowdeckers stood in pained silence as the lift took them ever downward, back to the squalor they were so desperate to escape.

*

"Show me the weak points," Alexis ordered as he stared at the vast schematics before him. The banquet table of the great hall was covered end to end by sheet after sheet of paper. The master's eyes took in every inch, studying the various lifts, maintenance tunnels, and access ports that crisscrossed Station Aelon. "I know we have secured all sectors on the western hemisphere of Aelon, but what about the eastern side? Steward Veschy? How have you fared with your mission?"

"My sectors are defended, sire," the squat, dark-complected man replied. Only a few years older than the master, Veschy had hair that was liberally streaked with grey. The same could be said of all the men that stood around the banquet table; the wages of war making them old before their times. "Ninn, Staben, and Lauchknit will hold against any attacks thanks to the squad of longslingers put in place."

"Yes, I understand that your sectors are holding, but have you made any headway with penetrating the lower decks? I sent you those longslingers as an offensive force, not to defend your interests with!"

"My apologies, your highness," Stolt said. "I gave the order for Steward Veschy to keep the longslingers back in order to conserve ammunition. Unfortunately, Gornish Wyerrn was struck ill and passed away last week. Production of the particle barb flechettes was halted due to unforeseen circumstances."

"Unforeseen circumstances?" Alexis snapped. "This is war! Death is never unforeseen in war!"

"If I may, sire," de Morlan said, in an uncharacteristic show of solidarity with Stolt. "The unforeseen circumstance is not the deck boss's demise, but the fact that he moved the exact specifications for the particle barb flechettes just before said demise. Until his daughters can find the specs, production of the flechettes has been halted."

Master Alexis looked at the two stewards in shock. He was used to bad news, having fought against the rebellion for over eight years, but the lack of ammunition for the longslings was almost too much to bear. The stewards' soldiers, as well as the royal guard, were well trained, but every one of the nobility had learned the hard way what training did against the full might of the lowdeckers' heavy blades.

Absolutely nothing.

"What do we have left?" Alexis asked as he took a seat, his body exhausted after days, weeks, months with little to no sleep. "Please tell me we have stockpiled the particle barbs."

"To tell you that would be a far cry from the truth, sire," Stolt said. "The royal armory reports we have enough to outfit a dozen squads and that is it."

"A dozen squads?" Alexis barked. The sound was like a mix between a laugh and snarl, and most of the stewards took an involuntary step back from the table. Alexis looked about the great hall until he found Corbin standing at the far end of the table. "Can we hold the lifts with a dozen squads?"

"We can, sire," Corbin said.

"I beg your pardon? Impossible!" Stolt blurted then cleared his throat. "I mean, it is not mathematically possible to cover all the sectors' lifts with a mere dozen squads."

"How fast we have become dependent on tiny pieces of metal," Alexis groaned. "As the *Ledger* says, 'From the highest mountains to the tiniest of molecules, Helios's will rules all.' We have forgotten to pay respect to those tiniest of molecules and now instead we pay a price."

"I'm not sure Helios's will is in play here, sire," de Morlan responded. "More like human folly."

"The folly would be to underestimate my men," Corbin said. "They have learned over the years the best strategical use of the longslingers. While the stewards worry about a proper show of force to prove their manhood, my methods are much more subtle."

"I don't believe that tone is called for," Stolt said. "You forget your place."

"He knows exactly where his place is," Alexis responded. "Advising me on matters of warfare that none of you seem to understand."

"Your highness," Corbin said. "The weakness of the rebellion has always been the lifts. They need them in order move out of the lower decks to attack us. Their weakness is ours as well."

"Are you suggesting the master is equal to a lowdecker?" Stolt challenged. "Saying as much could be considered a capital offense."

"Do you believe that is what I am saying, your highness?" Corbin asked.

"Of course not," Alexis snapped. "Continue."

"We shut down the lifts except one," Corbin replied. "We bottleneck the entire station. One way down, one way up."

"That's insanity!" Stolt shouted. "The passengers will revolt outright!"

"Not if we attack the lower decks before they can really protest," Corbin said. "That one and only working lift becomes ours. We start sending down regiment after regiment onto the middle decks, preparing them for a faster descent and assault once we begin. The lift will be tied up for days as we get men in place. The passengers will complain, yes, but they will also be wary to join the lowdeckers once they see the show of force we place on their decks."

"But what's to stop the lowdeckers from retreating deeper into their territory?" de Morlan asked. "We've tried something similar and they just get lost in that maze they call home."

"Because we cut off their avenue of retreat," Corbin answered. "With the longslingers. Before shutting down all the other lifts, we get them as close to the lower decks as possible without being detected. They then use the maintenance tunnels and access ports to get in position."

"You have lost your mind," Stolt said. "If the longslingers are found they'll be cut to pieces."

"Not in the access ports, or even the maintenance tunnels," Corbin smiled. "There isn't enough room for the lowdeckers to use their heavy blades. They'd barley get them out of their scabbards, let alone be able to swing with any lethality. They'll be banging elbows and raking knuckles while the longslingers pick them off, one by one."

Stolt started to respond then closed his mouth. He looked at de Morlan for help, but the older steward just shook his head.

"And to keep them from holding out too long," Corbin added, his eyes focused on Stolt. "You can make sure your man Diggory doesn't come to Langley's rescue. Without the backup he needs, Langley will be quickly cut off from the rest of the lower decks. We'll have him surrounded by longslingers while the main force runs him down from the front."

Stolt looked shocked. His mouth opened several times to speak, but only a small squeaking came out.

"What does he mean by 'your man'?" de Morlan asked Stolt.

"The steward has been cultivating a relationship with Moses Diggory, one of the major crew bosses down there," Corbin said. "He's considered to be Langley's successor if the man ever falls. Steward Stolt has made sure that Diggory is bought and paid for. I can't say exactly what the steward's end goal was, but I'm sure it was in line with the crown's needs."

"I'm sure it was," de Morlan said as he glared at Stolt then looked at the master. "Your highness? How should this be handled?"

"We use Corbin's plan," Alexis said.

"No, sire. I meant how should—"

"I know what you meant, Alasdair," Alexis responded. "What I'm saying is we use Corbin's plan, including the suggestion that Stolt here reach out to his turncoat and make the man an offer he cannot refuse."

Stolt swallowed hard, but composed himself quickly. "And what offer is that, sire?"

"That Diggory will become the next leader of the lower decks once Langley is in custody," Alexis smiled. "Making sure the lowdeckers are beholden to me and the crown as before, of course."

"Of course," Stolt nodded. "I'll dispatch a messenger immediately."

"I believe it would be safer if the steward took the message to Diggory directly," Corbin said. "I can vouch for the men in this hall, but I cannot vouch for any of Steward Stolt's messengers. I would hate for the entire operation to be jeopardized by the loose lips of a careless servant."

"Good suggestion," Alexis nodded then looked to Stolt. "Away this instant. Meet with Diggory and set everything up. Report back to me tonight."

"I may not be able to meet with the man tonight," Stolt said. "Communicating with the lower decks is troublesome, to say the least."

"I'm sure you'll work it out," Alexis said in a tone that told Stolt he had no choice in the matter. "Now go."

"Yes, sire," Stolt said and bowed low. He glanced over at Corbin and turned his lips up in a grimace. "I could certainly use an escort as my most capable guards are in the service of your highness at this moment."

"Very well," Alexis said. "Corbin? See to it that Steward Stolt gets to his meeting. I'll feel better with you there anyway."

Corbin glared at the steward, but nodded in agreement. "Yes, your highness, a wise decision."

*

"You think your influence is greater than mine, guard?" Stolt snarled as the lift descended quickly. "You think you can work your will upon the Master of Station Aelon? A pissant like you? What's your aim, Corbin? Looking for a sector warden position?" The steward leaned in close, his hot breath a menacing stench upon Corbin's cheek. "A stewardship? Is that what you want?"

"I want nothing more than the safety of the master and Station Aelon, my lord," Corbin said with a bow.

Stolt looked over at the lift operator and sneered. "A fine answer while ears are listening. But when we are alone, I will get the truth from you."

Corbin turned and faced the steward, his features calm, his eyes clear. "I would like that very much...my lord."

The lift ground to a halt and the doors slid open, showing they were expected. Corbin had both of his blades out and ready as men moved from the deck and into the lift, their heavy blades making Corbin's look insignificant and weak.

Yet not one of the lowdeckers underestimated the head guard. They knew him by reputation and experience. Even against five lowdeckers armed with blades that weighed almost as much as a small child, Corbin was hardly outmatched.

Diggory was the last man to enter the lift. The doors slid shut and the operator started taking them back towards the surface. Diggory turned slowly and faced the man.

"Do I know you?" he asked.

"No, sir," the operator answered. "I've only had the job for a week now."

"What happened to your predecessor?" Diggory inquired as he took a step closer to the man.

"He was killed, sir," the operator replied. "The Battle of Veber Listd. Took one of those particle barbs to the throat. Tore his head clear off."

"Like this?" Diggory asked and slashed out with his short blade. The operator's head fell to the floor, his body spurting blood high into the air before it too collapsed. Diggory gave it a nudge with his foot then looked at Stolt. "We can't afford loose ends anymore, can we?"

"Tell your men to put away their blades," Corbin said as he ignored the bloody corpse and kept his focus on Diggory. "Nonnegotiable."

"Nonnegotiable?" Diggory laughed. "Everything is negotiable, Mr. Breach. Or do I call you Head of the Royal Guard? Do you even have an official title?"

"Don't need one," Corbin replied. "You know who I am and that's all that matters."

"I suppose so," Diggory agreed. "I suppose so." He looked at Stolt and grinned. "I hear you have an offer for me?"

"I do," Stolt nodded. "Direct from the master himself."

"Oooh-la-la!" Diggory laughed and his men laughed with them. He waved at them and they sheathed their swords. "What is this offer direct from the master himself?"

"The lower decks," Stolt said. "They will be yours to run, as if you were a steward, sector warden, and deck boss rolled into one. The lower decks will be officially their own region and you get to be in charge. Under control of the master, of course."

One of Diggory's men snorted and got a slap to the face for it.

"We do not laugh at our friends, do we?" Diggory growled.

"No, sir," the man replied. "My apologies."

"Under the control of the master?" Diggory asked, focusing on Stolt once more. "What does Master Alexis have in mind with this control? Will I be a puppet? Or may I rule my people as they should be ruled?"

"You will rule as you see fit," Stolt responded. "As long as it is not at odds with the master's wishes."

"Which just circles me back around to another question," Diggory chuckled. "What are those wishes?"

"No more interruptions of the status quo," Stolt said. "Servants return to their jobs, lowdeckers make sure the rotational drive is maintained and running, no more talks of revolt or rebellion. The station returns to how it was, just with a new official region."

"I'll be your equal," Diggory stated. His eyes locked with Stolt's, begging for the man to challenge him on the point.

"Yes, precisely," Corbin spoke up. "But your seat will be part of the meeting of passengers, not the meeting of stewards."

"That's not equal," Diggory said as he turned to Corbin. "The meeting of passengers is a joke."

"No, it is not," Corbin responded. "Not once you are in charge of it."

"In charge of the meeting?" Diggory asked, puzzled and intrigued. "How is that possible?"

"Every group has its hierarchy or the assembly dissolves into chaos. Just as there is a hierarchy in the meeting of stewards, there will be with the passengers. You'll be at the top of that hierarchy."

"Is this so?" Diggory asked Stolt.

"What? Yes...yes, of course," Stolt nodded. "The only way to maintain control with the passengers is to make sure there is clear leadership. You will be that leader."

"Appointed by the master," Diggory said.

"Appointed by the master," Stolt agreed, smiling. "What say you?"

"I say I'd like a day or two to think about it," Diggory replied.

"You have until the lift reaches the next deck," Corbin responded.

All of the lowdeckers hissed then looked to Diggory.

"You are so sure of yourself," Diggory said. "I think we both know what happens to men that are so sure of themselves."

"They win," Corbin replied. "The lift stops in ten minutes. I hope you have an answer by then."

"No need to wait," Diggory said as he reached out and pulled the brake.

The sound of screeching metal and groaning cables made them all wince. The lift shuddered for a moment then stilled. Diggory cranked the throttle into reverse and the lift started to descend.

"I'll take the master's deal," Diggory said.

"Don't you want to know what Master Alexis wants in return?" Stolt asked.

"You really think I'm stupid, don't you?" Diggory said, shaking his head. "I know what the master wants from me. Betrayal."

"If you choose to call it that," Stolt nodded.

"I call it what it is," Diggory growled. "I'm a lowdecker and we say things as plainly as they are. We don't hide from the dirt and the grime like you surfacers. If it doesn't shine already, I sure as shit ain't going to waste my precious spit polishing it up."

"Very well then," Stolt said. "You get your men ready. Once we have everything in place, you will be notified. At the very least you'll be asked to just do nothing. At the most you will need to take up arms against Langley. Can you be counted on for that?"

"I can," Diggory nodded.

"Good."

"Good."

They waited in silence as the lift continued downward, the smell of sweat, fear, and distrust thick in the small space.

*

The swing was wild and raw, but the heavy blade didn't care, it did its job and took the man's head clean off. A fountain of blood gushed against the rusted metal of the passageway's wall as the headless body fell against it. The heavy blade was brought up again in a rough arc that was driven by desperation and panic.

"*Lucas*! *We must retreat*!" a man yelled as he watched as Langley removed the right arm from a soldier then looped the blade above the screaming man and come down to rip his torso in half. "*Lucas*!"

Langley looked over his shoulder to see that he was a good thirty yards ahead of his forces. He was the only one making a push for the lift; the rest of the lowdeckers were massed down the passageway, panic filling their eyes.

"*Come on, you cowards*!" Langley roared, parrying a thrust from a royal soldier then using the man's momentum against him to spin him about into the wall. Langley slammed the hilt of his heavy blade against the back of the man's head, crushing his skull and sending blood and brains spilling to the ground. "*Now is our time*!"

"Now is not your time." Alexis grinned behind a mask of blood as he pushed past his men to face the enraged lowdecker. "Your time is done, Langley. Give up and the rest of your men will be spared. Continue fighting and I show no mercy to a single soul."

"Mercy is not yours to give!" Langley spat as he gutted another soldier and shoved the wounded man towards Alexis. "You are not a god, Alexis. Just a man. Helios grants mercy, not men!"

"Today, I am as close to Helios as you will get," Alexis snarled. "I would advise you to take my mercy as if it was given by the Dear Parent. You will not get a better offer, Langley."

Langley began to walk backwards, his feet finding their own path between the dismembered bodies, severed limbs, crushed heads. The lowdecker's eyes were filled with nothing but hatred and disgust for the smug monarch before him. He knew he couldn't hold out long on his own, despite his skills with the heavy blade.

Alexis had the day.

"Take your wounded back to the surface," Langley said. "Or wherever you take them. To the middle decks? To some convalescence home on a Surface estate? Is there a stewardess doing her duty and giving her house over as hospital? That must be nice."

Langley walked past a lowdecker that still breathed, although most of his face was nothing but a tangle of flesh and bone. With a swift thrust of his heavy blade, Langley ended the man's suffering.

"We have no such luxuries down here," Langley said. "If you fall then you are done. Just like you will be one day, your highness."

"I think not, Langley," Alexis smiled. "At least not today."

A cry of pain from behind him made Langley turn to look at his men. He was instantly surprised to see them moving quickly towards him. He was even more surprised when they started to turn around and face the other end of the passageway, not towards Alexis and his soldiers.

"What are you doing?" Langley shouted. "Face these surfacers and fight!"

"*Longslingers*!" one of the lowdeckers shouted just before half his head was turned to pulp by a particle barb.

Langley whirled back to face Alexis and belatedly realized why the master smiled so broadly.

How did the longslingers get so far down into the lower decks?

Langley knew the lifts being shutdown was a prelude to the attack that came so he sent men to guard every maintenance tunnel and access port. Every way in and out of the lower decks had been covered. Diggory's forces had the entire place secured.

How did they get through?

Two possibilities flew through Langley's mind as he rushed towards Alexis, his heavy blade raised high: Diggory fell or Diggory turned.

Langley highly doubted Diggory had fallen.

"*Sire*!" Corbin shouted and shoved Alexis out of the way just as Langley attacked.

Corbin brought his short blade and long blade up in a cross, blocking Langley's heavy blade. The force of the blow nearly sent Corbin to his knees, but he held strong and shoved with all his might, knocking back the enraged lowdecker.

"Get him out of here!" Corbin ordered to the royal guard.

"I will not be removed from battle!" Alexis yelled. "*We* push the attack!"

Alexis moved forward, his blades already drawn and dripping with blood from his part in the fight. Corbin spun about and slashed madly at Langley's belly, forcing the man to jump back again and again. Alexis used that opportunity to rally his men forward and attack the exposed backs of the lowdeckers that had turned to face the regiment of longslingers that pressed at them from behind.

"Hold your fire!" Alexis ordered as a particle barb zipped by his ear. "The master is in the battle!"

Many of the lowdeckers whipped their heads about at the announcement, their panic replaced by bloodlust and fury. None wanted to give up the opportunity to take down the master. Whether for good or evil, the man that killed Master Alexis the First would be sung about for centuries. Eternal glory was just a blade slash away.

A dozen men rushed at the monarch, their mouths open and throats vibrating with war cries that drew power from the most primal instincts within them. There was no coordination to the attack, just unfettered fury and rage.

The carnage within the passageway slowed to quarter time as Alexis prepared himself for the attack. He could hear his men behind him, ready to join the fight, but they were a few steps back. When the lowdeckers reached him, he would be on his own for the first few blows.

Alexis was more than happy for that opportunity. His blood was at full boil with Teirmont anger. He could feel his veins burn under his skin. He was nothing but fire and wrath, ready to crush all who had defied him for so, so long.

The first man to reach Alexis lost his intestines with a swipe of a short blade as Alexis dove into a roll and came up swinging. The lowdecker's heavy blade met nothing but empty air. Alexis lurched to his feet, shouldering the disemboweled man back into his comrades.

Two lowdeckers fell as they became entangled in, and were tripped up by, their screaming brother's entrails. Alexis placed a boot firmly on one of the men's heads and crushed his skull like a shaow's bladder. The other man's throat was slit from ear to ear as Alexis's long blade rushed past.

Three down before the royal guards even caught up.

The world around Alexis became a dark void filled with the glowing red heartbeat of rage that burned in his soul. Wrath was all he knew. He'd felt it all before on Aelon Prime when he fought against The Way's Burdened. But then it had been a campaign driven by the holy desire to remove The Way's clutches from the throats of the primes on the planet and the stations in orbit. It had been different.

As Alexis slashed and hacked, stabbed and thrust, his conscious mind let go to the Teirmont beast that always dwelled on the edge. He had heard his whole life about his grandfather and great grandfathers before, who had ripped entire decks apart with nothing but their bare hands. He'd believed the stories to be fancies his father told him to boost his ego and self-importance, something Henry III was well known for.

Alexis knew the stories were not fancies of a troubled imagination as his short blade was knocked from his grip and he instinctively grabbed the attacker by the crotch and tore with all his might. The man before him would have wailed in agony if his throat had not been torn open by Alexis's teeth. The body fell to the ground, blood pouring from its neck and from between its legs, as Alexis stood there and roared.

It was a sound that stunned all who heard it. Lowdeckers and royal guards, all paused to gaze at the gore smeared monarch that held a pair of bloody testicles in one hand and pulled a hunk of flesh from his mouth with the other. The passageway was still for a split second that moved into an eternity until a battle cry from far down the passageway brought everyone out of their shock.

Alexis tossed the testicles aside, smirking at the loud splat they made against the wall, then fetched his blades from the viscera piled at his feet.

"We have been betrayed!" a lowdecker screamed just before his head was sent tumbling through the air by Diggory's heavy blade.

"Such harsh words from a dead man," Diggory snarled as he swung again, taking a man's arm off at the shoulder.

Heavy blades met heavy blades as the two lowdecker factions collided. Alexis watched with predatory detachment as men that had once been friends, many even extended family, tore into each other with viscous abandon.

Two men pulled away from the fray and came at Alexis, but even their weighty metal couldn't withstand the might of the man called Longshanks. Sparks flew as Alexis's weapons collided with the heavy blades. He towered over the squat lowdeckers, his powerful arms coming down again and again, bashing at the men's blades as if they were braids of scrim grass.

One of the men collapsed under the assault and Alexis pressed forward, sending his long blade through the man's heart. The second man took that opportunity to lunge, not with his heavy blade, but with a short knife he pulled from his boot.

Alexis looked down at the handle that stuck out from his side and frowned in disbelief. He dropped his short blade, yanked the knife free and returned it to its owner, blade first through the man's left eye. Without missing a beat, Alexis retrieved his short blade and looked for more men to kill. But the wound in his side wouldn't let him take more than a step or two.

"His highness has been wounded!" a guard yelled as Alexis dropped to a knee, one hand clutching the wound that leaked blood at an alarming rate.

"I'm fine!" Alexis shouted. "Continue the fight!"

"Sire, we must get you back," a guard said as he helped Alexis to his feet. "We have taken the day. There is no need for you to be here."

Alexis shoved the man away, staggered against the wall, regained his balance, and pointed at the lowdeckers ripping each other apart.

"We do not know how the day goes until the last man has fallen!" Alexis yelled. "Continue on and kill the rebels! Helios knows they deserve every cut of the blade we give them!"

The guard looked to three others that stood in a ring of protection around the master. "Sire, I cannot leave—"

"*You will do as I say*!" Alexis roared and the guards stumbled away from his fury, their eyes going to the blades he still held. "*I want nothing but pure victory*!"

The guards nodded and bowed then reentered the fight. Alexis watched them dive in with renewed drive and smiled. Then frowned as the pain in his side nearly sent him to the ground again.

A lowdecker slipped through the ranks and came at him, but hesitated, a rare thing for lowdeckers, as he saw the animalistic look in Alexis's eyes. That pause was the man's undoing as Alexis collapsed to the ground, but also lashed out, taking the man's legs off below the knees with one swipe of his long blade. The lowdecker's screams were cut short as Alexis pounced on him and buried his short blade up under the man's chin and into his brain.

A cry from behind him tore the master from his homicidal blindness, and Alexis whipped his head about to see Corbin being impaled upon Langley's heavy blade.

"No!" Alexis shouted, bringing Langley's attention from the stricken Head of the Royal Guard to the very man Corbin was sworn to protect.

"You," Langley sneered as he pulled his blade from Corbin's guts and shoved the man aside. "Now we end this."

Alexis stood back up and hobbled forward to meet the leader of the impossible rebellion. That leader strode forward confidently; his body crisscrossed with cuts and gashes, but none of his wounds were nearly as bad as Alexis's.

"Where is Helios's support of the monarchy now?" Langley laughed, pointing his blade at Alexis. "Look at you. You're just meat like the rest of us."

"I'm royal meat," Alexis replied, matching Langley's laugh. "There is a difference, believe me."

"There won't be when you're dead!" Langley shouted as he gripped his heavy blade with both hands and rushed towards the master.

He made it three steps before his right shoulder exploded into a mess of breen armor, shredded muscle, and spraying blood. Langley spun about and dropped, collapsing across a pile of corpses made up of both royal soldiers and lowdeckers.

Alexis glanced over his shoulder and saw a young woman standing there with a longsling to her shoulder. He nodded to her and she nodded back. Then her chest burst open as a heavy blade was thrust through her back. The lowdecker on the other end of the heavy blade smirked with malevolence then grunted in pain as he too was impaled upon a blade and cut down.

The master turned back to Langley, his concern for the rebel leader's demise more pressing than his concern for the outcome of what was happening behind him.

But Langley was nowhere to be seen.

Alexis rushed forward, his wound ignored as he began to shove corpses aside, turning them over with his boot, desperate to find one that would be Langley. Yet none were. The man was gone, a ghost lost from the battle, a specter that had retreated to a more familiar haunt.

The master swore he would destroy every possible hiding place Langley could have gone. Then he staggered forward and collapsed next to Corbin, his arms taking the man into his lap.

"Corbin? Speak to me, man," Alexis grunted. "Now is not your time. I swear to Helios you do not die today."

Corbin opened his eyes and coughed blood from between his lips.

"I failed you, sire," Corbin whispered. "You deserved more from me than my blood upon your trousers."

"You could never fail me, Corbin," Alexis said. "You have been nothing but loyal and trustworthy since I have known you. And you will remain so for the rest of your long life, I am certain."

Corbin smiled weakly and coughed. "You flatter me, your highness, but I am not long for this world. Let me die here and get yourself to safety. The battle is not done, sire. You are still in danger."

"No, no," Alexis said as he leaned back against the wall, his own warm blood mixing with Corbin's as it leaked from his wound. "I think I will stay and rest with you, if you don't mind. Just a short rest. I'm suddenly very tired."

He looked down and saw Corbin's eyes were closed. He pressed a palm to the man's nostrils and smiled as he felt the faint breath that came out. Alexis leaned his head against the wall and closed his eyes as well, thinking it really was a splendid idea to just rest, if at least for a minute or two, before getting back into the fight.

Chapter Six

"So much blood, my mistress," the nurse cried, huge, fat tears tumbling down her cheeks like liquid boulders. "It was everywhere...there was nothing the physician could do for him."

Eliza fell back into the chair, her hands clutched to her breast, stunned by the news.

"This can't be," she whispered. "He was still so young. He had so much of life to look forward to. Helios must be playing a cruel joke to take my beloved from me like this."

"I am so sorry, my mistress," the nurse sobbed. "We tried everything, but this strain of the weeping sickness is the worst seen in four generations. It's tearing the station apart."

"Take me to him," Eliza said as she tried to stand. Stewardess de Morlan hurried over and helped the mistress to her feet. Eliza looked at her like she'd had no idea the woman had been close at hand for the past five days straight. "Oh, Lesha, there you are. Will you come with me as I say goodbye to my boy?"

"I will, your highness," Lehsa said, her voice quavering with grief of her own. "Then I am afraid I must leave the court. I do not want to, but Alasdair's remains have been released from quarantine and arrangements must be made for his internment."

"Alasdair?" Eliza asked. "What has happened to your husband? Was he stricken as well?"

"Yes, your highness," Lesha replied. "He passed just before your Bora was taken."

"Oh...yes...that's right," Eliza sighed. "I'm sorry, Lesha. Do not bother with me. I can handle this on my own. Go to your estate and put your man with his ancestors."

"I will, your highness," Lesha responded. "Once I have done this task with you. I could not live with myself if I walked away. Alasdair is with Helios now. All that waits for me at the manor is an empty shell of the man I loved."

"We are all empty shells now," Eliza nodded. "Empty like the husks of dead honey wasp hives."

"Don't speak like that," Lesha said as she brushed a stray hair away from Eliza's forehead and tucked it behind her ear. "Alasdair and I lived a long, happy life. I have no regrets. You still have the rest of your children. Go to them, love them, hold them tight."

"Bora is gone," Eliza whispered. "My sweet girl. Helios took her and now the Dear Parent has taken my Thomas. Will Haley and James be next? Then my Esther and my Alexis? When does Helios's thirst for souls stop?"

"This is not Helios, your highness," Lesha replied. "This is just a disease. We have seen the weeping sickness before, we will see it again. It is a sad side effect of living in a station. Everything recycled, including illness. One day the physicians will know the cause."

"*The physicians know nothing*!" Eliza roared, slapping at Lesha as she shoved away from her. "*They just let it happen*! They should be ejected into space, *every last one of them*!"

A slight cough was heard from the doorway and Eliza turned to it, her eyes nothing but roiling madness and pain.

"Your highness," a man said, dressed in the robes of medicine. "I do not mean to interrupt."

"Perhaps now is not a good time," Lesha said, hurrying over to the physician. "Could you come back later when her highness is in a better state?"

"No, I am fine," Eliza insisted. "Tell me what it is you have come to say, physician. More death? More agony for me?"

"I am sorry, your highness..." the physician responded. "But...yes. The young minor, James, has been taken ill. It is early, and we may be able to stop the progress of the disease in him yet, but it is confirmed he has the weeping sickness."

Eliza looked at the physician then to Lesha. The mistress's face went whiter than it had been, turning almost translucent. A slight twitch at the corner of her mouth began then increased and soon her face was nothing but contractions. Her mouth opened in a silent scream and her whole body started to spasm. She was on the floor in the blink of an eye and Lesha rushed to her.

"Your highness!" she cried. "Eliza! *Eliza*!"

The physician rushed to her as well and gently, but firmly, pushed Lesha out of the way. He touched the back of his hand to Eliza's forehead then checked the pulse in her wrist while probing the glands under her chin.

"It has gotten to her as well," the physician said. "I do not want to be the one to do this, but we must quarantine the entire royal quarters. These floors of Castle Quent are to be sealed at once."

"I'll alert the master," Lesha said as she got up. "He'll want to be with his family."

"You will do no such thing," the physician ordered. "This floor will be closed off then the master will be told. His health is of the utmost importance. We cannot risk him falling ill because of sentiment."

Lesha's palm struck the physician's face across the cheek, leaving a red mark that equaled the sunsets on Aelon Prime. The man stood up, shocked and stared down at the stewardess.

"My lady," he said. "I do not think—"

"Shut your mouth," Lesha snapped. "And never call the love of a family 'sentiment.' Do you understand me? You physicians may be trained as cold, calculating clinicians, but the rest of us are not. Know your place, man, or find yourself stripped of that robe and assigned to the Vape mines on the planet. And not as a physician, but as a miner!"

"Yes, my lady, I apologize," the physician bowed. "I forgot myself there." He looked up and his eyes were fearful, but still determined. "This does not change the fact that the floor must be sealed off from the rest of the castle. As cold and calculating as that must sound, it is for the safety of the others at court as well as the master. This you must understand."

"I do," Lesha replied. "So go give the order. I will get word to the master once the job has been finished."

"Thank you, my lady," the physician nodded as he slowly backed out of the room. "I am truly sorry."

"I do not doubt that," Lesha said as a nurse hurried into the room and helped her get Eliza up and into the bed she shared with the master. "Just remember what I said and perhaps pass it on to your colleagues. Now is the time for discretion, not naked truths."

"Yes, my lady." The physician bowed just before leaving.

Lesha tucked the heavy breen comforter up to Eliza's chin and gently stroked her hair.

"Sleep, your highness," Lesha said. "I'll watch over your little ones."

Eliza opened her eyes and Lesha was shocked to already see the whites had turned blood red.

"Bring me my babies, Delihla," Eliza said. "Let me hold their tiny bodies in my arms."

Her eyes closed once more and Lesha sighed.

"Who is Delihla?" the nurse asked.

"It was the name of the nurse that accompanied her from Station Ploerv when she and Alexis were first wed," Lesha frowned. "She died shortly after from a tragic lift accident. The mistress was to be with her, and the others that perished, but she had missed the lift because she and Alexis were, well, indisposed. Those two were so in love as teens, it was almost laughable to watch."

"Are they not in love still?" the nurse asked then blushed. "Oh, I am sorry, my lady. That was rude of me to ask."

"They are still in love," Lesha said. "Deeply. I fear for Alexis's stability when he is given the news of this."

*

He rolled the plush leaves of the willow bush between his fingers as the servant stood there, legs shaking, eyes averted downward. Alexis didn't say one word, just locked his eyes onto the young man. Seconds went by then minutes and unfortunately for the servant, a large stain began to spread across his crotch. He let out a quiet whimper, but didn't move from his place in front of the master.

"Sire," Stolt said as he leaned close to Alexis's ear. "Can the poor boy be dismissed? I'm afraid he's had an accident while trembling before us."

"An accident..." Alexis mused. "Yes, I can see that. Do I strike so much fear in my subjects that they wet themselves when bringing me bad news?"

"It appears so, your highness," Stolt said. "These are terrifying times and those with weaker constitutions than the royalty and nobility have reverted to animalistic behavior." The steward glared at the still trembling young man. "Like shaows or grendts waiting for slaughter."

"My...my...my...apolo...apologies," the servant stammered. "I...was...I..."

"Begone," Alexis said finally. "From my sight and from the castle. Return to your home and be with your family. The Final Feast is upon us and we now wait for Helios to devour the rest of the System."

The servant's eyes went wide with surprise.

"Just go," Stolt said. "Be grateful you get to return to your loved ones."

The servant turned and sprinted from the two men, hurrying from the royal gardens as fast as his urine slick legs would take him.

Stolt looked up at the artificial clouds contained within the station's atmospheric shield. He'd always wondered what real clouds had looked like down on Helios before the Cataclysm changed the planet forever. His grandfather told him stories that had been passed down from generation to generation over the millennia about great puffy formations in the sky that looked like breen boles. Stolt wondered if the condensed moisture above him looked anything like those clouds from ancient times.

"I would like to see them," Alexis said. "I would like to talk to them."

He pressed his hand to his side and sighed. The wound he had been given during battle had split his body in the exact same spot as the assassination attempt so many years earlier. He had laughed about it causing not just "insult to injury, but injury to injury" and the court had found it very funny. But the jest was a rouse to ward off any suspicion of the true damage it had caused. The physicians had said he may never live without pain again; such was the extent of the wound.

Alexis turned to his now closest advisor. "Cousin? How do I see them? How do I speak with them?"

"We can connect you with them through the audio communication system," Stolt said. "I am unsure how to make that happen since the system is designed to work in the shuttles and environmental suits only, but I am sure a tech can make it work. As for seeing them...?"

"Video?" Alexis asked. "Can that be done?"

"It may be possible," Stolt said. "But the station's internal system is ancient and hasn't been used since your fourteenth great grandfather, uh, what was it called? Broadcast. Yes, since he broadcast his daughter's wedding to the entire station."

"Why did we not fix it sooner, cousin?" Alexis asked, his voice faded and far away. "A wonder of magic in small boxes. The world turned miniature and black and white."

"It is an unreliable technology," Stolt said. "A war of epic proportions was almost started because of the Grand Miscommunication between Thraen and Haelm. After that it was decided that we only communicate with other stations sparingly. Messengers and hard copies are more reliable within the station anyway."

"I knew that," Alexis snapped. "Do not school me like some child, Cousin! *I am not some child*!"

Alexis pressed harder against his belly and abruptly sat down in the neatly manicured scrim grass.

"Your highness!" Stolt exclaimed.

"Never mind about me," Alexis snarled. "Go see to it that I can talk to my family. Do that now, Stolt. A moment's hesitation may be too late."

"Yes, sire." Stolt bowed as he backed away. "I will fetch you when the preparations are complete."

Alexis gave him a weak smile and waved his hand, dismissing the steward.

Stolt hurried from the garden, a sly smile on his face.

*

The small screen in front of Alexis flickered madly, static lines shooting across Esther's grainy face.

"I haven't been allowed to leave this room for days, Father," Esther said, her eyes unsure of where to look. She kept flitting between staring directly into the camera or looking down at the screen that was provided to her as well. "They've given me Alexis to care for, but other than that I haven't seen another soul. Except for the tech that came in to set this contraption up, my door hasn't opened since Mother took ill and they rushed me and the baby here."

"They are feeding you, yes?" Alexis asked as he pinched the bridge of his nose. The poor video quality gave him a migraine and he struggled to focus on the flickering light. "I know proper food stores have been sent up to the royal floors. They have been ordered to make sure you want for nothing."

"They slide in food and drink through a hatch at the bottom of the door," Esther replied. She looked about the small room she was in. "What was this place? A jail cell? Where am I?"

"The third spire. It was originally a jail for Master Gordon," Alexis replied. "The one that went mad and killed his mistress and all but one of his heirs. He was held there until he passed."

Esther stared directly into the camera, her eyes wide and angry.

"You have put me in a haunted room?" she snapped. "My baby brother and I need all of Helios's help and you have them stick us in the Demon King's cell?"

"Esther!" Alexis hissed. "We never use that word! Kings do not exist any longer. We are masters and mistresses, nothing more."

"Same thing," Esther replied.

"It is not the same—"

"*It is so*!" Esther shouted. "Changing the name does not change the reality! A master is a king, pure and simple! The name 'master' was only used after democracy failed. It was a compromise on the surface. Know who you are, Father. Master in name, but king in power."

Alexis sighed and ran his hands down his face.

"I do not feel any power at this moment, my sweet girl," he replied, all anger and frustration gone. "Helios is taking all of it, piece by piece."

"Don't say such things," Esther responded. "The strength of the station is drawn from you. You cannot lose hope. If you do then all will and what will Station Aelon be then? Nothing." She leaned in close to the camera and her face distorted into a round blob of flesh. "I believe in you, Father. You will make it through this."

"Not if you die," Alexis whispered. "To lose my first...I can't..."

"You can," Esther insisted. "You can and you will! Stay strong and know one day you will see your family again."

There was a knock at the door and Esther turned.

"Who is it?" Alexis asked, hearing the faint voices that spoke to his daughter off screen. "Esther? What are they saying?"

The young woman tried to keep her composure, but the agony on her face betrayed her true emotions.

"Esther...?" Alexis asked as he heard his infant son start to wail. Esther stood up and left the picture as she fetched her baby brother. "Esther? Esther! What has happened?"

The minoress returned with baby Alexis in her arms and tears streaming down her cheeks.

"Mother..." was all she said.

Alexis pushed himself away from the small video screen and jumped to his feet. A deep rage filled his belly and he felt his wound burn with a hot agony that would have crushed any other man. But not Master of Station Aelon, Alexis the First. No, that man embraced the agony as his new direction in life.

If pain was all Helios wanted for him as master then pain was what he would become.

"Father?" Esther cried out. "Father, I can't see you. Are you there, Father?"

Baby Alexis started to whine then full on screech as he picked up on the grief and hurt his sister felt.

"Father!" Esther shouted. "Please don't leave us, Father! Please!"

*

The council sat around the long table, their eyes darting to the portraits of past masters that lined the great hall's walls, interspersed with the faded tapestries depicting triumphs of reigns long since past.

Then all eyes turned to Alexis as he sat at the end of the table, his face turned up to look at the murals painted onto the ceiling.

"We should have those restored," he said. "Return some life to the art of former reigns. History is important."

The council waited for him to continue, but when he didn't, Steward Stolt, seated directly to the master's right, cleared his throat.

"I believe the first order of business should be in welcoming Steward Veschy to the council," Stolt announced. "As well as Steward Alote. Their input is welcomed during these harsh and trying times."

"I am grateful for the honor," Steward Alote nodded. "And thankful the same was not extended to Steward Thierri, as his kind is not worthy to be in the presence of the master."

"Petty, petty shaowshit," Alexis said calmly. "So filled with it that I can see it leaking from your eyes like the blood that leaked from my late wife's and children's."

The table froze, silent and wary as the master stood up from his chair, the pain of the effort plain on his face.

"Do you think now is when we should air our rivalries, Steward Alote?" Alexis asked. "While my grief is thick like Vape fog? Are your words supposed to be ones of comfort while I digest the deepest sorrow any father or husband could possibly endure? Those are the words you so carefully chose to speak?"

"I am sorry for any disrespect, your highness." Alote bowed. "It was inconsiderate of me to—"

"Come here, Melco," Alexis ordered. "Stand before me so I can see your true nature."

The steward looked about the long table, but did not find a single ally ready to come to his defense. He slowly stood and made his way down the table to the master.

"Kneel," Alexis ordered.

"Yes, sire." Alote nodded as he took a knee.

"Do you feel superior now, Malco?" Alexis asked, almost spitting out the steward's first name like it was a hair stuck on the end of his tongue. "Is this the honor you deserve, but Steward Thierri doesn't?"

"Again, I am sorry for—"

"*Answer my fucking question*!" Alexis roared as his hand whipped down and gripped the steward by the throat. With a strength none of the council thought the master still possessed, Alexis lifted the man up to meet him eye to eye. "*Do you feel honored now*?"

There was a slight chuckle from the far corner of the great hall and Alexis looked over quickly then smiled as he saw who it was.

"Corbin, what shall I do?" Alexis asked the former head of the royal guard who sat bent over in a wheelchair. "Should I crush his windpipe so he only croaks like a swamp mucker? Or should I kill him outright?"

"Piss on him," Corbin slurred, his voice thick with a several days old gelberry wine drunk. "Or have a good squat and shit in his mouth." The man slapped about his lap for another flask of wine, but came up empty. "Where's my fucking drink?"

"Where's his fucking drink?" Alexis echoed, tossing Steward Alote aside with a flick of his wrist. He pointed at one of the servants that stood by the wall. "Get that man a drink! He is a station hero and will always, *always*, be taken care of!"

"My gratitudes, sire," Corbin said and attempted to bow, but only managed to half fall out of his wheelchair. "Oh, Helios, I pissed my trousers."

Alexis burst out laughing and slapped at his thighs as he sat back down and Alote hurried back to his seat. "Corbin! You are the only breath of fresh air in this hall! Never leave me, good sir! I treasure you almost as much as I treasure Aelon!"

"I'll promise never to leave you, sire, if you could have one of these worthless fucks fetch me some dry trousers," Corbin replied, hiccupping bile. "Otherwise I will be forced to leave in order to properly dress myself. A man should never be in the presence of greatness with urine in his trousers."

"Never wiser words have been said," Alexis agreed and snapped his fingers. Several servants hurried from the hall, eager to fetch new trousers and take their leave from the sad scene.

"Could I steer us back to station business, your highness?" Stolt asked. "We should speak of the crown's succession..."

Alexis slowly turned his head to face the steward, his royal eyes drilling into the man.

"Alexis will take the crown once I am gone," Alexis replied. "What is there to speak of?"

"Yes, of course, sire, but since the royal floor is still under quarantine...?" The steward left the question hanging, hoping the master would see the significance himself. When Alexis only stared, Stolt cleared his throat and continued. "If baby Alexis were to perish then there must be a second heir in place for when you pass."

"My son will not perish," Alexis said. "He is protected by the arms of his sister, the Minoress Esther Teirmont. She will not let her brother die."

"Sire, but Minoress Esther has been stricken as well," Stolt replied.

"As I was when I was young," Alexis said. "Yet I survived. It can be done, steward."

"Of course, sire. But my worry is that the physicians have tried to remove minor Alexis from their chambers, yet the minoress refuses to give them the baby. She will infect the poor lad. Then who shall take the crown?"

"Esther will," Alexis said and there were more than a few involuntary gasps from the council. The master smiled. "Oh, I'm sorry. Does that insult your sensibilities?"

"Your highness must know that is not possible," Stolt said. "A woman cannot hold the crown because she must bear children. Who would rule the station while she is pregnant or nursing an infant? A mistress cannot go to war when she is in a delicate way. That just cannot happen."

"Yes, yes, you are correct," Alexis said. "Which is why we will not speak of succession ever again, am I clear? My son will live. He will rule once I am gone."

"May that be many years from now," Alote responded.

"Oh, shut up, man!" Alexis said. "Your sycophancy is worse than your idiotic ego."

"Yes, sire," Alote nodded.

"I said to shut up!" Alexis yelled as he picked up a glass and hurled it at the man.

It struck the steward square between the eyes and knocked him from the table. The council stood as one and peered over at the man.

"Did I kill him?" Alexis asked.

"I am fine, sire," Alote replied as he gripped the table's edge and clumsily pulled himself back into his chair. Blood poured from a gash on his forehead. "But I may ask to be excused to make myself presentable."

"Sit and bleed, man," Alexis responded. "Braver men than you have done so. Right, Corbin?" A loud snore was his response. "He'd agree with me if he wasn't busy being so brave."

"Sire—"

"Oh, cram it up your Vape hole!" Alexis yelled. "No more about the succession! I want to know what is being done about Langley! Tell me you are close to finding that lowdecker bastard!"

"Diggory has all of his men scouring the lower decks," Stolt said. "He assures me the rebel will be found shortly."

"He assures you?" Alexis laughed. "Oh, well, if a lowdecker assures you then everything must be nothing but happy pillows and wet muffins!"

Corbin snorted in his sleep and then let loose with a long, wet fart.

"Exactly!" Alexis cheered. The smile on his face slowly faded. "I want Langley taken alive. I want him taken within the week. Crush the lower decks and leave them bleeding, if that's what it takes. The rebel will be kneeling before me in seven days or you will, Cousin Stolt. Understood?"

"Yes, sire," Stolt nodded. "I will add my own men to the search immediately."

"Your men haven't been party to the manhunt?" Alexis asked.

"Not all, your highness, which is my mistake," Stolt said. "A mistake that will be remedied as soon as I leave this hall."

"Then leave," Alexis said. "All of you. I call this meeting adjourned."

No one argued and no one dallied. The master was soon left alone, except for a smattering of servants and the flatulent Corbin.

*

The door blew inward, just missing Langley as he slept curled up on the sacks of flour piled in the corner of the storeroom. The former rebel leader tried to jump to his feet, but several fists, as well as feet and clubs, kept him down. Despite the ferocity of the attack, the man took the beating without uttering a single cry.

"Back off, back off!" Diggory ordered as he shoved them out of the way. "Let me see the traitor!"

The men parted so Diggory could look down on the bleeding man that had once been his ally. He shook his head as he hooked a toe underneath Langley's body and turned him over.

"Ah, look at that," he sighed. "You've almost killed the man. You best pray to Helios that he lives long enough to be brought before the master."

"As should you, Diggory," Stolt said as he shoved men out of the way and entered the cramped storeroom. "You were the one tasked to find Langley. It will be your head on the end of a pike if the man perishes before Master Alexis can order his execution."

"You forget that my position is equal to yours now, Stolt," Diggory grinned. "Do not speak to me as if I am below you."

"Yes, well, you are below me," Stolt replied, matching Diggory's grin. "As a lowdecker you will always be below me. Never think otherwise."

"Are you two going to swordfight with your cocks all day or take me to the surface?" Langley mumbled through broken teeth. "I'd much rather die than listen to you two twats."

"Then die you shall," Stolt said. "Get him up to the surface immediately. He has an execution to make."

*

"Your highness?" a man asked as he carefully walked into the great hall. "The work is complete, sire. The entire station will be able to watch the traitor's execution as you requested."

Alexis lifted his head from the long table as a string of gelberry colored drool dripped from his lip. He tried to focus on the man then gave up and laid his head back down.

"What's your name?" Alexis slurred.

"Lead Tech Jin Webley, sire," the man replied as he bowed. He glanced at the servants along the walls, but none returned his gaze. "I oversaw the work myself, your highness. If there are any problems then I take full responsibility."

Alexis rousted himself once more and leaned back into his chair. The stench of stale liquor and spoiled food filled the great hall, but the lead tech made sure not to show he noticed as the master drunkenly studied him.

"It's a rare thing these days for any man to claim full responsibility," Alexis sighed. "You are either a man of great foolishness or a man of great honor. Which is it?"

"I would have to plead the former, sire," Webley replied. "For no man could be of great honor when in your presence. To say so would be an affront to the crown."

Alexis laughed and clapped his hands together. "Well said, sir! Well said! Someone bring this man a glass and let him share drink with me!"

"I thank you, your highness, but I do not drink," Webley said cautiously. "My constitution does not agree with spirits in any form. My body would rebel instantly and I would embarrass myself in front of you."

"Oh? Is that so?" Alexis asked as he motioned for his own glass to be refilled. "Do spirits loosen your inhibitions? Make you dance like a whore wanting the credits dangled before her?"

"No, sire, it is my stomach," Webley replied. "I, well, uh, get sick."

"Sick?" Alexis snorted. "I know what sick is. I know all too well."

The lead tech did not respond, but stood there, waiting for his dismissal.

"Come, Womberly!" Alexis announced as he stood up. "Show me how this 'broadcast' will work!"

Webley did not correct the master as he snapped his fingers and two young men wheeled in a stack of electronic equipment topped by a large video screen. A third young man followed closely behind with a bulky square camera bolted to a tripod he had slung over his shoulder. The men, including Webley, quickly set up the equipment then stood to the side.

"Would you like me to do the honors, sire?" Webley asked. "Or would you prefer to be the first master in several centuries to activate this technology?"

"No, no, you do it," Alexis said as he stumbled closer and peered directly into the lens of the camera. "Can't risk my soul being stolen by this contraption."

Again, Webley kept his thoughts to himself. He nodded to one of the techs and the young man began flicking switches on the stack of equipment while Webley set about turning on the camera. A slight hum and buzz could be heard as the camera warmed up then the screen on top of the equipment came to life, showing an image of Master Alexis standing there in all his drunken glory.

The master nodded and waved at the camera, amused by the immediate response on screen.

"Just like the video communications I used to speak to my daughter when she was in quarantine," Alexis said. "Not so special really."

Webley smiled weakly and nodded then diplomatically said, "Yes, but the image this camera catches will be beamed to hundreds of screens set up in atriums and parlors on every deck of Station Aelon. A far cry from the closed circuit connection of the communication system."

"Same thing," Alexis responded dismissively. "As long as the passengers get to witness the traitor's execution then I am pleased."

"They will, sire," Webley said. "The only issue is there will be no sound. My deepest, deepest apologies, but the circuitry refused to behave and we found too many shorts in the wires to make it work."

"No worries on that," Alexis said. "As long as the people can see what happens, that is all that matters."

"Again, sire, they will," Webley nodded. "Where shall I set up the camera? Will it be in the main courtyard of Castle Quent?"

"No, no, no," Alexis grinned. "That is where all the executions have been held. No, this location will be special." He clapped his hands loudly and one of the techs squeaked with surprise. "Follow me, gentlemen. I'll show you myself!"

*

The lowdecker's mass of red hair was matted and flat against his skull as he was led towards the airlock. He kept his head down and refused to look at the nobility that had assembled in the passageway to see him die. It wasn't until he was directly in front of the airlock door did he look up.

"Hello, Lucas," Alexis said as the guards kept Langley just out of kicking range. "I have been looking forward to this day."

"As have I," Langley replied. "They are already writing songs about me. This will give the bards a fitting end to my saga."

"Well, far be it for me to deny artists their muse," Alexis responded. "I believe this execution will be legend for centuries to come. Shall I explain how it will go?"

"Your highness?" Stolt asked, stepping forward. "It would be more practical, and prudent, if you stood to the side and let the grand executioner take over from here."

"Today I am the grand executioner, cousin," Alexis stated. "Does anyone present have an issue with that?"

"Sire, please," Stolt said. "I am not arguing with you, but I believe your weeks of grief have left you without full use of your faculties. Again, I am not arguing or trying to insult you, sire."

"Stop sucking my ass, Stolt," Alexis said, his sour breath nearly too powerful for the steward to bear. "I'm not going to eject you into space for trying to give me advice. I'm not my grandfather."

"I did not mean to imply you were, your highness," Stolt bowed. "I shall step aside and let you commence with the justice. I have been informed that the camera is operational and we are now being seen by every man, woman, and child on the station."

"Are we?" Alexis asked as he turned to find the camera tucked to the side. He frowned and looked about the passageway. "Where is Wombley?"

"Webley, sire?" Stolt asked.

"Who?"

"Webley, the lead technician? Is that who you are asking for?"

"Right. That guy," Alexis said.

"I'm here, your majesty," Webley said as he pushed past the rows of nobility that blocked him. "How can I be of assistance?"

"Will the camera see what happens inside the airlock?" Alexis asked.

"No, sire, not until we wheel it forward."

"Then do so now!" Alexis ordered. "Because now this man dies!"

Guards opened the airlock and Langley got a good, hard look at his fate. For the first time since being held captive, he actively fought against his bonds and tried to dig his feet in as he was dragged forward.

"You are an animal, Alexis!" Langley yelled as he saw the heavy chains attached to large, metal weights. In the center of the airlock was a thick post, bolted directly into the floor. "What did I do to you to deserve such cruelty?"

"You pissed me off," Alexis stated. "Then my family died. I look at this as an exorcism of all the evil in this station. Once you are gone then all will return to normal and Station Aelon will be at peace once again."

"You are a mad fool if you believe that," Langley hissed as his back was forced up against the post so that he was facing the passageway. Heavy chains were strapped about his torso so that he could not budge a single inch.

"No, Langley, just a sad, tired monarch," Alexis admitted. "I hope this act will be enough to let me rest once again."

Langley started to argue, but a guard punched him in the mouth, sending the last couple of teeth he had left clattering to the floor. Alexis did not protest at the man's treatment, in fact he seemed to revel in it.

The nobility in attendance shifted nervously as they watched the guards attach the chains around Langley's forearms and calves. Alexis glanced over his shoulder to see what reception the rebel leader's treatment was getting and was disappointed by the preponderance of frowns.

"Cheer up, you lot!" Alexis yelled. "This is a celebration!"

Forced smiles bloomed like mold on week old bread and Alexis shook his head in frustration.

"Never can please the nobility," Alexis muttered to himself. "Father was right. There's no use trying."

Finished securing Langley to the post, and the chains with weights to his arms and legs, the guards exited the airlock and closed and sealed the door. The porthole into the airlock wasn't large enough for the crowd to see in so they all turned their attention to the boxy screen set up just to the side. Alexis, however, moved forward and peered through the porthole, his eyes locking with Langley's one last time.

"Your highness?" Webley said from behind him. "I need to place the camera now."

"Of course, Wombley," Alexis said. "My apologies."

There were barely contained gasps at the monarch's apology to a commoner, but all quickly shut up when Alexis turned towards the crowd. He bowed to all then placed his attention squarely on the screen while his hand was squarely on the airlock release lever.

"All set, Wombley?" Alexis asked.

"Yes, sire," Webley replied. "The subject is in focus and the camera is broadcasting. It is all in your hands now."

"Isn't it always," Alexis said under his breath. He looked at the assemblage and started to speak, but decided against a long speech and just slammed the lever down.

A claxon rang out as the opposite side of the airlock began to slide open onto one of the station's few access tunnels that led outside of the atmospheric shield. Although no sound came through the airlock door, Alexis imagined he could hear the roar of the wind as the air escaped around the condemned man and was sucked out into space.

Langley's mouth opened in an unheard scream as the weights attached to the chains were lifted into the air, pulled by the vacuum of open space. The man's arms were yanked backwards and legs lifted at unnatural angles while his torso stayed securely in place. Langley's extremities started to bend further until it looked like he was a child's toy that had met some irresponsible demise.

The crowd gasped as Langley's right arm began to tear away from his body. The blood was instantly whisked away by the vacuum, but there was still plenty of gore as muscles started to rip and tendons popped from the brute force. Langley's left arm joined the first, then his right leg followed by his left leg.

A few of the noblewomen, and more noblemen than would admit later, gagged and tore their eyes away from the screen, the horror too much for them. Alexis watched in fascination as one by one, Langley's limbs ripped off of him and flew through the tunnel and out into the cold of space, forever fated to float through the System.

Alexis reached out and shoved the airlock lever back into its original position. The claxon stopped and Langley's body sagged, held against the post only by the many chains.

"Open it," Alexis ordered and the guards moved forward and swung wide the airlock door.

Blood dripped from Langley's stumps as Alexis stepped inside the airlock and right up to the tortured man's face.

"Can you hear me, traitor?" Alexis snarled. "Show me you can hear the voice of the man that has beaten you."

"You...can...never...beat...me," Langley whispered. "I...will...die...your... equal. History...will prove...that."

"You flatter yourself and inflate your importance," Alexis sneered. "History is written by the victors, not the scum like you."

"You...assume...you...are the...victor," Langley said, still managing a smirk.

"Finish it," Alexis ordered as he turned abruptly and left the airlock. "Move it. Now!"

The guards dragged in one last chain and weight and affixed it around Langley's neck. Alexis stopped outside the door and once more placed his hand on the lever. Once the guards had exited and the door was closed, he wasted no time in slamming the lever down for the last time.

No gasps, no gags, no sounds from the crowd; they stood stunned as the chain crushed Langley's neck and sent his head flying out of the airlock. Alexis watched the flow of blood from Langley's headless torso slow then stop altogether. When the last drop was gone, Alexis closed the airlock and walked to the porthole.

"Take it away," he ordered and Webley did not hesitate as he removed the camera from the airlock door.

The nobility waited in silence as the master stared through the small circle of glass at what was left of his enemy.

"Your highness?" Stolt asked, finally approaching the monarch. "Shall I have the invited guests proceed to the great hall for the banquet?"

"Yes," was all Alexis said.

Stolt did not press the issue and turned to motion for everyone to leave. None of the nobility hesitated and soon the passageway was clear except for Alexis who stood stock still at the airlock porthole.

Seconds, minutes, an hour went by without the master moving a muscle.

"Father?"

"Mmmmm?" Alexis replied as Esther walked up behind him and placed her hand on his shoulder.

"Father, everyone is wondering where you are," Esther said as she moved next to the man and took her own firsthand look at the bloodless torso still held to the post. "Cousin Stolt has grown worried and some of the stewards are beginning to wonder if you haven't lost your mind."

"Are they?" Alexis asked, tearing his attention from the airlock so he could focus on his oldest child. He looked at her face and his heart nearly broke as he saw so much of his beloved wife looking back at him. "I will assure them later that I may have lost almost everything in my life, but my mind cannot be counted within that tally."

He frowned at Esther and looked about the passageway.

"Where's Alexis?"

"In our quarters. With three nurses," Esther stated. "And two physicians as you ordered he shall always be."

"Good," Alexis said. "That is good."

The man stretched and cracked his neck then rolled his shoulders and smiled down on the young woman who was his daughter.

"Escort me to the banquet?" he asked.

"But of course, Father." Esther nodded. "That is why I came to fetch you. This is a time when you need family."

"And Helios knows we are short on that, we Teirmonts," Alexis laughed hollowly.

"Family is not measured in numbers, Father, but counted in the love felt," Esther responded. "As long as there is you and me and little Alexis then there will always be a Teirmont family."

"And my sister," Alexis said. "Where was your aunt this evening? She did not attend the execution."

"She said she has had her fill of blood for a lifetime," Esther said. "I don't blame her."

"Neither do I," Alexis nodded. "Unfortunately, as master, there will be so much more blood in my future. There always is."

"Does there have to be, Father?" Esther asked. "Can this not end things?"

"No," Alexis said. "There are those that will always rise up against the crown. Not just in Station Aelon, but from the other stations. And the primes..."

Alexis and Esther walked silently the rest of the way to the banquet hall, trailed and watched over by royal guards the entire way. The added security disturbed Esther, but she kept that fact to herself. She knew, despite her wishful thinking, that the lower decks were not at rest. Even with Moses Diggory in charge, the lowdeckers would never forget the execution of one so beloved as Lucas Langley.

There was a huge cheer when the two royals entered the great hall, but Esther could feel the hollowness of it. Broad smiles didn't meet wide eyes, the clapping was wooden and automatic, the cries of "Huzzah!" rehearsed and forced. Esther wondered if her father might have made more enemies by killing just one.

"Thank you!" Alexis yelled as he raised his hands to quiet those assembled for the feast. "I thank each and every one of you for your loyalty and support!"

The hall quieted down and the nobles and gentry took their seats, all eyes on the master.

"Over the next few days I will be announcing some changes to Station Aelon," Alexis said. "The execution of the traitor does not mean the conflict is over. There is much that must be done to repair the damage, both physically and spiritually, perpetrated by Langley and his rebellion. Many joined him that did not wish to, but were forced to believe in his campaign. I will be listening to pleas of mercy and I promise to be fair."

There were some nods, but many grumbles as well. Esther could see the distrust in the nobles' eyes, but she could also see the bloodlust that still thirsted for "justice."

"The council will confer and decide the next meeting of stewards and meeting of passengers," Alexis said.

Someone coughed an expletive and Alexis frowned as he searched the hall for the offender.

"Did you think I would abandon the passengers?" Alexis asked. "All people of Station Aelon deserve a voice. I refuse to listen when that voice comes in the form of heavy blades, but I will listen when presented as reason instead of treason."

The hall laughed at the slight joke.

"Men are men and not animals," Alexis said. "Treating a man like a shaow or grendt is not how we as the royalty or nobility should rule. We give men a voice and they will give us their hearts."

"What about women?" a high voice asked from the back of the hall.

There were some audible gasps and angry rumbling instantly.

"Ha, yes, women need a voice as well," Alexis said. "But perhaps that voice is best left inside the family quarters? A woman's voice should be what children hear, what a husband hears, yet not what a meeting hears."

The men of the hall cheered at that proclamation, as did many women, but some held back. Esther was one that held back and she gave a sharp, reproachful look towards her father.

Then she caught sight of her aunt standing by one of the hall entrances. Their eyes met and Esther could see the sadness held there. Melinda turned abruptly and stalked away from the hall, leaving Esther alone to ponder the real meaning of her father's words.

"But enough of this tedious business!" Alexis called out. "Eat! Drink! Enjoy the night for the traitor is finally dead!"

That time the cheers and "Huzzahs!" were genuine and the entire hall got down to the business of celebrating. Alexis looked at his daughter and the twinkle of triumph in his eye that had been so present during his speech faded away quickly. Esther raised an eyebrow, but Alexis only shook his head as he sat down to the huge plate of food that was set before him, having to be carried by two servants.

A much more modest plate was set before Esther and she thanked the young man that brought it to her before taking her own seat. She picked at the food, pretending to eat with the same joy and abandon as the rest of the hall, but she mainly pushed the portions around. As the night continued, she laughed at the right jokes, blushed at the right compliments, acted offended at the right drunken insults, and ignored the ones that should have been ignored.

Yet, as the evening moved from night and into early morning, Esther couldn't help notice that her father kept glancing over at her. And as he drank more and more gelberry wine, it was obvious that something distressed him deeply. Esther knew it wasn't the usual pain of loss that had possessed him since her mother's and siblings' deaths, but something else. Something new...

"Over the next few days I will be announcing some changes to Station Aelon," Alexis said.

Esther had to wonder what those changes would be and how they affected her. A pit in her stomach opened as she considered the possibilities.

*

"I am master and the decision has been made," Alexis said as he drank his tea.

Two days had passed since the feast and he had been busy writing a speech that would let the people of Station Aelon know exactly what changes were to be made. Unfortunately for Esther, she would not be on the station to hear the speech as her father had just informed her.

"The prime?" Esther gasped. "I'm a minoress! You want me to go and live amongst the miners and planet trash?"

"There are some fine people down on Aelon Prime," Alexis replied. "I spent many a summer riding skids across the scrim grass plains and boating on the royal cutters. You and your brother will love the relaxed life the prime can bring."

"And I am to be their nanny, is that it Alexis?" Melinda asked from her seat in the corner. Her own tea had grown cold, just like the look she gave her brother. "Babysit the next master and train up the minoress so she can be married off to one of the other stations? I should thank you, but I just can't seem to find the words."

"Shaowshit!" Esther shouted. "How's that for a word?"

"It'll do the job." Melinda frowned.

"You two seem to believe this is a debate," Alexis said.

"No, dear brother, I have no illusions to that end," Melinda said. "I know your feelings on the standing of women on Station Aelon. Perhaps when I am in charge of the estate on Aelon Prime I can implement my feelings on the subject. Far away from the prying eyes of our benevolent master."

"Don't try me, Sister," Alexis grumbled. He barely dodged the teacup as it flew at his head. "Melinda!"

"You and me!" Melinda roared as she stood up and charged the master. "That is all that is left of our family!"

Alexis stood to meet her and the minoress slowed when she saw the rage upon his face. He was an imposing figure and even her fury couldn't dampen the fear he instilled as he towered over her.

"And now there is just myself and my brother," Esther said, placing a gentle hand on Melinda's shoulder. "Auntie? Father has made a decision and it is our duty, not just as women of the family, but as loyal subjects to the crown, that we obey that decision." She turned and smiled up at her father. "When does the shuttle leave?"

"First thing in the morning," Alexis said. "It is short notice, but it is the only window you have. The next few weeks of orbital synchronization and planetary access are taken up with shipments to and from The Way Prime. It is either tomorrow or three months from now. I prefer it happen immediately."

"Of course," Esther nodded then curtsied. "I will prepare my things."

"Your servants are packing as we speak," Alexis said then looked at his sister. "As are yours."

"Eliza would be furious with you," Melinda spat. The sudden slap from her brother rocked her head back and blood came away as she wiped her mouth. "You are lost."

"I am master," Alexis said and sat down. "It's the same thing."

Act III

A New Life, A Sudden Death

"The primes now are nothing as they were during the times of the Reign of Four. None, not even Thraen Prime, had even the inklings of the bustling, domed metropolises that stand on the planet now. They were wild and free, frontiers that had yet to be conquered fully. They were, to use a form of their very names, primitive. *This is what shaped a master and started Station Aelon on a course that would span many generations and see bloodshed like the System had never witnessed before."*

—Dr. D. Reven, Eighty-Third Archivist of The Way

"When your cousin does offend thee, then smite him down, for he should know his place. When your enemy does offend thee, then bring him close, for he should have a place. When you offend thyself, then look to Helios, for the Dear Parent will always know your place."

—Chants 3:25, The Ledger

"We cannot escape our history. Why try? As a master, I look to the future, but learn from the past. Just as masters and mistresses that come later will look back at my reign. What will they see? I cannot speak for them; only act now and speak for myself. Just as my great grandfather did in his time."

—Journals of Alexis IV, Master of Station Aelon

CHAPTER SEVEN

The master tugged at the bottom of the doublet, his face scrunched up in frustration as the new garment insisted on riding up around his soft belly.

"Why must we conform with these ridiculous fashions?" Alexis growled to Steward Stolt as the two men waited to be announced. "What charter did we sign that said Station Thraen dictates the clothing trends of the System?"

He pulled and pulled at the doublet, his anger rising higher and higher with every tug.

"And did we not send my dimensions to their tailor?" Alexis snapped. "If so then this blasted thing must have shrunk during shipment!"

"I understand your frustration, your highness," Stolt said as he resisted the same urge to worry at the hem of his own doublet, a new style of garment many of the various stations' nobility had begun wearing the previous season. "But we are here to keep friends and find you a new match. Not to have worn our gifts would be a massive insult to Master Paul."

Stolt looked about and made sure they were not being eavesdropped on.

"And my sources have confirmed what we have all heard," Stolt grinned. "That Paul the Fair has expanded considerably over the years. Not just in his famed cruelty, but in his girth as well."

"Has he really?" Alexis smiled, not feeling so self-conscious about the extra fifteen pounds he had put on since last seeing the monarch of Station Thraen. "Perhaps the sizing of this thing was on purpose?"

"So we all look to have ill-fitting clothing and a little extra around the middle?" Stolt smirked. "Sire, would a master stoop so low just to satisfy his ego?"

"No, never," Alexis laughed as they stepped up to the entrance of Station Thraen's great hall.

"Master of Station Aelon, Alexis the First!" the porter announced. "Accompanied by Steward Stolt of Sectors Kirke, Shem, Maelphy, Bueke, Gormand, and Trint on Station Aelon."

There was a large round of applause as Alexis bowed low, showing that even at the age of forty-two he could still exhibit grace. He straightened up and strode with purpose down the middle of the hall towards where Master of Station Thraen, Paul IV sat with his third wife, Carmnella.

"Your majesty," Alexis said as he bowed again. "It is an honor to be invited to your son's Blessing Day."

"I must wonder why you decided to attend this one, Master Alexis," Paul said, his cruel eyes hovering over a broad, empty smile. A smile nearly hidden in folds of indulgent fat. The master shook his head and his heavily jowled neck became an earthquake of flesh. "I have four other sons, all who had Blessing Days before this. Not to mention that you couldn't join me during my coronation either."

Alexis looked up from his bow at the master then turned his gaze to Mistress Carmnella.

"Nor did I attend your three weddings," Alexis said as he stood straight. "But if I had known the mistress would be this beautiful I would have dropped all matters of station and flown a shuttle here myself."

The mistress blushed and ducked her head. Alexis couldn't help but notice that her movements were away from Paul and not towards him. The master had to wonder what cruelties the woman suffered at the hands of her husband. He'd seen similar behavior in his grandmother when his grandfather's ire was up.

"Master Alexis had wanted to attend every single occasion, your highness," Stolt said as he moved in to smooth some of the tension. "But the life of a master is beyond complex and busy, a fact you are well acquainted with. Which is why we missed you at the funerals of Alexis's wife and children those many years ago."

"Or the wedding of my daughter Esther to Zaik, Minor of Klaerv, just last year," Alexis said. "We masters are so, so busy."

"Ah, yes, do give my regards to the minoress on her nuptials," Paul said. "Landing the heir to the crown of Station Klaerv? What an honor. I've always thought of Station Klaerv as such a quaint monarchy, living so close in the shadow of the much larger Station of Ploerv."

A few of the Thraenish attendants hid snickers behind gloved hands and Paul feigned anger and disgust instantly.

"I apologize for my court's reaction," Paul said. "You know how Thraen can be. We are just too prideful for decorum sometimes." Paul leaned forward. "But I am sure you know of what I speak since your late wife was Ploervian. She must have known all about the inadequacies of Station Klaerv. I am willing to bet she would have objected to such a union if she had been alive."

There was an audible hush from those within hearing distance. Even the snickers went quiet at that statement.

"Which is one of the reasons Master Alexis is here with you today," Stolt said, hoping to head his master off before the Teirmont anger could raise its head. "Master Alexis has decided that the royal crown needs a partner once again." He turned and spread his arms wide, taking in the entire hall, then looked over his shoulder and beamed at Master Paul. "And where else could my master hope to find a more pleasing sampling of royalty and good breeding? The court of Station Thraen has always been known for its standards when it comes to those who are considered the most noble of nobility."

"Which is why we like to include even the Aelish," Paul laughed. "To balance out the beauty!" He raised his hands high then slapped his thighs with a force that made the fat on his legs jiggle and roll. "I kid! A grand joke for such a grand guest! I hope you take no offense to my humorous ways, Master Alexis. We masters rarely get to jest back and forth."

"If I take offense at your words, Master Paul, you will be the first to know it," Alexis replied.

Stolt looked from one monarch to the other, his eyes trying to gauge the tenor of their moods. He had informed the shuttle crew to be on standby in case a hasty exit needed to be made.

"Well, hello there, Master Alexis," a woman in her late twenties said as she walked up to the royal party. "Such a pleasure to see you again. Time has been very, very kind to you."

The woman wore a wide, flowing dress of delicate breen thread like nothing Alexis had seen. Almost iridescent in color, shining bright blue then green then yellow all in a single blink, the woman drew every eye in the hall to her. Her auburn hair was pulled up into a tight bun that was studded with sparkling jewels from Thraen Prime. The woman's brown eyes watched Alexis closely and waited for his response.

"I...I am sorry, my lady," Alexis replied. "I am not sure we have had the pleasure."

"Oh, we have had the pleasure," the woman laughed. "You had the pleasure of meeting me when I was but eight years old. I had the pleasure of you saving my life. Although, I have to admit it was sort of your fault I fell prey to that attack that day since it was intended for you."

Alexis studied the woman's face, noting every curve and angle, dimple and ridge. He puzzled for several seconds as the woman waited patiently.

"Meredith?" he asked at last.

The woman curtseyed, but did not lower her eyes. "At your service, sire."

"My, how you have matured," Alexis said. "Of course I knew you would be beautiful one day, but I had no idea just how beautiful. It is always a pleasure to see one's expectations exceeded. Your husband must be full of pride."

"If she would take one," Master Paul snapped. "But somehow she has will to match her beauty. Don't you, dearest of sisters?"

"I'm sorry, but I am confused," Alexis said, looking from Paul to Meredith and then to Stolt. "I was under the impression you had married Steward Gramblitt of Station Haelm. Was that not part of your terms of treaty?"

"It was," Paul said, his voice cold. "But dearest sister here decided it was not a match for her. Thraen was lucky we were not plunged back into war, but Steward Gramblitt happily accepted the hand of my sister, Edwina. She is not as fair as Meredith, but she is younger by a decade and much more suited to producing heirs to those vast estates Gramblitt holds on Station Haelm as well as Haelm Prime."

"He smelled of gully fish and honey wasp liquor," Meredith said as she leaned in close to Alexis so only he could hear. There were instant whispers at the improper familiarity she took with the master, but she ignored them and instead looked up into Alexis's blue eyes. "I believe I deserve more than a steward who doesn't understand the meaning of proper oral hygiene."

"I believe so as well, my lady," Alexis said as he took the minoress's hand and kissed it gently. "It would be a crime to have a woman such as you clouded in a miasma of Haelmish stench."

Stolt cleared his throat and nudged the master. "The Haelm delegation is directly behind us, sire."

"Good," Alexis said. "Then they can witness how a woman such as this deserves nothing less than the highest royal honor, not another greedy steward looking to elevate his position within his station."

Stolt looked back at the stricken and angry faces of the Haelmish royals and tried to give them a reassuring smile.

"Master Paul, with your permission, I would be honored if your dearest sister would sit with me this evening during the feast," Alexis said, Meredith's hand still held within his own. "Unless you find objection to my attempt to make up for my previous royal neglect?"

Paul and Alexis stared at each other as only two monarchs could until finally Paul broke the gaze and waved his hand.

"Please do, Master Alexis," Master Paul said. "It would honor me if you would entertain my sister for the evening. I do warn you that she can be a handful."

"I am counting on it," Alexis said and turned quickly, leading Meredith away from her corpulent brother.

Stolt was left standing there with his mouth agape, trapped between an irritated Thraen master and an irate delegation of Haelmish royals.

"I, uh, well..." Stolt stuttered. He bowed low when he couldn't find words.

"Begone, steward," Master Paul said. "I will fetch you when I am ready to discuss business."

"Yes, your highness! Thank you, your highness!" Stolt said and hurried away as fast as he could to find his seat.

*

The two royals watched as the other nobility and members of station proceeded to attempt the steps of the newest dance.

The women twirled about, having pinned bright blue ribbons to their dresses, while the men stood stock still, nodding in time to the drumbeat. The melody of the song seemed to repeat itself over and over and over until it came to an abrupt halt and the men fell to their knees, hands out in supplication. The women mock-tittered, then turned and hopped to the center of the hall.

"Can a dance make one sick to one's stomach even if one is not participating?" Meredith mused. "I may need to fetch a porter and relieve my distress with some mid-course regurgitation." She turned her head and appraised Alexis. "Unless your highness enjoys this sort of thing. Then I apologize fully."

"I do not," Alexis replied. "My interest in forced gaiety left me several years ago."

"About the time your wife passed, I would suspect," Meredith said.

It was Alexis's turn for appraisal and he studied Meredith's face, looking for the smirk, for the sneer. But she only raised her eyebrows at the master then lifted her glass.

"I hate to waste time on the important matters," Meredith said. "Your love for your wife was legend. I have to know if it still burns or if there is room for another fire in your life."

"Legend?" Alexis asked. "When was my love for Eliza legend?"

"Oh, please, Alexis," Meredith said, going straight for the informal. "Bards have written songs about it for over a decade now. Maidens spend nights listening to the words, wishing they had what you had, while exploring their baser selves."

"Is that so?" Alexis smiled. "I never knew." He lifted his own glass and clinked it against Meredith's. "Were you one of those maidens that explored the baser self while listening to a fool's romantic notions?"

"Perhaps," Meredith said as her free hand found the top of his thigh under the table. "But I have never needed a prompt or excuse for such actions." She grinned and took a long drink from her glass then tapped it on the table so a servant could refill it. "Nor would I consider those actions base. I've always thought I possess a certain skill that elevates me above other women."

The servant's eyes went wide and he hurried off as soon as the glass was full.

"It's good to see you are just as shy now as when I first met you," Alexis laughed as his hand found hers and gave it a squeeze. "I would have hated for you to lose your innocence and tact."

"Tact is for the passengers," Meredith replied. "What's the point of putting up with all the shaowshit of being a royal if you have to be restrained by tact? If I have learned anything from my brother, it is that royals and tact need not be bedfellows."

"Then who should be bedfellows?" Alexis asked then turned to look across the hall before she could answer. "Perhaps that man and that woman there?"

"Sector Warden LeFlique and Madame Guntheest?" Meredith laughed. "It would take that man an hour just to find his own cock, let alone her jenny."

"Jenny? Is that what Thraens call it?" Alexis grinned. "Interesting..."

"Those two. See? Now they would be well matched bedfellows," Meredith pointed to a table where a diminutive man and a grossly obese woman sat, each looking in opposite directions. "The sexual tension is almost too much to bear."

"She'd crush him!" Alexis guffawed.

"Then he would be wise to think through his approach," Meredith nodded. "Perhaps a rear assault would work best?"

Alexis just shook his head as he tried not to choke on a sip of brandy. Meredith politely patted him on the back until he had himself under control.

"Oh, dear, I almost killed the Master of Station Aelon with crude humor," Meredith said. "Who knew I was so deadly?" She looked into his empty glass. "Another?"

"Oh, at least," Alexis said as he held his glass up and it was instantly refilled. "Leave the bottle."

The servant looked at Meredith then set the bottle of brandy between them.

"Do you enjoy your drink regularly, Alexis?" Meredith asked. "Or are you merely a social indulger?"

"I can put away a bottle now and again," Alexis said. "But I do not partake as much as I used to. I'll admit to quite a bit of debauchery during my lost years, though."

"Your lost years? That was when you sent your children down to Helios to live on Aelon Prime, am I right? That must have been hard to do."

"Keeping them with me would have been harder," Alexis said. "For them as much as for me. I was not in my right mind for a good long time after I lost Eliza and the others."

"No, I would think not," Meredith sighed. "And did the drinking work? Did it wash away the grief?"

"Of course not," Alexis said. "Only time can do that."

"Good to know," Meredith said. "Although I hope to never find out personally."

"Do you not want children?" Alexis asked.

"Oh, I do, very much," Meredith said. "I just don't want the heartbreak that can come with them."

"It is worth it," Alexis said. "In some strange way, at least."

"Do you see him?"

"Who?"

"Your son Alexis," Meredith replied. "Does he visit the station often or do you visit him on your prime?"

"There have been visits," Alexis frowned. "Not as many as there should be, but we enjoy each other's company when we can."

"And is he as tall and strapping as his father?" Meredith grinned.

"Much more so," Alexis admitted. "He is a very handsome young man. Fair-complected like me. Perhaps an inch or two taller, even."

"Already? How old is he?"

"Thirteen. No. Fourteen? My Helios, I can't remember my own son's age," Alexis laughed as he downed his brandy. "Probably a side effect of those lost years."

"Years of debauchery," Meredith added. "Your son is so young to be so tall."

"It's the way of the Teirmonts," Alexis shrugged. "We grow big."

"Do you?" Meredith responded, her hand moving along his leg. "Is that so?"

"It is," Alexis nodded, letting her do as she pleased. "I would never brag about something that could so easily be disproved."

"Sire?" Stolt interrupted as he stepped up behind the master. "I believe Master Paul would like to discuss business now. Shall I tell him you are coming?"

"Must we do that now?" Alexis asked. "I have been sitting here enjoying the minoress's company."

"Which is why Paul wants to talk now," Meredith said, keeping her eyes averted from the sight of her brother sitting at the front of the great hall. "He's been watching us have fun and now wants to take that away. One thing you must know about my brother is he is perpetually five years old and hates it when others have fun that he is not a part of. He will kick your sandcastle over, Alexis, for no other reason than just to see you cry. Be warned."

"I know how to protect my castles, my dear," Alexis said as he reluctantly stood up. His lips found her cheek and brushed it lightly. "I protect everything I care for."

His words sent a small shiver down Meredith's spine and for the first time that evening she looked like she was at a loss for words.

"Yes, well, he is waiting," Stolt said, unsure of what he had witnessed. "Shall we, sire?"

"Lead the way, Cousin," Alexis said as he rolled his eyes and then winked at Meredith. "You will be here when I return, I hope?"

"Oh, I have no plans to abandon you, Alexis," Meredith replied.

"Good," Alexis said and bowed low. "Until then, my lady."

Stolt waved towards the front of the hall and Paul gave a perfunctory wave back as the steward and master walked towards the Master of Station Thraen.

"You seem to be getting on well with the minoress," Stolt said. "She seems like a lovely person. You know who else is a lovely person? Stewardess Vla—"

"Stop, Cousin," Alexis interrupted. "I have no interest in any stewardess, no matter what wealth and holdings she has."

"But, sire, part of why we are here is to shore up Aelon's treasury," Stolt said. "And in order to do that we must find you a match that has sufficient resources."

"And the entire station and Prime of Thraen is not sufficient enough for you, Stolt?" Alexis asked.

"Sire? Minoress Meredith is out of the question. Her reputation as a firebrand precedes her. I believe, if you must choose from Station Thraen, perhaps one of Master Paul's less spirited sisters would be better suited for Aelon's needs."

Alexis stopped and looked at Stolt. The steward tried to smile, but the withering gaze Alexis gave him made it difficult.

"Or you could do as you see fit for the station, sire," Stolt said quickly. "Your happiness is always what is best for all of Aelon."

"It's also what is best for you, Cousin," Alexis stated. "Always keep that in mind."

"Oh, I do, sire, no worry there," Stolt said then gestured towards the waiting master. "Shall we complete the main part of why we have come to Station Thraen?"

"Yes, please," Alexis said, looking over his shoulder at where Meredith sat, her eyes watching him closely. "The sooner we conclude this part the sooner I can get started on the next."

*

She slammed him up against the wall as soon as the door closed to her quarters. Their mouths pressed hard against each other, as did their bodies, while their hands fumbled at laces and clasps.

"Damn this dress!" Meredith snarled as she pushed Alexis away. "It takes three of my ladies to get me into the stupid thing!"

She grabbed Alexis by the collar and yanked him back towards her mouth. She nearly devoured him as his hands lifted her layers of skirts only to find even more layers.

"Use your blade," she gasped.

"I plan to," he replied.

"No, moron, your actual blade," she laughed. "Cut me out of this Helios forsaken dress!"

Alexis stepped away and grabbed the hilt of his short blade. It was a ceremonial one, only brought out on official business, but it was still plenty sharp.

"Are you sure? That is quite the dress," Alexis said.

"You'll buy me another," she said as she turned around and pointed to the long row of laces that went from the nape of her neck all the way down past her lower back.

"Will I?" Alexis chuckled as he hooked the tip of the blade under the very bottom lace. "That's presumptuous of you."

"This entire encounter is presumptuous," Meredith laughed. "There is only one way forward from here, you know. Too many people saw us leave the hall together, stagger down the passageway together, and will soon hear how loud we are together. You will ask me to be your wife and you will buy me a new dress."

"I don't think we have anything as beautiful as this dress on Station Aelon," Alexis responded, not quite grasping what she said, as he slit every lace up her back with a quick swipe of his blade. "But I will make sure to change that."

"Yes, you will," Meredith said as she turned about and shimmied out of her dress.

She stood there in her undergarments which hugged her long torso and muscular legs. Alexis was on her at once, but she shoved him back, her eyes looking him up and down.

"You've seen me in my dainties, now let's see the legendary Master of Station Aelon in his," Meredith smirked. "Fair is fair, Alexis."

"You don't want to see this old man's broken body," Alexis replied as he stepped back from her.

"Alexis," Meredith said as she moved towards him and took his hands, pressing them to her chest. "If this is going to go where I think we both expect it to go, then you'll have to undress in front of me at some point. Husband and wife can't remain modest for long."

"Husband and..." he trailed off, finally catching up and realizing the true implications of what was occurring. "So you would consider it?"

"Consider it?" Meredith laughed. "I've dreamed of it since that day on Helios. I was a minoress rescued by a master. Please, you can't top that for an adolescent girl's fantasy."

"But we barely know each other."

"Oh, shut up," Meredith said as she gripped his tunic and tore it open. "You know familiarity plays no part in matches of royalty. We should feel lucky we feel anything for each other at all."

She pulled his tunic off then struggled not to gasp at the stained dressing that covered part of his side and abdomen.

"Is that...?"

"Where I was stabbed on Helios by a traitorous gatekeeper and then stabbed again by the rebel Lucas Langley," Alexis nodded. "Damn thing refuses to heal all the way. I have to clean it daily and be careful not to allow any contaminants to get inside. It's a burden that I do not wish to force on anyone."

"Burden, my ass," Meredith smiled as she led him over to the bed. "Lie down. I'll clean it for you now."

"That's not necessary," Alexis said as he tried to pull away from her, but was firmly shoved down onto the mattress. "I should leave. I'm afraid I have spoiled the mood."

"Again, shut up," Meredith said as she went to a side table and fetched a washcloth and basin of clean water. "You don't know me well enough to say what mood you have spoiled. Perhaps I like to tend to weak and feeble older men?"

"Weak and feeble?" Alexis laughed, grabbing her in his arms and pulling her on top of him. "I'll show you weak and feeble."

"Not yet, you won't," Meredith smiled softly as she extricated herself from his grip. "Let me take care of this, since you have neglected it today obviously, and then perhaps I'll let you prove my words wrong."

Meredith carefully removed the dressing and tossed it aside. She studied the wound, which was streaked with black lines and wept a clear liquid from the edges. She hissed at the sight, but didn't let it stop her as she wet the washcloth and set about gently cleaning the wound from edge to edge.

"You are a different sort of woman, aren't you?" Alexis asked. "I wonder why no other man has snatched you up."

"Because I haven't been waiting for another man," Meredith said as she rinsed the washcloth and started again. "I've been waiting for you."

"Have you now?"

"I have," she nodded. "And not very patiently. I do hope you aren't offended when I tell you that I lost my maidenhead a long while back."

"I'd be surprised if you hadn't," Alexis laughed.

"And what does that mean?" she glared. "Is his highness calling me a slut?"

"On the contrary," Alexis replied. "A slut is a woman that indiscriminately gives herself to men. I highly, highly doubt you do anything indiscriminately, nor would you give yourself away. You take what you want, and that is not a slut, but a woman with confidence and power."

"You have no idea how sexy you sound right now," Meredith smiled as she finished her second round of swabbing the wound and set the cloth and basin aside. "Luckily for me, you are all clean. Let me redress this and then you can experience my confidence and power."

Alexis watched her walk across the quarters and into the bathroom. He could hear her opening and closing drawers until she finally came out with a fresh dressing in one hand and absolutely nothing on.

"I decided to save you the effort of removing my dainties," Meredith grinned as she slowly walked over to the bed, making sure he saw every inch of her.

She was not a skinny woman at all, but strong and made of curves. Her legs, belly, arms rippled with muscle and Alexis couldn't help but wonder how a woman like her could stay confined in a station. She had the body of a prime explorer and from what he'd witnessed, the temperament as well.

Neither of them spoke a word as she covered his wound with the dressing, making sure it was secure, but not too tight.

Her hand reached out and dimmed the lights then she climbed onto the bed, her legs straddling him. She shook her head and her auburn hair dangled down, tickling his cheeks as she slowly lowered herself to him, pressing her breasts into his chest.

Alexis wrapped his arms about her as she reached between his legs and joined them together. They did not move, they just stayed that way, one being of flesh, connected in the most intimate way possible. Their breathing began to synchronize and then Meredith started to move up and down upon Alexis, making both of them suddenly gasp at the same time.

Neither was in a rush, and all the talk of confidence and power was forgotten as they found a rhythm that was the complete opposite of the hurried, sweaty lovemaking each was used to. They stared into each other's eyes as they indulged their passions with a leisurely casualness that made both of them smile broadly.

"Do I look happy?" Alexis asked.

"You do, sire," Meredith said, her voice breathy and catching slightly on the downstroke. "Do I?"

"I believe so, my lady," Alexis responded before his own voice was stolen by a move from Meredith that left him tingling and almost helpless under her. "That was new."

"I saved the best for you, my dear Alexis," Meredith giggled. "Told you, I had been waiting."

"And am I thankful," he replied just as he threw her to the side and rolled on top of her. "Now, how about I show you my best?"

*

"Well, isn't this an unexpected delight," Paul said as he sipped from his glass while servants laid out an elaborate brunch before him, his wife, Steward Stolt, Alexis and Meredith. "I hope it's not just because of the immense dowry that has been accruing interest since my sister was of marrying age." He laughed and snapped his fingers. "Quick! Someone do the compound calculations! After all the years of rejected suitors, the amount must be enormous!"

Alexis bristled at Paul's words, but Meredith's firm hand under the table stayed the biting response he had ready.

"Station Aelon will be happy with new wealth in their coffers," Stolt nodded. "But, as we can all see, I believe this matter was of the heart and not the pocketbook."

"Every matter is of the pocketbook," Paul snickered. "Especially matters of the heart. You know that, steward. Your strategic marriages have made you a man of wealth that even some masters of station would envy."

"I have been fortunate in my holdings, but unfortunate in my loss of spouses over the years," Stolt replied. "How I would give up every credit to take just one of my wives in my arms again."

"Your last wife was taken in the weeping sickness outbreak that stole all but one of Master Alexis's heirs, am I right?" Paul asked, draining his glass. "Yet you have stayed a bachelor all these years. May I ask why?"

"I have not found the right partner," Stolt responded. "And my duties to the crown have prevented me from having much of a private life. Perhaps when I am ready to retire from court I will find someone suitable."

"Well, the best of luck with that, steward," Paul said, raising his refilled glass. "And the best of luck to the newly betrothed."

"Thank you," Alexis said, raising his own glass. "Which brings me to a request. We would like to wed as soon as possible, possibly tomorrow, if we can. I must return to Station Aelon right away and there is no reason why Meredith should not accompany me."

"Oh, that is much too soon," Paul said, waving his hand in the air dismissively. "She will remain here so we can plan a proper wedding and invite all of the heads of station."

"Understood, but the majority of them are already here," Alexis said. "Why waste the opportunity, and time, to do this now? Stolt has already conferred with the other stewards and there have been no objections from a single station. Many will gladly remain an extra day to attend."

"Conferred already, has he?" Paul asked, locking eyes with Stolt. "Well, aren't you the busy little honey wasp." Paul's face was nothing but conflicted emotions until he sat up straight and pounded a fist on the table. "Tomorrow it is! We had a Blessing Day and now we'll have a blessed day! Helios will shine on us for our show of love and devotion to the Dear Parent's grace!"

No one at the table bought into the master's feigned piety, knowing full well the man only praised Helios to keep the High Guardian and gatekeepers of the Way happy and content.

"Thank you, sire," Alexis said as he raised his glass once more. "Your devotion is a testament to us all." He downed the glass and then yawned. "But if you will excuse me, I believe I will rest a bit before I dive into preparations for the ceremony."

"I'll join you," Meredith said as she stood up from the table. All eyes fell on her and she shook her head. "For the preparations. The master is capable of resting on his own." She leaned in close so only he could hear. "Not that we would rest much if I joined you now."

"Is your wound acting up?" Paul asked. "I hear the thing is stubborn and refuses to heal properly. Maybe you should give some extra credits to your station gatekeepers so they may pray harder. I have always found the gatekeepers willing to pray for near about anything when properly motivated."

"I wouldn't burden the gatekeepers with something so trivial as my scratch," Alexis said, standing as well. "But feel free to pay yours on my behalf. An early wedding gift, if you will." He extended his arm and Meredith wrapped hers about it. "I'll walk you to your quarters on the way to mine. We can talk wedding plans."

"A lovely idea," Meredith said as he looked at her brother. "I shall dine in my rooms tonight, brother. So much work to do."

"Of course," Paul said. "I understand."

*

The two royals lay entwined on the bed, sheets wrapped about their naked, sweaty bodies as they breathed hard from the hour's exertion.

"We are going to use all of our passion up before I even get you back to my station," Alexis laughed. "Then what will we have to look forward to?"

"Travel," Meredith said. "To the primes."

Alexis pushed up on his elbows and looked at her as she lay her head on his belly, mindful of his wound, and let her hair splash across his skin.

"The primes? Why would we want to visit there?" he asked.

"Because I love the primes," Meredith said. "The wildness, the freedom. Isn't your son on the planet? We could visit Alexis at his estate and then tour the rest of Aelon Prime, not to mention the leases you hold on Thraen Prime. I can show you some wondrous sights from my homeland."

"Homeland," Alexis said, letting the word roll about his tongue. "Such a strange thing to say since there hasn't been a royal born on the planet in millennia."

"Well, maybe one day there will be," Meredith said. "Our children could be born there. Wouldn't that be something?"

"Our children?" Alexis asked then smiled. "Yes, our children. I forget how much younger than me you are. You have such an old and wise soul for a woman that hasn't even seen her thirtieth birthday."

"You won't see your next birthday if you ever use the word 'old' when describing any part of me again," Meredith laughed, kissing his soft skin. "With that said, thank you. It's nice to be appreciated for who I am instead of being perpetually treated like a child."

"Why anyone would treat you as such is a mystery to me," Alexis laughed. "Even when you were a child you insisted on being in charge. But then I'm sure that has always threatened your brother, hasn't it?"

"Dear Helios, you have no idea," Meredith laughed as she scooted up so her head could rest against Alexis's shoulder. "I think the imbecile has always thought I would take the station from him, despite the fact that women cannot lay claim to the crown."

"Such is the way of the system," Alexis said then cried out as Meredith pinched his nipple.

"What you are supposed to say is that is something you will change on Station Aelon," Meredith said.

"Change? Change what? The line of succession?" Alexis laughed after swatting her hand away. "No, that is not something I plan on tackling during my reign. The meeting of stewards would eject me out the airlock. They would never allow their daughters to take control of their estates."

"Then only make it for the crown," Meredith said. "Damn the stewards. They can let their spoiled sons keep the estates. But I believe any daughters I give you should at least be in consideration of the crown."

"Hmmmm," Alexis said. "That would mean Esther would become mistress upon my death. I'm not sure she's suited for it."

"Is Alexis?" Meredith asked. "I don't mean to pry, but there are rumors of his less than regimented upbringing on Aelon Prime."

"My sister is overseeing his education and making sure he is molded into a proper minor, ready for his duty as master one day," Alexis replied.

"Yes, of course," Meredith nodded. "Your sister..."

Alexis sighed. "Ignore the rumors, they are only that."

"Who else handles Alexis's schooling?" Meredith asked.

"The men of the estate," Alexis said. "Specifically my old friend Corbin. At the very least they will teach him how to be a man. Prime men are not known for their coddling of anyone, even the women of the estate. It's a rough life I have left my son in the care of, but a life that will build character at least."

"But will it be the right kind of character?" Meredith asked, nuzzling her lips against his neck.

Alexis didn't try for an answer since he had none to give.

*

Nobility, gentry, and even passengers lined the grand promenade that led from the main shuttle bay to the lift that would take the royal party up to the Surface and Castle Quent.

Meredith happily waved to the people that were her new subjects, a broad smile on her face and happy lift to her step. The cheers around her were exuberant and she was amazed at the extravagance of blossom petals and breen boles that were thrown in the air as she passed by. But she was also puzzled by the many passengers that pointed and chattered away, their eyes wide as they saw her dress.

"Did I dress too boldly?" Meredith asked, leaning in close to Alexis as they walked the long, wide passageway. "Why does everyone stare?"

"Look about you," Alexis said. "Station Aelon is not known for its fashion sense. Despite providing some of the highest quality breen to the stations in the System, our tailors and designers have yet to match the sensibilities of Thraen, Ploerv, or even Klaerv. We are but simple folk, her in Aelon."

"Simple yet dangerous," Meredith replied. "Everyone knows that picking a fight with Station Aelon is not the wisest choice."

"Do they?" Alexis smiled, feigning humility. "I didn't know."

"Oh, shut up," Meredith said as she swatted his arm. "You know you are the tough guys in the System. It is whispered in parlors all about Station Thraen that you have weapons at your disposal that none of the other stations possess. Is it true?"

"Perhaps," Alexis said. "But how about less talk of fighting and more talk of loving? I'm certainly ready to retire to Quent and get lost in her lusciousness for at least a week."

"Only a week?" Meredith smiled, giving him a peck on the cheek which resulted in several rounds of loud cheers from the crowd. "I have lusciousness to last much longer than that."

"Unfortunately, Stolt has only given me a week's reprieve from the duties of master," Alexis sighed. "Not that I expect him to wait even that long before interrupting us."

"Well, if he does interrupt then he better knock first," Meredith laughed. "Or he'll get an eyeful of some of the private duties a master must see to."

"Mmmm, I can hardly wait," Alexis grinned.

*

Meredith looked about the quarters, a forced smile on her face.

"Do you approve?" Alexis asked.

"It's quaint," she replied.

"You mean, it's Quent," Alexis joked then saw the lack of enthusiasm that was his new bride's response. "Sorry. Like I said, simple folk, including our lodgings."

"Is the castle safe?" Meredith asked as she traced her finger along a long crack in the wall. "The place looks as if it will crumble with a hard sneeze. I don't dare wonder what will happen if you take me to bed. Will the structure implode around us?"

"My father spent most of his life trying to redesign and rebuild Station Aelon," Alexis said. "Yet he barely spent a moment's thought on the royal lodgings."

"I can see," Meredith said then shook her head and smiled. "I apologize, Alexis, I'm being rude. Wherever we are together will be fine for me. We could live in the swamps of Aelon Prime and I would be content."

"No, you wouldn't," Alexis laughed. "You'd be miserable."

"But you would be miserable right there with me, yes?" she asked. She began to undo a lace at her shoulder, but the knot was too snug. "Where are my ladies? I may need help with this."

"I have sent your ladies away," Alexis said. "We have the entire floor to ourselves. That way I can show you all the rooms without worry of being overheard."

"All the rooms?" Meredith smiled. "How many are we talking about?"

"I can never quite recall," Alexis said as he walked over and helped his wife with the knot that vexed her. "We'll have to count them one by one as we go."

"So our adventure begins at home, does it? And then when do we go down to the planet and visit the primes?"

"Are you that anxious to leave Station Aelon already?" Alexis freed the knot then began on the other shoulder, in a hurry to get Meredith free of the elaborate dress she wore. "Can we make plans for that after our week of bliss?"

"We will plan during the week," Meredith said. "I will lie upon the bed, wrapped up in your arms, while we decide where exactly we will travel. I've never seen Flaen Prime and I hear it has incredible geysers of hot steam that erupt like clockwork. Wouldn't that be fun to see?"

"You realize that I will have to run all plans by Steward Stolt, right?" Alexis sighed. "A master and mistress cannot just visit another station's prime without there being an immense amount of bureaucratic fuss."

"Oh, I know," Meredith replied as the dress was finally freed from her shoulders and she was able to push it down over her chest, her hips, her legs. "But a mistress can wish, yes?"

"Yes," Alexis said. "A mistress can always wish, and a master can always try to grant those wishes."

"I like the way you think, husband," Meredith said as she sauntered over towards the bed. "Can you guess what I'm thinking right now?"

"I have an idea," Alexis said, following her over.

"Then perhaps you should put that idea into practice," she responded as her undergarments were removed and tossed across the room. "You're going to have to get those trousers off first, though."

"Of course, my lady," Alexis said as he took a deep bow. "I live to serve."

"We'll see about that," Meredith said. "Words are good, but actions are much, much better."

She drew back the comforter and climbed into bed, pulling the bedding up to her chest, but not over. Alexis kicked his trousers off and hurried to her, jumping onto the bed like a teenager and not the middle-aged monarch that he was.

Chapter Eight

The two towheaded children dashed between the furniture, dodging comfy looking breen chairs, climbing over the long lounges and couches that were spread throughout the wide, open room. They laughed and called to one another, playfully taunting and teasing as they traded positions on who was being chased and who was doing the chasing.

"Thomas! Eliza!" Meredith called as she walked into the room. "There you two are! I have been calling on the intercom for ten minutes now! Lunch is ready!"

"Yes, Mother," the siblings replied.

"We'll be right there," Thomas said, the older at six years.

"I want juice!" Eliza stated, her hands on her five year old hips. "Lots of juice!'

"Come eat lunch and you'll—" Meredith started then stopped when she turned and saw the state of the intercom console on the wall.

Wires and polybreen plastic littered the floor, having fallen from the gaping hole in the wall where all of the components should have been.

"What happened here?" Meredith asked, her voice low and menacing. "I expect an answer this very second!"

Eliza looked from her mother to the hole in the wall to her older brother, then burst out crying. Meredith rolled her eyes and turned her attention to her son.

"Explain," she demanded.

"We were just playing," Thomas said. "I told her not to throw it, but she did and then I ducked and it hit the intercom and then it broke and all the pieces feel to the ground and we didn't say anything because we wanted to keep playing and then we forgot and now you're here yelling at us and Eliza is crying and I have to go pee."

Meredith struggled not to smile. She kept her lips firmly pressed together until she had it under control.

"And what did your sister throw at you that could break hard polybreen?"

Thomas glanced over towards the corner of the large room and Meredith followed his gaze.

"Oh, Thomas! No! Do you have any idea how angry your father will be over this?"

"Angry over what?" Alexis asked as he walked into the room, his breen environmental suit covered in dirt and pollen. "What did my little devils do this time?"

"Alexis," Meredith frowned. "Look at you. You are tracking that in everywhere."

"It's the prime, dear," Alexis smiled. "This is where we get to be dirty and nasty and not worry about decorum."

"I could give a grendt's ass about decorum," Meredith said. The children snickered at her use of "ass", but she held up a finger and they quieted instantly. "I care about having you track mud all over the compound. As you have said, this is the prime, and not only do we have to deal with dirty and nasty, we have to clean it up ourselves."

"You have four servants, the children each have one, I have six, and that doesn't even count the kitchen staff or maintenance crews," Alexis frowned. "You shouldn't be cleaning anything up yourself."

"Easy for you to say," Meredith scowled. "You're used to this place. On the Thraen Prime estate, the compound is kept spotless at all times. Just because we were planetside never meant we sacrificed comfort or hygiene. You and I need to sit down and talk about some changes that need to be made."

"You've never complained before," Alexis replied, eyeing his wife. "What's different this time?"

"Nothing," Meredith said. "This is the third time we've come down from the station since we've been married and it is time to civilize this place."

"Ugh. Civilize?" Alexis the younger said as he walked into the room and stood next to his father.

At twenty years old, he was a couple of inches taller than his father, but not quite as broad. The same fair looks, but with a dangerous twinkle of mischief in his eyes, Minor Alexis had been turning heads for years. Rumors quickly spread of his less than discrete exploits amongst the miners' daughters on the lease holdings on Thraen Prime. There were also a few rumors that said exploits may have been made up to hide certain dalliances that the nobility and gentry preferred not to speak of.

"Civilizing the prime would be like trying to pump air into space," Minor Alexis laughed. "You can try all you like, but you'll never get anywhere."

"You are supposed to be on a cutter to The Way Prime," Alexis the senior growled. "You know how dangerous it is for the station to be left without a regent in place."

"Cousin Stolt is up there running things," Minor Alexis said. "Don't you trust Cousin Stolt to handle the affairs of the crown while you are gone?"

Alexis and Meredith shared a quick glance that Minor Alexis didn't catch.

"I trust you to handle the affairs of the crown," Alexis responded. "That is why I appointed you regent and you were supposed to be on a shuttle rocketing up to Station Aelon! If you miss your window then it will be at least another week before you can leave!"

"Then it's another week," Minor Alexis shrugged. "I hate it up in the orbiting death trap, anyway. I much prefer the land down here with all the wide open spaces, huge breen fields, vast seas, and dark, scary mines."

He leaned down and wiggled his fingers at his half-siblings, making them giggle. Then he stood and clapped his father on the shoulder.

"Plus, I want you to meet my dearest friend," Minor Alexis said. "Gannot? Where are you, brother?"

"Sorry," a young man said as he hurried into the room, a slice of pie in his hands and berry juice running down his chin. He wasn't as tall as Minor Alexis, but he was obviously muscular and athletic. Dressed in a bright yellow tunic with trousers that seemed to be made of multi-colored patches instead of whole cloth, the young man obviously cared about his dress much more than he cared about his eating habits. "Found myself to be a little peckish and swung by the galley. Are these your parents?"

"They are," Minor Alexis said, wiping the juice from Gannot's chin and licking his finger. "This is my father, Master of Station Aelon, Alexis the First."

"An honor, sire," Gannot said, taking an exaggerated bow. "I have heard nothing but wonderful things about you."

"Have you?" Alexis replied. "Because I have heard nothing about you."

"Ally? Have you not informed your father of all the adventures we've had over the years?" Gannot asked, his face contorted with mock pain. "And to think I have called you brother for this long and it has meant nothing."

"Oh, shush," Minor Alexis said. He turned back to his father. "I've told you about Gannot. Remember when I crashed the skids on Thraen Prime last fall? That was me and Gannot. Oh, and the time I was caught playing a joke on the gatekeepers here in the compound? Us again."

"Such an amazing joke that was going to be," Gannot sighed. "We spent two weeks planning it. Had half the staff in on it."

"Which is why we were found out," Minor Alexis said. "Too many fingers in the pie."

"I do love pie." Gannot smiled, his teeth and lips dark purple. "Don't you, sire?"

Alexis glared at the brash young man that stood before him, pie juice once again escaping his lips to find its way onto his chin. Minor Alexis started to reach for it, but Alexis the senior slapped the young man's hand away.

"I do love pie, *Gannot*," Alexis growled. "But I know the proper time and place to eat it."

"Ouch," Gannot laughed. "I know a reprimand when I hear one. Helios knows I've had enough of them in my short, fun-filled life."

"A life that could end up much shorter if you are not careful, you Thraenish bas—"

"I'm Mistress Meredith," Meredith said, interrupting and stepping between her husband and the brash youth. "Also, Minoress of Thraen. It is good to see another Thraenish face again. What sector of the station are you from?"

"Me, your highness?" Gannot asked as he took the mistress's hand and kissed it gently. "Oh, I'm from the prime. Born and raised on the planet. My father is the steward assigned to the lease holdings. I'm sort of a hybrid, if you will. I'm Thraenish, but technically, while Aelon holds the leases on that part of Thraen Prime, I am also Aelish. A man with two stations."

"Your father is Steward DuChaer?" Alexis asked, surprised by the revelation. "I would think you a miner's son with the way you act."

"Everything is much freer down here on the planet," Gannot said, ignoring the insult. "You learn to go with it or get left behind. And when you can't breathe the atmosphere, swim in the water, or descend into a Vape mine without special equipment, you come to understand that there are more important things to life than which teacup to use during lunch."

"Yet, I have managed to navigate both worlds," Meredith said, giving her husband a reproachful look. "Alexis, dear? How about you clean up for lunch and join us in the banquet hall?"

"I believe I am better needed—" Alexis began.

"I'll escort Minor Alexis and young Gannot to the meal," Meredith said. "It'll give me time to get to know my fellow Thraen. Hurry along now."

Alexis stared at her, but when she didn't budge or even blink he realized that he didn't stand a chance of arguing the point.

"Fine," Alexis said. "I'll be along shortly. Don't wait for me. Feel free to begin eating."

"Of course, dear," Meredith said. "Come along children."

Thomas and Eliza, glad that their mishap was completely forgotten, bolted from the room and sprinted down the passageway towards the banquet hall. Meredith held up an arm and looked at Gannot. The young man just smiled at her until Minor Alexis coughed and cleared his throat.

"Oh, yes, of course," Gannot laughed. "Forgive me, your highness. My wild habits are hard to break. There are some women on this planet that would crack my nose and snap my arm for offering to escort them."

"I am not one of those women," Meredith said. "As you will learn while we get acquainted."

"Alexis? A brief word?" Alexis said, his eyes locked onto his son and heir. He saw Meredith's face start to cloud over and he bowed. "Very brief, my love, I promise."

"Very well," Meredith said, pointing towards the door. "Shall we, Gannot?"

"It's my pleasure," Gannot replied, giving Minor Alexis a wink as he escorted the mistress from the room.

"Father, I—" Minor Alexis started, but was quickly interrupted by a slap across the face.

"When I tell you to be on a shuttle, I expect you to be on a shuttle," Alexis snarled low. "Is that understood?"

"Yes, Father," Minor Alexis replied instantly. "It won't happen again."

"No, it will not," Alexis said. "As soon as lunch is finished you will be on our fastest cutter to Way Prime. You'll still have time to make the shuttle before the planet rotates and we lose our scheduled departure window. I am not asking the Thraenish to let you ride on theirs to Station Thraen and then take a shuttle from there to Aelon. Do you know how humiliating that would be?"

Minor Alexis prudently stayed silent.

"Eat your lunch, say goodbye to your...friend, and then get your ass on the cutter," Alexis said, turning his back on his son as he walked from the room.

"Father!" Minor Alexis cried. "About Gannot..."

"What about him?" Alexis asked, whirling on his son. "What? Out with it!"

"I would request that he accompany me to the station," Minor Alexis replied. "I don't really know any of the stewards there except for Cousin Stolt and it would be good to have someone I trust around in case I need counsel."

"Counsel? From that roughneck? I think not," Alexis laughed cruelly.

"No, no, not in an official capacity," Minor Alexis pushed. "Just as a sounding board. So I can think things through out loud."

"Yes, well, I'm not sure I want his sort on Station Aelon," Alexis said.

"His sort?" Minor Alexis asked. "What does that mean?"

"I'm not sure I know," Alexis replied. "Nor do I want to."

The two Alexises stared at each other, old eyes to young eyes, locked in a power play that had been repeated by fathers and sons for generations.

"Fine," Alexis conceded. "The Thraen can accompany you. But he does not attend any official meetings and he is not there in any diplomatic capacity. He is your friend only and will be expected to behave himself and tame that prime streak in him. If I get one hint of impropriety, I will order the royal guard to shoot him out an airlock."

"I'd expect nothing less, Father," Minor Alexis bowed. "Thank you."

"Fah," Alexis grumbled and waved his son away. "Let me go get cleaned up as your mother has ordered."

"Step-mother," Minor Alexis corrected.

"*Mother*," Alexis replied. "The woman married to me is your mother and she will be respected as such."

"Of course," Minor Alexis said. "Better get cleaned up then, before *Mother* gets upset."

Alexis pursed his lips and shook his head, but said nothing else as he turned and strode down the passageway. Minor Alexis watched him go then burst out in a huge grin and hurried towards the banquet hall.

*

"Do you think he will be alright with that Thraen?" Alexis asked as he lay in bed with Meredith, a breen wax candle burning and flickering on the table beside them. "There is something about him I do not like. And did you see what he was wearing? What insane style is that?"

"You're talking about the trousers, aren't you?" Meredith asked.

"Yes, I'm talking about the bloody trousers!" Alexis snapped then took a deep breath. "Sorry."

"The patched trousers are the latest trend in the court of Station Thraen," Meredith said. "They may look silly, but apparently each patch is carefully placed so that the positions have some sort of meaning."

"Meaning? What meaning?" Alexis asked.

"That I don't know, my love," Meredith said. "I'm an old woman now and not privy to the secrets of the youth."

"Old woman, my ass," Alexis laughed as he ran his hand up and down Meredith's thigh. "You are barely older than thirty. I'm the old one in this marriage, not you."

"Thirty is old," Meredith sighed. "If you were to pass, Helios forbid, I would not be much of a catch. Not with much younger and firmer examples running about the stations. I'm afraid two children have ruined my firmness."

"Oh, be quiet," Alexis laughed as he rolled on top of her. "Any man would be lucky to have you, *with* your firmness." He kissed her and then rolled back to his side of the bed.

"That's it? A kiss?" Meredith asked, this time rolling on top of him. "We have been on the prime for six days now and we have yet to consummate this trip."

"What about in the third floor closest the afternoon we arrived?" Alexis asked as he lay under his wife, his arms pinned by her hands. "I'd say that consummated things quite nicely."

"That was for you, dear," Meredith said. "I knew you wouldn't rest until you'd gotten in me. Tonight, my love, tonight is for me." Her hands found him and she smiled as she gave him a squeeze. "And that is for me, as well. You better be up to the task, dearest of loves, because I had a quick nap earlier and I'm rested and ready to get my turn."

"Oh, the torture you put me through," Alexis said as he leaned his head up and nipped at her lips.

Meredith laughed and bent down, her mouth parted and tongue wet. But they were interrupted by a loud knock at the door before they could go any further. Alexis sighed and Meredith swore as she rolled off him and he swung his legs from the bed, looking for his trousers.

"Hold on!" Alexis snapped as he stood and found his trousers peeking from under the bed.

He hop-footed into them as he made his way over to the royal bedchamber door. He winced slightly as the skin around his ever present wound stretched tight. He stopped in front of the door, took a deep breath, steadied his anger, and then yanked open the door.

"This better be good," Alexis snapped.

"Sire," a guard said. "We are getting reports of some disturbances on the lease holdings. A message was received by the communication system that Thraen troops have moved into the region and are demanding back taxes."

"Back taxes?" Alexis asked, truly puzzled. "What in Helios's name could they be thinking of? We pay no taxes on the lease holdings. That's what the lease payments are for!"

"Yes, sire," the guard said, bowing. "I am just relaying what I have been told."

"Fine, right, yes," Alexis growled. "I'll be to the communications room shortly. Let me get dressed."

"Yes, sire," the guard said as he hurried away.

Alexis looked over his shoulder at his obviously disappointed wife.

"I'm so sorry," he said as he walked over and found his tunic. "I'm sure it's some general or commander trying to make a name for himself. I'll get it sorted out and be back right away. No falling asleep. I promise to perform my husbandly duties immediately upon my return."

"Yes, well, don't be surprised if I get started without you," Meredith smirked. "A mistress cannot be left waiting."

"I'll hurry," Alexis grinned. "That is a promise."

*

The paper in his hands shook as he tried to keep his boiling rage from spilling over. Alexis read the message for a fifth time before wadding the paper up and tossing it across the meeting room.

"What in Helios's name is the man thinking?" Alexis shouted. "Taxing me? Taxing the Master of Station Aelon? It's never been done! A master cannot tax another master!"

"He is not considering you a master, but a tenant just like any other lease holder," Stolt said, having just arrived on the planet. "He does have the High Guardian's approval. You can see by the official seal that—"

"Oh, fuck off, Stolt!" Alexis roared. "That whore of a gatekeeper puts his official seal on anything someone pays him enough for! He'd stamp my cock if I gave him enough credits! I could have the only cock in the system that is ordained by the High Guardian! Only the Dear Parent would have a more holy cock than mine!"

"Does Helios have a cock?" Meredith asked, smiling. "I never really thought about it before. Do you think it glows?"

"Not now, wife," Alexis snapped. "This is not the time for jokes or lev—"

"Oh, shut up, Alexis," Meredith said. "This is the time for jokes because this entire situation is one giant joke!"

"Excuse me, your highness, but I think it is more complicated than mere humor," Stolt said. "Don't you agree, gentlemen?"

The other men seated at the table looked from Stolt to Mistress Meredith then to the master, who was busy pacing back and forth, his anger blinding him to half of what was happening in the room.

"I believe the mistress may not grasp the scope of the dilemma," a man said. Younger than Alexis and Stolt, the man kept his shoulders bunched and head down in order to seem subservient at all times.

The prime administrator, Jorben Tallaly was tasked with making sure all Aelish planetside operations ran smoothly and efficiently. That included the lease holdings on Thraen Prime. His body language gave the impression he knew he was not doing his duty.

"General Herlect is very serious about the payment of the taxes, sire," Tallaly said, turning his attention to the master. "He does have sufficient forces to take and shut down our operations on Thraen Prime."

"But he won't do it," Meredith said. "I know Staunchton better than anyone in this room. My cousin is a taint. Pure and simple. He's always wanted claim to the Thraen crown, but being one step removed from it, he's decided that he'll kill and blow things up instead. The silly twerp has always been a sadist and a bully. He killed one of my trollen birds when I was a child, just to make me cry. Punch him in the nuts and he'll crumple like any man."

"We can hardly punch the commander of the Thraen Prime forces in the nuts," Stolt said.

"Well, not sitting there like a lump, you can't," Meredith said. "You'd actually have to get up off your old, fat ass to do it."

"Mer," Alexis warned. "Please."

"Oh, don't Mer me," Meredith responded as she stood up and looked the men in the eyes.

Besides Stolt and Tallaly, there was Steward Hylora, a thin man of indiscriminate age; Steward Prochan, a young man who had just taken his birthright after his father had fallen from a balcony one drunken night; and Steward Exchester, a man as round as he was tall.

"I may be Mistress of Station Aelon, but I am also Minoress of Station Thraen, don't forget," Meredith snapped. "You men sit here and wonder what Staunchton's motivations are when you should be focusing on my brother's. Paul is toying with our cousin, making him feel important and worth something other than a babysitter for a hunk of rock stuck on a planet worth nothing except for Vape and breen."

"Uh, those two items are quite important, your highness," Steward Exchester said. "Breen is a valuable commodity that can be made into—"

"Shut up, Exchester," Alexis said. "My wife knows what breen is and she knows how important Vape is. What she's trying to say is that Master Paul of Thraen wants something other than taxes and probably has not let his cousin know that yet. Am I right, dear?"

"You are, as always," Meredith said. "My cousin thinks he's collecting taxes when he's actually just a distraction from the real goal."

"Which is what, your highness?" Stolt asked.

"Marriage," Meredith said, shocking even her husband with her answer. "I still have my sources in the Thraen court. Paul feels that the lease holdings on Thraen Prime are too important to be in constant negotiations. He wants a more permanent arrangement. I believe he's willing to give them as part of a dowry, with the explicit precept that a Thraenish team mine the land and proceeds are sent to Station Aelon, not raw materials."

She laughed at the looks on the men's faces.

"Oh, close your mouths, you'll collect honey wasps," Meredith smiled. "My brother loves to scheme and figure out a way to skim off the top. He can't do it to the Thraen stewards or he'll risk an uprising, so that leaves Thraen Prime, specifically the land leased to Aelon. Are you seriously telling me you never saw this coming?"

"No, we did not," Stolt replied. "But, whether true or not, it does bring up a topic I wanted to talk about."

"Don't we have enough topics to deal with?" Alexis growled.

"This touches on what the mistress has said," Stolt replied. "It is in regards to the minor, your son."

"I assume you mean Alexis and not Thomas," Alexis replied.

"I do, sire," Stolt nodded. "As you know I was with the young man for a week until you called me down here. I have to say I witnessed some rather, well, *disturbing* behavior."

"He's a spirited lad," Alexis said as he stopped his pacing and took his seat next to his wife. "What trouble did he get into?"

"That list would be too long for the time we have available, sire," Stolt said. "Let me just say that all troubles the minor may have placed himself in were always with the company of that young man, Gannot DuChaer."

"Yes, they are fast friends," Alexis sneered. "And it is not a friendship I condone. I'll have the Thraen removed from the station as soon as I return there."

"I'm afraid the damage may already be done, sire," Stolt said. "The DuChaer boy has his hooks in Minor Alexis. And I do not believe the minor cares or is inclined to remove said hooks."

"Sycophants come and go, Cousin," Alexis smiled at the steward. "You of all people should know that."

"Right you are, your highness," Stolt replied. "It's just that, well, I believe this is more than sycophancy. The two young men's relationship may be more complicated than that."

"More complicated?" Alexis asked. "What in Helios's name are you babbling about?"

"Oh, knock it off, Alexis," Meredith said. "Take the blinders from your eyes and admit that you know well and true what Stolt is saying. Alexis and that DuChaer boy are more than friends. They are lovers and you know exactly how dangerous that can be."

"Lovers..." Alexis said, sighing deeply. "I may have suspected, but I wasn't sure."

"I'm not condemning the minor in any way," Stolt said. "That is up to Helios to do, but the meeting of the stewards, not to mention the meeting of the passengers, will not stand for a queer master. I am above such judgment, but others are not."

"You son needs to stop slapping blades or we'll lose the station," Meredith said, causing everyone, except Alexis to gasp. "Oh, don't be prude or act like this is the first time two men have ever had a lustful relationship. Please, I'm from Thraen. Half the men there prefer cock to twat most days of the week."

"Dear Helios," Steward Prochan exclaimed. "Such language! And from a mistress!"

"Oh, grow up, Prochan," Meredith said. "Everyone knows your own brother likes the rod. Don't act all offended."

"Mer, stop," Alexis said softly, touching his wife's arm. "They get the point."

"But the point, sire, is that the minor's proclivities put the station at risk," Stolt said. "If Mistress Meredith is right, and I have no reason to doubt she is, then a marriage between stations may be just what the crown needs. The minor gets a wife, and shows the stations he's not what he is suspected to be, and we get long term stability with our lease holdings on Thraen Prime."

"We were supposed to have stability when I married Meredith!" Alexis snapped.

"Yes, well, that marriage was not of Master Paul's choosing," Stolt said. "It was your personal choice, sire."

"At a significant cost to the crown, I know, I know," Alexis sighed. "Master Paul will want terms that benefit Thraen and not Aelon. Who knows the amount of revenue that will be lost when he takes control? And why would we let him do that, anyway? If his daughter is to marry my son then he should be giving me the lease holdings as part of the dowry!"

"Precisely, sire," Stolt said. "Don't worry about the details of the transaction. I will make sure that, in the long run, Station Aelon comes out ahead and profits from the arrangement."

"Transaction? Arrangement?" Meredith scowled. "You men have no idea what it's like to be a woman in this age. Even one like me, born into royalty and privilege, is nothing more than a bargaining chip. My niece could be a prize shaow for all you care. And don't forget that fact, gentlemen, that the woman you are negotiating for is my niece. She is my blood, more so than Minor Alexis."

"Meredith!" Alexis snapped. "You forget your place!"

"And you forget your heart!" she snapped back. "Look to it, Alexis. Make sure that this decision I can see you are about to make will not crush two souls all for the price of a piece of land."

"Only Helios need worry about the souls of royals," Alexis replied. "We are here to do our duty, nothing more."

"Nothing more..." Meredith repeated and trailed off. Then she slapped her hands on the table. "Well, I can see my counsel has been used up. I'll let you men get to work on the trading of human beings. Just remember that you need a plan for when it all falls apart. I have been lucky with my marriage, but I doubt my niece will feel the same way. Good night."

*

"I'm sorry for that," Alexis said as he climbed into bed.

"Sorry for which?" Meredith replied as she scooted away from him and tucked the covers around her body, making it quite known she had no interest in royal affections. "I counted at least three offenses that should have me dragging your ass out of this bed and into the passageway."

"I'd like to see you try," Alexis laughed and reached for her, but was rebuffed by a nail rake to the forearm. "Ow!"

"What terms did you decide on?" Meredith asked.

"A quarter million credits for a dowry," Alexis said. "As well as Station Aelon keeps the current lease holdings on Thraen Prime in perpetuity. With future options of expansion."

"Future options?" Meredith asked, her interest piqued despite her irritation with her husband. "What future options?"

"Permanent title bestowed upon Alexis's heirs," Alexis smiled. "They will be of Thraenish blood, after all."

"So despite what may happen between Alexis and my niece, their children will be the title holders?" Meredith laughed, reached over and grabbed Alexis's arm, tugging him to her. "I forget just how smart you are sometimes."

"Whether the rumors about my son are true or not, it won't matter," Alexis grinned as he felt his wife's warm body press against his own. "If for whatever reason the marriage doesn't work out, as long as there are heirs, then Station Aelon will always have a claim to the lease holdings on Thraen Prime."

"If my brother agrees," Meredith said as she climbed on top of Alexis.

"When I'm only asking for a quarter of a million credits as a dowry?" Alexis laughed. "If Paul doesn't agree, his advisors will force him to. Your brother likes his lavish lifestyle and a proper dowry would hurt the treasury enough that he'd have to make some cutbacks on his daily feasts and barrels of wine."

"Which the fat shaow would never do," Meredith said. "Yet another reason I am glad I married a man of action and not sloth. Dear Helios, could you imagine what my life would be like with one of those layabout masters or stewards from the other stations? I'd probably have hips wider than a cutter and an ass as big as Thraen Prime itself."

"Mmmmm, I might let you do that," Alexis said, his hands gripping her hips then her ass. "More for me then."

"I'd crush you with one thrust," Meredith said, leaning over him and kissing his lips. "Because I certainly wouldn't slow down or take it easy on you."

"I would expect not," Alexis said. "That wouldn't be you at all."

BOOK I

*

"You are forcing me to do something I am not ready for, Father," Minor Alexis said as three attendants busied themselves about the young man, making sure his trousers were free of any dirt and his tunic was perfectly tucked about his torso. "I have so much more to do before I settle down and marry."

"I was several years younger than you when I was married," Alexis said, as he sat sipping gelberry wine and watched the attendants make the final alterations and adjustments to his son's wedding outfit. "Getting married doesn't mean your life ends. In many ways it actually starts."

"So the occasional dalliance is permitted?" Minor Alexis grinned. "Did you ever stray from Mother?"

"From Eliza? Helios no," Alexis said. "I'm not that type of husband. I was lucky with your mother and found a woman that I loved with all of my heart."

"And my current mother?" Minor Alexis asked. "Has the royal eye perhaps realized the amount of eligible beauties that grace our station?"

"Again, I have been lucky," Alexis said. "Meredith is the only woman for me. I can barely keep up, to be honest."

"No need to explain," Minor Alexis said. "Really, don't. That's something I don't need to hear."

"What about you, son?" Alexis asked. "Any beautiful young ladies catch your eye? Not that I would officially approve of any extramarital affairs, since that could undermine the marriage agreements and the crown, but I know a hot blooded youth like you must have his eye looking about."

The three attendants tried to look as if they weren't listening intently, but their faces fell far short of feigned indifference.

"There may be someone," Minor Alexis answered. "But it wouldn't be a union possible, whether officially or unofficially."

"A commoner?" Alexis asked. "One of the passenger girls? Your late Uncle Derrick was known for his trolling the decks for a taste of passenger meat. He once worked his way through an entire sector, going from woman to woman, until I think half those decks knew his privates intimately."

"Not a passenger," Minor Alexis replied. "But not one of the station's nobility, either."

The three attendants shared a look, which Alexis caught instantly, causing him to set his glass down harder than he intended.

"Leave us," he ordered and they scurried from the room without question.

Minor Alexis stood there on the wide, tailor's stool and waited for what was to come.

"You know you are the heir to one of the most powerful stations in the system, right?" Alexis asked as he sat there, his fingers steepled, his eyes boring into his son. "Everything you do, every word you say, everything you wear, you eat, you drink, you sing—all of it is scrutinized down to the most insignificant detail. You do not lead a private life, son. Nor will you ever lead a private life. Image is what counts with us royals, almost more than actual substance."

"Yes, I have been made aware of this my entire life, Father," Minor Alexis replied. "Auntie Melinda drilled it into me before she left for The Way. As did Corbin, that old crippled souse. Always telling me that I wasn't living up to my potential, that I needed to take more interest in affairs of station and less interest in racing skids across the prime or even the science of agriculture." Minor Alexis changed his voice into a gruff, old drunk's. "Alexis! Stop dreaming of tilling soil and playing farmer! You're going to be master one day, so Helios damn act like it!"

"You sound just like him," Alexis sighed. "I regretted sending him to the prime estate with you, but he was the only one I could trust."

"Yes, that's what he reminded of me also," Minor Alexis said. "Not to knock the poor sod. I did learn how to fight with every type of blade invented, plus shoot a sling better than any Aelon master."

"Is that so?" Alexis laughed. "Then why do you refuse to join in the tournaments the stewards host?"

"Boredom," Minor Alexis said. "I'd either win outright, they'd let me win outright, or I'd lose and look like a fool. The last two aren't acceptable to me, and the first one is an almost foregone conclusion. I know the outcomes and I don't care for any of them. I'd rather sit and drink and watch the others fight for their supposed honor."

"That isn't a bad analysis," Alexis responded. "I give you points for that."

"Do you? How generous."

"You know, I don't have to be," Alexis snapped. "I could just shove you out that door right now and make this ceremony happen today. I wouldn't be the first upset royal parent that accelerated a wedding. It would be awkward for all involved, but then it would be done."

"The minoress and her father just arrived today," Minor Alexis said. "I would guess Master Paul doesn't like to be hurried for any reason. You'd risk the agreement, and all the hard work Cousin Stolt has put into this, just to prove a point to me? I don't think so."

"No, I don't think so either," Alexis said. "But I always have the option. As long as I am master, I will be in charge of your future."

"Then when you are gone, no one is in charge of my future except me," Minor Alexis said.

"I'll let you believe that," Alexis smirked. "As an early wedding gift."

"Again, how generous," Minor Alexis said then looked down at his clothing. "Do you think we could call the attendants back in so I can get out of these blasted garments? While I do enjoy the prints, the cut is riding up my craw something awful."

"Of course, son," Alexis said. "We wouldn't want your craw to be uncomfortable just before your wedding. An uncomfortable craw isn't going to produce heirs. That's a solid, royal fact."

*

Meredith gripped her husband's hand as he sat there in a huff. The entire great hall of Station Aelon was lined with The Burdened, a faction of The Way that Alexis was not exactly fond of, especially since some of their members had tried to kill him, and almost killed the very woman that gripped his hand like a vise.

"I should have put my foot down," Alexis whispered. "Seeing those holy thugs just makes me want to grab a long blade and kill every one of them. I could do it, too. I still have what it takes to kill."

"In here, yes," Meredith said, tapping the master's chest. "But I think the rest of your body would disagree. When was the last time you sparred with anyone from the royal guard?"

"I don't know," Alexis sulked. "It hasn't been that long."

"It's been two years, love," Meredith said, trying not to smirk. "You haven't touched a blade, other than what's between your legs, in two years. You'd be on your ass before you even got your blade out of its sheath."

"Oh, I'd take a couple with me," Alexis insisted. "A warrior never forgets how to fight."

"No, they just forget they no longer can fight," Meredith said. "So be quiet about it all. The Burdened aren't going away, not until the High Guardian leaves the station. And the High Guardian isn't leaving until after the ceremony."

"Right after the ceremony," Alexis said. "Since his holiness is needed elsewhere in the System. Would it kill the man to stay for the reception and feast? Maybe bless some of the nobility and gentry for me? The political capital generated from that would last me the rest of my reign."

"So now you want him to stay?" Meredith said, beyond exasperated. "You are a tangle of contradictions, Master Alexis Teirmont. Good thing I like working out knots."

"All rise for his Holiness, the Pontiff of the One True System and all systems under Helios's watch, the only human being deemed worthy enough to protect the portal to the planet and gateway to the primes! All rise for the High Guardian!"

The entire hall stood and turned towards the entryway. Instead of wearing plain, drab robes as most of the gatekeepers wore, the man that walked through was dressed in brilliant colors of varying iridescence and shades. Spotlights placed strategically throughout the hall shone down from above, creating an almost blinding, dazzling effect of reflections from the pontiff's attire.

As well as wearing the head to toe show robes, the High Guardian also wore a hat that was nearly as tall as he was. Attendants walked behind the man, staves in their hands; ready to push the hat back into place should it shift or start to fall. Clutched in the man's hand was a staff of glass that swirled with contained Vape. All that attended the ceremony were wealthy enough to appreciate the cost of the staff. Containing Vape that was not compressed was not an easy task to accomplish and the artisan who made the staff must have charged a fortune.

Or donated it to The Way, as was usually the tradition.

"Be seated," the High Guardian said once he had made his way to the front of the hall, climbed the dais, and turned to address the crowd. "Helios blesses you all and thanks you for your attendance to this most holy of ceremonies."

The hall echoed with the sounds of shuffling feet and rustling clothing. Many a cloak and dress had been brought out of storage, more than likely expanded to fit the increased girths of the owners, and were still stiff from their cleaning. While official galas and banquets were common in the Aelon court, nothing so special had been held in Castle Quent for some time.

"Let the betrothed walk to me," the High Guardian said, his voice more a reedy rasp than the commanding tenor one would expect from such a figure.

He was severely old, and rumored to have been undergoing treatments for various life threatening illnesses, but he still stood tall and clutched the Vape staff in a grip that showed he could deliver a blow or two if needed.

"If he dies here then Helios will never forgive me," Alexis whispered to his wife, who in turn swatted his arm.

"Don't even say such a thing, Alexis," she hissed, causing more than a few eyes to turn her way.

Eyes such as her brother's, who sat across the aisle from her, his wife Carmnella by his side. The Master of Station Thraen nodded to his younger sister then turned his attention back to the High Guardian. Knowing full well that Meredith held no real love for him, Paul had stepped onto Station Aelon with nothing but a formal attitude to the whole proceeding as if he were merely attending the signing of some new declaration and not his daughter's wedding.

The High Guardian droned on for close to twenty minutes, espousing the greatness of Helios and why all beings owed their immortal souls to the Dear Parent. He paused for a moment, giving everyone the impression he was ready to move onto the actual nuptials, but it turned out he was only thirsty and once given a drink of water he continued on for another twenty minutes.

Alexis had to guess that the man read half of the *Ledger* before he finally clacked the end of his staff onto the dais and called out that the bride and groom be brought before him so he might bless them with Helios's permission to marry.

"Alexis Teirmont, heir to the crown of Station Aelon, do you swear before Helios that you choose to marry this woman of your own free will?" the High Guardian asked.

Minor Alexis stood there for a split-second, a split-second that everyone in the great hall noticed instantly, then puffed out his chest, grabbed the young minoress's hands, and said, "Yes. Before Helios, I swear it."

There were more than a few loud exhalations throughout the hall.

"And do you, Bella Herlect, Minoress of Station Thraen, do swear before Helios that you choose to marry this man of your own free will?"

"Yes, before Helios, I swear it," Minoress Bella replied immediately.

Alexis and Meredith looked on as the couple performed their duties and recited their memorized vows, most of which were straight from the *Ledger*, but some were surprisingly original. Both the master and mistress had to wonder if the young minoress had heard any of the rumors about her almost husband. If she had, she never showed any indication to either of them when they spoke briefly at the welcome dinner.

By the time the exchanging of the rings, crowns, scepters, cloaks, armbands, and belts had taken place, Alexis was close to falling asleep. Meredith kept nudging him, making sure he didn't snort or snore as his eyes refused to stay open. The High Guardian frowned as he looked down to see the master's head start to nod, but he didn't increase his tempo one bit and continued the litany of royal ancestors from both stations that would now be joined as one with the union of the minor and minoress.

"With all of Helios's love and trust, I now pronounce you husband and wife," the High Guardian stated finally. He snapped his fingers and a long privacy screen was brought before the newlyweds, blocking them from the view of the entire hall. "You may now kiss."

The hall waited, all completely silent to see if they could hear anything from the lips of the two royals, but the screen was quickly removed and by the looks on the minor's and minoress's faces, some had to wonder if they kissed at all.

The High Guardian stepped down from the dais and looked at Master Alexis then Master Paul.

"The Way thanks you for your generosity today, masters," he said. "Your endowments will help fund many a holy endeavor. Bless your reigns forever."

The masters bowed to the pontiff as he made his way down the aisle and back out of the great hall. As soon as he was gone then the newlyweds turned and looked at the assembled guests. Minor Alexis held out his hand and Minoress Bella took it willingly, if not completely enthusiastically. Music started up and the two walked down the aisle, heads held high, eyes forward until they too left the hall.

"Shall we?" Alexis said as he looked over at Master Paul.

"Please, Alexis, lead the way," Paul responded. "I could certainly use a refreshment or two."

"I could use the whole damn bar," Meredith muttered.

"The same with me," Alexis replied. "The same with me."

CHAPTER NINE

"The hard part is acting sad," Meredith said, her hands in her lap as she sat at the end of the bed, the letter bearing the news crumpled next to her. "I think I loathed the man more than many of his enemies."

"He wasn't easy to like, that is for sure," Alexis said, propped up by a stack of pillows, his face trying to hide the pain that plagued him. "But he was your brother, and Master of Station Thraen, so we are obligated to attend the funeral service."

"What if we sent Alexis and Bella in our stead?" Meredith suggested. "Let this be the heir's first official business. He's had it easy so far, except for a couple stints as regent."

"Which were really overseen by Stolt," Alexis replied. "Not that I don't trust Alexis to make the right choices, but..."

"You don't trust Alexis to make the right choices," Meredith said. "I do not blame you. He is a bright and merry young man, but I do not believe he takes any of his responsibilities seriously. And that 'brother' of his..."

"DuChaer," Alexis almost spat. "Making him part of his entourage shows bad judgment of character on my son's part. The flip parades around as if he is royalty and heir to my crown. My gut says to have the boy ejected into space as soon as possible before he does some real damage to Station Aelon."

"Your gut needs to rest," Meredith responded as she turned and looked at her husband. "That's not just me, but all of your physicians' orders. You are not young anymore, Alexis. And neither is that wound."

"My double wound," Alexis laughed. "What master is unlucky enough to survive an assassination attempt only to have the same wound pierced while fighting off rebels? Helios laughs at me, for sure."

"The Dear Parent does no such thing," Meredith said. "You are still alive despite the insults to your body. If Helios were laughing he would have put you in your grave before Alexis was of age so that Cousin Stolt could run the station as regent."

"You do not like Cousin Stolt at all, do you?" Alexis smiled then waved his hand. "No need to answer, I know the truth. And, since you were honest about your brother, I'll be honest about my cousin. I don't trust him either. Never have. I know he's worked behind my back to undermine me at times. But he's also worked with me to help keep Aelon secure. The man doesn't know his own ambitions sometimes. I'll take advantage of that as long as I can."

"But what about Alexis? What about how impressionable your son is? If Stolt outlasts you then he will have his hooks in Alexis before your body cools."

"Aren't we a morbid pair this morning," Alexis laughed.

"The news of a death does that to people," Meredith said.

"I am not worried about Stolt so much as I am about DuChaer. Stolt may be a self-serving noble, but he is a noble of Aelon. He'll do everything he can to bolster his position and fill his coffers when I am gone, not unlike what he has done during my reign, but I believe, in the end, he will do what is right for Station Aelon as well."

Alexis shifted his position and winced. He took a couple of long, deep breaths before he continued.

"Gannot DuChaer will devour this station with reckless abandon. He will use up my son, and the power he wields, until there is nothing left. Then he will move on, leaving Station Aelon a dried out husk of a monarchy. Stolt is an evil that is known, and an evil that has limitations. I don't believe DuChaer understands what limitations are."

"So what do we do about it, husband?" Meredith asked, gently moving to his side. She nuzzled her face against his neck, careful not to bump or move him. "How do we make sure DuChaer does not destroy everything you have worked for once you are gone?"

"I don't know," Alexis replied. "Stolt may be our only choice. I could grant the meeting of stewards additional powers. He holds the most sectors so he is the defacto leader of the meeting. By elevating the meeting, I limit the reach of the crown."

"You'd cut off your nose to spite your face?" Meredith asked, alarmed. "I am all for limiting what a monarch can do, especially after the havoc my brother caused when he banished the gatekeepers from his court and seized their Vape wealth for himself, but diluting the crown's power because of some common thug's hold on a minor? What precedent does that set? You give Stolt more power and he will use it to destroy the monarchy and take everything for the stewards."

"What would happen if Alexis died without an heir?" Alexis asked. "After I am gone and he becomes master? What then?"

"Then our son Thomas takes the crown," Meredith replied.

"And Stolt knows he cannot control Thomas while you live, so what is the next logical conclusion?" Alexis said.

"Stolt removes me from the equation," Meredith responded. "Then he has Thomas to himself."

"Or he removes you and Thomas," Alexis said. "Then the crown is up for contention. He does have a blood claim. He is a true cousin. Yes, there are other cousins on the station that could also throw in for the crown, but Stolt has his feet firmly planted in court. There would be few to oppose him."

"You scare me, Alexis," Meredith whispered. "All this talk of you dying and Cousin Stolt scheming."

"These are things we have to discuss," Alexis said. "I know my infirmity will pass, as it always has, but one day it won't. One day this cursed wound will be the death of me and I need to know that those I love will be safe and taken care of."

"Oh, speaking of curses," Meredith said, her mood changing instantly. "Did you hear of what Gatekeeper Schlecht said upon my brother's death?"

"I did not," Alexis smiled. "Please, let me in on the royal gossip."

"He said that it was proof of Helios's anger at what Paul had done," Meredith said. "And that a curse is on the crown of Station Thraen."

"And what curse is that?"

"That none of my nephews shall produce a male heir," Meredith said. "That the Herlect line would die out with the males already born."

"That is quite the curse," Alexis laughed. "Just goes to show that you never take credits from a gatekeeper. They always go straight for the Helios's damnation every time."

"But, do you see what this means?" Meredith said. "If none of my nephews produce male heirs, but your son and my niece do, then your grandson would actually have a legitimate claim on the crown of Station Thraen."

"Helios, you are right!" Alexis exclaimed. "My grandson could end up ruling two stations! And their primes! Wouldn't that be something? Do you think The Way would allow it? Having one master lord over two stations would constitute a concentration of power that might make the High Guardian nervous."

"It should make everyone nervous," Meredith said. "For it has never been accomplished before. No one knows what could happen."

"So much chaos and uncertainty," Alexis sighed. "It's a wonder my mind doesn't succumb to a daily stroke."

*

"We attend his father's funeral service and then his coronation, but the son of a bitch doesn't have the balls to confront me face to face?" Alexis roared as he stared at the proclamation he had just been handed. The council sat quietly as the master punched the table with his fist again and again. "The bastard is lucky! If he'd told me, then I would have handed him his head right there in his own station!"

"Sire, calm down," Stolt said. "You have pushed yourself these past weeks and you can't afford a relapse."

"I'm fine, Cousin," Alexis snapped. "If I wasn't, then I wouldn't be here. My health is not of concern at this moment."

"Not to argue with you, but your health is always of concern, your highness," Stolt replied. "Men of our age cannot ignore the march of time. Helios's calling is only around the corner."

"For you, maybe, but not for me," Alexis stated. "I have much to accomplish before I am gone. First of which is to teach this new master a lesson in keeping one's promises!"

"If I may, sire," Steward Hylora said. "Master Charles did not make any promises, his father did."

"The Thraen crown did!" Alexis shouted. "And it is the Thraen crown we are dealing with! Are you too stupid to understand how this all works, Hylora? Should I have you replaced on the council?"

"Sire, he was only suggesting an explanation to Master Charles's motivations," Steward Exchester said, coming to his colleague's defense. "We are all trying to find reason in such an unreasonable action."

"There is no reason to find!" Alexis shouted. "Except that the Thraenish whelp wants his ass handed to him by a man that truly knows what it means to be a master!"

"Uh oh," Minor Alexis said as he walked into the great hall and saw the dark looks upon the council's faces. "Bad news for the elite?"

"Can there ever be bad news for the elite?" DuChaer asked as he followed right behind the minor. "I mean, we are elite, after all. How bad could things get?"

"Helios has truly blessed us," Minor Alexis said, his voice dripping with mockery.

"All praise the Dear Parent!" DuChaer added.

"Why is he here?" Alexis growled, an accusatory finger pointed towards the Thraen. "This is a council meeting, Alexis, not a trip to the pub."

"Or brothel," Stolt muttered under his breath. Alexis caught the words and whipped his head about, a glare of pure rage on his face. "My apologies, sire."

"Even though your tone is insulting, I will answer your question, Father," Minor Alexis said as he took a seat at the end of the long table. "Brother DuChaer is my official advisor. When I take the crown, Helios forbid, he will be my right hand, ready to advise me on all matters of station. I thought it best he understood now how those matters work."

"I need to be prepared if I am going to be as efficient and trusted an advisor as Cousin Stolt," DuChaer said as he sat next to Minor Alexis and promptly propped his feet up on the table. His boots were shined to perfection, but he still wet a thumb and wiped at an imaginary smudge before looking directly at the master. "You don't want your son's reign to be in the hands of the ignorant, do you, sire?"

"I fear it already is," Alexis spat. "Get your fucking boots off my table."

DuChaer held up his hands and set his feet back on the floor. He looked at Minor Alexis and frowned. "Perhaps we have hurried this along. I shall retire to my quarters and wait for your call, my lord."

"No, Brother, you shall stay where you are," Minor Alexis insisted. "My father had his advisor when he was only a minor and I will have mine."

"My advisor was your late uncle!" Alexis yelled. "He was my real brother and had as much right to be present during a council meeting as I did! This...this...this flip does not!"

There were controlled gasps by the council at the slur; more because of the implication towards Minor Alexis than the insult to DuChaer.

"A flip?" DuChaer asked with surprise. "I can have half the Sector Forbine pleasure girls dispute that accusation, your highness."

"And that statement is to convince me of your higher character?" Alexis asked. "That instead of buggering my son, you spend your time buggering whores? You wouldn't be fit to advise the court fool, let alone a master."

"Father, please," Minor Alexis laughed. "Brother DuChaer is my trusted friend and nothing more. He is not a flip, I am not a flip, and there is only the love of comrades between us. You forget that you exiled me to Aelon Prime, leaving me with your sister and an estate filled with ruffians and drunks. Brother DuChaer was my only salvation from a life of true depravity. He is the son of a steward, you know. He brought civilization into a world barely elevated above primitive savagery."

"I tried," DuChaer said. "Ah, how I miss those days sometimes."

"Do you?" Alexis asked then grinned wide. "Do you miss the freedom of living on the prime?"

"At times, sire," DuChaer nodded.

"Good," Alexis said. "Then you shall accompany me down to the planet as I retake what is mine."

Alexis couldn't help but smile at the shock that faced him. From the council stewards to his son and son's friend, not a single face was able to remain composed after Alexis's statement.

"What? Surely none of you expected me to take this insult lying down? I have done enough of that lately," Alexis said. "No, I will descend on my lease holdings on Thraen Prime and return them to Aelish control. I plan on showing this new master just how hard the job really is."

"Your highness," Stolt said. "I do not think it wise for you and your son to leave Station Aelon. Despite my serious misgivings about a military campaign against Thraen Prime, I have even more misgivings about leaving the crown unprotected here."

"You misunderstand me, Cousin," Alexis explained. "My son will remain here on station as regent. He will rule in my stead while I beat the ever loving shit out of some Thraens and take back land that is mine in perpetuity."

"But you said Brother DuChaer is to accompany you, Father," Minor Alexis said. "Or did I hear that wrong?"

"You heard correctly," Alexis said as he left his place and walked the length of the table down to his son.

He motioned for the minor to stand up and Minor Alexis, after a couple of puzzled frowns, did so. The entire table watched as Master Alexis circled the minor, seeming to study him with serious interest.

"As I thought," he finally said. "You two are not joined at the hip as half the station likes to say."

Alexis walked back to the head of the table, all jest gone and done for good.

"No, I mean as I said," he stated gruffly. "DuChaer will accompany me to the prime while you, my son, remain here and rule for me. Being from Thraen Prime, DuChaer will be a great asset to have. He'll know the land better than most of my generals and commanders. If he is to be a trusted advisor of the crown of Station Aelon then he will have to prove his loyalty before I pass and you take my position."

"But, Father, Brother DuChaer is not—"

"*Brother* DuChaer is a subject of the Master of Station Aelon and he will fucking do as I fucking say!" Alexis shouted, his palms slapping the table top with every word. "That is unless you don't feel he is up to the task. If that is the case then please make your voice heard now. Is he up to the campaign I propose, which would prove he is up to being a royal advisor, or is he not man enough to handle the basics of what it means to stand by a ruler? Please, Alexis, my son and heir, tell me which is it."

DuChaer started to speak, but Alexis's lifting of a single finger shut him up instantly.

"Son?"

"He is up to the task, Father," Minor Alexis replied. "He will help with everything you need. Despite the accusations of Brother DuChaer being a flip, he is an accomplished bladesman and fighter. He will not disappoint you. Or me."

"Good," Alexis said as he slowly sat down, his eyes never leaving his son's. "That is what I was hoping to hear."

There was nothing but silence in the great hall. Not a creak, not a groan from the old castle could be heard as the council sat there, their minds reeling from everything that had occurred.

"Cousin Stolt," Alexis said calmly. "Please inform the generals that we will be going to war. Also inform the meeting of Stewards and meeting of passengers that I expect their full support. That includes their financial support. The lease holdings on Thraen Prime benefit the entire station, not just the crown. We will all share in the cost of this campaign is that understood?"

"Explicitly, your highness," Stolt nodded. "I will see to it immediately."

"And I will see to it that my wife does not hear of this from other lips," Alexis said. "That would be almost as dangerous as going to war."

*

The Aelish destroyer, Malachai, cut its way through the boiling waters of Channel Blaern, its bow like a massive knife pointed at the coast of Thraen Prime. Behind it were eight more destroyers, each as impressive and dangerous as the lead ship.

Unlike the cutters of the Aelish Navy, the destroyers didn't have protective atmospheric shields to cover the exposed upper deck. This meant that only a polybreen environmental suit and helmet were what stood between Master Alexis and certain, painful death. Several generals stood behind the master, their body language stating their disapproval of Alexis putting himself at so much risk, especially as they grew closer to the landing site of their attack.

"I have missed this," Alexis stated as he looked over at the equally suited DuChaer. "The poisonous mist as it rises off the water; the never ending cloud cover draping the planet in a shroud of grey; the fact that all that is between me and asphyxiation is a suit made of polybreen, woven by hands in my lower decks that at one time wanted nothing more than to strangle me." The master laughed and clapped DuChaer on the shoulder. "I haven't felt this alive in a long time."

"Yes, sire," DuChaer replied, his ever present bravado lost, weighted down by fear of the coming fight. "The planet Helios is a test of courage and conviction."

"Yes, it is," Alexis said then spun about and faced his generals. "Are we ready, gentlemen?"

A man easily as tall as Alexis took a step forward and bowed slightly. His dark skin made it almost impossible to read his features inside his helmet.

"All forces are prepared for the landing, your highness," General Umphrey Ryan stated. "Once the destroyers reach the shallows then the attack skids will be sent out. We know that General Staunchton Herlect and his men are waiting, but reports say that his numbers are woefully inadequate to fight us off."

"Their very beings are woefully inadequate," Alexis replied.

A sharp pain stabbed at his side and he had to use all of his self-control not to grab at it. He took a deep breath, hoping those around would interpret it as patience and resolution, and not a reaction to an alarming discomfort that quickly escalated into agony.

"You do not need to wait for my orders, General," Alexis said. "Once in place I expect you to attack with all the force and might that Helios has granted this righteous army."

"Yes, sire," General Ryan said, bowing slightly once more. "We will not disappoint you."

"This is not about me," Alexis said, teeth gritted. "It is about the honor of Station Aelon and its people. From the stewards to the passengers, I do this because they deserve the respect of every station in the System. A move against our holdings is a move against our very existence. That cannot be tolerated."

"No, sire, it cannot," General Ryan agreed. "For the glory of Aelon!"

"For the glory of Aelon!" the rest of the generals echoed.

"If you will excuse us, sire, I will now join my men below as the other generals return to their destroyers and their men," General Ryan said. "The war begins within the hour."

"Helios's blessing to you all," Alexis said and nodded towards the men as they turned crisply and left the deck.

"Uh, your highness?" DuChaer asked. "Am I to accompany the first wave or remain here by your side?"

"You, *Brother DuChaer*, are to remain by my side," Alexis replied. "Then when this conflict is over, you are to remain here on the planet, banished to the lease holdings on Thraen Prime. You will not step one foot outside of the boundaries without the threat of execution. Your time with my son is over, you sick little flip. I don't care how many whores you say you've fucked, I know you covet my son for his title and his body. You are an abomination to Helios and I will not stand for your presence in my court."

DuChaer stood stock still as he looked out at the ever approaching piece of land. Despite the coastline being technically assigned to Station Aelon and an extension of its prime, DuChaer was a Thraen and he knew the land was a part of him, not the master that stood menacingly close.

Yet he replied, "Your son is not like you, sire. He is a man that loves the land underneath his feet. He likes to live with a thrill in his heart and a cheer in his throat. Your son was raised by soldiers and men that understood what it meant to face death each and every time you walked out of an airlock. Alexis is a lover of the poetry of living, whether that means digging trenches in the breen fields or catching gully fish with his hands in the swamps. You want to bind his spirit to a floating ball of metal and polybreen stuck up in the heavens, when all he wants to do is live free down here on the primes. With me."

"My son will never set foot on this planet again, as long as I am alive," Alexis replied. "Nor will he ever set eyes on your smug face. Those well-rehearsed words of yours mean so little to me. I bind my son to nothing, it is his heritage that binds him; binds him to his destiny of taking the crown and learning that being a master of station is not a position of freedom, but a position that grants freedom. He doesn't have a choice in the matter, just like I had no choice."

"There is always a choice, your highness," DuChaer replied. "You choose to not exercise it. Do not project your cowardice onto my Alexis. He is much greater than your failures."

Alexis's first instinct was to pick the lout up and throw him over the railing, sending him to a messy death in the waters of Helios. But the pain in his side prevented him from even turning on the impertinent youth. To have shown weakness in front of such as DuChaer would have been too much for Alexis to bear, so he remained still and let silence be his response.

It did the job as DuChaer grew increasingly ill at ease while he waited for an outburst or some type of retaliation. For a split second it seemed as if the Thraen would have preferred to throw himself overboard than stand and wait for retribution.

"Does your father still live?" Alexis asked, finally breaking the silent treatment.

"He does, sire," DuChaer responded.

"And does he know what you are?"

"He knows I live my life the way I want," DuChaer replied.

"Yes, but does he approve of that way?"

"Not entirely, sire," DuChaer said. "He has expressed concerns over the years."

"Yet he hasn't disowned you? Surprising."

"He made a promise to my mother that he would always keep me in his life," DuChaer explained. "My father has never broken a promise to my mother; not when she was alive and certainly not while she rests in peace."

"Too bad you did not get your sense of honor from your father," Alexis said. "You might have had a great future to look forward to. Now, all you have to look forward to is a life far removed from my court. Or any court, really, as I doubt any of the stations will look kindly on an exile."

"When you pass, your highness, you do know that your son will recall me, right?" DuChaer asked. "He will not leave me down here to rot."

"He will leave you," Alexis said. "For I will make him swear an unbreakable oath to Helios and all that is holy to uphold my final wishes. Your exile will be last on my lips." Alexis laughed and clapped his gloves together. "Plus, I have left instructions with Stolt to make sure you never set foot on Station Aelon again. If you do, you will be executed on the spot by the royal guard."

"You really hate me so much?" DuChaer asked. "Why?"

"Because you are not a man," Alexis said, finally risking the pain and turning his body so he could look the young man in the face. "You are a parasite that has latched onto my son and is sucking him dry of all that makes a Teirmont a Teirmont."

"And what is it that makes a Teirmont a Teirmont?" DuChaer asked.

"Our independence," Alexis replied. "We are beholden only to Helios, and even the Dear Parent's grasp on us is tenuous. A leech like you puts that legacy of independence at risk. That is what I am putting a stop to."

"And nothing I say can change your mind, sire?"

"Nothing Helios could say would change my mind," Alexis said, his face a mixed grimace of triumph and torment. "Which is a statement my son will not be able to make as long as you are in his life. I hope you said some type of goodbye to Alexis, because your influence on him is over."

DuChaer swallowed hard under the intense gaze of the master, bowed, then turned and fled the deck of the destroyer. In seconds claxons started to ring as the ships made their final approach towards the prime coastline. Alexis knew the young man would immediately try to contact his son and was glad he already gave orders to imprison the youth in the brig until the conflict was all over.

Alexis the First, Master of Station Aelon was done playing games and indulging the whims of those around him. He was ready for war and his soul burned to conquer and kill, even if he himself would not join in the actual battle.

*

The screen before Alexis showed a grainy image of the Aelon council, his son sitting at the head of the table, all eyes on Steward Stolt as the man pleaded with the master.

"The treasury is nearly bankrupt, sire," Stolt said. "As much as I would like to teach Thraen a lesson for trying to rescind our lease holdings on their prime, I cannot condone an all out war and seizure of the entire continent! It would be grossly irresponsible of me to agree with you, my liege."

"Some would say it would be irresponsible of you to *disagree* with me, Cousin," Alexis glared, hoping the fury he felt could be conveyed across the transmission from the meeting room he sat in on Aelon Prime to the great hall of the station orbiting above. "I may be on the planet, but I am still Master of Station Aelon. You will rally the sectors, levy the taxes needed to fund this campaign, and make sure I have the resources sent to me that I need to crush Thraen Prime and show Master Charles the First of Thraen what happens when you pick a fight with a Teirmont!"

Stolt sighed, but nodded. "Yes, sire, I will see to it at once. Is there anything else I can tell the meeting of stewards? Maybe something to lessen the blow of this edict?"

"Tell them that I will be leading the charge this time," Alexis said. "I will no longer be sitting back and watching this conflict, but actively participating so that the soldiers of Aelon know they have a master that puts station before his own life."

"Your highness!" Stolt shouted. "That cannot be allowed! You are not a man in his youth! Whether you see combat or not, you risk your very life just by exerting yourself! Need I remind you about—"

"That is all, Cousin," Alexis said. "My mind is made up. And you need not remind me about anything. I am well aware of who I am and what exertions I can handle."

He clutched at the wound that seeped fluids into the heavy breen bandages wrapped about his torso. Even though he was fully dressed, Alexis could tell some of the council caught the movement. He doubted his wife would be spared the observations. Alexis knew to expect a transmission from Meredith in the very near future.

The image started to waver and fade and Alexis leaned forward.

"It appears our talk is about to be cut short as the station's orbit moves from range," Alexis said. "Do as I have commanded and all will be well. We are Aelish and we will bow to no one."

"Yes, sire. We are Aelish, but...cannot...landing..."

The transmission hissed and popped then went to nothing but static as Station Aelon, thousands of miles above, moved out of orbital synch. Alexis leaned back in his chair, nearly crying out as his side protested angrily, and looked at the wide window before him. Aelon Prime stretched and stretched for miles, making him wonder if masters of old, the leaders that ruled before the planet was torn apart by the Cataclysm, only needed to gaze upon the land to find inspiration.

If so, he knew how they felt, for his whole body hummed with inspiration and drive. He understood he was living his last days, and despite his need to see his wife one last time, he did not regret the choice to spend those last days fighting for the honor of family Teirmont and Station Aelon.

*

"*Push forward*!" Alexis shouted from the front of his royal skid as rows and rows of Aelish soldiers before him engaged with the Thraenish troops. "*Drive them back*!"

"Sire, you must get down!" General Ryan yelled, yanking on the master's arm. Several flechettes pinged along the railing. "*Sire*!"

The general forcibly pulled the master back towards the armored enclosure set up around the skid controls. The flat vehicle used the same rotational drive that allowed the stations to orbit the planet and maintain artificial gravity, but on a fraction of the scale. Hovering just above the ground, the royal skid was three times the size of an average skid, able to hold the small group of generals and advisors that watched the battle rage.

"Let go of me," Alexis hissed despite his obvious pain. "I am Master of Station Aelon and I will rally my troops as I see fit!"

"Sire, we are taking heavy fire from their slingers," General Ryan said. "While they do not have particle barbs, there is always the chance your suit will be pierced, even with your royal armor."

Alexis smacked his chest, refusing to wince at the pain it caused his wound, and stared the general in the eyes, the visors of their helmets almost touching.

"I am a Teirmont and a Teirmont does not run from tiny pieces of metal, General Ryan," Alexis said. "This armor is the best polybreen in the System. Their little slings can do nothing to me. They'd need a hundred long blades to even get to my flesh!"

The generals and advisors looked at each other, worry clouding their visored faces.

"Sire, are you feeling well?" General Ryan asked. "Your face is flushed and you are sweating."

"We are at war, Ryan! There are sweat and tears and blood in war! Would you prefer I was safely back on Aelon Prime, sitting in my quarters with a cold tea and haunch of shaow leg? I bet you would," Alexis glared. He cocked his head and narrowed his eyes at the men about him. "I bet you all would. Then you could take your time with this war, drag it out so that more Aelish men die while you get the glory."

"Your highness," General Ryan said as he reached out to take the master's arm once again. "You aren't making sense. We are here to do as you bid, that is all. We want this day to be a decisive win for Aelon. The fewer men we lose the greater the victory. It is not about our glory, but about the honor of Station Aelon and Aelon Prime."

Alexis watched the man for a long, silent minute, the gears in his head grinding together as he tried to make sense of the feverish jumble that was his mind. The master sighed and clapped the General on the shoulder then turned to look out at the battlefield.

"The only way to glory is to fight," Alexis said, holding out his hand. "My long blade, General. Now."

"Sire?"

"My long blade," Alexis said, his hand waiting there, empty. "I would like my long blade. Is that difficult to understand?"

"No, sire, I just wonder for what purpose you need your long blade," General Ryan replied. "Surely you aren't thinking of joining in the fight. If so then I would have to protest greatly."

"I will tell you my purpose once I have been given my long blade," Alexis said. "Place it in my hand now!"

The general looked over at one of the royal attendants, but the man only shrugged and shook his head.

"It appears your blades were not brought with us, your highness," General Ryan said. "They must be back on Aelon Prime in your quarters." The attendant nodded in confirmation. "I am truly sorry, sire. I take full responsibility for this oversight. No one expected you to need them."

"No one expected me to need them?" Alexis echoed, his voice mocking and cruel. "No one expected me to need them? I'm master of this battle! Of course I will need them!"

He whirled on the men and looked about the small space.

"Where is Corbin?" Alexis asked. "Corbin! Correct this at once!"

"Corbin Breach, sire?" the attendant asked. "The former head of the royal guard?"

"No, Corbin Willymuck, that stupid clown that performs during the Last Meal celebrations each year," Alexis spat. "Yes, I mean Corbin Breach! Where is that man? He should be by my side as he was when we fought the accursed lowdeckers. Now that was a battle!"

The master swayed and clutched his side. Attendants moved forward, but he shoved them back, his eyes filled with anger and contempt.

"You dare to grab a master?" he shouted. "You think because you dress me and watch me crap that you are equal to me? You are all nothing but siggy worms eating at a corpse! You are the droppings of trollen birds left for the wind and waves to clean from the pristine deck of my royal cutter! You are walking louts of flame that eat at my...eat at my..."

The master didn't finish.

His eyes rolled up into his head and he collapsed onto the deck of the skid. His attendants were at his side instantly and they held him as they looked up at General Ryan for instructions.

"Take him back to Aelon Prime," General Ryan said to the skid pilot, his face drawn and exhausted. "Get him to his quarters and into bed. Make sure the physicians know you are on the way. Hopefully he will not expire before we can get him up to the station. This is not how greatness should leave the world."

The generals quickly got down off the skid and moved out of the way as the vehicle spun about and shot away. The men of war looked at each other then at General Ryan as they stood in the scrim grass.

"We'll regroup on my skid," General Ryan said. "There is nothing we can do."

"Should we contact the station?" one of the men asked.

"Not until we know if he survives the journey across the water back to Aelon Prime," General Ryan replied. "When we have confirmation then I will contact Steward Stolt. He can inform the council and Mistress Meredith."

"If he dies then Minor Alexis becomes master," a general said. "Will he continue this campaign or call it to a halt?"

"No way to know," General Ryan said. "It depends on how he is advised."

The old soldiers stood there, solemn with the thought of who Minor Alexis received his advice from.

*

The wound continually oozed green puss and brown liquid. Despite everything the physicians tried, they could not stop, or even slow, the infection that had raged in the master's body for so many years.

"Am I to die today?" Alexis asked, his eyes blurred by pain and fever. "Rick? Tell me the truth. Am I to die today?"

"Rick?" a physician asked.

"His brother, the late minor," another physician replied. "Long since dead."

"His mind is burdened by memories," a third physician suggested. "We could sedate him so he sleeps and is not troubled by such thoughts."

"We cannot sedate a master," a physician from the back snapped.

The man, Xander Vlerara, was the youngest of the physicians, but stood and held himself as if he had always been in charge. The other physicians looked at him, six in total, and waited for him to finish. Despite his young age, he had risen quickly in the medical ranks of Station Aelon and had specifically requested he be assigned to the master during the prime campaign. From a long line of physicians, he was the latest in his family to serve the crown and he took the honor as seriously as he did his own life.

Perhaps more so.

"A master must not be put under unless the regent has been informed," Vlerara stated. "Have we been able to establish communications with the station?"

"We are still out of orbital synch," an attendant said from the doorway. "Communications with Station Aelon will be restored in the next few minutes, though, sir. I was under orders from General Ryan to let the mistress speak to his highness first."

"Very well," Vlerara replied. "She can speak to him then the minor. Once the regent gives his assent then we can sedate the master. If he lives long enough for that."

"He must have been in great agony for weeks, if not months," the first physician stated. "Were the physicians on station not aware of this?"

"They were," Vlerara replied. "But he is the master and told them to do nothing. Not that anything could be done. The master has been treated for his wound since he was young. When it was re-injured it sealed his fate. I believe only willpower has allowed him to last this long."

"Father? Father, did I finish your work?" Alexis asked, gripping one of the physicians by the collar and pulling him close. "I tried, Father. I made sure your remodeling of the decks continued. Did I do you proud, Father?"

The physician looked back at Vlerara in horror and confusion.

"Answer him," Vlerara said. "Give him some comfort."

"Uh...yes...Son," the physician responded to the delirious monarch. "You did me proud. All of your work was exactly as I envisioned."

"Was it? Excellent," Alexis said as he relinquished his grip on the poor physician. The man scuttled away, his robes nearly tripping him up in his haste. "Where are my children? I want to see them so they can hear it from your lips that I did you proud. Where are little Thomas and James? Where are my girls, Bora and Haley? Bring them to me. I must hold them."

"They have been detained by the shuttle, your highness," Vlerara responded. "But they are on their way. I believe you can speak to Minor Alexis soon, though, sire. He will be grateful to hear your wise words one last time."

"One last time..." Alexis whispered as a hint of clarity came to him. "Yes, of course. One last time." The master looked about and shook his head. "My death began here, you know. On the planet. So many years ago when I was young and still innocent. So young..."

"The communications have been restored," the attendant said as he wheeled over a video screen and large microphone. "The minor is waiting to speak with his father."

"Leave them in private," Vlerara said to the physicians. "This conversation is between royals."

"I will stay," the attendant said. "I am required to, as witness to any royal proclamations."

"Of course," Vlerara nodded as he hurried the other physicians from the room. "But alert us immediately if the master's condition worsens."

The attendant nodded then waited for the door to close before gently placing the bulky microphone in the master's hands.

"Sire? Minor Alexis is waiting to speak to you. He is on the screen here." The attendant tapped the grainy image then stepped away from the bed and into the shadows of the royal quarters.

"Father?" Minor Alexis asked, his voice tinny and thin from the weak connection. "Father, they say you are dying. Is this true?"

"Can a master ever die, Son?" Alexis chuckled. It sounded more like a harsh rattle of pain than anything born of mirth. "A master lives on in history forever, Alexis. Know this, understand this. What you do with your reign will always be remembered. You control your immortality."

"Yes, Father, of course," Minor Alexis nodded. "But your story isn't finished. You must get better and return to me. I have so much more to learn."

Alexis laughed hard, which turned into a coughing fit that sent him writhing with pain on the bed.

"Father!" Minor Alexis yelled. "Fetch the physicians back! Call them to help!"

"No...no," Alexis replied as he settled himself. "There is no point." He breathed deeply and tried to focus on the video image. "Let me speak with your mother."

"Meredith is in the other room," Minor Alexis said. "I'll get her."

"Meredith? That child? No, no, your mother, Alexis. Let me speak with my Eliza."

The minor paused, unsure of how to respond.

"What is it? Why do you not fetch her immediately? I am dying, Son. I do not have time to wait."

"Mother passed years ago, Father," Minor Alexis said. "Your wife is the Mistress Meredith now, remember?"

"Meredith..." Alexis said. "I saved her. She was so young, perhaps eight or nine, I can't remember. I saved her when they tried to assassinate me. Those bastard gatekeepers wanted me dead so they could give Derrick the crown and keep me from making changes. I know the stewards were behind it, but could never prove a thing."

Minor Alexis narrowed his eyes and leaned closer to the camera on his end.

"The stewards, Father? Which stewards?" he asked. "Was it Cousin Stolt? Did you know even then that he had an agenda against the crown?"

"Cousin Stolt," Alexis nodded. "Yes, I believe it was. I kept him close all these years. Made sure his fate was intertwined with mine. I know he worked behind the scenes during the lower decks uprising. I know it."

Minor Alexis smiled. "I have always suspected. Is there proof, Father? Tell me where you have the proof. I will need it to fight him off when he comes after me."

"No, Son, there is no proof other than my gut feeling," Alexis said. "Which is quite diseased at the present time." Alexis laughed weakly then reached out to touch the screen. His fingers ran down the black and white image of his son's face and he tried to smile. "Do not fight the man, Alexis. Let him have his little glories. Just steer him in the direction you want. His ambition will always look to keep the crown strong, no matter his own intentions. He does not want a weak Station Aelon anymore than you or I do."

"Yes, Father," Minor Alexis nodded. "I thank you for that counsel."

"And kill them all," Alexis snarled. "When they try to kill you in your sleep! When they box you in on a lift! When they hold you down and fill you with Vape! Kill them all, my son! *Kill then all*!"

The master's body began to convulse and shake and the attendant ran to him.

"Your highness!" he shouted. "Oh, Helios! Physicians! Vlerara! Physicians, help!"

"Father? Father!" Minor Alexis yelled from the screen, but the cart was shoved aside as the bed was surrounded by harrowed physicians. "*Father*!"

Alexis screamed as the pain raged through his body. The wound in his side began to pour blood, dark, heavy blood, and no matter the number of towels pressed against it, they were not enough.

With one last, long scream, Master Alexis of Station Aelon left the world of the living and joined Helios in the One True System for eternity.

When Vlerara was certain that the master was dead he turned to the screen to see Minor Alexis watching it all, hands covering his mouth, his eyes wide with fear.

"I am sorry, your highness," Vlerara said. "Your father has passed on. The master is dead, long live the master."

He quickly took a knee and the other physicians, as well as the attendants in the room, joined him.

"The master is dead, long live the master!"

*

"Your highness, the treasury cannot handle the expense of such a lavish coronation," Steward Stolt said as he stood in front of the new master. "With the expense of the campaign against Thraen Prime, we barely have enough to keep basic operations going on the station."

"And whose fault is that, Stolt?" Alexis the Second asked. "Don't think I don't know that you have been pilfering credits from the crown for decades."

"I have vast holdings in all of my sectors, sire," Stolt replied, his voice even and calm. "I do not need to pilfer from the crown. My wealth is all my own."

"Then perhaps it is time you shared some of that wealth with the crown," Alexis grinned, delighted that Stolt had fallen right into his trap. "I am sure you could finance the coronation expenses all by yourself, don't you think? As a gift to me?"

"Even I am not that wealthy, sire," Stolt said and bowed. "I am sorry."

"That you are, Stolt. That you are," Alexis sighed as he crossed his legs and started to drum his fingers on the long table in the great hall. "So, the only recourse is to raise taxes so we can pay for the coronation. I refuse to be crowned like a simple master. Do you think I'm a Flaenian? Those garment makers and tailors can live like the common folk, but here on Station Aelon we treat our masters like...kings."

Stolt stood and had to use every ounce of his willpower not to reprimand the young master for his almost blasphemous use of the word "king."

"Sire, as much as I want to please you, I cannot make credits appear in the treasury," Stolt said. "The only way possible would be to end the prime campaign and call a truce with Master Charles."

"A truce? Is that possible?" Alexis asked.

"Well, of course, your highness," Stolt said. "We could recall all of our troops and end the conflict with a simple declaration. But the council would be against it, sire. They have fully committed to the campaign. Not to mention the generals. From what I have seen of this morning's report, we are close to actually taking all of Thraen Prime."

"But if we stop now then the treasury would have enough money for my coronation, yes?"

Stolt hesitated. He wanted to answer truthfully, to do otherwise would be very dangerous, but what the new master was hinting at was beyond irresponsible and bordered on complete corruption of power. A master ending a military campaign to finance his own coronation? Station Aelon would become the laughingstock of the System.

Stolt swallowed hard and pushed on. "Yes, sire, if we end the campaign against Thraen Prime then the treasury could afford your coronation."

"Then make that happen," Alexis said, pushing around a stack of papers as he searched the table for a pen. "Get me something to write with and I will declare it done today."

"Sire, this would require the approval of the meeting of stewards as well as the meeting of passengers. You cannot just—"

"Am I master of this station or not?" Alexis shouted as he stood and shoved all the papers onto the floor. "If I decide to end this silly campaign then the silly campaign is ended! Bring me a pen so I can put this to writing and not have to think of it ever again!"

He looked about the great hall at the stunned faces.

"Why is no one moving? *I want a pen now*!"

Half of the servants jumped into action, each finding a pen and hurrying over to offer it to the master.

"See, Stolt," Alexis smirked as he picked one of the pens and sat back down. "Was that so hard? Paper. Now."

Stolt just smiled as he bent to the floor and found a clean sheet of paper from the mess Alexis had created. He set the paper directly in front of the master and stepped back. It took Alexis all of two minutes to write out his declaration. He signed it, blew on the ink, then set the pen down and leaned back in his chair.

"The war is over," Alexis said. "Let the station celebrate. No one likes a silly war anyway."

"Yes, sire," was all Stolt said as he nodded to the master. "Is there anything else?"

"Not that I can think of at the moment, Stolt," Alexis replied. "But I am sure the council will want to have words with me after they hear of this."

"As will the stewards, your highness," Stolt replied.

"Yes, them as well," Alexis said. "Go ahead and schedule the meetings today. Let's get this business behind us so I can be properly crowned without the shadow of nonsense floating above me."

"Yes, sire," Stolt said. "I will make it all happen."

The steward turned and strode towards the entrance to the great hall. Just as he was about to leave, the master called for him one last time.

"Stolt! Hold!" Alexis yelled. "There is one thing that needs to be done. I want this to happen before we announce the end of the war."

"And that is, your highness?" Stolt asked, turning to face the master.

"Send word to the sectors that Brother DuChaer has been returned to Station Aelon," Alexis said. "The dearest friend a master could have is no longer in exile. He is home, Stolt, he is home."

"Is home, your highness?" Stolt asked. "When did he return?"

"That does not concern you, Cousin," Alexis said. "Just make sure the meeting of stewards knows. I don't want it to be a surprise when he is seated at my right hand."

Stolt bowed low, looked at the floor, and waited for the opportunistic grin on his face to fade away before he stood straight again.

"It will be a pleasure to have Gannot DuChaer back at court," Stolt responded. "Every master should have a friend and confidant they can turn to. I can think of no more worthy candidate than DuChaer."

"Well said, Stolt," Alexis agreed. "He gives nothing but the best advice. Oh, and Stolt, there is one more thing."

"Yes, sire?"

"Bestow upon Brother DuChaer some title. I know he is heir to a Thraenish stewardship, but that is Thraen," Alexis said. "Find him an eligible woman with solid holdings here on the station. A man of his breeding mustn't stay a bachelor, don't you agree? How would that look? The advisor to the master should be a full steward with all the rights and privileges."

"You couldn't be more correct, sire," Stolt said. "I will find him a worthy spouse. I am sure women will line up for the honor of being his wife."

"I would if I were them," Alexis said then cleared his throat. "Now go. You have much to do."

"Yes, sire. Thank you, sire," Stolt said as he backed out of the great hall and shut the doors behind him.

The steward stared at the carvings on the door for a long while, his mind working through the implications of what had just happened.

"Steward Stolt?" a servant asked. "Are you well?"

"Oh, I am more than well," Stolt said. "I am elated. It is an exciting time on the station, my boy. Do not forget where you were when this day happened. It will be remembered throughout history."

The servant frowned as Stolt walked quickly away, ready to do as the master bid and to set his own plans into motion.

It was an exciting time indeed.

REIGN OF FOUR

BOOK II

Act I

A Suspect Beginning

"For most monarchs, their legacy is what helps define them through history. Not just their policies and proclamations, their accomplishments and failures, but their actual heredity. For Alexis I, his dreams of a positive legacy must have seemed lost. Little did he know who would be born from disappointment and failure."

—Dr. D. Reven, Eighty-Third Archivist of The Way

"As for the father, so for the son. Let there be no distinguishing between the two for the son is not but an extension of the father. And let the son know that to act is to act as if he was the father. Triumph be divided, shame be shared."

—Book of Porticus 3:12, The Ledger

"The fool fought wars when he could have let others do the work. Is it no wonder he died and yet I still live? Is it no wonder that I enjoy the spoils of my Station while his eternal soul looks down at his own folly? I loved my father, but he was a man that refused to see the future. I will not make the same mistakes."

—Coronation speech of Alexis the Second, Master of Station Aelon

CHAPTER ONE

The Vape swirled and churned about the planet, its grey mass a thick blanket of protection and oppression. The atmosphere was nothing but toxic hell and not a person could live on the surface of Helios exposed. They'd burst open and burn in a raging conflagration of oxygen ignited Vape.

Vape.

The gas that powered everything.

Mined by the workers who rarely saw daylight, other than brief, grey glimpses as they went from skid to deep, dank hole in the ground.

Compressed by the factory workers who at least could look at the line of window slits at the top of the factory walls and know that it was still day.

Transported by barges across the boiling seas of planet Helios, to be delivered to waiting shuttles that would take the precious gas up to one of the six stations.

Thraen. Flaen. Ploerv. Klaerv. Haelm.

Aelon.

A station for each of the masterships. A station to match each prime on the planet. A station, an artificial celestial body that rotated as if it was set there by Helios, God of all, Dear Parent, Creator. But the stations were not set there by the hand of Helios. Instead, they were built by an ancient civilization long gone.

Powered by Vape, kept rotational by technology that the current occupants only had a slight understanding of. Enough understanding to make repairs, but not improvements.

BOOK II

Six stations, floating like satellites in the starry sky above a planet that had one way off and one way on.

The Way Prime.

A meteorological anomaly.

Of the seven primes—lands that once were part of a massive continent, but were separated into smaller continents after the Cataclysm that forced humanity to flee the planet—the Way Prime was the only piece of land with a clear sky. It allowed The Way to control what left the planet and what arrived on it. Making the religious order more powerful than the stations combined.

It was that portal of turquoise sky that lay directly below the royal shuttle that plummeted from Station Aelon down to the planet. An almost perfectly round hole in a cocoon of Vape was what the shuttle aimed for.

Minoress Esther Teirmont, first born to Master Alexis, the First of Station Aelon, held her hand against the environmental pod that housed her baby brother. She looked down at the small window in the pod and frowned as she saw the scrunched up face of the screaming infant, silent to her ears since there was no communication system in the pod to broadcast his wails to her environmental suit's helmet.

"I know, Alexis," she said to the heir to the crown of Station Aelon. "I don't want to be here either."

The shuttle clanged and rocked as it hit the outer atmosphere of the planet. Esther gripped the metal handles by her shoulders and said a prayer to Helios, the Dear Parent. She prayed that the shuttle wouldn't fall apart on its descent. She prayed that once she and her brother arrived on Helios, the gatekeepers of The Way would let them travel immediately and not hold them until her father made an "offering" to the holy men and women.

Mostly she prayed that her father would come to his senses and recall her and her brother from the planet, and Aelon Prime, where they were headed, instead of banishing them to a primitive life for their "protection."

Protection from what, she didn't know. There were far more dangerous elements on Helios than on Station Aelon. But then there were far less politics and intrigue. The station was never truly safe for any royal, regardless of how much power they wielded.

"Relax," a woman's voice said in Esther's ear, amplified by the communications system in her environmental suit's helmet.

The minoress turned and looked at the helmeted face of her aunt, Melinda Teirmont, older sister of Alexis the First. The woman had aged considerably the past few months, having had to deal with the deaths of so many friends and family from the Weeping Sickness that swept station Aelon. Melinda tried to smile at Esther, but it merely looked like she had gas.

"We are already on our journey, child," Melinda said. "There is no going back now. Prepare yourself for a life on the Prime instead of fretting over a shuttle ride."

"I'm not a child, Auntie," Esther responded. "I'm a teenager of marrying age according to The Way. If I can take a husband then I can be considered a woman."

"You can be considered a woman when you've lived a woman's life," Melinda said. "Bleed from your first copulation and then we'll talk about who is a woman."

"Many of the female gatekeepers have never copulated, but they are considered women," Esther countered.

"Dear Niece," Melinda sighed as she patted Esther on the shoulder. "If you believe the gatekeepers don't copulate then you have more to learn than I thought. Have you not heard of the Taking? How do you think the Burdened are made? By Helios's will? No, they are born from the wombs of gatekeepers. Born into a life of soldiering, sworn to protect The Way with their lives, all because of the sins that their parents committed in the name of our Dear Parent."

"You lie," Esther snapped. "The gatekeepers are holy people. The High Guardian would never allow such animal instincts to be present on The Way Prime."

"The High Guardian gets his pick of the gatekeepers," Melinda laughed. "Whether male or female. He does as he pleases with his cock just as he does with his proclamations and religious orders. Stop being a naïve station girl and prepare yourself for real life. This is the planet Helios! Once the home to all of humanity, but now a frontier meant to be mined and exploited for its resources. Grow up, *child*."

Esther looked about the compartment at the others strapped to the walls, expecting to see shocked faces, but all she saw was fear and apprehension of an uncertain future. The royal servants hadn't heard a word and Esther realized that she wasn't just isolated by a private communication channel; she was isolated by an ignorance of how things worked.

She glanced back at her aunt and nodded.

"I will, Auntie," Esther said. "I'll grow up. Fast."

"Good," Melinda replied as she closed her eyes. "Now try to rest. It'll be an hour before we land. Once we hit the ground, we will head straight for the royal cutter and Aelon Prime. I have no intention of being a bargaining chip for some gatekeeper with ambitions of High Guardianship."

"But won't Corbin protect us?" Esther asked, nodding her helmet towards the former head of the Royal Guard of Station Aelon. The man was sound asleep and drooling into his own helmet a few seats away. "Father sent him down here to make sure we are not harmed in any way."

"That drunk cripple?" Melinda laughed. "We'll be lucky to avoid stepping in his puddles of piss. Forget Corbin, girl. He is a lost cause and only sent with us so he could retire. Goes to show you who your father cares about more, doesn't it? Now close your eyes and rest. You'll need it."

"Yes, Auntie," Esther said and closed her eyes.

But she didn't rest.

She just counted off the seconds and minutes as the shuttle rocketed towards the surface of the planet and her new life.

*

The boy, only six, but hardly considered small, stayed hidden behind his sister's legs, his bright blue eyes and head of blonde hair all that could be seen from around Esther's breen skirts.

"Don't be shy, Son," Master Alexis said as he towered over his children.

At nearly seven feet with legs that seemed to never stop—giving him the nickname "Longshanks"—Alexis the First was an imposing figure. Especially due to his children having only seen him in person twice since leaving Station Aelon years before. And the fact he reeked of gelberry wine.

"Come and give me a hug, boy," Master Alexis said as he crouched and held out his arms. "Greet your father proper."

"He's like this around people he doesn't know," Esther said, her eyes narrowed and full of challenge. "It'll take him a bit to warm up to you."

"I don't have a bit," Master Alexis snapped. "This is a huge risk leaving the Station without an heir onboard. The meeting of stewards could take control in 'station interest' at any moment if they liked."

"But what about Cousin Stolt?" Esther sneered, her hands on her hips. Hips that had widened over six years into a woman's hips, despite her aunt's insistence that a nineteen-year-old virgin was not a woman. Little did her aunt know. "Isn't Cousin Stolt always looking out for our interests?"

"You know perfectly well that the only interests Cousin Stolt looks out for are his own," Master Alexis said. "That is why I keep him so close."

"One day he'll be the death of you," Esther said.

"I doubt that," Master Alexis replied, as he stood up, tired of waiting for a greeting from his son and heir. "I have been stabbed twice through the gut and still live. Stolt wouldn't dare tempt Helios with an assassination attempt on my life. Then little Alexis here would become Master of Station Aelon. And no one is ready for that."

"You think Stolt wouldn't put himself in power as regent?" Melinda asked as she strode into the small banquet hall of Aelon Prime's estate house. "He'd have the documents drawn up in a heartbeat. If he doesn't already have them waiting."

"Yes, but I have documents putting you in place as regent, Sister," Master Alexis said as he walked over and embraced Melinda warmly. "Which I have made sure he knows. The last thing Stolt would do is go to war with you, Mel. He'd have to walk around the Station with his hands cupping his nuts, ever ready for them to be snatched from his grasp."

"I wouldn't touch that weak man's balls for all the credits on the planet," Melinda laughed. "I prefer my men with some heft and strength. Real men, not sycophantic toadies like Cousin Stolt."

"Toadies?" Alexis asked from behind Esther. "Can I see the toadies?"

"The heir speaks," Master Alexis laughed. "You like toads, son? Maybe I will send a guard out to find you one."

"Please don't," Esther sighed. "He's already gone through six bog toads, two trollen birds, and a shitload of siggy worms. You think it's easy keeping creatures alive in here that were meant to live out in the wilds and breathe Vape? It's not. Yet he's always bringing the things inside and we have to scramble to get them in a Vape tank so they don't explode in the airlocks."

"An adventurer and man of the land, eh?" Master Alexis smiled. "Excellent qualities for a future master."

"Know what else would be an excellent quality? Knowing how to pick up his room himself," Esther snapped. "Another one of my jobs since we don't have enough servants down here on the Prime."

"Esther," Melinda warned. "Now is not the time. Your father has just arrived and must be exhausted from the shuttle and the cutter ride across the sea."

"I am at that," Master Alexis said, fixing his eyes on his daughter. "Let me rest and freshen up and then we can discuss matters of the estate, alright?"

Esther glared for a second then nodded.

"Come Alexis," Esther said, taking her brother's hand. "Let's have you take a rest as well. That way you can be full of energy for Father. Then he can really see just how adventurous you are."

She gave a weak curtsey then left the royal quarters quickly, barely acknowledging her aunt.

"Is she always like that?" Master Alexis asked.

"Only when she's awake," Melinda said.

"We'll have a hard time marrying her off with that attitude," Master Alexis said as he pulled off his breen tunic and threw it across the room. He flopped into a less than comfortable chair and looked up at his sister. "Good thing I am thinking ahead."

"Are you now?" Melinda asked, taking a seat across from him in an even less comfortable chair. The breen upholstery was worn and the springs were starting to poke through, but she ignored the discomfort, quite used to the scarcity on the Prime. "What noble have you promised her to this time?"

"Not a noble," Master Alexis smiled, leaning forward and resting his arms on his knees. "A royal. Zaik, Minor of Station Klaerv, to be precise."

"The Infant Heir?" Melinda laughed.

"He is eleven now," Alexis replied. "No longer the infant."

"But she is nineteen," Melinda replied. "Tell me you are joking, Alexis."

"I am not," Master Alexis said and leaned back. "It is all still in negotiations and the marriage will be years off, so I trust you to keep her nose, and all other parts, clean until then." He frowned as something jabbed him. "I hope to Helios that the whole estate isn't as bad as this chair."

"Some of it is worse," Melinda said. "I'd divert funds for repairs, but you gave financial powers to Corbin. What an enlightened decision."

"How is the man?" Master Alexis asked. "Still ornery and wishing he could get back to the Royal Guard."

"If by 'ornery' you mean drunk and 'by get back to the Royal Guard' you mean had the strength to pull himself from his wheelchair to take a shit instead of doing it in his trousers, then yes, he's all of that," Melinda scowled. "He's out of control, Alexis. The man needs to be retired. Permanently."

"Did I just overhear the plotting of my death?" Corbin asked as the door to the royal quarters was shoved open and he slowly wheeled himself inside. "I can leave if you need to work out more details."

"Oh, I already have the details worked out," Melinda sneered.

"And you wonder where Minoress Esther gets her attitude," Corbin said as he pulled out a flask and took a long drink from it.

"I have never wondered," Master Alexis said. "She is all Teirmont fire. My dear, sweet Eliza wasn't like that at all."

"There's room for debate there," Melinda said, her sneer becoming a smile at the memory of her late sister-in-law. "Eliza was not weak-willed."

"No, she was not," Master Alexis nodded then looked at Corbin. "Going to share that flask or what, man?"

Corbin tossed it over to the master, a sly grin on his face. Master Alexis unscrewed the top, took a pull, then coughed hard enough to make the chair beneath him creak in protest.

"Dear Parent! What is that?" Master Alexis gasped. "Did you liquefy Vape?"

"My own concoction," Corbin said as he snapped his fingers for the flask to be returned. He caught it easily, opened it up, wiped the rim with the soiled sleeve of his breen tunic, and then proceeded to finish it off without a single hiccup. "I learned how to make liquor from honey wasp nectar then combine that with boiled and distilled scrim grass seeds. Plus a few drops of gelberry wine. Let that ferment for a month or two and you have the best damn drink in the whole System."

"You have something, alright," Master Alexis laughed. "Don't know if I'd call that a drink or a form of torture."

Corbin shrugged and fished out a second flask from a trouser pocket.

"How many of those do you have?" Master Alexis asked.

"Enough to get me through the day," Corbin replied. "You should really try it. Makes living so much more bearable."

"For you, maybe," Melinda said. "It's unbearable for the rest of us."

Corbin replied with a loud fart.

"You are lucky I like you, Corbin," Master Alexis said. "The stench of that flatulence is a capital offense. I could have you thrown outside the estate house without an environmental suit."

"He'd only poison the air more," Melinda sighed. "Trust me, I've already thought of it."

"Suck my shriveled cock, you harpy," Corbin said as he farted again. "You can't kill me. No one can. I'm the invincible idiot."

Master Alexis looked at his sister, his features trying to hide the sadness he felt from the state of his old friend and bodyguard. He only looked back at Corbin when the man started to snore loudly.

"I'll take him," Melinda said. "It's part of my daily routine. You rest so you can spend some time with your son later."

"Thank you, Mel," Master Alexis nodded as he got up and walked to the large bed. "I appreciate everything you do down here. I hope you know that."

Melinda only nodded in response as she wheeled the passed out Corbin from the quarters.

Master Alexis fell across the bed and closed his eyes. Sleep took him quickly.

*

"My Helios, look at him go!" Master Alexis exclaimed from the bow of the large skid as he watched his son race through the scrim grass of Aelon Prime on a single seat skid, its hover drive glowing bright blue. "I've seen soldiers lose control at that speed!"

"Well, racing skids is one of the few pastimes here on the Prime," Esther said as she stared out of the protective dome that enclosed the royal skid's deck. "I've left more than my share of royal guards in the dust, you know."

"Have you?" Master Alexis asked as he continued to watch his son zig and zag in front of the royal skid. "A minoress out on a skid? Wouldn't that be a scandal on the Station?"

"Would it?" Melinda asked. "How little it takes to offend the nobility these days."

"Never takes much," Master Alexis said. "Which is why I have to return at the next scheduled rotation."

"You what?" Esther cried. "You only just got here!"

"I know, I know," Master Alexis said, holding up his hands. "But word has reached my ears of certain matters that must be taken care of. I'd trust Stolt to handle them, but I don't trust Stolt. I have to leave on the next orbital rotation in order to go straight back to Station Aelon."

"One day someone will create a shuttle that can actually be flown where we want it to go instead of just a straight line," Melinda said. "Station to planet, planet to station. Station to station. Our ancestors mastered the technology to allow all of this, surely we can master the technology to adapt and fly a shuttle as if it were a skid."

"Perhaps someday, Helios willing," Master Alexis said. "But for now our scientists are too busy maintaining the Station rotational drive and keeping it operational. I'd prefer they focus on that, and the life support systems, than worry about being able to zip around the System at will."

"So you leave in four days?" Esther asked, unable to keep the hurt and disappointment from her face and voice.

"I do," Master Alexis said. "With great regret. I always forget how wonderful and wild the Prime is."

"Try living on it and see how wonderful it is," Melinda smirked. "I have a feeling even the next four days will become trying."

"Well, at least I have four days with my family," Master Alexis said. "Can we spend it in peace? Or will we have to trade barbs back and forth the entire time?"

Melinda and Esther looked at each other then at the master.

"We'll keep the barbs down to only a couple of times a day," Melinda said. "Now watch your son. He's starting to get too daring, as he always does. The crash should be entertaining."

"The crash?" Master Alexis asked just as the single skid out front took a hard turn and flipped onto its side. "Dear Helios! Someone get out there and make sure he's alright!"

"He's fine," Esther and Melinda replied at the same time just as Alexis jumped up out of the scrim grass and gave them all a big wave.

"Gonna take a lot more than a tipped skid to kill that little shit," Corbin said from his wheelchair positioned back against the wall of the skid's pilothouse. "Trust me, I've tried."

Master Alexis turned slowly and looked at the former royal guard. "Did you just admit to trying to kill my son?"

"Oh, keep your blade in its sheath," Corbin replied. "I mean in training. He can take on two servants at once with a short blade now. Of course, they are required to lose, but I watch his form. He's a natural, like his father."

"Isn't it time you graduated him to real opponents?" Master Alexis asked. "He is six, after all."

"In good time," Corbin said. "I'm waiting for him to draw blood. Right now, he's just fighting them off. Once he's able to slip their guard and give a wee nick, then I'll put my men on him. I know how to train a fighter, sire, don't you worry your crown."

"I am not worried," Master Alexis said. "I just need him ready as soon as possible. You never know when my time will be up."

"Not for a long while," Melinda said. "So let's stop talking about this, shall we? And it's time to head back to the estate house."

"Why don't we have a castle on our prime like Thraen does on theirs?" Esther asked.

"Because the Thraenish are vain people and need big castles to make up for their deficiencies elsewhere," Master Alexis replied, eliciting a loud guffaw from Corbin.

"Or it could be that Station Aelon doesn't have the funds to build a new castle, or give us the proper style of the day, due to Cousin Stolt's management of the treasury," Melinda responded. "But what do I know of such matters? I'm only a woman."

"Stop it," Master Alexis growled.

"The minor has loaded his skid onto the back, sire," the pilot said as he leaned his head out the window of the pilothouse. "Shall we return?"

"Yes, let's do," Master Alexis said.

"Did you see me crash, Father?" Alexis asked as he ran up and jumped into the master's arms. "I really ate shaowshit that time, didn't I?"

"That mouth!" Master Alexis laughed as he spun his son around. "Who taught you that?"

"Corbin did," Alexis grinned. "And Esther and Auntie Melinda. Oh, and the miners in the barracks and the servants in the kitchen. And Mrs. Pleep. She's my nurse."

"Welcome to the Prime, Brother," Melinda smiled. "We don't mince words down here."

"I can see that," Master Alexis laughed.

*

"Will he come back?" Alexis asked as his sister tucked him into bed having sent Mrs. Pleep off after the minor's bath was done. "I miss him already."

"You don't know him enough to miss him," Esther said. "He's visited us only three times since we came here to live."

"But we can talk to him on the communication system, right? Even use the video?" Alexis asked, his face bright with hope and anticipation.

"Perhaps," Esther said. "It depends on when he has time. Masters are busy men."

"I'll be a master one day, won't I?"

"One day," Esther said. "A long ways off. Father isn't going to die anytime soon. He'll live long enough to make sure you are of age before you take the crown."

"But he has to die for me to take the crown, doesn't he?" Alexis asked.

"Yes, he does," Esther replied.

"That's kind of sad," Alexis frowned. "I don't want to be master if it means Father has to die."

"Those are the rules of succession," Esther said. "Unless he was to be deposed or he abdicated, but that won't ever happen. No Master of Station Aelon has ever been deposed and Father would have no reason to abdicate the crown."

"Desponsed?" Alexis asked. "What does that mean?"

"*Deposed*," Esther corrected. "It means the meeting of stewards, with the vote of the meeting of passengers, decide that a master is no longer fit to lead the Station."

"Oh," Alexis nodded, obviously not understanding. He lay there in his bed, breen sheets pulled up to his chin, and thought about it all very seriously. "Esther? Why can't you be master?"

"You mean mistress," Esther replied. "Women are mistresses. Only men are masters. And I suppose that answers the question. Only men can be masters. It's the law of the stations and the edict of The Way. It would be in defiance of the High Guardian for a woman to take the crown. And if you defy the High Guardian then you defy Helios, our Dear Parent and God."

"Ugh, why does everything have to be named Helios?" Alexis grumbled. "The Star, the System, the Planet. Even God is named Helios. It's very confusing."

"You seem to understand it just fine for being six," Esther smiled. "And it's better not to question. There's little point."

"Like questioning why women can't have the crown, right?" Alexis asked.

"Right," Esther smiled then leaned in and kissed his brow. She stood up and dimmed the Vape lamp by his bedside then walked to the bedchamber door. "Sleep well, little brother."

"Esther?" Alexis called just as the door almost shut.

"What now?"

"If I have a daughter born first, then she will get to be Mistress of Station Aelon," Alexis announced. "I don't care what the stewards say or what the old High Guardian says. She will have the crown. It's only fair."

Esther paused at the door for a long while before she composed herself enough to answer.

"That is very kind of you, Alexis. I hope you actually do it. You have no idea how much your daughter will love you for that."

She closed the door and left Alexis to his thoughts in the dark.

"I'll also name her Alexis," Alexis said. "It's a boy's name, but maybe that will trick them." He looked up at the shadows on his ceiling from the swirling Vape fog that had descended on the estate outside. The windows of his quarters looked like video screens filled with very dim static. "Or I could kill them all and then they couldn't argue."

That was the thought that echoed in Alexis's head as he drifted off to sleep.

*

The long blade flew from Alexis's hand and stuck squarely in the groove between wall panels of the training room.

"Don't see that happen every day," Alexis said as he jogged over to the blade and yanked it free. "What do you think the odds are, Corbin? That a blade could fly twenty feet and stick in the one spot it can fit? A hair over and it would have bounced off the panel."

"I'll bounce my fist off your forehead if you don't start paying attention," Corbin snapped from his wheelchair. "I should let my men cut you a few times and then see how obsessed with the odds you are."

"Helios, Corbin, have a couple more drinks and relax," Alexis said. "Don't stay sober on my account. I prefer you drunk. You're easier to get along with."

The two guards that had been training with the twelve-year old-minor covered their mouths quickly so the former royal guard couldn't see their smirks.

"You think you are so smart, don't you?" Corbin sneered. "We'll see how smart you are when you take a blade to the gut, you whelp."

"Corbin Breach," Esther snapped as she entered the training room. "Do I need to have you escorted from the royal compound? Should you be tossed outside the gates in nothing but an environmental suit and your wheelchair? That is what I'll do the next time I hear you call my brother a 'whelp,' are we understood?"

"Can I call him a little shit?" Corbin smirked. "Or a gully fish turd? What about shaow spunk?"

"Only if warranted," Esther said as she leaned down and picked up a discarded long blade. "Now, let's see what you have been teaching my brother lately."

"Really, Sister?" Alexis laughed. Despite being only twelve, he had sprouted quickly and looked his twenty-five year old sister straight in the eye as he lifted his own blade. "I couldn't possibly spar with a woman."

"Not this woman," Esther said as she bent over and pushed her skirts up between her legs then tucked them into the waistband at her back. "You'd have to know how to spar with a long blade to beat me."

"You should have worn trousers," Alexis said as he started to circle his sister, the tip of his long blade bobbing along as if to some tune in Alexis's head. "Hardly fair of me to engage a woman that's all trussed up like that. And why your good skirts?"

Esther circled with Alexis, her eyes locked onto his chest, waiting for the attack.

"An envoy from Klaerv is to arrive today," Esther said. "Apparently one of them is a minor and Auntie wants me to look my best."

"You're what? A hundred years old?" Alexis laughed. "Who'd marry you?"

"I'm not even twenty-six yet," Esther replied. "And no one said anything about marriage. They are here to see the breen fields and our production facilities."

"Not the Vape mines?" Alexis asked, continuing to circle.

"If they wanted to see Vape mines they'd go to Thraen Prime," Esther replied. "Not Aelon Prime. We're known for our breen crops."

"Oh, will you two dolts shut up and fight," Corbin snapped. "This circling, circling, circling is going to make me puke."

Esther thrust towards Alexis and he easily parried it, dodging to the side as he came in low at her knees. To his surprise, Esther easily jumped his attack and came at him faster than he thought she was capable of. In less than a couple of seconds, he found himself with the sharp edge of a long blade against the side of his neck.

"That's more like it," Corbin said. "Now do us all a favor and finish him, will ya?"

"He's the man in charge of my safety," Alexis laughed as he gently placed his thumb on the blade and pushed it away from his skin. He wiped at his neck and was surprised to find a small amount of blood. "You actually cut me."

"A reminder," Esther said as she untangled her skirts and let them fall back in place. A guard handed her a towel and she dabbed at the light sweat on her brow and upper lip. "Never let your ego get in the way of reality."

"Reality," Alexis scoffed. "That's for passengers and the lesser folk."

"Hey!" Corbin snapped. "Listen to your sister! You are not invincible, no matter how much you think of yourself!"

"Do I need to order you to take another drink?" Alexis growled at the old cripple.

Corbin glared, but did take a flask from his pocket and drink half of it before capping it and sticking it away.

"There. Satisfied?" Corbin said. "Now get back in form so my men can show you some reality."

"I'm afraid he's done for the day," Esther said. "That's why I'm here. As much as I love seeing your grizzled face, Corbin, I'd only set foot in this stinkhole with good reason. Minor Alexis needs to make himself presentable so he can receive the Klaervian delegation by my side."

"Then go," Corbin grumbled. "I was tired of seeing your faces anyway. I have work to do as it is."

The two royals raised their eyebrows at him, looking very much like siblings.

"What? I work," Corbin protested. "Who do you think informs his highness of your progress? I write reports, you know."

"Good for you, Corbin," Alexis laughed. "Paperwork. It's a nice change from your drinking and...what else?"

"Kiss my shithole," Corbin said. "And get the fuck out of my training room."

Alexis bowed low and backed out with his forehead almost touching the ground. Once out in the hall, he stood upright and turned to his less than amused sister.

"I do love that man," Alexis said. "He has such charm."

"He takes too many liberties," Esther replied. "He needs to remember his place here. As much as he likes to think he's in charge, he is not."

"No, I am," Melinda said as they rounded a corner and almost ran into their aunt. "Not that it seems to make a bit of difference. I sent you to make sure Alexis was getting cleaned up and I find you still in the hallway chatting? Care to explain why?"

"Because she decided I needed a shave," Alexis said, pointing to the nick on his neck. "She's not a very good barber."

"Esther," Melinda hissed as she grabbed Alexis's chin and turned his head so she could get a better look at the cut. "Well, at least it isn't bad. I doubt the Klaervians will even notice."

"Why should they care?" Esther asked. "Minors spar; it's what they do in order to train to be master. He has to know how to kill, kill, kill, doesn't he?"

Melinda eyed her niece for a second then sighed. "Tell me what's on your mind, girl."

"First, not a girl," Esther said. "Girls aren't in their twenties."

"Yes, but women in their twenties are already married with children," Melinda said. "Since you do not live up to either of those criteria. I will refer to you as a girl. Unless there is some other qualification that you feel I should know that makes you a woman?"

Esther glared. "You know damn well there is. No need to rub it in, Auntie."

"Oh, but there is," Melinda said. "The entire reason the Klaervians are here is so the minor can get a look at you. Their morals are a little less stringent than ours, so he will not insist on proof of your purity before marriage. What happens after marriage is between a husband and wife, and not my responsibility."

"But...you said they were here to tour the breen fields," Esther replied, stunned. "We talked just last night. You were very specific."

"Because there were ears besides ours in the banquet hall," Melinda snapped. "I'm not exactly going to shout out that you lost your virginity to two guards while high on willow bush leaves, now am I? It's a wonder the entire estate doesn't know by now."

"They promised to stay quiet," Esther whispered.

"Have you seen them since that night?" Melinda asked.

"No, of course not," Esther insisted.

"What I mean is, have you seen them anywhere in the compound or on the estate since that night?" Melinda pushed.

"No, Auntie, not at all."

"Do you know why, Niece?"

"Because you ordered them to stay away from me," Esther replied.

"No, because I had them stripped of their suits and thrown into the sea," Melinda replied, her voice cold. "Corbin saw to it that only his most trusted men did the job. I am sure they screamed your name as their skins was boiled off their bodies and their internal organs burst into flames from the Vape. How very romantic, don't you think?"

"You didn't," Esther gasped.

"Oh, I did," Melinda said as she got in her niece's face. "I most certainly did. And you should be thanking me. Two men of low caste like that would have bragged about sticking themselves in you. Maybe not at first, but after a little gelberry wine, they would have talked. Then you'd have been lucky to be accepted into The Way. Even the gatekeepers have standards. Surprising, considering the initiation is the Taking, but who am I to question Helios's way?"

"Stop it," Esther said, her eyes welling with tears. "You're just being cruel."

"No, I am being protective!" Melinda nearly shouted as she grabbed Esther by the shoulders. "I once had a husband and children, but they were lost before your time. You do not want to be a single woman in this world, Esther. There are cruelties waiting for you as you age, believe me. There comes a day when you can't get two guards to even look up your skirts, let alone desecrate your holes."

"Auntie!" Alexis exclaimed. "You go too far!"

"And you," Melinda said, turning her attention onto her nephew. "Don't think I don't know about your late night escapes on your skid. Did you really think you were the first minor to try to sneak out on his own? Please! You are only one of a long line of bored royals looking for thrills out in the open lands."

"You follow me?" Alexis asked.

"No, I have you followed," Melinda said, shaking her head. "I sometimes wonder if your helmet doesn't leak in that environmental suit of yours. Do you actually think these old bones are going to hop on a skid in the middle of the night and chase after a fool like you?"

"I have never seen anyone following me," Alexis said.

"Good, then I don't have to toss more guards into the sea," Melinda replied. "Now, enough nonsense from either of you. Go get prepared for our guests." She returned her focus to Esther. "And wear that scent I gave you."

"It smells like musk," Esther said, wrinkling her nose.

"That's because it is," Melinda said. "And if it does its job you'll be fighting Minor Zaik off of you."

"What kind of name is Zaik?" Alexis asked.

"What kind of name is idiot?" Esther responded as she smacked her brother upside the head.

"Enough. I'm tired," Melinda sighed. "Go now. The next time I see you both it will be in the entry hall with huge, welcoming smiles on. Do not disappoint me or your father."

"Hard to disappoint a man that we never see," Alexis said.

"You'd be surprised," Melinda smirked. "Now, go!"

*

The door flew open and Melinda rushed in with several guards close behind her.

"Grab that man and pull him off the minoress!" she shouted as she pointed an angry finger at the two naked royals on the bed. "And fetch the Klaervian envoy! I have words for Steward Gloesman!"

"Auntie!" Esther nearly screeched. "Get out of my quarters at once!"

She grabbed up the bed sheet and wrapped it about her chest, very aware of the leers coming from the guards. The man next to her, Minor Zaik of Station Klaerv, just sat there, his manhood on display and his mouth wide open in shock. Esther looked down, saw he was still at attention, and spread some of the sheet over his lap.

"I can attest that the minor did not—" Esther started.

"Do. Not. Say. Another. Word," Melinda hissed as she closed the distance between the door and the bed. "You will keep your mouth shut from this moment forward. You say nothing unless I tell you too. Do you understand me?"

"Minoress," Zaik said, finally finding his voice. "You have to know that—"

Melinda produced a short blade from somewhere and placed the tip just above Zaik's covered crotch. The minor gulped and shut up instantly.

"You will want to wait for your advisor to arrive, Minor Zaik," Melinda said. "The wrong words spoken could be considered an act of war. Would you like to declare war on Station Aelon and its Prime? Is that your goal for this trip?"

The minor did not respond.

"What is this? Unhand me!" Steward Gloesman cried as he was shoved into the quarters. "Minoress? What is the meaning...of...all... Oh, Dear Parent, what have you done, boy?"

"He is far from a boy," Melinda said. "As I unfortunately witnessed for myself. Your minor has shamed the Minoress of Station Aelon. He has forced himself upon her and taken what only Helios can give. I expect our earlier discussion to go beyond consideration and into full planning, Steward Gloesman. These two will be wed before the month is out or I will be forced to inform Master Alexis that his daughter was raped by Minor Zaik."

"He did not!"

"I would never!"

"Shut up, the both of you!" Melinda shouted. "Steward Gloesman understands what is at stake, don't you, steward?"

"Yes, minoress, I do," Steward Gloesman replied. "I'll inform my master that his son has proposed marriage and that we should approve it post haste. Will a wedding held on The Way Prime be acceptable? I believe it is how we will get both families together in such a short time."

"I have the authority to agree to that," Melinda said. "Tell your people and I will tell mine." She yanked the sheet away from Minor Zaik. "And please take the rogue with you. The next time these two are allowed to be alone in a room together will be their wedding night!"

Melinda waited for the Klaervians to leave then shooed the guards out as well. When she turned to her niece, a huge smile was on her face.

"I couldn't be more proud of you," she said.

"You...what?" Esther cried, so very confused. "But you said... I'm supposed to... I don't understand."

"Let me explain it to you," Melinda said as she sat down on the bed. "You were upset at me over our confrontation in the hallway earlier, yes?"

"Yes," Esther nodded.

"And before you even set eyes on Minor Zaik, you were thinking of being inappropriate with him, weren't you? As a silly way to get back at me, right?"

Esther hesitated then nodded. "Right."

"Then you saw the minor and realized he wasn't an ugly troll, but a very handsome young man. Maybe a little too young since you are his elder by about seven years, but that isn't your fault and it isn't his. Of course, as beautiful as you are he instantly became enamored of you. Everyone saw that. All I had to do was seat him next to your side during dinner and let the musk do its work."

"You think he slept with me because of that stupid musk?" Esther laughed. "I never put it on. He slept with me because I grabbed his cock under the table during dinner, turned and whispered in his ear how much I wanted him inside me. I do not need musk to get a man into bed."

"No, apparently not," Melinda said. "As we have established. But you need a clever aunt to capitalize on that man in your bed. Because of this indiscretion, not only will you get a husband that is heir to the Klaervian crown, but I will now be able to renegotiate the union without a dowry. Station Aelon will not pay a dime to have you wed despite negotiations made all those years ago for your betrothal."

Melinda stood up and went to the door.

"Stay in here until I call for you," she insisted. "Do not answer the door, do not think of leaving. The timing of this situation is delicate, despite my planning. You mess this up, girl, and you will spend the rest of your life as a gatekeeper." Her features softened and she took a deep breath. "Do you like him?"

"Wh-wha-what?" Esther stammered.

"Do you like him? Is he nice? Is he smart? Can you make a life with him?"

"I, uh, yes," Esther nodded. "I like him. A lot."

"Good," Melinda said. "I was hoping so. You may hate me right now, but I do love you more than words can express. One day you'll understand."

Melinda opened the door and strode from the room, leaving Esther still tangled in bedsheets, tears streaming down her face.

*

"But why do you have to leave?" Alexis whined. "What will I do all by myself here?"

"You won't be all by yourself, my silly little brother," Esther smiled a she hugged the boy. "Auntie will still be here. And Corbin and the others you've grown up around."

"But they don't love me like you do," Alexis said.

He hugged her back so fiercely she thought he'd crack a rib. It took some work, and strength, to get free from him.

"No, they don't," Esther said. "Always remember that."

She started to turn as a loud whistle rang through The Way Prime's shuttle dock signaling that it was time to depart to Station Klaerv. But instead, she took Alexis by the shoulders and stared right into his eyes.

"You remember how you swore you'd make your daughter Mistress of Station Aelon if she was born first?"

"Yes, of course."

"Promise me right now that you will not break that oath."

"I don't think it could be called an oath."

"Then call it that now," Esther insisted as voices started to call to her. "Swear an oath right now that that is what you will do."

"Alright, I swear it," Alexis nodded.

"No, say the words," Esther said. "Say them."

"I swear that if my first born is a girl, she will be heir to my crown on Station Aelon," Alexis said. "No matter who objects, she will be mistress of station, with all of the rights and privileges."

"Good," Esther nodded. "Because what is happening to me should never have to happen to her. I like Zaik, but I do not love him. Maybe in time I will, maybe. Your daughter should be able to know her heart and find her own love. Don't take that from her."

"Never," Alexis growled with a fierceness that surprised his sister.

"That's time enough," Melinda said as she came up to them. "You cannot wait any longer. Go to your husband, Esther, and start your new life."

"Goodbye, Brother," Esther said as she kissed him on the cheek and hurried off. "Remember your oath!"

"Always!" Alexis called after her.

A claxon blared and everyone not boarding the shuttle was escorted from the platform and inside the shuttle dock building.

"What was that about?" Melinda asked.

"Nothing," Alexis said. "Just a promise I made."

They stood there for a long while until the shuttle engines roared to life and the vehicle was thrust high towards the only open sky on the entire planet. It took several minutes, but finally the shuttle was lost from sight and Melinda took Alexis by the shoulder to lead him back to their skid.

"Do you think I will see her during Last Meal?" Alexis asked. "I hope I see her sooner, but Last Meal will do."

Melinda didn't answer.

"Auntie? What are your thoughts? Will I see here during the holiday?"

"I don't know when you will see her again, Alexis," Melinda admitted. "She is a minoress of Station Klaerv now. It could be years before you see your sister again."

"What? Years?" Alexis cried. "I can't go years without seeing her! She's my sister!"

"I know," Melinda said. "But our first duty is to the crown and Station Aelon. One day you'll see that. When you do, just know that you have my deepest sympathies."

"Years..." Alexis muttered under his breath as the royal guards led them to the skid. "Too long. Too long..."

CHAPTER TWO

Melinda stared at the pitiful video screen, her eyes refusing to focus as she processed the news.

"You can't be serious?" she said, trying to find the meaning in the order. "Who will run the estate? Who will look after your son, the next Master of Station Aelon?"

"I was hoping it would always be you, Mel," Master Alexis said, his face a grainy blob of static as the approaching Vape storm caused havoc with the transmission. "But now, with what I have learned, I can't trust you. I need someone down there I can trust. I'm turning it all over to Corbin."

"Have you lost your fucking mind, Alexis?" Melinda roared. "That drunk can't supervise his own bowel movements! You think he'll keep the estate in order? You are insane."

"This is how it has to be," Master Alexis said, ignoring the insults. "What you did to Esther cannot be forgiven, Sister. You whored her out to Klaerv. You set up the minor to believe he took my daughter's virginity when you knew all along it was already gone. The levels of deceit you went to have brought only shame on the Teirmont name!"

"I did what was best for the family and for Esther!" Melinda insisted. "I did the only thing that could be done! She is a minoress that will one day be mistress, Alexis! And they are in love! She told me so in our last correspondence! Tell me how that is a bad thing?"

"Because she is barren!" Master Alexis shouted, causing the small speakers under the video screen to pop and hiss. "The physicians have confirmed it. She can't have children. When they questioned her about her sexual history with the minor, she volunteered her past indiscretions.

Why? I don't know. Maybe she thought it would help them find a way to conceive."

"Oh, Helios, that silly girl," Melinda said. "She was supposed to take that to her grave."

"Yes, well, she may very well do that if they convict her of conspiracy to defraud the crown of Klaerv," Master Alexis said. "The only way she has out of this is if you come forward and say you had been training her from a young age and it was your fault she was promiscuous. You have to say it was all part of your plan so she could seduce the minor and Aelon wouldn't have to pay a dowry. Which we now have to pay, of course. Then you say that she wanted to back out because she had feelings, honest feelings, for Zaik, but you forced her to go through with it."

"Alexis..." Melinda began, but trailed off when she realized he was right. There was no other way. "Fine. I'll do it. Draft up the confession and I'll sign and seal it."

"Good. I'm glad you see reason."

"You know they'll want my head instead of hers, right?" she said. "You are condemning me to death."

"You condemned yourself to death when you played a game you couldn't win."

"I saved your daughter from shame and humiliation, you bastard! I had men killed to keep her secret! You know I did this for you, for us, for Family Teirmont! I will die knowing in my heart I am innocent!"

"You will not die at all, Sister," Master Alexis sighed. "Did you think me so cruel that I would send my last sibling to her death? No, a different fate waits for you. This one should satisfy your desire for intrigue."

"I have no desire for intrigue," Melinda said. "All I want is peace, Alexis."

"And you shall find it," Alexis said. "In the saving hands of Helios."

"What...?" Melinda asked. "That makes no... No. No, Alexis, do not do this to me."

"Would you rather be ripped apart in an airlock? Because that is the fate you will be looking forward to. My airlock form of execution has become quite the rage in the System. It appears every monarch is using it now."

"The Way? You want me to become a gatekeeper? That's absurd. No one in their right mind would believe I'd choose The Way this late in life. They will all know something is wrong."

"Not if you sell it, Mel," Alexis said. "Just sell it. Convince them it is what you want. Leave no doubt in their minds that you have chosen a new path for your life."

"And how do you propose I do that? Flagellate myself in front of the High Guardian? I'm sure the sick, old pervert would love that. But it would only convince him, not all the gatekeepers and royals."

"Then go to the extreme," Alexis said as he looked away from the camera. "You know what has to be done, Melinda. And it is no worse than what you did to Esther."

"No worse than—Alexis?" she shouted as the screen went black. "Alexis! No worse than what I did? What in Helios's name does that mean?"

Melinda got up and started to pace her quarters. She ran his words through her head over and over. There was a solution there, but she couldn't grasp it.

She used Esther's sexuality to set up the marriage. How could she use that to convince The Way she was coming to them in all honesty and sincerity?

How could she...?

"No," she whispered. "He can't mean for me to take part in that. With all of those men and women? No. No, no, no."

She sat down on her bed and hung her head as the tears started to fall. Sobs racked her body and she rolled onto her side and tucked her knees up to her chest, letting the pain and feelings of betrayal wash through her. After several minutes, she sat back up and pulled herself together.

"Three days," she said as she stood and walked over to the full-length mirror on the wall.

She undid the clasps and let the dress she wore fall away. Melinda studied her body in the glass, her fingers tracing the tight muscles, and also loose skin, that was her belly. She turned and looked at her ass and frowned, but shook it off as she cupped her breasts, lifted them then let them fall back to her chest.

"Who would want this body?" she asked herself. "The repressed, that's who."

*

"This is so exciting Auntie," Alexis said, nearly jumping in his seat as the royal skid maneuvered its way to the dock specifically reserved for Aelon Prime. Each prime had their own dock on The Way Prime; it kept things civil.

"Stop fidgeting and don't call me auntie," Melinda said, dressed in her finest gown and adorned with almost every jewel she owned. "You are sixteen, Alexis. You are a man of marrying age and will be Master of Station Aelon. Address me as Aunt Melinda or as minoress, but not as auntie."

"What about when we are alone?" Alexis asked, his eyes studying the bright lights of The Way's massive cathedral complex. "Can I call you auntie in private?"

"After tonight, there will no longer be a 'private' for me, Alexis," Melinda sighed. "After tonight, everything about me will be very, very public."

Alexis turned his attention to his aunt despite the spectacle of the royals and dignitaries that mingled on the docks, disembarking from their own skids for the evening's festivities. The young minor studied Melinda for a good long second then frowned.

"Why do I think this is goodbye?" Alexis asked.

"It isn't really a goodbye," Melinda said. "It's more of a change of situations."

"No, no, I know a goodbye when I hear one," Alexis said. "I've heard a lot in my life. Everyone leaves me, Auntie. Everyone. Now you are leaving me as well. Just tell me why."

Melinda started to protest, but thought better of it and just sighed. "I have done some things that need to be rectified. Tonight is my rectification. I am joining The Way. They will remove my jewels and take them for the church. They will remove my gown and take me as well."

"The Taking? You are participating in the Taking?" Alexis gasped. "But, you can't! I've heard the stories and they...they do things to each other during the Taking."

"Yes, Alexis, they do," Melinda said. "And as a result, the Burdened are conceived. Tonight is a holy night for all of us. Take solace in that. If I am lucky, I will carry a child once again and it will be born to grow up as a protector and warrior of The Way."

"Can you still have children? At your age?" Alexis asked.

"Biologically, yes, I can," Melinda said. "Would it be safe? Hardly. If I were to become pregnant tonight, then it could very well be my death sentence."

"Then don't do it," Alexis pleaded just as a guard opened the partition.

"It is Aelon's time to disembark and greet the others," the guard said. "We cannot wait any longer."

"What I wouldn't give for Corbin to be here now as a distraction," Melinda laughed. "That crippled drunk would certainly divert attention from me, but he's gone ahead to 'secure' the box."

"What do you mean?" Alexis asked. "Why do you need a distraction?"

"You'll see," Melinda said. She stood up and held out her arms. "Come here."

Alexis stood and hurried into her arms. He was taller than his father, a full seven feet, but not as wide of shoulder and thick of neck. He leaned his head down and nestled it into Melinda's hair, taking a long sniff of a scent he'd known his entire life.

"You made your sister a promise once. Can you make me one as well?" Melinda asked, pushing back from him.

"Anything," Alexis said.

"Follow your heart," she said. "Ignore the politics and shaowshit of the court. Do what feels right to you. Be honest with yourself. Can you do that for me?"

"Yes, Auntie, I can," Alexis nodded.

He started to cry and she reached up and gripped his face in her hands.

"Stop that now," she ordered. "You are a minor, not some sissy boy from the Lower Decks."

"I've never seen the Lower Decks," he sniffed.

"No, I suppose you have not," Melinda said. "But one day you will rule them, and all the decks of Station Aelon. When you do, you remember your promise to me."

"Yes, Auntie," Alexis nodded.

"Good," she said and took a deep breath as she stepped to the front of the skid and climbed the steps up to the airlock that connected to the covered and protected docks.

Minoress Melinda Teirmont stood on the dock, her arms raised high above her head, and looked towards The Way's cathedral complex.

"I give myself to you, Helios!" she shouted at the top of her lungs. "Take me tonight as your bride! Take me as your vessel so that I may carry your child! I give myself, Helios! I give you my soul!"

The crowds quieted down, shocked at the sight before them. Some had witnessed passengers making pilgrimages to The Way Prime to give themselves over, but none had ever seen a royal do it before. It was a spectacle that all would talk about for generations.

A group of soldiers, the Burdened, rushed over to Melinda and grabbed her by her arms. While two held her, the rest stripped her of all her jewelry, setting the valuables in a large breen sack. Then, right there in front of all, she was stripped naked; her gown tossed aside for whomever wanted it.

None touched it, for fear of catching whatever shame Melinda was trying to rid herself of.

*

"Not going in to watch the show?" a young man, very close to Alexis's age, said as he walked along the balcony just outside the box seats reserved for the royalty and nobility. "This only happens once a year, you know? And it's quite...enlightening."

"I'm not in the mood for enlightenment tonight," Alexis replied, refusing to look at the young man.

He kept his eyes focused out at the grand entrance to the cathedral and watched the hundreds of commoners make their way into the building, all talking and gesturing excitedly in anticipation of the night's events. Men, women, children—all were going to watch as the gatekeepers and initiates joined in the Taking.

The walls of the cathedral were painted in bright reds and oranges, deep yellows and golds. They were adorned with ornate carvings, representations of the many forms of Helios, from Planet to God, Star to System. Jewels and precious metals were woven into the designs, creating a majestic view that dazzled the crowds, hypnotizing them with the sheer opulence of it all.

Yet, standing along the walls were the gatekeepers—men and women dressed in simple, grey robes. They nodded and gave their blessings to all that approached them, making sure Helios was in the hearts of the crowd.

And watching it all were the Burdened, the elite guards and soldiers of The Way. Their deep, blood-red breen armor shone in the light, their faces obscured by helmets. The crowd kept their distance from those men, none wanting to risk offense; none wanting to find themselves on the end of a long blade.

"Ever been to a Taking before?" the young man asked, moving to the balcony railing, only a couple of feet from Alexis. When there was no answer from the minor, he looked about and frowned. "Either I'm not seen as a threat, or your bodyguards could care less that I have a six inch blade in my boot. Your men are nowhere about."

Alexis finally turned and considered the person he was quickly seeing as an annoyance. Several inches shorter than Alexis, the young man was dark complected, with deep olive skin and brown hair. He was muscular, fit, and dressed impeccably in a bright orange tunic and blue striped trousers. His boots were of the finest shaow leather with matching gloves tucked into his belt. His eyes, a strange gold/brown, danced with mischief and the young man's body radiated chaos.

"Do you know who you are addressing?" Alexis asked. He had a quick glance around and realized the young man was right, that his guards were nowhere to be seen. "I could have you killed on the spot for admitting you have a knife on your possession when all weapons are to be left outside the cathedral."

"Is that what you are going to do? Have me killed?" the young man asked, pushing away from the railing and taking two steps closer to Alexis so that they stood only a couple of inches apart. "Will I be held down so your guards can gut me? Or will it be swift with a good, old fashioned decapitation?"

The young man held up a finger and wagged it, turned and walked a couple of paces away.

"No, no, you aren't boring like that, are you? No, you'd find some special way to have me executed. Perhaps a Vape nozzle shoved where Helios doesn't shine so that my innards boil and flame and not a mark on the outside of my body can be seen."

The young man turned and regarded Alexis, looking him up and down.

"Yes, I think that's what you'd do. I hate to disappoint you, Minor Alexis, but I already have several marks upon this body. Life on the Prime, you know." He walked back to Alexis and smiled, showing just a hint of perfectly white teeth. "But you know all about life on the Prime, don't you? I'll bet you have some marks of your own."

"Who are you?" Alexis asked, his voice low.

"Gannot DuChaer, at your service," the young man bowed. "And I do mean that, my lord. I am at your service. Literally."

DuChaer stood straight and waited for an answer, but all Alexis did was narrow his eyes at the young man.

"You aren't having a fit, are you?" DuChaer asked. "You seem out of sorts."

"DuChaer!" Alexis exclaimed suddenly. "Is your father Steward DuChaer, the Thraenish governor of the lease holdings we control on Thraen Prime? Is that him?"

"It is," DuChaer replied, bowing again. "And since he is technically a part of those lease holdings, that makes my father, and myself, your subjects. You see. I literally live to serve you."

"You're different," Alexis said. "Your clothes, your manner, everything. You say you grew up on the Prime, but you don't act like it. You aren't rough or cold. You're...I don't know."

"Alive?" DuChaer laughed. "Not a constipated bureaucrat looking to make a credit or two and then bail back to the stations? Not a hardened miner or crop worker with dead eyes and the rotting disease eating away at my organs?"

"Something like that," Alexis replied.

"Something like that," DuChaer echoed, but with his voice, it sounded forbidden, like a secret between the two of them. "Join me in my box, will you? Watch the Taking with me as my honored guest."

"I cannot," Alexis frowned. "I have my own box that I must be present in. The High Guardian will be looking to make sure I am in attendance. I'm Minor of Station Aelon; I can't be someone else's guest without causing all kinds of political waves."

"Then I'll join you," DuChaer said. "Unless your box is full."

"Full? No," Alexis sighed. "It is just me. Well, and Corbin, but he'll be passed out and snoring most of the time. And farting. The old man has wicked gas."

"Delightful," DuChaer grinned. "I can suffer by your side."

Alexis cocked his head and studied the young man once again. Those eyes, that chaos.

"Fine," Alexis nodded. "You will be my guest. It will be nice to talk to someone my age for a change that isn't a servant sent to empty my chamber pot."

"Chamber pot?" DuChaer laughed. "Have you no plumbing at your estate?"

"It's a figure of speech," Alexis said. "Although the plumbing on Aelon Prime isn't always up to snuff."

"Then we forget about plumbing and chamber pots and we talk about other things," DuChaer said. "What interests you, Alexis?"

"You really could care less for protocol, couldn't you?" Alexis laughed.

"What is protocol amongst new friends? Just an obstacle that eventually is removed once familiarity is established. Why wait for that when we could be familiar now? Life is for living, not waiting."

A chime sounded and the crowds making their way into the cathedral quieted instantly, leaving only the occasional hushed whisper to drift up to Alexis's ears.

"It is starting," Alexis said.

"Then show me to my seat, my lord," DuChaer said. "Tonight will be a night neither of us will forget."

The thought of his aunt flitted through Alexis's mind and the frown returned.

"We will need to do something about those lips," DuChaer said.

"Excuse me?" Alexis asked, taken aback.

"That frown that keeps showing up," DuChaer responded slyly. "It will not do. I can guarantee that by tonight's end you will never frown like that again."

"That is not a guarantee you can make," Alexis replied as he walked towards the ornate double doors of his box seats. "I don't think anyone can."

"We'll see," DuChaer replied. "I'm very resourceful."

*

The room was massive, more an indoor arena than a theater or auditorium. The lower levels were filled with long benches that curved around the huge space and the commoners quickly took their seats, their attention on the empty area in the middle of it all, where cushions and pillows were piled high.

The next level was made up of balconies that also curved around the arena. The balconies did not hold benches, but plush, comfortable chairs made of the best materials that Helios could provide. There sat the nobility—stewards, sector wardens, and deck bosses down from their stations. Some lived on their primes full time, as Alexis did, but most had paid large sums of credits for space on the crowded shuttles. And even larger sums for a seat at the spectacle.

But, above it all were the private boxes for the nobility that were more than just landholders. And station royalty, of course. Most of the boxes were empty; since only on the rarest of occasions did masters of station attend the Taking. In certain circles, it was considered an old tradition that no longer had its place. But some of the boxes did have occupants.

One of those being the royal box of Station Aelon and its prime.

There sat Alexis, with DuChaer by his side, and a sleeping Corbin in his wheelchair tucked into the corner, a bottle of gelberry wine perched precariously on his lap.

Without saying a word, or asking royal permission, DuChaer got up and expertly removed the bottle from Corbin's drunken grasp. Alexis watched him in awe.

"I tried that once and had my face slapped ten times before I could take a single step back," Alexis said. "I didn't know the man could be parted from his drink."

"Be the drunk," DuChaer laughed quietly. "Be the drunk."

"I don't know what that means," Alexis said, but laughed along with DuChaer anyway.

The lights in the arena began to dim and a single spotlight lit up a platform that was slowly lowered down to the center of the arena floor from the ceiling. Sitting on the platform, decked out in gilded robes and layers of jewelry, was the High Guardian, a middle-aged man of considerable girth. He held in his right hand a scepter of a dull metal that looked like it had been forged centuries earlier, which it had. It had neither shine nor jewels, but all eyes were fixed upon it.

"Welcome," the High Guardian said as he brought the end of the scepter down six times.

The crowd clapped their hands six times in return, then waited in silence.

"It is the custom of the High Guardian to give a long speech about Helios the Planet, the Star, the System, the God, but tonight is not a night of speeches. It is not a night of words we have all repeated a thousand thousand times since we were born. It is not a night for words that may have lost their meaning to many of you."

The High Guardian looked about the arena and closed his eyes.

"Tonight is one of the most holy of nights. It is the one time a year that the gatekeepers are allowed carnal interactions. But this night, this Taking, is not about sexual pleasure. No, the Taking is about the men and women that serve without question the holy order that honors our Dear Parent Helios. It is about them bringing their bodies together in the hopes that children will be conceived and the Order of the Burdened will be replenished and add to its ranks."

The man stood and waved the scepter outward, pointing it randomly at people seated on the low benches.

"You will witness acts that many of you have never dreamed. You will watch as skin touches skin, flesh melds with flesh, and you will be silent. This night is not about you, whether commoner or nobility."

"I have always found it interesting that we call the lower castes 'commoners' on the planet, and not 'passengers' like on the stations," DuChaer whispered.

Alexis was shocked that the young man would dare speak during the High Guardian's speech, but still he turned and addressed his new friend. "I agree. Are they not passengers on the planet, just like they would be on a station?"

"Precisely," DuChaer said and patted Alexis on the knee, before returning his hand to his lap.

"This night is about the gatekeepers giving themselves—body, mind, soul—to Helios so that the Dear Parent may fill them with holy energy and allow them to copulate until conception is achieved. As you know, exclusive partners are not allowed. Everyone must experience, and be experienced, by everyone else. This way, when the children of this night are finally, blessedly born into this world, they will not have two parents, but hundreds! For the Burdened must know they serve us all! In Helios's name, they serve us all!"

The arena stayed silent, none clapped or cheered, but sat and waited.

"I leave you now, as I cannot participate," the High Guardian said. "Before I go, I give you one last chance to remove yourselves from the holy arena. For when the Taking begins, those doors will not open until the evening is through. Go now, if you must. Stay, if you are willing."

The High Guardian sat down and the platform was lifted back into the ceiling.

The people waited.

Eventually there was the sound of locks being thrown, and doors opened in the curved walls of the arena. Men and women, naked except for a thin, breen rope tied about their throats, walked into the center of the arena. They turned about so that all could see them then sat on the floor in a circle, their legs crossed and arms held up high.

"Helios, is that your aunt?" DuChaer whispered. "She's an initiate? That explains what that commotion on the docks was. She is a handsome woman for her age."

"Quiet," Alexis hissed. "Do not test me on this subject."

DuChaer smiled broadly at the reprimand then took a drink from the wine bottle and handed it to Alexis. The minor glanced at the bottle, looked back down at the arena floor, glanced back at the bottle again, then took it and drank some as well.

More men and women filed into the arena from the side doors. They were all of various ages, sizes, colors. They strode towards the circle of initiates, their own bodies completely devoid of clothing, and began to fill the arena floor. Hundreds and hundreds of naked men and women crowded into the space that only seconds before had looked so empty and open.

Not a sound was made by the crowd as they watched.

The arena filled almost to the very walls, forcing many of the gatekeepers to climb onto the piles of pillows and cushions. None smiled nor showed any emotion on their faces. They were blank slates, ready for their holy night of carnal duty.

Six chimes rang out and then, as one, the gatekeepers raised their arms into the air. They swayed back and forth as more chimes rang out, still in groups of six, coming faster and faster until all that was heard was one long, single chime.

The chimes stopped and the gatekeepers lowered their arms.

Then they moved even closer to the initiates' circle, which was completely blocked from view at that point. Lines started to form out of the crowd and Alexis realized that each line was directly behind an initiate. His throat grew dry and he grabbed the bottle and took another drink of wine as the sounds from the arena floor drifted up to him.

"I could think of worse ways to be initiated into something." DuChaer smirked.

Alexis couldn't believe his eyes as cries of passion, and perhaps pain, started to grow in volume until it was unmistakable what was happening in the arena. Those that were being initiated into the The Way were being had by every single gatekeeper, whether male or female. The minor shook his head and wanted to look away, but he couldn't. The spell had been cast and he was caught in its trap.

"How freeing it must be," DuChaer said, his voice a normal volume since no one could hear him from up there, especially with the cacophony of cries and moans down on the floor. "To let yourself go and know you are doing the work of Helios. Appetites get to be satisfied without worry of blasphemy or shame. Almost makes me want to join The Way just so I can take part in this one night of the year."

Alexis couldn't respond. His eyes were locked onto the movements and gyrations of the bodies below. There was so much action and motion that he couldn't keep up with it all. It became a chaotic sea of writhing flesh. Men with women, women with women, men with men. Many on one, one with many. There was no way to tell where an individual began and the group ended.

"Do you sometimes wish we could have freedom in our lives always?" Alexis asked, finally able to gather the strength to speak.

"Every day of my existence," DuChaer said. "And, personally, I don't see why we cannot. We aren't commoners, we aren't passengers, we aren't gatekeepers beholden to one night a year. I am noble born and you are royal born. We are above these rules that govern our passions and desires. We were born to be free."

"Were we?" Alexis asked as he looked over at his new companion.

Those eyes, that chaos.

"We were," DuChaer said as he placed his hand on Alexis's cheek. "We have no one to blame for not seeing it sooner than now."

Alexis glanced over at the cripple in the corner and DuChaer followed his eyes.

"Do not worry about him," DuChaer said. "He won't wake up for a long time."

"How can you be certain?" Alexis asked.

"Because I may have put something extra in the first bottle of wine he finished off." DuChaer smiled.

Those eyes, that chaos.

"The guards," Alexis argued, yet didn't remove DuChaer's hand from his cheek. "They will check on me."

"No, they won't," DuChaer said, pulling Alexis towards him. "I have paid them enough to keep their distance for the entire night."

"They could be executed for that," Alexis said.

"And, technically, we could be executed for this," DuChaer said as he pulled Alexis all the way to him until their lips met.

Alexis resisted at first, but the longings in him would not be held back any more.

The kiss went from tentative to passionate to ravenous. Hands moved, tunics were pulled free, belts unbuckled, and trousers unclasped.

And in the corner, a cripple pretended to sleep, a puddle of what any observer would think was piss underneath him, which was actually dumped wine.

*

The two single passenger skids raced across the scrim grass, pointed directly at the fields of tall breen that covered the majority of Aelon Prime. The riders of the skids laughed and jabbed at each other, their voices only heard inside each others' helmets.

"You'll turn," DuChaer said.

"I will not," Alexis replied. "You will turn first. You don't have the courage needed to drive blindly into a breen field."

"Blindly, you say?" DuChaer chuckled. "You assume I haven't already done this."

"No one has," Alexis said as his skid continued to rocket forward. "I would have been told about an idiot racing a skid into a breen field. I am Minor of Aelon Station and Prime."

"Perhaps that idiot bribed any witnesses so he could have an advantage when he challenged the Minor of Aelon Station and Prime," DuChaer responded. "Especially since the winnings from the wager made between myself and the Minor of Aelon would more than cover the expenditure of these theoretical bribes."

"What is it with you and bribes?" Alexis asked as he lowered his head and leaned over the handlebars of the skid controls. "You are a noble, son of a steward, you could just order the workers to keep their mouths shut."

"But then they wouldn't be complicit in the crime," DuChaer said. "By paying them I bring them into the fold with me. Ordering them around does nothing but add to the list of injustices heaped upon them during their miserable lives. Bribes keep me off that list."

"Injustices? Are you sympathizing with the commoners?" Alexis asked as he swerved to avoid a clump of rock that had been hidden by the long scrim grass. The back corner of his skid didn't quite clear the clump, but the contact was insignificant and didn't alter Alexis's course in any way.

"Helios, you are a shite driver," DuChaer guffawed. "I saw those rocks a hundred yards back."

"You did not!" Alexis yelled. "Don't be an ass! And answer my question!"

"What question? The one about me sympathizing with the commoners? Please, Alexis, don't you be an ass. Understanding my marks is not sympathy, it's practicality. I know what motivates them and what doesn't. Makes it so much easier to manipulate who I want, when I want. You should try it sometime."

"Try what? Bribing field workers and servants?"

"No, understanding them. One day they will be your loyal subjects, you know."

"I have zero desire to understand any of them," Alexis scoffed. "Personally, I could care less what they want or don't want. They do what I ask, and when I am master. they will do what I ask without question."

"Well, there's always that approach, I guess," DuChaer replied. "It is tried and true and hasn't let a master down yet. Just know, I will never do a damn thing you ask of me unless it corresponds with what I want."

"Of course, Brother, of course," Alexis said. "I'd expect nothing less from you."

"Nor I from you, Dearest Brother," DuChaer responded. Just then, the two young men braced themselves as they both shot into the tall breen.

With thick, fibrous stalks and multi-pointed leaves, breen was one of the few species of life that survived on planet Helios. Despite the poisonous air and constant cloud cover, breen thrived and flourished. And nowhere else on the planet did it thrive more than in the soil of Aelon Prime.

The plant could be made into almost anything, from clothing, to hard polybreen plastic. It was essential to human life on the primes and in the stations, giving Aelon a distinct economic edge. But it was an edge that could easily cut both ways. For while Aelon was supreme in the cultivation of breen, it relied on other stations, specifically Station Flaen, to turn the raw crop into finished goods.

A power amongst the stations, Aelon was still an agricultural driven monarchy that needed to trade continuously to keep its coffers full. That made the lease holdings on Thraen Prime so essential. With the Vape mines that lay on that land, Aelon kept itself from being beholden to any one station or crown.

That was what Alexis should have been thinking when he was with DuChaer—the tactical advantages of having the heir to the lease holdings' stewardship by his side.

Instead, he saw only a playmate who was able to keep up with his never-ending appetite for adventure and mischief.

The breen leaves whipped across Alexis's helmet, making visibility more a concept than a reality. The minor twisted and turned the skid, trying to find the widest spaces between the rows. Workers, people only one step up from slaves, dove and ducked out of the way, their screams muffled and contained inside their environmental suits.

A glimpse of bright purple caught Alexis's eye and he looked to his right to try to catch sight of his compatriot, believing the color was the Thraen's gaudy environmental suit that he had colored differently for every outing.

But it was only a gelberry-stained blanket someone had draped over a cargo skid.

That slight distraction was all it took for Alexis to miss the other cargo skid in the area. The one that lay directly in his path.

"Mother of Helios!" Alexis shouted as he tried to steer around the vehicle, but only ended up whipping the side of his skid into the rear of the other.

Chopped breen went flying, along with the minor, as metal tore and polybreen cracked. Alexis watched in wonder, as if he was outside himself, as his body tumbled through the poisonous air and landed in a heap of limbs and breen stalks.

"Brother? Alexis? Talk to me!" DuChaer cried over the communication system in his helmet. "Tell me if you are injured!"

"Only my pride is, as far as I can tell," Alexis laughed as he lay there, arms and legs akimbo. All around workers hurried to his side, standing around him in a circle, afraid to lay a hand on the minor, even in help and assistance.

"I'm coming to you," DuChaer said, and the whine of his skid could be heard from several rows over.

"No need, no need," Alexis replied. "I'm fine. Just let me get up and check on my—Ow! Shit, my leg!"

Alexis tried to stand, but his left leg wouldn't hold him and he collapsed back onto the spilled breen. This was enough to force the workers into action and several of them hurried forward, but Alexis waved them off. He tapped at his wrist and switched the communications system to an open channel.

"I'm fine, I'm fine. Just a sprain," Alexis said. "I can walk on my own."

"But, my lord, you do not look well," a man said as he came forward and offered to help again. "You should let us put you on the cargo skid and take you back to the compound. Your leg may be more hurt than you think."

"Is that so?" Alexis snapped. "More hurt than I think? That's your medical opinion, is it? Are you a physician?"

The man just looked at him, blinking with confusion behind his helmet's visor.

"Answer my damn question!" Alexis yelled. "Are you a physician?"

The man shook his helmet. "No, my lord."

"So then you have no clue what you are talking about, do you?" Alexis pressed.

"No, my lord."

"So it would be wise to keep your mouth shut and not address me again, wouldn't it?"

The man began to reply, but kept his mouth shut and just nodded.

"Good," Alexis grinned. "Bring me my skid. That is something I know you can do, since all it takes is you moving your ass."

The man hurried off to fetch the crashed skid and Alexis looked about at the other workers. "Don't you have jobs to do?"

They scattered like fleas and Alexis sat there and waited for his skid. He could see the man trying to get it upright, but the nose of the skid was buried deep into the soil. Alexis glared, his patience already gone.

"What is taking so long?" Alexis roared.

"I'm right here, brother," DuChaer said as he drove his skid right over a row of breen and into the space next to Alexis. "Calm yourself, you spoiled little brat."

"I wasn't talking to you, DuChaer," Alexis said. "Although I should have you whipped for calling me a spoiled brat."

"Spoiled *little* brat, were my exact words," DuChaer said. "If I'm to be whipped, then I want the specifics of the offense to be known." He hopped off his skid and crouched next to Alexis. "And don't call me DuChaer. You only call me that when you are mad at me. You know how much it pains me when you are mad at me."

"Well, get used to the pain," Alexis said. "Because I intend to follow through with that whipping."

"Will you be doing it yourself, my lord?" DuChaer smiled.

Alexis's eyes widened and he tapped at his helmet then wrist. DuChaer frowned then nodded.

"I wouldn't stoop so low as to carry out a whipping myself," Alexis said. "I will have a guard do it once we return to the compound and estate house."

"Of course, my lord," DuChaer replied.

"My lord, I am sorry, but I cannot free the skid from the dirt," the worker said, his voice trembling with fear.

"Then get back to work, you worthless siggy worm," Alexis snapped. "What is your number?"

"Fourteen-seventy," the worker replied, his head held low.

"Well, fourteen-seventy, your wages will be docked for the cost of the repairs of my skid, is that understood?"

"Yes, my lord. My apologies, my lord," the man replied.

"Your apologies are worth less than nothing to me," Alexis said as he held out his arm and DuChaer helped him up. "That means you are now in my debt. Your credits will be held until the skid is paid for. I hope your wife knows how to make water taste like soup because that is all you will be eating until I am satisfied."

DuChaer helped Alexis onto his own skid then climbed up and turned the vehicle around the way he had come.

"That was harsh," DuChaer said once they were clear of the breen field. "That man and his family will likely starve to death before he has worked enough hours to pay for your skid."

"Do you question my rule, Gannot?" Alexis asked.

"Far from it, Brother," DuChaer replied. "I applaud it. I was just making an observation."

"But you do not disapprove?"

"No, of course not," DuChaer said as the skid moved slowly across the scrim grass and back to the state house. "You have chosen what kind of ruler you plan on being and I support your choice. I also support you calling me Gannot. I like how my name sounds coming from your lips."

"So many things I could say in response to that," Alexis chuckled. "Too many, in fact."

"Good," DuChaer smiled. "Keep some of those things in mind. Once we get you looked over by a physician, I will insist on doing my own examination. I plan on making it very thorough."

"Such is your duty, Brother Gannot," Alexis laughed, then winced. "As long as the examination includes multiple bottles of wine."

"Oh, surely it will," DuChaer responded. "But as a medicinal prescription, of course."

"Of course."

*

Alexis stared at the piece of paper in his hands, reading it over and over until the words blurred before his eyes. He finally tossed it aside and looked across the table at the man in the wheelchair.

"Have you given this to my father yet?" Alexis asked.

"No, my lord," Corbin replied.

Alexis narrowed his eyes at the formal response. This was a man who had once lifted him up onto his knee so he could whip his ass red after Alexis had set fire to the pantry.

"So, this is your way of showing me courtesy then, Corbin?" Alexis asked, tapping the letter.

"It is my way of turning in my resignation," Corbin replied. "It is time I retired fully and officially from the Royal Guard and took care of myself for a change. You have grown into a...capable man. You don't need a cripple hovering by your side."

"No, I do not," Alexis responded. "But I'd be lying if I said this wasn't a surprise. Why now?"

"Why not now?" Corbin said. "As good a time as any."

"Stop it, Corbin," Alexis sighed. "You have been like a father to me over the years. An angry, unreasonable, drunk, crippled, sometimes cruel, sometimes caring father, but a father nonetheless. I learned what it means to be a man from you. Please show me some respect and be honest with me."

"Honest?" Corbin asked as he leaned back in his wheelchair and eyed the minor carefully. "Are you sure you want honesty? I'll be honest if you answer one question for me."

"Certainly," Alexis nodded.

"Where are you supposed to be right now?"

"Now? How do you mean?"

"You know what I am talking about. Answer the question."

Alexis sighed and looked down at the table like a chastised boy.

"I am supposed to be on a cutter to The Way Prime so I can take a shuttle off planet back to Station Aelon," Alexis said. "Where I will sit as regent while my father is down here on the planet."

"Yet, here you are," Corbin said. "Your father, his wife, and your half-siblings will be here soon. I will hand the same letter you have to your father at that time. Then I will be off to a small plot of land that I have and live out my retirement drunk as all Helios."

"You're staying on the Prime?" Alexis asked.

"I am," Corbin said. "There is nothing for me up on Station Aelon except pain and regret." He smacked the sides of his wheelchair. "And a lot of narrow passageways."

"You said you'd be honest if I answered your question," Alexis said. "So be honest and tell me the real reason you are retiring."

"Because I can no longer sit here in this blasted thing and watch you soil your title and position," Corbin said. "You are an amazing fighter with a blade, probably one of the best I have ever seen. You can out eat and out drink my stoutest of guards. Despite the way you treat the field workers, you know more about agriculture and breen crops than any master before you. Yet you piss all of that away for that...boy."

"Ah, there it is," Alexis said and smiled. "The bias against Brother Gannot."

"*Brother Gannot*," Corbin sneered. "That opportunistic flip will be the death of you, of that, I have no doubt."

"A flip!" Alexis shouted as she stood up and smacked his hands on the table. "You will take that back, Corbin! A slur of such magnitude will not be tolerated against a friend of the crown!"

"A friend of your cock, you mean!" Corbin snarled. "The *man* is a Thraen, you fool! He may live on land leased by Station Aelon, but in the end, he is nothing but a Thraenish steward's son! He will turn on you and he will bring down the crown if you do not rid yourself of his influence!"

"What influence is that, Corbin Breach?" DuChaer asked as he strode into the room dressed in a bright green tunic with trousers that seemed to be made of multi-colored patches instead of whole cloth. He spun about to show his new clothing and smiled at the man in the wheelchair. "I hope it is my influence on Aelish fashion. Or lack of fashion, as the case may be down here on this rock."

"Dear Parent, save me," Corbin hissed. "The flip is dressed like a trollen bird fucked a gully fish."

"I'm sorry...did he just call me a flip?" DuChaer growled as he glared at Corbin. His hand went to the hilt of the long blade strapped to his belt. "I would think cripples had more sense than to pick a fight with their superiors."

"Superiors?" Corbin roared as he drew his own blade from the sheath on the back of his chair. "Come at me, you willy taster!"

Before Alexis could protest, DuChaer lunged at Corbin and the crash of metal echoed about the room. Corbin fended off the attack skillfully, but DuChaer was not lacking in his own skill, and having two working legs, was able to dance about the old guard with ease and practice.

Once blood was spilled, Alexis threw himself between the men, his face a mixture of rage, shock, and sorrow. He pulled a handkerchief from his pocket and dabbed at the gash across Corbin's right forearm.

"I accept your resignation, Corbin," Alexis said. "Reluctantly and with a heavy heart, but I accept it. I apologize for the way my friend has acted. A man of your honor should not be treated in such a way."

"Seriously?" DuChaer said, but the look he received from Alexis shut him up quickly.

"If you will do me one last favor and not tell my father about this, I would appreciate it," Alexis pleaded. "One last bit of protection from the greatest of royal guards?"

Corbin shook his head, but smiled slightly. "I think you will have more than your share of troubles with your father without me getting involved. Just make sure that painted bastard stays away from me until I am gone. I don't want to see his face again."

"I am requesting that Brother Gannot accompany me to Station Aelon," Alexis said. "You will not have to deal with him again."

"But I have to deal with this shirt," DuChaer mumbled. "Got blood all over it."

"Then go and change," Alexis said, waving his hand towards the young man. "But be ready at my call. Father will be very angry with me when he arrives. I'll need your support."

Corbin sneered at the Thraen as DuChaer turned and strode from the room. Alexis took a deep breath and then stood tall. He saluted the wheelchair bound guard and took six steps back.

"I will miss you, Corbin," Alexis said.

Despite his anger, Corbin saluted back and nodded. He took the handkerchief from his arm and tried to hand it back to the minor, but Alexis waved him off.

"Keep it, please," Alexis said. "I'll get you a better going away gift when I return from the Station."

"Be safe up there," Corbin said. "There are dangers on that station that you know very little about. As much as I agreed with many of your father's arguments as to why you should be raised on the Prime, he has done you a disservice by not letting you experience the nest of honey wasps those stewards are. When you become master, I hope you know that, no matter what any of them say, they are not to be trusted."

"All the more reason I need Brother Gannot by my side." Alexis grinned.

"You cheeky shit," Corbin replied, grinning in spite of himself. "You are a smart one. You'll probably do just fine."

A loud bell rang and Alexis paled.

"They are here," he said. "Go have a physician look at that cut. Then get blind drunk and forget about your duties for the rest of your time here."

"Yes, my lord," Corbin said and bowed his head.

Alexis looked down at the man until a second bell rang then he turned and hurried from the room.

Corbin sat there for quite some time and listened to the hustle of the servants and the marching of the guards outside the room. He would have liked to go see the physician right then, and take the minor up on his order to get blind drunk, but there was no way he would allow himself to be seen. Not with the tears that streamed down his cheeks and splattered onto his old and worn uniform.

CHAPTER THREE

The two young royals looked at each other, alone truly for the first time since their engagement. It had always been improper to allow the minor and minoress to be unattended, but with their wedding finished only hours earlier, they finally would be able to speak freely.

Yet they stood there, still clothed, still several feet apart, like strangers, not close and ready to consummate a holy union, like newlyweds. The awkwardness nearly filled the room as much as the piles of gifts and vases of flowers.

"You were very beautiful today," Alexis said, trying not to sound like a lost child. "I thought the color of your dress perfectly fit your eyes."

"Thank you," Bella replied. She was former Minoress of Station Thraen but with the marriage to Alexis, she became the Minoress of Station Aelon as well.

A woman with royal standing on two of the most powerful stations in the System, but feeling as if she had no power while she stood in front of her new husband. He was incredibly handsome, as all the Teirmonts were, but there was an air about him that put her off. Not that she wasn't physically attracted, considering his broad shoulders, long legs, blonde hair, and blue eyes. It was just that there wasn't a spark between them.

The Minoress Bella felt no passion for her husband, and that terrified her.

As if reading her thoughts, Alexis turned and walked to the row of decanters set on a side table in their honeymoon suite. He checked the small tags on each, making sure he knew exactly whose gift each was, before he selected a brown liquor that seemed to coat the sides of the crystal decanter when he swirled it. He quickly poured two glasses and walked back to his new bride.

"Here," he said as he handed her one. "This will ease our tension. Perhaps wash some of the stress away and put us in the mood for...well, you know what mood we are supposed to be in."

"Yes, it is expected of us," Bella replied, taking the glass and sipping at it quickly. She coughed a little, smiled with embarrassment and then took another drink. "We have to prove to them that this is a real marriage."

"Prove?" Alexis blanched as he looked about for a hidden camera. "I thought that old tradition was long gone?"

"What? Oh, no, I don't mean literally prove," Bella laughed. It was a rich sound, filled with the fullness of a light storm on the primes, but without any of the menace. "We have to produce an heir, is what I meant. Both of our stations expect us to have children right away."

"Right, right. Sorry," Alexis said. "Which I'm fine with, you know. I love children. And I think ours would be beautiful, if we are lucky and they take their looks from you." He finished his drink and hurried back to the row of decanters. "Would you like another?"

"You think I'm beautiful?" Bella asked as she finished her own drink and walked to her husband, setting the empty glass by his so she could take his hand with both of hers. "Do you, Alexis? Find me beautiful?"

He turned and looked at her and saw the fear in her eyes. So many words were on his tongue that he could not say. So he went with the truth.

"Yes, I do," he said. "Your hazel eyes, your auburn hair, the graceful cheekbones and strong chin. How your nose comes up at the tip just so. Those tiny ears that match your tiny hands. You are gorgeous."

"You sound like you're admiring a painting," Bella replied. "Are you? Am I aesthetically pleasing, but perhaps not...sexually pleasing?"

"Why do you ask such a thing?" Alexis spat, then quickly got himself under control. "I mean, it is strange to say. We are husband and wife and I have already said you are gorgeous. Of course, I want to be with you... sexually. What man wouldn't?"

"I've known a few in my time," Bella said quietly. "They preferred the company of, well, other men."

"Did they? How disgusting!" Alexis crowed. "I couldn't imagine being with another man. How is that even possible? Where do the parts fit?"

He laughed loudly and poured more drinks, making sure the glasses were full. He handed Bella one, then grabbed a decanter and maneuvered her with his elbow towards the huge bed set against the far wall.

"I am Minor of Station Aelon and I am a Teirmont," he said. "I can assure you that I only have eyes for the female form. And now that we are married, I only have eyes for your female form." He finished his drink and poured more. "Which, my dear, I have yet to see."

"Would you like me to undress, Husband?" Bella asked.

"Oh, how I would," Alexis replied. "Do you need help out of your gown? It isn't nearly as ornate as your wedding dress was, but still it looks like it took more than a couple of attendants to get you in there."

"You do have an eye for fashion," Bella laughed. "I have heard that about you. That you prefer the look of Thraen to the look of Aelon."

"Yes, while it is true, that is a preference we should keep to ourselves," Alexis laughed. "The Aelish are a more modest people and we will be expected to tone down our garments for their uninitiated eyes. I would hate to flaunt it in my people's, *our people's*, faces. So, let me see you as you were born and we will rebuild from there."

"You as well," Bella said as she handed him her glass.

Alexis nodded and fumbled with the two glasses and decanter, barely able to get them to the bedside table before they fell from his grasp. He gave her an apologetic look then stood up straight and started to unbutton his dress shirt.

Once Bella saw he was willing to undress, she too began the process of removing herself from her reception outfit. It wasn't as easy for her as it was for Alexis, but she didn't ask her husband's help and struggled through the outer dress, the tight corset (a new undergarment that she was not happy had become the style), the under dress, the light chamois, the two slips, and finally the pantaloons.

There she stood, in a pile of garments, bare naked and more vulnerable than she had ever felt in her life. Standing before her was her husband, a man whose body was truly a specimen of male perfection. She couldn't help but tingle when she looked at what was between his legs. He was a man of size in all ways.

But still she hesitated.

"You said I am beautiful, that I am gorgeous," Bella said. "What do you think now? Now that you see me as Helios intended me to be seen by my husband?"

"I think I am the luckiest man in the System," Alexis replied then glanced down at himself. "But I believe the stress, and drink, of the day may be playing a trick on me. Let us relax in bed, and turn down the lights, and perhaps my mind will cease its endless chatter and I can truly perform like a husband."

The two newlyweds climbed into bed, she from one side and he from the other. Alexis twisted a switch above the bedside table and the lights dimmed almost to off. They both lay there under the covers, a vast expanse of bed between them.

"I know we are allowed now that we are married, but I feel like I must ask your permission to touch you," Alexis said. "It's silly, I know."

"No, no, not silly at all," Bella laughed. "I feel the same way. We have only spoken to each other a few brief times and now we are to hold and love each other as spouses do. I envy the passengers and their easy way of finding love with their marriage. How nice it must be to know a person truly first before wedding."

They lay there, both looking up at the ceiling.

"Can I make a confession?" Alexis finally asked, breaking the silence.

"Of course," Bella said. "The marriage bed is the place for confessions. Whispered between lovers late at night as they fall asleep in each others' arms. Their bodies entwined and still warm from lovemaking."

"Now I'm not so sure about the confession," Alexis said, slightly alarmed. "You sound like you have experience in this sort of thing."

"What? Oh, no! Helios, no!" Bella exclaimed as she rolled onto her side and reached for her husband's hand. She found it and squeezed it tight. "I read! That is all! My confession is that I read those horrible little books that all the servants read. Filled with romance and sex and adventure. I was actually quoting one of my favorites."

"Oh, thank Helios," Alexis said. "Because to find out that you may have already, well... But you haven't, so I can tell you my secret. A confession in the marriage bed."

Alexis gulped and squeezed her hand.

"I have never been with a woman," he said. A weight seemed to lift from his chest and he continued quickly. "I know it is expected of royal men to find a woman they can practice with while young, but that is more a myth to boost reputations than anything. The truth is that I grew up on Aelon Prime, and let us say the women and girls are cut from a different cloth. One might say an ugly, ugly cloth."

"Alexis!" Bella giggled. "That is nothing to be ashamed of! You have no idea what a relief that is!" She sighed deeply and moved herself closer to him. "Have you ever even touched a woman? I mean, in that way. Do you know how a woman feels?"

"I do not," Alexis replied. "Your body is a true mystery to me."

"Then here, let me teach you," she said as she lowered his hand to between her legs. "I will show you what my body feels like. It is yours now, Alexis. My body is yours to own and you may treat it as such."

"I don't know," Alexis laughed. "I haven't always treated my body so well. Perhaps you should think of only loaning me your body now and then. Perhaps full ownership should come later once I have some more experience."

Bella giggled again and then moved even closer, pressing him to her down there. She inched her face towards his and closed her eyes as their lips met.

Alexis was terrified.

That was the only way to put it.

But he knew what he needed to do. So he closed his eyes and pretended that her lips were someone else's lips; that her thighs were someone else's thighs; that her tongue was someone else's tongue.

With those thoughts and images in his head, and the warmth of liquor in his belly, Alexis brought himself to the task. He could feel Bella smile and knew she was happy he finally was showing his arousal.

"There," she said as she guided his hand. "Like that."

"You seem to know what to do," Alexis said.

"Yes, well, I bet you know what to do with yourself as well," Bella replied.

Alexis laughed and took her other hand and placed it between his legs. Together they learned about each other and learned what they already knew how to do to themselves.

It wasn't what he desired, but as the night progressed, it wasn't what he feared either. He could do it; he could be a married man and please his wife.

He just hoped that the person he really held in his thoughts, and his heart, would understand.

*

"Oh, well, look at the two lovebirds," DuChaer said as he came around the corner of the passageway and nearly bumped into Alexis and Bella. "Heading to breakfast, are we? I was just on my way also. May I accompany you?"

Bella took her new husband's hand and squeezed it tight.

"We are dining in private this morning," Bella said. "The observatory in the third spire."

"The third spire?" DuChaer laughed. "Seriously? The third spire is a prison, not an eatery."

Bella looked at Alexis and frowned, her rosy, cheerful demeanor gone almost instantly.

"You'd have our first breakfast be in the castle prison?" she asked. "Are you mocking me, Husband?"

"Mocking you? No!" Alexis protested, giving DuChaer a harsh glare. "There is no one housed in the third spire as of now. Yes, it is a prison, but for nobility only. And rarely do they stay long. My father has made an art of extorting levies from stewards that haven't been exactly forthcoming in handing over their share of the taxes."

"So we will not see any prisoners? You're not going to lock me up in a cell and throw away the key?" Bella asked.

"What? Helios, no! What a horrible thing to—Oh, now you are mocking me," Alexis sighed. "It will take me some time to get used to your Thraenish wit."

"Why is that? You didn't take long to get used to *my* wit and I'm a Thraen," DuChaer said.

"Not of the station proper," Bella said. "You grew up on the Prime. Hardly a haven for intellectual exercise. Did you try to match wits with a crop of breen? Or perhaps play word games with some of the miners?"

DuChaer eyed the minoress carefully then stepped back and gave an exaggerated bow.

"I have been properly put in my place, my lady," he said. "I would never assume to have anywhere near the learning or grace such a royal as you could possess. That is why you are perfect for my brother here."

"Brother? What is this brother nonsense? You are not royal blood, DuChaer. Do not expect to have the same privileges."

"Bella. Gannot," Alexis said, stepping between the two. "We have all gotten off on the wrong foot. Let us breakfast together and see if we cannot mend this schism between the two most important people in my life. I know by the end of the meal we will all be fast friends."

"Or even worse enemies," Bella stated.

"Even worse?" DuChaer asked. "Are we enemies now, minoress? I can't understand why. I have only your best interests in mind." He looked at Alexis. "And heart."

"Stop it, both of you," Alexis laughed, although it was hollow and held no mirth. "Join us, Brother. I believe this is best."

"If you insist, my lord," DuChaer replied. "But only if the minoress wishes it as well."

DuChaer held an open smirk that rankled the minoress. She didn't know what it was exactly about the young man that she detested, other than the rumors and suspicions regarding his relationship with her husband. Bella couldn't put a finger on it, but she knew a bad seed when she saw one.

"I think I will actually retire back to our quarters, Alexis," Bella said. "That headache I woke up with will not let go and I think some more rest is in order. Too much wine, I guess."

"And perhaps you were up too late exercising your newly found marriage privileges?" DuChaer grinned, the smirk growing wider.

"That is not something a lady speaks of, sir," Bella replied, her tone nothing but hostility. She turned to her husband. "Will you walk me back, Alexis?"

"Yes, Alexis, will you walk her back?" DuChaer asked. "The boss needs you."

"She is not my boss," Alexis snapped then got his temper under control, instantly regretting the words. He looked at Bella. "You should rest alone. I'll be by to check on you after breakfast. Perhaps if your headache is gone we can, well..."

"I don't believe so," Bella said, her eyes locking on DuChaer. "It is quite the bad headache that just refuses to go away."

"Yes, well, I will check on you anyway," Alexis said. He leaned in to kiss her, but she turned her face so he was forced to give an awkward peck to her cheek. "I won't be long."

Bella gave a weak smile and a nod then turned and headed back the way they came. Alexis and DuChaer watched her go and once she was out of sight, they turned to each other, DuChaer still smirking, Alexis seething with anger.

"You test our friendship, Brother," Alexis said.

"Do I? How about what we have that is deeper than friendship?" DuChaer asked. "Do I test that? Because from where I stand, you tested it until it broke."

"Stop," Alexis said as he took DuChaer by the arm and marched him down the passageway towards the third spire. "You know my feelings. They have never wavered."

"Oh, I believe they wavered last night," DuChaer said. "I can almost smell her musk on you. How was she? Everything you'd hoped for?"

"Stop it," Alexis whispered. "There is no need to be cruel."

They reached the stairway to the third spire and DuChaer yanked Alexis into the alcove at the bottom of the stairs and shoved him against the wall.

"I am not being cruel, Brother. I am dealing with cruelty," DuChaer said, his hands gripping the minor's arms, squeezing and kneading the muscles under his tunic. "I am dealing with it the only way I know how."

"Then find another way," Alexis said as he shoved DuChaer away. "Because if you keep going down this path you will force my father's hand. He will banish you."

"He can banish me from the Station," DuChaer said. "But he can't banish me from your heart. Only you can do that."

"Don't..." Alexis pleaded.

"Say the words," DuChaer insisted. "Say them to me and I'll promise to hang back in the shadows."

"You couldn't hang back in the shadows if you wanted to," Alexis laughed, looking DuChaer up and down, smiling at the man's bright clothing.

"Just say the words," DuChaer said. "Say them, or you never see me again."

"Gannot, no, do not make threats like that," Alexis said as he grabbed the man and pulled him close. "I would die without you."

"I doubt that," DuChaer said.

"I would! To not have you in my life would be the greatest torture. Greater than being forced to marry a woman I cannot truly have love and affection for," Alexis said.

"Then say the words," DuChaer ordered. "I am not going to wait a second longer. Say them or you never see me again."

Alexis looked up the stairs then peeked his head out of the alcove to make sure they were alone.

"I love you," Alexis said. "There. Now stop trying to sabotage my life."

"How was she?" DuChaer asked, his face filled by that smirk once again. "Better than me?"

Alexis rolled his eyes. "You'll never stop asking, will you?"

"Never."

"Then let's ascend to the observatory and eat our breakfast," Alexis said. "I'll tell you all about it there. And there is much to tell. I had no idea a woman's body was so complicated. My Helios, do they have a plethora of parts!"

DuChaer laughed heartily at that and the two men quickly raced up the stairs.

*

The Teirmont men faced each other like two mountains, towering above everything, their very presence filling each nook and cranny of the great hall.

"Her father has passed," Alexis said. "My wife is minoress to Station Thraen and her father, the master, has passed. You will allow her to attend the funeral."

"No, I will not," Master Alexis said. "She will remain here, by your side, while you sit as regent."

"I do not need my wife with me to perform my duties as regent," Alexis snapped. "I am perfectly capable of handling the intricacies on my own!"

"Yes, but you will not be on your own," Master Alexis said. "You will have that DuChaer with you. I would prefer you listen to your wife's counsel than that braggart and lout."

"Father, you insult me when you insult Brother Gannot," Alexis said.

"I am not going to dignify that with a response," Master Alexis said. "It has been decided. Now, where is your wife?"

"My wife? Bella? Why?"

"Because I will tell her in person," Master Alexis said. "As you just stated, she is Minoress of Station Thraen. She is also a Minoress of Station Aelon. That position comes with an expectation of respect, even from a master."

"I, well, I believe she is in our quarters," Alexis replied. "The news has hit her hard."

"I would expect it has," Master Alexis said. "Stay here, I will not be long, we still have much to discuss before I leave with your mother for Station Thraen."

"Yes, Father," Alexis nodded.

"And where is DuChaer now?" Master Alexis asked.

"Gannot? I am unsure," Alexis replied.

"He is visiting the Sector Forbine girls, your highness," Stolt said from his seat at the long table. "Or he is visiting the brothel, at least."

"And what does that mean?" Alexis snapped.

"Calm yourself, Son," Master Alexis said. "It is Cousin Stolt's job to know the comings and goings of those that stay here at court."

"Yes, of course." Alexis glared.

"Sit and talk with Cousin Stolt while I am gone," Master Alexis said. "I won't be long."

The master turned and quickly left the great hall, his long legs moving him so much faster than the royal guards behind him that they struggled to keep up. The man smiled at his ability to still show up the younger men that were sworn to protect him.

It did not take him long to traverse the passageways of Castle Quent and soon he was standing at the door of Alexis's and Bella's quarters. A quick knock and a woman servant answered.

"My liege," the servant said, dropping into a hurried and awkward curtsey. "You were not expected."

"Is the minoress decent?" Master Alexis asked. "I wish to speak with her if she is not indisposed."

"She is dressed and decent, your highness," the servant said and quickly stepped aside.

The master strode into the quarters and barely gave the furnishings and accouterments a glance. His attention was instantly turned to the woman who had stepped through the bedchamber door.

"Your highness," Bella said as she curtsied. "A pleasant surprise."

"There is nothing pleasant about any of this business," Master Alexis frowned. "You do not have to stand on ceremony with me while you mourn. I too know what it feels like to lose a beloved father."

"I thank you for your kind words," Bella said. She gave a quick glance to the servant. "Leave us in private, please."

The servant nodded and hurried from the quarters.

"I suspect you are not here to offer only condolences," Bella said as she gestured towards two chairs by a large hearth. "Please, sit and tell me what is on your mind, sire."

"Yes, I must remember you are used to court intrigues and politics," Master Alexis said. "I am sure you saw my intentions upon my face the moment you walked into the room."

"No, sire, you are too seasoned to give anything away so easily," Bella replied. "But I do know royal men and the way they carry themselves. Your shoulders tell me conflict and your hands speak of repressed anger."

Master Alexis looked down at his aging hands and clenched then unclenched them.

"You do not miss much, do you Bella?" Master Alexis laughed. "Which is exactly why I am here."

"Oh? Is there some mission that my powers of observation are needed for?" Bella grimaced. "I am afraid my faculties are not fully my own right now. Mourning sadness seems to affect me in waves. It comes and goes like the tides on Helios."

"How are things with you and my son?" Master Alexis asked abruptly.

"With Alexis? Wonderful, sire," Bella stated.

"Shaowshit," the master replied. "Your whole body told me that lie. I want honesty."

"Every new marriage faces challenges," Bella said. "We barely knew each other when we were wed. It takes time to learn each other's personalities and...quirks."

"Yes, I suppose it does," Master Alexis replied. "And my son does have his...quirks. Tell me, how are things between you as far as intimacy?"

"Sire," Bella gasped. "I couldn't answer that!"

"I know it is deeply personal, but being master of station I need to know that the succession will be secure before I go," Master Alexis replied. "I assume you are actively trying to produce an heir."

"We have, yes," Bella replied.

"But...?"

"Well, sire, while Alexis is very attentive to me in our day to day lives, he is not exactly forthcoming in his responsibilities in the bedchamber," Bella replied, her entire face turning red.

"You aren't telling me the marriage was never consummated, are you?" Master Alexis asked.

"No, no, it was. I can assure you of that," Bella said. "It's just that, since our wedding night we haven't...well..."

"It's been that long? Dear Helios," Master Alexis sighed. "Are you trying to encourage him? You are a beautiful woman, so I can't imagine why he isn't wanting you in bed twenty-four hours a day."

They both let the reality of that statement hang there between them.

"I encourage him when I can," Bella said. "When he is with me."

"Does he not sleep here every night?" Master Alexis asked.

"Most nights, yes," Bella nodded.

"Most nights? Another lie, but I can understand why you tell it," Master Alexis said as he stood up. "I will speak to him about his husbandly, and royal, duties."

"No, sire, please do not," Bella pleaded. "We are happy. Your son is smart and charming. He makes me laugh and when we are together, we truly enjoy each other's company. He just needs time."

"A minor in line for the crown does not have the luxury of time," Master Alexis said. "I am not getting younger. When I am gone there will need to be an heir in place in case something were to happen to Alexis. You know how courts are. No one is safe."

"Yes, I am well aware of that, sire," Bella said. "Thank you."

"Yes, well, do not thank me yet," Master Alexis said. "I have also come to inform you that I need you to remain here with Alexis while he is regent. I cannot risk other influences whispering in his ear. I know what a burden this is on you, and how disrespectful it may seem, but there are forces at work that—"

"Stop, sire, I understand," Bella said as she stood up and took Master Alexis's hands in hers. "I understand all too well what forces are at work. If I were to leave now, then any progress I have made with my husband would be undone before the shuttle reached Station Thraen. If I am to be the mother of the heir to Station Aelon, then I must be willing to sacrifice everything for the Aelish crown. My brothers will be cross, but I am sure you can take the brunt of that for me."

"It would be the least I could do, my lady," Master Alexis bowed. "Not a negative word will be said against your character as a daughter and minoress. The fault and blame will be all mine."

"Thank you, sire," Bella said. "Now, if you do not mind, I believe I will contact my brother to tell him the news. It is better he hears it from me so it does not sound like we are colluding against Thraen."

"Right you are, my dear," Master Alexis said and bowed again. "I leave you to your familial obligations."

"Thank you."

*

The bedsheets were a mess, half of them thrown to the floor, the other half knotted and roped about the young royals' calves. Alexis waited a moment, his chest heaving from the exertion, then rolled off his wife, his body radiating heat and sweat.

"That was nice," Bella said as she turned her body about and placed her feet up on the headboard of the bed. "I have missed that."

"Have you?" Alexis asked as he looked over at her then frowned. "What in Helios's name are you doing?"

"Tilting my pelvis," Bella replied. "The physicians and midwife say it helps with conception."

Alexis gave a bark of a laugh and swung his legs over the side of the bed. He grabbed the large goblet from the bedside table and drained the last bit of wine it contained.

"Well, so much for romance," Alexis said as he looked over his shoulder at his wife's naked body, her legs propped up in the air. "Good to know the royal bed is nothing more than a fertility clinic."

"Oh, don't be cross," Bella said. "The evening has been so pleasant. No need to ruin it."

"Pleasant? Yes, that's exactly what a man wants to hear from his wife after he has made love to her," Alexis laughed again as he got up to fetch another bottle of wine from the tray set near the door. He looked down at the remnants of the meal they had shared just an hour earlier and grimaced. "But we must do our duty, mustn't we? Can't leave Station Aelon without an heir."

"You think that is all this evening was? Us, performing our duty? We had fun tonight, Alexis. Fun like we haven't had in a long time."

"Oh, now it's fun?" Alexis snapped as he lifted the wine bottle from the tray, realized it was empty, then threw it aside, letting it shatter on the hammered metal floor of their bedchamber. "I guess fun is better than pleasant!"

"What is wrong with you?" Bella shouted as she whipped about and lunged off the bed towards her husband. "Is making love to me so awful that you must create an argument every time? Not that there have been that many times!"

"Put something on," Alexis said as he searched for a full bottle. "You shouldn't stand there naked like that. It's shameful."

"Shameful?" Bella scoffed as she looked down at herself. "Men would kill for this shameful body! You think I haven't had overtures from others? You think there haven't been whispers in my ear? Notes left on my meal trays? This body is far from shameful, you ass!"

Alexis started to respond then stopped himself as he realized the true extent of his wife's fury. He gave up looking for the bottle and instead held out his arms.

"I am sorry, my love," he said, his tone and demeanor changing instantly. "I am the one that should feel shame. This is not how a husband treats a wife. And certainly not how a minor treats his minoress."

He kissed her brow and then worked his way down to her lips. They held the kiss for a long moment before finally pulling apart.

"Go lie back down," Alexis smiled. "Prop up that ass and make us an heir."

"Join me," Bella said. "It can't hurt to try again. Just in case."

"Yes, but let me use the facilities first," Alexis smiled. "I hate to be crude, but the wine is knocking and must be let free."

"Well, yes, please take care of that," Bella laughed. "I'd hate for an accident to happen."

"Then there truly would be shame, wouldn't there?" Alexis said as he grabbed a robe and threw it around himself. "I'll only be a minute."

He smiled at her broadly and quickly left the bedchamber. Alexis shut the door and hurried through the quarters, ignoring the bathroom door to his right. He carefully opened the main door and peered into the passageway.

"I'm right here," DuChaer growled. "Waiting like a thief, hiding from the law. First a stowaway on the shuttle, and now a shadow forced to skulk in the passageway."

"I am sorry, Brother," Alexis said as he pulled the man into the quarters then made for the bathroom. Alexis pushed DuChaer inside, turned and locked the door behind them. "I am so sorry I couldn't meet you at the airlock. I didn't know dinner would turn into something more. Once I realized what she was up to, it was too late to get a message to you."

"No, I understand," DuChaer said and smiled at the surprised look on Alexis's face. "Honestly, I do. There is talk in the court lately about why it is taking so long for you two to produce an heir. The talk has even reached ears down on the primes. If it is there then it has reached the other stations, I am sure. It will only get worse unless the bitch pushes out a whelp or two."

"Do not talk about Bella in such a manner, Gannot," Alexis said. "She is my wife and she is a good woman."

"Really? How good?" DuChaer asked, moving closer. "Is she as good as me?"

"Stop. Not here," Alexis said and then almost screamed when there was a loud knock upon the door. "Helios!"

"My lord?" a servant called through the door. "I apologize, but your presence is needed immediately in the communications room. There is an urgent call from the planet."

"Just one moment!" Alexis called out and then glared at DuChaer. The man shrugged and tucked himself away in the linen closet. "I'll be right out!"

Alexis looked at himself in the mirror and then opened the door quickly. He stepped into the main room of the quarters just as Bella came out of the bedchamber, busy wrapping a robe about herself.

"What is it?" Bella asked the servant, a young man obviously embarrassed to be in the presence of the royals as they stood there with nothing but robes on. "Has the master died?"

"I do not know," the servant replied. "I was only told it was urgent and the minor must come at once."

"Fetch me some clothes," Alexis said to Bella. "I'll have to dress on the way."

Bella nodded and hurried back into the bedchamber.

"Who told you to come and get me?" Alexis asked the servant.

"Steward Stolt did, my lord," the servant replied. "He was quite adamant that you not hesitate for a second. I don't know anything else."

"Yes, well you have done your job, you may leave," Alexis said, dismissing the man with a wave. "Tell them I am coming."

"But, my lord, I was told to—"

"Go!" Alexis snapped just as Bella came back out of the bedchamber. "I will follow right behind!"

The servant bowed and rushed from the quarters.

"Was that necessary?" Bella asked. "He was only doing his duty."

"Just as we did ours tonight and will do for the rest of our lives," Alexis replied, but not in an angry way. His shoulders slumped as the weight of realization settled upon them. He looked Bella in the eyes and tears were close to spilling out. "What if he is dead? Or dying? I don't know if I am ready."

"You, my dearest husband, were born ready," Bella said, crossing to him and handing him his clothes. "You are Minor Alexis Teirmont. This is your birthright. You have been regent with great success on many occasions."

"With help," Alexis replied.

"Of course with help," Bella sighed. "That is what a council is for. It is also why a master holds court. He must hear many opinions and many points of view in order to come to a sound decision. I grew up watching my father do it, and I know you can too."

"But I did not grow up watching my father do it, don't you see?" Alexis pleaded. "I was down on Aelon Prime! I know how to ride skids and how to grow breen! I know when a Vape storm is coming and I know how to tell if a miner is cheating at cards!"

He threw the clothes on the floor and held out his hands.

"I know how to use these, Bella! I know how to farm and how to fight, but I have never learned how to rule! I don't belong here! I belong down there!"

"No, you belong right here," Bella said as she knelt and picked up his trousers. She tapped his left leg and held the trousers under him. Alexis smiled and stepped into them. "You are ready for this. Just as you have been ready for everything that life and duty has thrown at you."

She shimmied the trouser leg up and then helped him with the other. Bella shoved his robe aside and let it fall to the ground as she buckled his trousers then knelt and picked up his tunic. She kissed his chest several times and gently placed the tunic in Alexis's shaking hands.

"Go, husband," she said softly. "You knew this day would come. You are ready. I feel it in my soul."

He leaned down and kissed her hard then took a couple of steps back and breathed deep.

"Yes," he nodded. "I am ready. I love you."

"I love you too, Alexis," Bella said. "Now hurry! You don't know what time you may have left!"

Alexis pulled on his tunic and ran to the door. He was out before he had both arms in the sleeves and Bella had to close it behind him. She leaned her back against the door and closed her eyes for a minute. After she had time to gather her thoughts she opened her eyes and looked towards the bathroom door.

"You can come out now, Brother Gannot," Bella called. "No need to keep yourself hidden."

A couple of seconds passed, then the bathroom door opened and DuChaer stepped out, a smug, satisfied look on his face. He raised his hands and clapped mockingly.

"Lovely speech, my dear," DuChaer said. "Very rousing, very stirring. But then rousing and stirring was your goal tonight, wasn't it?"

"How are you even here?" Bella asked. "You were banished from the Station by Master Alexis."

"Was I? Oh, dear, I do hope he doesn't catch me," DuChaer replied. "Oh, wait, he's not on the Station, but dying down on the planet."

Bella rolled her eyes. "You mentioned my having a goal tonight, Gannot. And you were quite right, I did have a goal." Bella's hands instinctively went to her belly. "My goal was to try for an heir. And I am more than confident that I have achieved that goal."

"Are you?" DuChaer laughed. "How very optimistic of you. His seed has been in you for less than an hour, but you are certain it has taken hold. Helios must be whispering prophecies in your ear."

"Do not take the Dear Parent's name in vain around me, Gannot," Bella said. "We both know your lips do not deserve his grace upon them."

"I do not care about Helios's name upon my lips," DuChaer said as he waved a hand and crossed to one of the chairs. He plopped down in it and reached for a decanter that was close by. He pulled the stopper and gave a sniff. Satisfied, he drank straight from the vessel, smacking his lips when finished. "Do you know what I care about being on my lips?"

"Don't be disgusting," Bella said as she rushed over to him and yanked the decanter from his grasp. "You will hold your tongue about such things when in my presence."

"Oh, is that so? Did Alexis hold his tongue in your presence? Or did he use the skills I taught him to take you to your special place?"

Bella turned away as her face burned.

"Oh, dear me," DuChaer snickered, sitting up and leaning forward in the chair. "You haven't ever been to your special place, have you? Not even by yourself?"

"Shut your filthy mouth," Bella spat. "And get out of my quarters now."

"Oh, the poor, poor minoress," DuChaer frowned. "Did no one show you the art of self-pleasure? How very, very sad."

"I said to get out, Gannot!" Bella shouted. "Or I will call the Royal Guard in here and then we'll see what happens when I say you tried to force yourself on me!"

DuChaer held up his hands and stood. He backed his way to the door and stayed facing the angry minoress.

"One day, Bella, you will know who really holds the power in this court," he sneered as he reached back and opened the door. "And I truly hope it doesn't come as a surprise that it isn't you."

"Just get out," Bella hissed.

"As you wish, my lady," DuChaer said. He bowed and casually left the room, blowing her a kiss before the door closed behind him.

Bella looked at the decanter in her hands then threw it as hard as she could. It shattered against the door and the gelberry wine ran down to the floor, pooling at the bottom like purple blood.

*

Steward Stolt stood by the doors of the great hall, busy shaking hands with nobles and visiting dignitaries. He looked back over his shoulder and was glad to see the great hall was almost empty of the spectators that had come for the coronation of Alexis the Second, Master of Station Aelon. His eyes looked at the elaborate decorations that adorned almost every surface and he grinned, knowing that once the cost of the coronation reached the ears of the passengers there would be near riots.

He already knew the mood of the meeting of stewards and it was not in favor of the new master at all.

"Stolt," Steward Prochan said as he stepped up next to the former advisor to the crown. "Not the best of circumstances for you, yet here you stand, shaking hands and smiling like a child with a pile of presents on Last Meal day."

"Not the best of circumstances?" Stolt asked as he shook the very last hand and turned to the young steward. "I don't know what you mean. Yes, it was disappointing that the High Guardian did not come in person to crown the master, but I believe the gatekeeper he sent in his stead did a fine job. What was the man's name again?"

"Oh, who cares, they all look alike to me," Prochan replied.

"Well, well, haven't we become jaded," Stolt laughed. "A far cry from the young man that first sat down on the council thinking he knew everything there was to know about this court."

"We have a new master in place," Prochan replied. "And with that new master comes a new royal advisor. I believe it is safe to say that none of us want that man anywhere near power, but there he will be, whispering whatever he wants into Master Alexis's ear."

"Such is the way of politics," Stolt shrugged. "What could we possibly do about it? The master has spoken."

"Yes, he has spoken," Prochan sneered. "And given fealty to Master Charles of Thraen. I will concede it was a foolish war that the late master fought, but he had the Thraens beat. All Alexis had to do was keep pushing. But instead he bends over and not only does he give up the ground won, he tells Master Charles that Station Aelon will always swear fealty to Thraen as long as Station Aelon holds the leases on the Thraen Prime. It stinks, Stolt. It stinks like shaowshit!"

"Calm yourself, my friend," Stolt responded. "I have a feeling that the fealty issue was created by her highness. A way to let her brother save face after such a near defeat."

"Bah, it's all crap," Prochan said.

"I agree with you," Stolt said. "But there is little we can do about it."

He glanced around and leaned in close.

"Have you heard the news? It just reached my ears this morning."

"What news is that?" Prochan asked. "The master is bleeding from his anus and only has a couple of days to live?"

Stolt's eyes flashed with anger. "Hush, you idiot!" he hissed low. "I will chalk that up to too much drink during the coronation. Despite my personal feelings, or yours, Alexis is still master. If one of the royal guards overheard you say that, while I am standing here speaking to you, then we'd both be in the third spire waiting to be jettisoned out the airlock. Do you understand me?"

"Most of the guards despise Alexis as much as the stewards do," Prochan said.

"True, but many of them have been bought by Brother Gannot," Stolt said, smiling as he saw the look of surprise on Prochan's face. "Didn't know that? The man is a devil, but he is a sly devil."

"Fine, fine," Prochan said. "Tell me this news of yours. Out with it."

Stolt's entire demeanor changed and he grinned from ear to ear.

"The mistress is with child," Stolt said. "Soon there will be an heir to the crown of Station Aelon."

"This is good news to you?" Prochan asked. "With your blood ties you could have made a claim for the crown if Alexis were to die prematurely."

"Yes, true, true," Stolt shrugged. "But being master would be such a tiring job. I believe regent would be a much better position."

"You are one scary bastard, Stolt," Prochan said. "Remind me to stay on your good side."

"Oh, Steward Prochan, if I have to remind you of that then it is already too late," Stolt responded. He clapped the man on the shoulder then rubbed his hands together. "I believe it is time for the feast to begin. I'm sure Alexis has already said a dozen idiotic things and Brother Gannot has supported each of them. Shall we go watch the fun?"

Act II

An Uprising From Above

"One reads the accounts of those days and wonders how Station Aelon survived. It almost seemed incompetence was in the water. Yet it did survive, and for a while, so did Alexis II. For a while."

—Dr. D. Reven, Eighty-Third Archivist of The Way

"From Helios to master; that is the word of the Dear Parent."

—Creation 10:18, The Ledger

"I almost have to wonder if it wouldn't have been better for my father if the stewards had succeeded in their original efforts. They would have given my father a much more respectful end."

—Journals of Alexis III, Mistress of Station Aelon

Chapter Four

The teenage minor and minoress stood there before their half-brother, their eyes wet with tears, but chins held high. Thomas wasn't nearly as tall as Alexis, having taken his height from the Thraen side of his heritage, but he was fair of hair and eyes like his half-brother. Eliza was a beauty that turned heads in court and it was a miracle she hadn't been married off. But that wasn't Alexis's way, not towards his family.

The siblings' mother, Meredith, breathed deeply and smiled at Master Alexis.

"Thank you for allowing this, Alexis," Meredith said. "You have saved my life and the lives of my children. I will be forever in your debt."

"Nonsense," Alexis replied. "The threats against you are all rumor and I put no trust in them. But you have asked to return to Station Thraen and who am I to go against your wishes."

"You have always been kind to me, Alexis," Meredith said. "Despite a few headstrong spells here and there."

"We all have our weak moments, Mother," Alexis said, making the woman smile even wider at the use of the familiar. "I have yet to see yours, though."

She embraced him warmly, resting her cheek against his chest.

"You are like your father in so many ways," Meredith said. "But you are unlike him in others. I have always worried that this royal life would be the end of you, as it has been for so many monarchs. Tread carefully, Alexis, please. The decisions you make, even the small ones, can have deadly consequences."

"You are not leaving because I am making a small decision," Alexis replied. "You are leaving because I am making one of the largest decisions a Master of Station Aelon has ever made."

"So very true," Meredith said as she pushed away. "Please be careful, please. You are up against almost the entire meeting of stewards on this. You may have the support of the majority of the meeting of passengers, but their power is so limited that even if they rally behind you they cannot stop the stewards from taking control."

"I am painfully aware of this," Alexis said. "It's a good thing the longslingers of Middle Deck Twenty are on my side. If it does come down to war then I will be able to put up a fight."

"Not against the numbers the stewards control," Meredith said, shaking her head. "Or the resources. Even longslingers must eat and drink. All it takes is three stewards to give the order and the Middle Decks starve."

"The lowdeckers would rise," Alexis said.

"We have been through this so many times that I won't repeat myself again on that point," Meredith said. "Just remember that the lowdeckers are not your allies. What your father did to them will always be a thorn in their sides."

"We'll see," Alexis grinned. "I may have a way to remove that thorn."

Meredith narrowed her eyes and studied her stepson's face.

"What are you up to, Alexis?" she asked then shook her head again. "No, no, don't tell me. It's better I don't know."

"Grandmother!" a girl's voice screeched from down the passageway.

Meredith looked around the master to see a young girl of seven sprinting towards them and the shuttle dock's airlock.

"Alexis! What are you doing here?" Meredith cried, unable to hide the alarm in her voice.

At hearing his daughter's name, Alexis spun about and hurried to meet the girl, scooping her up in his arms the instant she was close enough.

"You little grendt," Alexis snapped. "Do you know how unsafe it is to have all heirs that can lay claim to the crown of Aelon in one place right now?"

"I do, Papa," Minoress Alexis smiled. "You have told me a billion times."

"So then why are you here?" Alexis asked.

"I wanted to give my aunt and uncle these," Minoress Alexis said as she fished in the pocket of her trousers for the woven breen bracelets. "I made them and I thought if they wore them they'd never forget me."

"Oh, dearest little one," Meredith laughed as she looked over her shoulder and motioned for her children to come forth. "They would never forget a precious miracle like you."

"Never," Thomas said as he reached out and took one of the bracelets.

"Not in a billion years," Eliza added, taking hers. "I promise never to take it off."

"You can take it off when you shower," Minoress Alexis said. "Or it will get all gross."

"Well, we wouldn't want them to get gross, would we?" Meredith laughed as she leaned in and gave her step-granddaughter a huge kiss on the cheek. "Although I don't think anything you make can ever become gross, beautiful girl."

"Set me down, Papa," Minoress Alexis ordered. "My trousers are riding up my craw."

"Alexis!" Meredith exclaimed. "Manners! You must remember your manners. You have been around your father and the court too much. You are a minoress and must uphold standards of behavior."

The little girl belched and none of them could contain their laughter. They continued laughing, enjoying a last moment of lightheartedness before the departure, until they heard the sound of heavy boots coming towards them.

"Your highness!" a royal guard yelled, then stopped as he saw who the master held in his arms. "Oh, thank Helios! The mistress reported her missing and we have been scouring the Station."

"You didn't tell your mother you were coming?" Alexis glared. "Alexis, we have talked about this a billion times as well. You cannot run off without one of us knowing where you are—"

"At all times, I know," Minoress Alexis interrupted. "One day I won't have to tell anyone where I am going."

"If only that were true, my silly biscuit," Alexis said. "But I'm afraid that day will never come. Not if you are to be Mistress of Station Aelon."

The royal guard took a step back, but composed himself quickly. Alexis caught the movement and turned to the man.

"Is there something you'd like to express, guard?" Alexis asked.

"No, sire," the guard replied quickly.

"Are you sure? This is the time to do so. As my family is my witness, no harm will come to you if you speak freely. In fact, I welcome your opinion, since this decision affects everyone on Station Aelon."

"It's just that...well, sire..."

"Out with it, man," Alexis snapped. "There is a shuttle about to leave, and despite my regrets, I must make sure my mother and siblings are on it."

"When you say Mistress of Station Aelon, you are talking about her becoming ruler, just like you, yes?" the guard asked.

"I am," Alexis replied.

"But it has never been done. Not in the history of all six stations," the guard said.

"Then I shall make history," Alexis smiled.

"I will be the one making history, Papa. You'll just be making an announcement," Minoress Alexis said.

Alexis smiled even wider and looked back at the guard.

"Do you have any doubt my daughter can lead?"

"No, sire," the guard nodded. "I do not. I have watched her for years now and never seen a more capable child."

"So you would approve and support my decision?" Alexis asked, careful to keep his voice even so he did not sway the young man too much.

"I would, but..." the guard hesitated.

"But? There is always a but, isn't there," Alexis sighed.

"But the stewards would not, and I know the sector warden and deck bosses from where I come from in the Station would fight it tooth and nail," the guard replied. "But they don't know the minoress like I do."

"Would you fight to protect her?" Alexis asked. "Put your life on the line for my daughter even if it meant fighting your friends and neighbors from your sector?"

"Yes, sire!" the guard said as he stood at attention and saluted. "My dying breath would be hers!"

"Ewww," Minoress Alexis said.

"Thank you, guard," Alexis replied. "You may return to your post. I'll bring Alexis back with me."

"Yes, sire!" the guard said and saluted once more. Her turned on his heels and marched quickly down the passageway.

"Well, he's an eager one," Meredith laughed, leaning in to kiss the minoress once more. A chime rang and she frowned. "That's us. We have to go now, little one."

"Don't go, please," Minoress Alexis pleaded.

"We have to," Meredith said, despite the look she got from the master. "It's been decided."

"Travel safe, and may Helios be with you," Alexis said.

"Thank you, Son," Meredith said.

"Goodbye, Brother," Thomas said as he clasped Alexis on the shoulder and nodded.

"I will miss you, Alexis," Eliza said, standing on tiptoes to kiss him on the cheek.

"I will miss you all," Alexis replied. "Goodbye."

The three entered the airlock and waited for the door to the shuttle to open. They were quickly swallowed up inside the metal tube and lost from sight. The minoress, still in her father's arms, sniffled, but did not cry.

"We won't see them again, will we?" she asked.

"I don't know," Alexis replied. "You might since you have a very long life ahead of you. I could easily not."

"Don't you have a long life ahead too, Papa?" Minoress Alexis asked.

"Maybe," Alexis said as he started walking down the passageway so he could get them clear of the shuttle dock and safely into the full station proper. "A master doesn't always choose when they get to leave this plane and join Helios."

"But I thought a master could choose whatever they wanted," the minoress said.

"With most things, yes," Alexis replied. "Which I'm about to prove to a roomful of angry men."

"Don't prove it, Papa, just do it," Minoress Alexis said. "You're the master, not those menfolk."

Alexis laughed as he walked with his daughter. He hugged her tight and reveled in the feeling of her youth and energy.

*

There they sat, every steward from every sector of the Station. The meeting of stewards, all lined up next to each other, up and down the extended long table that filled the great hall. Alexis studied their faces, seeing many, many more foes than friends.

"It has been decided," Alexis said from his seat at the head of the table. "The meeting of passengers has already passed it and now you must do your jobs and pass it as well."

"Without debate?" a steward from down the table called out.

"Debate is for sissies and women!" DuChaer shouted from his seat to Alexis's right. "Action is for men! So act like it and pass the master's order!"

"Order," another steward sneered. "The master does not order the meeting of stewards. This body is here to keep the crown in check and make sure the will of the people is looked out for. And the will of the people will not stand for this radical change to the crown!"

The table erupted in applause, cheers, and fist pounding.

Alexis just sat where he was, a small smile on his lips. DuChaer started to stand up, but Alexis put his hand on the man's shoulder and kept him in place.

"Let them wear themselves out, Brother," Alexis said. "I want them to get whipped into a fervor. That way I am the cool head at the table." Alexis caught Steward Stolt's eye and nodded. "Or one of the cool heads."

"You know the snake is scheming behind your back, right?" DuChaer spat. "My wife is a Stolt and that's all they talk about at tea, apparently."

"Stolt's daughter has confessed to this?" Alexis asked, stunned. "What folly."

"Eh, not so much," DuChaer replied. "My wife hates me, all of the Stolt's hate me, so it's natural they should talk about issues that could lead to my downfall."

"If your wife hates you then why would she tell you that information?" Alexis asked, still amused by the continuous jeers and outbursts from the stewards. "Seems counterproductive on her part."

"Simple," DuChaer said, picking at some dirt under his fingernails. "I beat it out of her. Strip her to her waist and take a breen broom to her tits. Or I did. I just have to touch the broom now and she spills everything."

"You do that?" Alexis asked. "Honestly?"

"Sure," DuChaer shrugged. "Not like I love her."

"You'd beat your own wife for me?" Alexis said. "Your devotion knows no bounds."

"Why would it?" DuChaer smiled. "You have given me everything I have. My devotion is eternal."

"*Are you listening, sire*?" a tall steward roared from halfway down the table. "*This will not stand*!"

Alexis turned away from DuChaer, his head moving slowly, methodically, fluidly on his neck. He sized up the steward and frowned.

"Do I know you?" Alexis asked.

The steward gaped at the master, his mouth hanging open, ready to catch honey wasps.

"That is Steward Jackull Beumont, sire. He is new to the meeting," Stolt said. "His wife was the daughter of Steward Lei of Sector Norbrighm."

"Norbrighm?" Alexis laughed. "You make those children's toys! That's your sector, isn't it?"

Beumont was young, close to Alexis's age, in his mid-twenties. He stood there, healthy and angry, his hands shaking as a vein pulsed in his neck.

"I believe the fool is having a stroke," DuChaer said, then sat up and cupped his hands around his mouth. "I say! Beumont! Are you having a stroke? Blink three times if you are!"

DuChaer and Alexis watched the man then both shook their heads.

"Maybe the stroke is affecting his eyelids?" Alexis said.

"Or perhaps he's just stupid," DuChaer replied. "Hey, Beumont! Are you stupid?"

"I am neither stupid nor having a stroke," Beumont said, his teeth gritted together. "I am simply trying to find a reasonable way to respond without committing treason."

"Well, that's nice of you," DuChaer said. "Very considerate, Beumont."

"Now, now, Brother Gannot," Alexis said. "The steward wants to express something. Let's not mock him a second longer. Please go on, Steward Beumont. I believe you were asking if I was listening."

"Yes, sire," Beumont replied, the tendons in his neck taut with frustration. "I was asking if you were listening, because your noble servants are outraged that you would bypass us on such an important decision. Especially when the crown does not have the legal authority to do what it has done."

"Ah, yes, I see your point," Alexis said.

"You do?" DuChaer asked.

"I do," Alexis nodded. "Now, let me make a point of my own, steward."

Alexis stood up and fixed his eyes on Beumont. The steward, to his credit, did not flinch or look away.

"Were you a rich man before you married into Sector Norbrighm?" Alexis asked.

"I was not rich, but I was not poor, your highness," Beumont replied.

"Are you from Sector Norbrighm, Beumont?" Alexis asked.

"I am, sire," Beumont responded. "Born and raised in the Middle Decks. Worked my way up in the costume factory until I was the youngest foreman they'd ever had. That's how I met my wife."

"Yes, your wife," Alexis grinned. Many at the table that knew the master well enough felt a chill run up and down their spines. They all knew a trap was being set. "And your wife is the daughter of the former Steward of Sector Norbrighm, correct?"

"Correct, sire."

"And when you married her you obtained the title of steward, since she was the only child of Steward Lei and had inherited his estate," Alexis smiled. "This is true also, is it not?"

"Yes, sire," Beumont replied, his shoulders sagging slightly as he caught on to where the master was going with his questions.

"So, let me get this straight, if I might," Alexis said as he walked around the table, his hand lazily trailing from shoulder to shoulder of the seated stewards until he reached Beumont. "You are only here because a man died, left his estate to his only child, who happens to be female—a female you married—which means you take control of the estate as well as the title, and yet you argue against me passing on my title to my only child, who just happens to be female also?"

"Sire, if I may explain?" Beumont said.

"Please do, Beumont," Alexis said as he took Beumont's unoccupied chair, slid it out away from the table, then sat down with his fingers steepled and elbows on his knees. "I am looking forward to this explanation very much."

"It is true I was given title of steward when I married Terla," Beumont said. "But it is a title that she did not have, but was holding until she wed. If she had not wed within two years of her father's death then the title would have been forfeit and she would have lost everything."

"And you think that would be fair, do you? For your wife to have lost everything if she hadn't found her one and only true love in you?"

Beumont hesitated, knowing he had one foot in the trap already. He wanted to step out, but that escape had long fled and the only way to proceed was to put the other foot in.

"No, sire. I do not think that would have been fair to her," Beumont replied finally. "Her father may have held the title, but she ran the sector, and oversaw the success of the factories, almost on her own."

"So your wife is a capable manager and would have actually handled the affairs of the sector just fine without having married you? Is that what you are telling me, Beumont?"

"My wife is an amazing woman, sire," Beumont said. "And, luckily for both of us, we are in love. With that love, comes respect and honor. I hold title, but we run the sector together."

"He's dodging, Alexis," DuChaer said.

"Hush, Brother," Alexis said without turning from Beumont. "I am well aware of that. Answer my question, Beumont. Would your wife been able to handle the affairs of the sector without having had to marry you?"

"Yes, sire," Beumont replied, knowing he had no other option. "She is more than capable of running the sector without me. But we are a true partnership."

"I don't doubt it," Alexis said as he stood up and clapped his hands. "I don't doubt it at all! A capable woman such as her would not choose an idiot to wed. She would want a partner. She would want someone that knew she had all the skills and intelligence to run the sector on her own, and was willing to allow her to do so, if needed."

Beumont didn't respond. He knew his time was done.

Alexis walked back to his chair and sat down, all teeth and smiles. Then the smile fell as Alexis looked down the table at the stewards, all of whom had seated themselves as understanding of what the master had accomplished hit them.

"Your wife is lucky to have your support and love," Alexis said. "Just as my daughter is lucky to have mine. And all of your daughters are lucky to have your support, dear stewards. Do you believe what I propose only applies to the crown? No, it does not. From this day forward, daughters may inherit their fathers' titles as well as estates."

The great hall was silent.

"With this caveat," Alexis said. "The father must bequeath the title and estate to his daughter. If, of course, he does not feel she is up to the task then the first-born son will inherit everything as it has always been. If there are no sons, then the steward's last will and testament shall decide who gains control of the sector and holdings. No will and testament, and the crown gains control."

He met each and every gaze at the table.

"Any objections?"

There were none voiced.

"Then let it be law from here forward," Alexis grinned. "What a happy day."

He stood and turned his back on the meeting, striding out of the great hall without another word.

DuChaer stood and gave a low bow. "Refreshments will be in the secondary banquet room, if anyone cares to join us."

The Thraen exited as well, but with much more flourish and drama.

The stewards all sat there, stunned. None could speak. They just seemed to exist.

Stolt stood up finally and looked about at his fellow nobles.

"I do not believe the last word has been spoken on this matter," Stolt said. "Let what happened today sink in and then we will discuss it amongst ourselves in more private settings. I for one, would never speak ill against the master and his edicts. At least, not in public."

The old steward nodded and then left the table, his dark cloak flapping behind him as he walked through the doors, leaving the meeting of stewards to their stunned silence.

*

"She will be Mistress of Station Aelon?" Bella asked for the third time, not believing what her husband had told her. "All rights, privileges, and power that a master would hold?"

"That is what I have said," Alexis replied, amused at his wife's shock. He stood up from the small chair that was against the wall in their bedchamber and crossed to her as she sat in front of her vanity, a forgotten hairbrush halfway pulled through her hair. "Our daughter will become Alexis the Third when I die."

"Helios forbid," Bella said. "That you die. Not that she becomes mistress. This...this is incredible, Alexis!"

"Yes, I know," Alexis smiled as he rubbed her shoulders, feeling the deep, deep tension she held there. "But it wasn't easy."

"I do not doubt it," Bella replied.

"I am quite certain I have made enemies of a majority of stewards," Alexis frowned. "I know I have some allies, but if the rest were to band together, I feel the crown would be in jeopardy."

"A coup?" Bella asked as she tossed the brush onto the vanity and turned to look up at her husband. "Would the stewards dare?"

"Of course they would," Alexis said. "They hate me. It's that simple. I do not hold the same control over them that my father did, despite all my efforts."

"I do not believe they hate you, Alexis," Bella said as she stood and pressed herself against him. "It is DuChaer that they hate. And with good reason."

"Shaowshit!" Alexis snapped and pushed away from his wife. "Brother Gannot is my most trusted advisor and a great asset to the crown!"

"Brother Gannot is bilking the treasury for every credit he can get his greedy hands on," Bella insisted. "He collects taxes at random from various sectors, yet does not deposit them as he is supposed to. Business leaders from the surface down to the Lower Decks have been complaining for years, Alexis. You can't have been blind to this."

"The Lower Decks have business leaders?" Alexis asked. "Who knew?"

"I am serious, dammit!" Bella yelled. "DuChaer is a threat to your rule! If he is not held in check then his corruption will taint the crown and become fuel for the stewards to revolt as you fear!"

"And I am serious, as well!" Alexis shouted back. "Brother Gannot has been a dear friend to me since my time on the Prime. He has always been there for me and always will. There is a bond between us that transcends the crown or this blasted station!"

Bella shook her head and sat back down. "Dear Helios, listen to yourself, Alexis. Do you even hear the words coming out of your mouth? You are Master of Station Aelon. Nothing transcends that except for Helios the Dear Parent. Nothing."

Alexis began to reply, but stopped as the weight of what his wife said hit him.

"Yes, yes, of course," Alexis sighed, the fight gone from him.

He may have had the handsome looks of a Teirmont, but he did not have the famed rage. Alexis was more willing to follow the path of least resistance than go to battle. Except when it came to his daughter.

"Please tell me you understand what I am saying about DuChaer," Bella pleaded. "The danger he poses is far greater than the danger the stewards pose. He will chip away at your authority until he thinks *he* is the master, not you."

"Let's not speak of Brother Gannot any longer," Alexis said. "The subject is no longer up for discussion. Ever."

"Ever? Ever!" Bella snapped. "Be careful, *husband*, that you do not add me to the list of your enemies."

"Oh, and what would you do? Divorce me? You would need permission from your brother as well as the High Guardian to do so. And we both know they will not let it happen."

"They might," Bella smiled. "Once they realize the threat your edict presents. Did you think of that, Alexis? That perhaps allowing our daughter to take the crown might be bigger than only Station Aelon? I'm a Minoress of Thraen. In fact, if none of my brothers were to produce heirs then I would be in line to take the crown. If Thraen followed the same rules you just put in place. Which they do not. But that wouldn't stop our daughter from making a claim once she is Mistress of Station Aelon."

Alexis studied his wife as the gears turned in his head. His ego had always allowed him the comfort of believing he was smarter than all of the stewards, and his title had always allowed him to force the issue if he needed. But in the royal bedchamber, he quickly realized that he wasn't the smartest person present and a small kernel of fear took hold in his gut.

Bella continued, seeing that she had rattled her husband for once. "Alexis the Third could declare war on Thraen, with legitimate reason. The High Guardian would have to get involved, as would the other stations. Your decision to change the rules of succession here could end up throwing the whole System into chaos and war. Did your trusted advisor tell you that?"

"No," Alexis replied quietly. "He did not."

"Then cut him loose," Bella said. "If only for his lack of qualifications as advisor than for nothing else. As much as I want Alexis to be mistress, your decision has taken us down a path that will run with blood at some point. Do your duty and send DuChaer away. That will calm the stewards long enough to booster support amongst the other stations and perhaps create a system wide change. You have no choice."

"You are right," Alexis replied. "I have no choice. The choice was never with me."

"What? I don't understand," Bella said.

"The choice has always been yours, *wife*," Alexis sneered. "One child. That is all you chose to give me. A girl child, whom I dearly love. But because of the difficult birth, you are now barren. I have no choice but to force this on the stewards because you cannot give me a male heir! You took the choice away from me by failing in your wifely duties to provide more children!"

"My wifely duties? My wifely duties!" Bella roared as she lunged for Alexis.

Her fists pounded his chest and the master stumbled back, falling onto the bed. Bella leapt on top of him and ripped open her robe. She grabbed her breasts and shoved them towards Alexis.

"I am more than willing to perform my wifely duties right now! Take me, Alexis! Ravage my body and make me scream with passion! Do your husbandly duty and fuck your wife!"

Alexis held his hands across his face in horror at the half-naked mad woman that straddled him. He kept his eyes averted from her chest, only looking at her anger-filled face.

"That's what I thought," Bella said as she climbed down off him and the bed. She wrapped the robe about herself and stood there, seething. "We don't know for sure that I am barren, do we, Alexis? That is what the physicians say. That is what the midwives guess. But you and I know the real reason there are no more heirs. Because you have not been inside me since Alexis was conceived. You speak of duty? You know nothing of duty, you fucking flip."

Alexis stood up and crossed to the bedchamber door. He cleared his throat several times before speaking.

"You are distraught and upset," Alexis said. "I am leaving and won't be back until I know for sure that you have calmed down. Feel free to go to bed without me. I may be late as I have a lot of thinking to do."

He opened the door and turned to leave. His eyes went wide for a second then he left the bedchamber. Bella, seeing his expression, followed immediately and prevented Alexis from closing the door behind him.

"*You*," Bella hissed as she saw DuChaer sitting out in the main room. "I'm guessing you heard everything."

"Of course I did, what with the way you too were carrying on," DuChaer grinned as he lounged in a large chair with both legs hanging over the arm. "It is my duty as royal advisor to know everything going on in court. How else am I supposed to advise his highness? I can't very well do it from my bedchamber, now can I?"

"Where I am sure your wife is sleeping right now," Bella replied. "Alone."

"Could be," DuChaer shrugged. "I wouldn't know having not been home in ages. So much to do here at court. The estate house her father gave us in Sector Trint is so far from Castle Quent that there is almost no point in ever going home except for special occasions."

Bella looked at Alexis and then back at the Thraen. "Yes, I am sure that is why you stay away," she smirked. "Because of the distance."

"And duty," DuChaer said as he quickly stood up. "Don't forget my duty. Speaking of which, Alexis, I believe we have an appointment."

"We do? At this hour?" Alexis asked.

Bella and DuChaer both sighed.

"Yes, your highness, at this hour," DuChaer replied. "That thing with the deck boss, or something."

"Oh, right, yes that," Alexis nodded. He turned to Bella. "It appears I will be later than I thought. I have an appointment."

"Oh, dear Helios, just get out," Bella said as she shoved Alexis fully into the main room and slammed the bedchamber door.

She turned and stared at the bed for a couple of minutes then rushed to the vanity, picked up a pair of scissors, stormed over to the bed, and began to shred the comforters, the pillows, the sheets, everything.

Her anguish was so great that she raged with her mouth open in a silent scream that she knew she could never voice. A new future might have been made for her daughter, but she was still a prisoner of the old ways.

*

The old steward looked up from his desk, not surprised at all by the knock at the door.

"Enter," Stolt said as he closed the account book he had been working on.

"Steward Stolt?" a servant asked. "There is a Steward Beumont here to see you."

"Send him in, if you please," Stolt said as he leaned back in his chair and waited for his guest.

Tall and dark, Steward Beumont was like a negative image of Master Alexis. A fact that Stolt was very aware of.

"Jackull! What a pleasant surprise! Please, come in and have a seat," Stolt said as he held his hand out over his desk. "I would stand to greet you, but my back isn't what it used to be. I hope you don't see my staying seated as a sign of disrespect?"

"Not at all, Steward Stolt," Beumont said as he hurried over to the desk and shook the senior steward's hand. "My father has back troubles and spends many days lying in bed. I completely understand."

"Oh, dear, I hope I don't get to that point," Stolt said. "As much fun as staying in bed all day sounds, I think I would grow dreadfully bored. Drink?"

"Uh, yes, please," Beumont said.

Stolt nodded to the servant and the man quickly fetched a tray with a decanter and two glasses. He set it on the desk in front of Stolt then backed away.

"Thank you, that is all," Stolt said and the servant quickly left, shutting the door behind him. Stolt looked at Beumont and waved at a chair in front of the desk. "Sit, please. My apologies for not offering right away." He pointed at the decanter. "You can see where my priorities lie once evening has come."

Beumont took his seat, then leaned forward to take the glass he was offered. "Thank you." He sipped and his eyes went wide. "Is this what I think it is?"

"It is," Stolt nodded. "And I am surprised you know it, having come from humble beginnings. There are many a noble born steward that wouldn't know Klaervian whiskey from gelberry wine."

"I did some traveling when I was younger," Beumont replied.

"Traveling when you were young? How old are you now? Sixteen?" Stolt chuckled.

"Twenty-four, sir," Beumont replied. "Same age as the master."

"Please, call me Girard," Stolt said. "We are equals in the meeting, so there is no need to be so formal. You are a steward, the same as I, and you should learn to embrace and fill that role and the privileges that come with it."

"There seem to be fewer privileges these days, I'm afraid," Beumont responded.

"I assume you are referring to the business that was brought before us yesterday," Stolt said, watching the young man over the rim of his glass. "It was a shock, but Alexis is the master and he will rule as he sees fit."

"But aren't the meeting of stewards, and meeting of passengers, there to keep masters in check when they behave this way?" Beumont insisted. "To be spoken to the way we were was unacceptable."

"Unacceptable behavior is a long tradition amongst masters," Stolt laughed. "And not just on Station Aelon."

"But will the High Guardian stand for this?" Beumont asked. "Surely the man will see that this is an affront to Helios."

"Yet you agreed with the master's point yesterday, did you not?" Stolt asked. "Are you saying you changed your mind and would look your wife in the face and tell her she is not capable of running the sector as well as you?"

Beumont took another drink and swallowed hard. He cleared his throat and fidgeted in his chair.

"I'll take your silence as a no," Stolt said. "Best never to speak ill of one's wife's abilities, I always say. Even when it is just two gentlemen having a polite conversation. You never know who is listening at the door, do you?"

Beumont blanched and looked over his shoulder, causing Stolt to chuckle again.

"Calm down, Jackull," Stolt said. "My servants wouldn't be caught dead within fifteen feet of that door. So consider my office an exception to such a sound rule of discretion. You can speak freely here, my boy, as I shall do now."

The old steward stood from his chair, his back cracking in protest, and walked over to a draped window.

"Dim that lamp for me, will you?" he asked as he pulled the drape aside. He waited for the light to go down before he spoke again. "Come here, Jackull, and look out at the Surface with me."

The young man stood and walked to Stolt's side, his eyes looking out the window at the surface of Station Aelon. Directly before them, but not obscuring the view, were several wings of Castle Quent, but beyond that was nothing but darkness except for the occasional twinkling light.

"Why do we have a monarchy, Jackull?" Stolt asked.

"I'm sorry?" Beumont replied.

"Simple question, although there is no truly simple answer," Stolt said. "So give me your opinion of why we have a monarchy?"

"Because when our ancestors fled the Cataclysm to live in the stations, they quickly realized that democracy would not work," Beumont said. "Too many voices vying to be heard. There was chaos and no structure. And chaos, when living on an artificial planet in space, is never a good thing."

"No, it is not," Stolt said. "And that was an excellent definition. Straight out of the schoolbooks. But, how about you tell me the real reason?"

"The real reason, sir?"

"Girard, remember?" Stolt smiled.

"Girard, yes," Beumont nodded. "What is the real reason?"

"That the passengers have never wanted to have a voice," Stolt said. "Some do, yes, but the majority would rather not concern themselves with affairs of station. They have children to raise and jobs to do. They want someone else to do the work of making decisions."

"Yes, of course," Beumont nodded. "I can see that."

"But, hold on," Stolt said as he looked out at the dark night. Far above them was the environmental shield that kept the atmosphere from dissipating out into space. The rotational drive kept Station Aelon spinning so there was artificial gravity, but it was not strong enough to make the Surface's atmosphere inhabitable on its own. Stolt pointed up at the faint glow of the shield. "Do you see that?"

"The environmental shield? Yes," Beumont replied. "What of it?"

"Think of that shield as the monarchy," Stolt said. "It covers everything and maintains the atmosphere on the Surface, but is it really necessary?"

"Well, no," Beumont admitted. "The rotational drive engines keep gravity in place and we could conceivably seal off the Surface and all live below in the decks."

"Yes, we could," Stolt said. "And since you come from the Middle Decks, I am sure you see that as a perfectly reasonable option."

The steward turned and looked at Beumont, making the man slightly uncomfortable with his intimate assessment.

"But you would be hard pressed to get the stewards to give up their lives on the Surface," Stolt continued. "Just as the environmental shield is needed for us to maintain our lives of comfort and security, away from the decks and the, and I mean no offense here, away from the lesser classes of the passengers, the monarchy is needed for us to maintain our power over said classes."

Beumont frowned and stepped away from the window. Stolt closed the drapes and returned to his chair behind the desk.

"So, if the monarchy was gone, we as stewards would have no power? Why would that be? I have always thought we derive our power from the passengers we represent," Beumont said as he too returned to his seat.

"We do, we do," Stolt replied. "If the monarchy is the shield then the meeting of stewards is the rotational drive itself. And you, of course, need passengers to keep the drive functioning, just as you need passengers to keep a sector functioning and a stewardship healthy. Helios knows I couldn't do every job myself! This station would fall apart in a second!"

"Then I'm afraid I am missing your point," Beumont said.

"My point is that the monarchy is there so we can have our place on the Surface, and the passengers can feel more secure that they are protected by the shield, even if technically they do not need it to survive."

Beumont sighed and shook his head in frustration.

"Hmmm, my apologies for not making myself clear," Stolt said. "Let me be more blunt. If the monarchy falls, then we are all that stand between the passengers and oblivion. Where do you think they will focus if things do not go as they would like?"

"They'd blame the meeting," Beumont said.

"Yes, exactly," Stolt said. "And it is much easier for them to destroy the rotational drive by either refusing to maintain and repair it, or by rising up and smashing the blasted thing than it is for them to come to the Surface, a place many have never seen except in books, and reach up and tear down the shield."

"But doesn't the shield derive its power from the rotational drive?" Beumont asked. "They destroy the drive and they destroy the shield as well."

"Very true," Stolt grinned. "Now you are getting it."

"So, stewards and master are in this together, and if one goes, then eventually the other will follow," Beumont said. "Yes, I think I do get it."

"I said you are getting it, not that you have gotten it," Stolt responded. "Because you are still missing the most important point I am trying to make. Let's see if you can work it out."

Beumont frowned and took a long drink from his glass. He thought for a while as Stolt sat patiently and let the man work it out for himself.

"If very few of the passengers have actually seen the shield then they really only know of it because they are told it is there," Beumont said. "So the solution to our problem is not to remove the monarchy, but to keep up the illusion that it exists. Keep the crown, but give all the real power to the stewards."

"And there you have it," Stolt said as he finished his drink and set the glass down. "Of course, I could never be a part of such an undertaking directly. Not with my long career as former advisor to the crown. That would get the attention of the passengers immediately. But, if say, a young steward—a steward who married into his title and came from the ranks of the passengers—were to approach this, then perhaps things might shift in the right direction."

"But in order to keep up the illusion of the monarchy being in power, we would surely have to have the master agree to this," Beumont said. "Which would never happen. Alexis would fight us tooth and nail. He may be shit for a master, but he is a Teirmont. The man knows how to fight."

"Then the fight must be taken out of him," Stolt said. "And there is an easy way to do that."

"Which is?"

"That, I'm afraid, is for you to figure out," Stolt said. "Like I said, I can't do all the work myself. Everything would just fall apart." Stolt grinned with contentment as he reached for the decanter. "Another drink?"

*

The three skids flew across the scrim grass, their front lights blazing before them in the pre-storm gloom. If not for the environmental suit helmets, laughter would have been heard echoing across the lands of Aelon Prime as the three vehicles zipped in and out of each others' paths, just barely avoiding collision and certain death for the riders.

"You two drive like old ladies!" Minoress Alexis shouted through the helmets' communication systems. "Look at you! Barely able to make turns without slowing down! Are you sure you know how to ride? Maybe you two should be driving a full skid and not single rider ones? You could take turns steering!"

"She is a cheeky little thing, isn't she?" DuChaer laughed as he braked hard and flipped his skid about so he could rush back towards the minoress. "I guess I will show her what riding really looks like!"

"Be careful, Brother Gannot," Alexis said. "She is wily as well as cheeky. If you plan on playing a game of grendt with her, then you better be prepared to lose!"

"I have never lost a game of grendt in my life," DuChaer replied.

"You're about to now!" Minoress Alexis laughed. "I hope you brought plenty of undergarments on this trip because you're going to need them!"

Alexis stopped his skid and let it hover above the brown grass, his eyes twinkling with delight as he watched his daughter and dearest friend race towards each other. He knew he should be put a stop to it, since the only heir to Station Aelon was driving at a very dangerous speed towards a man who was driving at an equally dangerous speed. But where was the fun in that?

"Last chance, little girl," DuChaer cackled. "I'm not swerving."

"Neither am I, Gannot!" the minoress replied, her voice having turned to steel. "So think it through. If you crash into me and I die then you'll be guilty of assassinating a Minoress of Station Aelon. Is that how you want your legacy?"

"How old is she, Alexis?" DuChaer asked.

"I'm eight!" the minoress yelled.

"Almost eight," Alexis corrected.

"Almost eight and she has the guts to put me, a grown man, in my place? What a mistress she will make!" DuChaer said.

"Then please try not to kill her, Brother," Alexis said as his insides clenched from the stress and suspense. "I worked very hard to crush the meeting of stewards' opposition to her taking the crown. It would all be such a waste if she died here on the Prime."

"It would also be sad since I would be dead, Papa," Minoress Alexis said, her body leaning forward over the handlebars of the skid. "That would be the really bad part, yes?"

"Of course, my dearest love," Alexis laughed. "I would be heartbroken."

The two skids were only fifty feet away then thirty then twenty.

"I'm not swerving, Gannot!" Minoress Alexis shouted.

Fifteen feet, ten feet then DuChaer's skid suddenly lurched to the side. The Thraen was sent flying through the air as his vehicle tumbled across the scrim grass, just missing the minoress's skid.

"Brother!" Alexis shouted.

"*Yes*!" Minoress Alexis cheered.

"*Who dared attack me*?" DuChaer shouted as he picked himself up out of the grass. He checked a small screen on his wrist and was glad to see his suit hadn't been compromised, but that relief was gone in an instant as rage poured through him. "*I swear by Helios, I will kill whomever attacked me*!"

Alexis raced his skid over to DuChaer and sat there staring at the wrecked vehicle.

"Attack? What are you talking about?" Alexis asked as he reached out a hand for DuChaer.

The Thraen slapped it away and spun about, his eyes searching the landscape.

"Gannot, what are you looking for?" Alexis asked. "You lost control."

"I did no such thing!" DuChaer snapped. "Look at the side of my skid! That was a particle barb shot, if I ever saw one!"

The master stepped down off his skid and looked at DuChaer's. The vehicle wasn't a complete loss, but it was severely damaged and there was a large hole in the side that was obviously not from the crash.

"Papa, I know what happened," Minoress Alexis said.

Alexis turned from DuChaer and looked out through the gloom towards his daughter. She was a good twenty-five feet away and was not alone.

"What is the meaning of this?" Alexis shouted.

"Sorry, your highness," a royal guard's voice said over the communication system. "We were coming to fetch you and saw the skid going towards the minoress. I assumed she was under attack and fired my longsling. I did not know it was Steward DuChaer, sire."

"I will have your head!" DuChaer yelled. "You are a dead man!"

"What in Helios's name do you want, guard?" Alexis asked, not even bothering to get the man's name. They all looked alike to him anyway, and since Corbin's departure he could care less who they were as individuals. "Why would you come out here when I expressly said we were not to be disturbed?"

"An envoy from the Station has arrived, sire," the guard said. "He wishes to speak to you immediately and will not be put off."

"An envoy? From what station?" Alexis asked.

"Station Aelon, sire," the guard said. "It is Steward Beumont, sire. He says he is on official business from the meeting of stewards and you must speak to him now or be banished to the planet."

Alexis stood there, stunned. His mind had a hard time wrapping itself around the guard's words.

"No one banishes the master!" DuChaer shouted. "Tell Beumont that—"

"Stop, Brother," Alexis said as the shock of the statement subsided and he climbed back aboard his skid. "See to it that Alexis is returned safely to the estate."

"The minoress is not to be in the presence of the traitor, sire," the royal guard said, his voice sounding like he enjoyed using the word. "That is the meeting of stewards' orders. We will take her back with us."

"Papa?" Minoress Alexis asked as two guards helped her down from her skid then set her on the back of the main guard's. "Papa? What do I do?"

"You stay calm and know I am right behind you," Alexis said. "We will return to the estate and sort this all out. I promise you that no harm will come to you."

"We can make that promise as well," the guard said. "She is under our protection, sire. That is not what you need worry about."

The guards spun about and their skids shot across the land back towards the royal estate house, leaving Alexis to gun his drive and hurry after them.

DuChaer stood there next to his broken skid then looked at the one the minoress had abandoned. He felt a shiver go up his spine, but he shrugged it off as he walked through the scrim grass to the vehicle, his mind whirling with ideas of violence and revenge.

*

"You will be put to death for this," Alexis snarled as the reality of what Steward Beumont had just told him sank in. "This is treason."

"No, sire, your relationship with DuChaer, and inability to see his corruption, is treason," Beumont said as he stood before the master. The two men stood alone in a small study off the main room of the estate house. "I have the official proclamation here, if you want to read it. It is signed by every steward, and also by every member of the meeting of passengers. This document and order meets all legal requirements needed to exile DuChaer to the lease holdings on Thraen prime and to banish you here permanently, should you try to fight it."

"You cannot do this, Beumont," Alexis said.

"As one steward, no," Beumont replied. "But like I said, I have the full support of both meetings, sire. DuChaer goes to the lease holdings or you are relieved of your crown."

Alexis felt numb inside. He wanted to feel pure rage, he wanted to feel something that would propel him across the room so he could throttle the smug steward, but the drive wasn't there. In fact, the master felt his strength quickly leave him and he had to stumble back to a chair or risk his legs going out from under him.

"This...this...can't be happening," Alexis said.

"It is, sire," Beumont replied. "I wish it didn't have to, but it is."

"Is it because I named my daughter as my heir?" Alexis asked. "Is that why you are doing this to me?"

"It is what started it, yes," Beumont replied. "I am man enough to admit to that. But it is DuChaer's behavior that is really at issue."

"He is a steward as well," Alexis said. "Did he sign it? You said all stewards signed the proclamation, but I think you missed one."

"He has been stripped of title and lands," Beumont responded. He took a deep breath and looked down at the master. "You must see this as a compromise, sire. You get to remain master, your daughter will still be considered your heir. All we are asking is that DuChaer never be allowed on Station Aelon or Aelon Prime."

"I may remain master, but I have to give up all power and authority to the meetings," Alexis said. "You forgot to say that."

"That's not completely accurate," Beumont said, barely able to contain a grin. "The meeting of stewards will have all authority, not the meeting of passengers."

"How in Helios's name did they agree to that?" Alexis asked.

"Such is the extent of loathing felt for DuChaer," Beumont said. "The meeting of passengers threw in with the stewards just to get rid of the man. That should tell you all you need to know right there, sire."

Alexis sat there, deflated, defeated, dejected.

"What now?" Alexis asked, his eyes rimmed with tears.

"You accompany me back on the next shuttle to Station Aelon and make a declaration that you are in full agreement," Beumont said. "Then we continue as we have for centuries, just without the Thraen and without the crown wielding all the power."

"Without the crown wielding any power, you mean," Alexis said. "Be honest, at least."

Beumont didn't respond, only smiled.

CHAPTER FIVE

The master wanted to hold his head up high, but he could barely meet the gaze of his wife as she glared at him, her eyes daggers of resentment. He sat in a less than comfortable chair in the main room of the royal quarters, his face haggard and tired looking.

"This will not stand, Alexis," Bella snapped. "She is turning ten years old! To not celebrate her Decade before Helios would be tantamount to blasphemy!"

"Do not exaggerate, wife," Alexis sighed. "They are not saying we cannot celebrate, just not as elaborately as we had hoped."

"They have no right to do this to us!" Bella shouted. "The meeting of stewards has gone too far! Look at this place! Look at how we are dressed! We have been shoved aside like orphans and made to live as paupers!"

"Yes, well, that I can agree with," Alexis said as he pressed his fingertip against a worn spot on his sleeve. The spot gave way immediately and his finger slid right through. "I will ask for a larger clothing allowance."

"But you won't fight them," Bella stated. "You'll just beg like a lowdecker."

"They have stripped me of my power, Bella," Alexis said. "I am a figurehead master. They keep me around so that the other stations do not feel threatened."

"Threatened? Threatened by what?" Bella laughed. "My brother Harry would crush any hint of uprising by the Thraen stewards. He would send them all out the airlocks! But then he is a real man."

"I am a real man," Alexis hissed. "I am just biding my time until the opportunity comes to retake everything that was once mine."

"Oh, you're *biding your time*, is that it?" Bella spat. "Waiting for Helios to come visit you and hand you what? More divine power? You are a master! The stewards cannot be allowed to stand between you and the Dear Parent! Your power is ordained, not theirs!"

"Yet the High Guardian refuses to get involved," Alexis snorted. "Matters of station do not interest him. You would think the man, having just been installed in his position, would want to solidify the will of Helios and banish these accursed traitors. But, no, he says that I am still master so I have not technically been removed or wronged. Who runs the Station is an internal administrative issue, not something The Way need bother with."

"The Way will not get involved because that damned DuChaer is down on the planet causing chaos," Bella said. "Even exiled to the lease holdings on Thraen Prime, that man is still a thorn in our sides."

"Do not speak ill of Brother Gannot," Alexis said. "It has been just over two years since I have seen my friend. He is not a threat to you so you can at least do me the courtesy of being civil when talking about him."

Bella shook her head without responding. She sat down in a chair across from Alexis and lifted the teapot that sat on the small table between them. Empty.

The teapot had shattered against the wall before Alexis knew his wife had even thrown it. He jumped, a small squeak escaping his throat, and looked at his wife in shock.

"That was a gift from your father for our wedding!" Alexis cried. "What has gotten into you?"

"That piece of shit?" Bella laughed. "That was an insult, is what that was. The Thraenish lowdeckers churn them out by the hundreds. It was worthless crockery and nothing more."

"But the design work was Haelmish, not Thraenish," Alexis said. "He said it was a piece from his own collection."

"He was mocking you," Bella sneered. "It is an inside joke amongst us Herlects. When we give that crap to someone, it tells everyone in the family how much we disapprove of them. Father hated you."

"And you stood by and let me think otherwise?" Alexis snapped. "How could you?"

"Oh, now you are upset?" Bella laughed. "The stewards take your station and you mope about our quarters for two years, but when you find out some stupid teapot isn't what you thought then you get upset?"

Bella threw up her hands and bolted from the chair.

"Now it all makes sense!" she continued. "I should have just dressed as a teapot with a cock hanging out of the spout and then you'd have shown me the attention a minoress of Thraen deserved!"

"Stop being hysterical," Alexis shouted. "You produced an heir as you were supposed to. You did your job. No one expected any more from you, so you can quit pretending that I have dishonored you in some way. I haven't."

"But you haven't honored me either, Alexis. And a mistress should be honored!"

"As should a master!" Alexis roared as he stood and raised his hand. Bella didn't flinch. She only smiled as she looked past Alexis to the bedchamber door beyond.

"Hello, sweetheart," Bella said. "I am sorry that mother and father disturbed your sleep. We forget ourselves sometime and get over-exuberant."

Alexis slowly let his hand fall to his side and turned around. He saw the wide, shocked eyes of his daughter as she stood in her bedchamber doorway, dressed in her nightgown and slippers.

"There is my girl," Alexis said as he turned from his wife and hurried over to his daughter. "Let's get you back in bed. Tomorrow will be a big day. It's your Decade."

"Were you two fighting again?" Minoress Alexis asked as her father picked her up. She wrapped her arms about his shoulders and nuzzled into his neck. "You know I hate it when you two fight."

"I know, I know," Alexis said as he carried her into her bedchamber and set her down on her bed.

The minoress scooted back under the covers and Alexis sat down, his hand going to her head. He stroked her hair, her cheek then gave her chin a playful tug and wiggle.

"Your mother and I do not always agree on how the monarchy should proceed," Alexis said. "But one thing we do agree on is how much we love you. That can never be argued or debated."

"Until one of you insists you love me more than the other," Minoress Alexis replied.

"Why on Helios would you say that?" Alexis asked. "The thought has never crossed my mind. I love you as much as my heart can ever love any living soul. Your mother feels the same way. Our love for you is not a competition, my dearest love. Not ever."

"One day it will be," the minoress said. "I can see it coming."

"Nonsense," Alexis laughed as he tucked the covers up around her. "Your love is not a toy to be fought over like toddlers. You are free to love your mother as much as you want and you are free to love me as much as you want. I could care less about who says they love you more as long as I am always in your heart."

"You are my heart, Papa," Minoress Alexis grinned. "The day you die will be the day I die."

"Alexis!" Bella hissed from the doorway. "You knock six times and take that back!"

"But it's true, Mother," Minoress Alexis replied. "When Papa dies then I will no longer be the girl I am now. I will be a new girl. I will be Mistress of Station Aelon and the old Alexis will die away. When you die, Papa, I die. But then I am born anew."

Alexis looked back at his wife and they locked eyes, both sharing the same thought. Bella walked to the bed and sat down across from Alexis, her eyes softening and her face taking on a sad, knowing look.

"You will always be the same person, Alexis," Bella said. "You will just have grown and changed because that is what life does to you. You will not die and be reborn. You will be you."

The minoress smiled up at her mother and shook her head.

"No, Mother, that's not true," she said. "I can feel it in my soul. When Papa dies and I take the crown, I will change. I don't know if it will be for better or worse, but I will change so much that who I am now will never, ever be able to exist again. This is truth. This is Helios's will."

"I never know who the parent is half the time with you, my little minoress," Alexis chuckled. "You carry wisdom in you that many adults never find."

Bella snorted at his words, but then frowned in apology.

"I don't need a big Decade celebration," Minoress Alexis said. "I would be just as happy staying here in our quarters and having tea and cakes. Helios knows my age, and that is all that matters."

"No," Alexis said. His face was firm and resolute as he stood up, leaned over, and kissed her on the forehead. "You will have your Decade celebration. It is your Helios-given birthright as Minoress of Station Aelon. I will make this happen for you."

"Alexis, do not make promises you cannot—" Bella started, but was silenced by a sharp look from her husband. A look she hadn't seen in quite some time.

"I promise you, my dear, sweet girl, that the meeting of stewards will not only allow the expense of your celebration, they will all be in attendance," Alexis grinned. "Every single one of them."

*

The great hall was filled with angry men, to say the least.

All of the stewards sat at the long table, their heads turned to look at Alexis as he stood at the end.

"We had an agreement," Alexis said. "Brother Gannot would be stripped of title and land, I would be stripped of all power, but able to keep my title. This I agreed to because the main part of the deal was my daughter would take the crown when I pass. Is there anyone here who disagrees with my recollection of the terms?"

No one spoke up, they just glared.

"Good," Alexis continued. "So, as future Mistress of Station Aelon, my daughter deserves the respect her position and title affords her. However, you feel about me, and the way I have ruled this station, you have no right to treat my daughter as if she were party to any of it. She is an innocent little girl who turns ten today. As a minoress of the Family Teirmont, it is her birthright to a Decade celebration. You, as honorable men and nobles, will see to it that she has her celebration or I will see to it that the agreement we have is null and void and this station is plunged into anarchy and chaos."

That got the stewards talking and the great hall erupted with shouting and calls for the master to be removed. Several guards stepped forward, but Alexis whirled on them, long blade drawn. The table quickly went silent as they watched the threat of bloodshed unfold before their eyes.

"Master Alexis," Stolt said as he stood. "There is no need for histrionics. No one here wants to deny the minoress her Decade celebration. It is just that the treasury cannot handle the burden at this time. It has taken two years to undo the damage that DuChaer did. Station Aelon is just now getting to a point of financial stability."

Alexis put his long blade back in its sheath and turned to look at the old steward.

"While I will admit that finances bore me more than having to listen to you lot prattle on," Alexis said. "I am not so naive as to believe that you all have stood by and kept your fingers out of the pie for the sake of the Station. You do not have the funds for my daughter's Decade celebration because the pilfering from the treasury has never stopped. You pushed me aside, and exiled Brother Gannot, so that there would be no one standing between you and the Station's coffers. That is why I live like I'm a deck boss and not master of this station while all of you sit there with your new clothes and fineries."

"That is a powerful accusation," Beumont said as he stood and faced the master. "And a powerful threat. Unfortunately, sire, you no longer have a way to make good on your threat. How would you plunge this station into anarchy and chaos? The passengers do not listen to you any longer. You can shout until you are blue in the face, but the leadership of this station is in our hands and our hands alone."

"Unless I decide to give it to the passengers," Alexis smiled.

Stolt narrowed his eyes. "How do you mean, Alexis?" He received a glare so sharp he almost wiped at his face to see if it had drawn blood. "My apologies. How do you mean, *your highness*?"

"Oh, that is simple." Alexis grinned. "All I have to do is declare it so. I am still the master, after all."

Stolt watched the master for a minute, then began to laugh. Slowly at first then with more and more force, the old steward laughed and laughed. The table watched him, many faces showing they thought he might have gone mad.

"Sire, how will you tell them?" Stolt asked, finally able to get himself under control. "Will you visit every single passenger, one by one? Because you will have to. You cannot use the broadcast system and not a single sector warden or deck boss will let you gather the passengers together. You would have to act like a simple passenger yourself and go door to door.

And even if you did lower yourself to such behavior, no one would listen or follow a master that would act in such a manner. You forget that the passengers want a master to be in charge, they just do not want you."

"Then I will have to find a way to change their minds," Alexis said. "So I advise you give my daughter her Decade celebration, or consider yourselves at war with the crown."

"This is not what we agreed to!" Beumont shouted. "You are out of order and in direct violation with the decree—"

"Calm yourself, steward," Stolt interrupted. "You are shouting for no reason. Master Alexis offers us empty threats. Let him try, but as we have all witnessed, the man knows nothing of politics or real power. He just knows how to dress like a flip and play with skids on the Prime."

"If that is how you feel, and we have nothing more to discuss, then I will give the bad news to my daughter," Alexis said. "The same daughter that will become mistress and is not beholden to your decree. That agreement was between myself and the meetings, nothing more. Read your own document, you pompous fools. Once I die, it becomes invalid and your power goes away. Then you will be dealing with a daughter whose beloved father was so terribly wronged. How do you think things will turn out for those of you here that live to see that day? I believe you will become intimately familiar with the airlocks."

Alexis smiled wide then bowed, turned and strode from the great hall.

*

"Thank you, Papa!" Minoress Alexis exclaimed as she collapsed onto her bed after a full day of parties, games, singing, dancing, and more food than she could possibly have dreamed of. Not to mention the piles of presents heaped on her by nobles and passengers alike. "You made your promise come true!"

"I said I would," Alexis replied. "But I didn't have to do much. The stewards just had to be made to realize that they wanted to make you as happy as I wanted to make you. They had forgotten their loyalties and I simply reminded them."

"Yes, you did," Bella grinned at him from the minoress's bedchamber doorway. "Now it is time to let the Decade girl go to bed."

"But I can't be expected to sleep after a day like this," Minoress Alexis said. "It was all too exciting. I don't think I'll sleep for a whole month!"

"Whether that is the case or not, your father has guests, and the adults need to talk before we go to our bed," Bella said, her eyes locking onto Alexis. "I'll have the nurse read to her and tuck her in. You are needed in the parlor presently."

Alexis frowned at his wife, but her expression did not change.

"Very well," he said as he leaned over and kissed his daughter's brow, feeling the hum of energy that still buzzed inside her. "Be good for the nurse and go to sleep when she says. Do you hear?"

"Yes, Papa," Minoress Alexis smiled. "Thank you and I love you so very much."

"As I do you, my dearest, sweetest love," Alexis grinned. He stood up and walked to his wife then turned and blew a kiss to the minoress. "Sleep well, Alexis, future Mistress of Station Thraen."

"Papa, you said Thraen and not Aelon!" Minoress Alexis giggled.

"Did I?" Alexis replied. "Well, maybe you can be Mistress of Station Thraen in addition to Station Aelon one day. You do have a claim, you know."

The minoress's eyes went wide with the thought and Alexis could see the wheels turning in his daughter's head.

The nurse came in and the two parents quickly left, both surprisingly content at that moment.

"What is this business?" Alexis asked as he walked towards the door that led from the main room to the side parlor of the royal quarters. "The hour is late. Who would come to see me at such a time?"

"That is a surprise," Bella said. "Apparently for the both of us."

Alexis frowned at her cryptic statement then crossed the room and opened the parlor door.

"Ah, Master Alexis," a short man said as he stood up from one of the chairs. He was a couple of decades older than Alexis with salt and pepper hair and small, beady black eyes. His stomach was very round, but tight like a boulder and he stood on almost stick thin legs. "It is so wonderful to finally meet you in person. My son and I have heard so very much about your infinite capacity for generosity and understanding."

"We have, sire," a second man said as he stood as well. He was closer to Alexis's age and was thin and wiry, the complete opposite of his father.

"Despite the ugly business of the Station, the only truth we have heard has been nothing but glowing."

Alexis looked from the men to his wife and back.

"I am sorry, but you have me at a disadvantage," Alexis said. "Who are you?"

"They are our saving grace, my Brother," a very familiar voice said from a shadow in the corner of the parlor. "And they have come to get your crown back."

"The master has not lost his crown," Bella said, her voice even and controlled. "Let's not forget that. What he needs back are his people, so that they may rise up against the corrupt stewards, and the balance of power can once again be where it is ordained to lie."

"That is exactly what I meant to say," DuChaer replied as he stood and stepped out of the shadows. "That my Brother Alexis should once again reign without worry of old fools trying to usurp his crown."

"Gannot?" Alexis whispered. "But how...?"

"It was really quite simple, actually," DuChaer frowned. "So simple that I have to wonder if there might be some stewards that are none too happy with how things have turned out."

"Well, I look forward to hearing the details," Alexis said. Every fiber in his body wanted to rush to the man and take him in his arms, but he restrained himself and looked at the two strangers. "But I think the first details should be these gentlemen's names."

"Oh, look at me," DuChaer laughed. "I'm so happy to be back that I have completely forgotten how things work. Master Alexis Teirmont, I bring to you your saviors—Herlen and Deran Spiggot. These two men are why the lease holdings on Thraen Prime produce so much Vape at such a fast rate and low cost."

"We control the labor of all of Station Aelon's mine interests, whether on the Thraen Prime or on the Aelon Prime proper, even though those mines are meager pickings," the older man, Herlen Spiggot, said.

"But they do still produce," the younger man, Deran Spiggot, added. "And with the right application of pressure and resources, sometimes the Aelon Prime mines are actually more profitable than the lease holdings."

"I am sorry, gentlemen," Alexis said. "But I grew up on the Prime, have spent a considerable amount of time on the Prime, and am Master of

Station Aelon. How in Helios's name is it possible that I have never heard of you?"

"If you had, sire, then we wouldn't have been doing our jobs," Deran responded. "We are men behind the scenes and off the books. We keep things running so others can believe they are in charge."

Alexis looked from DuChaer to the new men and shook his head.

"That doesn't answer my questions, of which I have many," Alexis said. "But it does pique my interest. If Brother Gannot has risked his life to bring you here, then there must be some good you can do. Let us sit and discuss it."

The Spiggots' eyes went to the mistress.

"This should be a private conversation," Herlen suggested.

"It would be best if the mistress was not present as this is sensitive information," Deran added. "The less she knows, the less that she can admit to. Plus, if things do not go our way, she has deniability and will be able to be there for your daughter."

"Deniability?" Alexis asked. "If things do not go our way?" He focused on DuChaer. "Brother Gannot, what are you up to?"

"I will leave you gentleman so that my husband can get an honest answer to that question," Bella said. "Just know that if at anytime I want information, you will give it to me. I won't ever explain that again."

"Of course, your highness," Herlen said.

"We mean no offense," Deran said.

The two men bowed low and waited for the mistress to leave.

"I will not wait up," Bella said to Alexis. "Remain as long as you need to conduct whatever business this may be." She glanced at DuChaer. "Or whatever business may come up."

She quickly left the parlor and Alexis moved to make sure the door was locked and shut tight. He turned and gestured to the chairs and all men sat. Alexis took a seat next to DuChaer and patted the man on the knee.

"It is good to have you back, Brother," Alexis said, beaming.

"It is good to be back," DuChaer replied. "But we need to discuss business immediately. What the Spiggots have to say is time sensitive, and must be implemented within the next three days."

"Three days?" Alexis asked. "This is all very rushed now, isn't it?"

"It has to be, sire," Herlen said. "Just as DuChaer here is not exactly welcome on the Station, neither are we. There would be more than one steward we may have crossed who would love to see our heads rolled down the passageways of this station for the wee children to play with."

"That's a grim picture," Alexis said. "Now, explain yourselves."

Herlen and his son looked at each other then the younger man sat forward.

"We are lowdeckers by birth," Deran said. "And it just so happens that my sister is married to the brother of Steward Klipoline."

"Steward Klipoline?" Alexis laughed. "The Steward of the Lower Decks? That is the only title with less power than mine! The meeting won't even notify him when they are gathering for business."

"Yes, and he is none too pleased with that treatment," Herlen responded. "In fact, he is none too pleased with being a steward."

"Is he now?" Alexis said. "How ungrateful. He could always go back to being just a common lowdecker, if he wants. No one, and I do mean no one, is going to stop him."

"No, sire, you misunderstand," Deran said. "He doesn't want to retire from being a steward, he wants to be a master. The man is ambitious, to say the least."

"He wants to be...?" Alexis said, the words catching in his throat. His body began to shake with rage and he was afraid he'd burst into flames right then.

"Calm yourself, Alexis," DuChaer said, his hand going to the master's leg. "It is not what you think."

"No, it is not," Herlen said. "Klipoline doesn't want your mastership, he wants one of his own."

"My brother-in-law's brother would like to be master of the Lower Decks," Deran said. "With all rights and privileges that a mastership is granted."

Alexis looked from DuChaer to the Spiggots, from the Spiggots to DuChaer. Then he stood up abruptly, his face red with anger.

"You have come to mock me," he snarled. "I have been reduced to almost nothing on this station and you three come to kick me even lower." He whirled on DuChaer. "I cannot believe you would do this, Gannot. Your cruelty has no bounds."

"Sit down and stop acting like such a drama flip," DuChaer barked. "This is legitimate, and your only chance at crushing the meeting of stewards so you can regain your place in this station! So sit your royal ass in that chair and listen to what is being offered to you!"

Alexis fumed. He was so enraged that he couldn't see straight and had to reach out to the chair back to keep from falling as the parlor swam about him. DuChaer was suddenly in his face.

"Sit down, Alexis," DuChaer whispered, the harshness gone from his voice. "Please. I have risked everything these past two years to get us to this place. Even though you tossed me aside and forgot all about me. The least you can do is listen for five minutes."

"I...I never forgot you, Brother," Alexis whispered back. "Never. Not a single moment."

"Then sit and calm yourself," DuChaer said. "Trust me with this. I am not steering you wrong."

"I'll fetch you a drink, sire," Deran said as he stood and moved to a sideboard against the wall. "Anything in particular you'd like?" He looked at the decanters and realized quickly they were all filled with the same liquor. "Oh...right."

Alexis, with the help of DuChaer, sat down once again. He took the glass offered to him by Deran, but didn't drink from it, just held it in his hands as he stared at the two men.

"So...what is it you have to offer?" Alexis asked.

"We can offer every man in the Lower Decks," Herlen said. "We can also make sure that the Wyaerrn longslingers of Middle Deck Twenty remain neutral throughout the conflict."

"And how in Helios's name can you offer that?" Alexis asked, beyond skeptical.

"Simple," Deran replied. "I am married to a Wyaerrn, the youngest daughter of old Gornish, Helios rest his soul. Middle Deck Twenty will not join the fight."

"And that is not all," Herlen smiled. "Every mine worker on Aelon prime and the lease holdings on Thraen Prime will stop working as soon as I give the word. Vape production will grind to a halt. We will bring the stewards to their knees in a matter of months. Most may be rich from breen plantations, but they cannot farm that breen without Vape."

"They can buy Vape on the open market from other stations," Alexis said. "It will cost them more, but they will do it."

"Except that no one will sell to Aelon while we are at civil war," Herlen said. "Trust me, I have already put the feelers out and gotten word back that the other stations would rather we rip ourselves apart so they can pick at the carcass when it is done. None believe you can lead a revolt against the meeting of stewards."

"The other masters talk of my situation?" Alexis asked, his face going pale. "How embarrassing."

"No one makes any disparaging remarks, if that is your worry, sire," Deran responded. "Well, no more disparaging than they make about each other."

Alexis turned to DuChaer and finally took a sip of his drink. He didn't say a word, as the question was clear in his eyes.

"This is your chance, Alexis," DuChaer said. "All you have to do is say yes."

"And turn a commoner into a master," Alexis said. "How will that work? There would be two masters on Station Aelon? That dilutes my power right there."

"No, no, no," Herlen smiled. "Klipoline would only be master of the Lower Decks. They would become a fully autonomous region with their own rule and governance. You would never have to worry about them again."

"Except the rotational drive is down there," Alexis replied. "What's to stop the man from holding the rest of the Station hostage once he comes into power?"

"Because, no matter who he thinks he is, the rotational drive runs on Vape," Deran said. "And we control the Vape."

"It is your choice, Alexis," DuChaer said. "But it could be the last one you ever get. And the last chance for your daughter."

"For my daughter?" Alexis asked.

"Do you think they'll let the terms of the decree expire when you die? They'll either force Alexis to agree to new terms or they'll kill her," DuChaer answered. "You know it's true. In your heart, you have always known that."

Alexis looked from one man to the other, sighed, downed his drink, sighed again, set the glass down then stood up and offered his hand.

"Gentlemen," he said. "Let us go to war!"

"Well, there are still some preparations to make." Herlen smiled as he sat back in his chair and relaxed. "A couple of key players will need to be removed from the board before we can truly strike."

"Key players?" Alexis asked. "Which key players?"

"The less you know the better, sire," Deren replied. "The stewards will accuse you of the...removals, so it would be wise if you can honestly feign ignorance on the subject."

"But what if they ask about the entire plot?" Alexis asked. "I am a shit liar."

"It is true," DuChaer agreed. "The man can't lie to save his soul. It's so damn cute."

"Yes, quite," Deren smiled. "But that is not a problem. Just don't give away our names, or the fact that Gannot has returned to the Station, and all will be well. If Stolt asks what you know, just tell him that wheels are in motion for the end of the meeting of stewards and, unless he returns full power to the crown, he can expect to be dead within a year."

"A year? Is that how long you expect it to take?" Alexis asked. "Can we hold out for a year? What do I do? Where do I go with my family? How will we be safe?"

"We'll see to your safety, sire," Herlen said. "The Lower Decks are impenetrable."

"That's not true," Alexis argued. "My own father took down the Lower Decks himself."

"No, he did not," Deren said. "And I mean that with all due respect. Your father had Diggory. Diggory was how the royal soldiers really gained access and took the Lower Decks during the uprising. That is one reason Klipoline came to us. He wants out of that dark shadow in history, and would like to forge his own monarchy and rule. As we all would. The stain of Diggory is a sore spot for many a lowdecker."

"So, everything my father worked and fought for will be undone?" Alexis responded.

"Will that be a problem?" Herlen asked.

"I do not think so," Alexis smiled. "I loved my father, but we had our differences." He looked over at DuChaer. "I think it is time I moved past those differences and stepped out of my own dark shadow in history."

"We feel the same way, sire," Herlen said, grinning. "The very same way."

*

The bodies were mutilated almost beyond recognition. Not a single one was left intact.

"Who would perform such a heinous act?" Stolt asked as he covered his mouth with a handkerchief. He tried to look away, but everywhere he turned was blood and gore, limbs and entrails. "Steward Exchester had no enemies that I can think of."

"He was on the council," Beumont replied, trying to breathe through his mouth to avoid as much of the rotted meat stench as he could. "There are always enemies of the council, even within the meeting of stewards."

"Sweet Helios," Stolt muttered. "You cannot believe that a steward ordered this, can you?"

"How else would they be able to gain access to a steward's estate house?" Beumont replied. "Simple thugs could not do this. Someone with credentials gained entry and then went to work. Look about and tell me what you see."

Stolt stood stock-still. "I'd prefer not to look about at all, thank you."

"Stop being such an old man, Stolt, and look!" Beumont snapped.

The old steward narrowed his eyes and turned, but didn't look about the room, instead he looked directly at Beumont.

"You have changed, Jackull," Stolt said. "You have sharpened your claws and shielded your heart. You are not the same, naïve steward who came to me years before. I wouldn't go so far as to say you have become cynical, but you certainly have embraced the ways of the Station."

"I have done what has needed to be done, Stolt," Beumont replied. "That is all. Now look and tell me what you see."

Stolt reluctantly studied the room and the dismembered bodies. He spun all the way around then closed his eyes.

"I see nothing but death, young man," Stolt said. "Hideous, brutal death."

"Look at the entryway to the room then," Beumont said. "The answer is there."

Stolt opened his eyes and turned towards the gruesome scene at the room's entryway. Four guards were spread across the floor, their bodies shredded.

"I see men who failed in their duties," Stolt replied.

"You see men who came to help when they heard what was happening," Beumont said. "Then they were killed. The guards had already let the killer, or killers, inside. This proves my point that whoever did this was known on this estate."

"Then it could be a servant, could it not?" Stolt replied. "A worker gone mad? Have all been accounted for?"

"No," Beumont said. "There are two missing. Lowdeckers."

"Lowdeckers?" Stolt gasped. "Who in their right mind would hire lowdeckers as estate servants? The pigs can barely wash themselves."

"Be that as it may, I think we know who the killers are," Beumont said. "Now we must find out who ordered them to do this."

"They are lowdeckers!" Stolt snapped. "The animals didn't need to be ordered! They just went mad and showed their true selves! All we need to do is have all lowdeckers on the Surface and in the Estate Decks rounded up and questioned! Then we will have our killers and this business will be done!"

"You are slipping, Stolt," Beumont said. "These people did not act alone or on impulse. This was a message being sent. What we need to do is have our own estates locked down and secured. Only trusted servants and guards. No one goes in, no one goes out. We are under siege, Girard. That is the only way to put it."

"Nonsense," Stolt responded. "This is just—"

"They have gotten steward Prochan as well," Beumont said. "And I have not heard from Luviester or Tollmay. My men are hurrying to their estates as we speak. I expect to find the same scene as here and at Prochan's."

"My family," Stolt whispered.

"Already safe," Beumont said. "Or as safe as can be for now. Like I said, we must remove any and all persons from our estates who we do not trust implicitly. Then we meet with the rest of the stewards and decide how to coordinate our campaign. We cannot trust the master's soldiers, so we will need to use our own men only."

"Cannot trust the soldiers? Our own men?" Stolt asked. "You are talking of war, aren't you? But with whom?"

"I have an idea, but need a day or so to confirm it." Beumont sighed. "Hopefully we *have* a day or so."

"War," Stolt whispered. "A civil war, at that. This will tear the Station apart."

"It may very well do that," Beumont agreed. "So we must act fast."

*

The terrified faces that ringed the Middle Deck Twenty-Eight, Sector Maelphy atrium looked down at the men armed with various blades and shook with fear. Mothers clutched at children, husbands pulled their wives close, friends and siblings grabbed onto each others' hands and held tight.

"If you give fealty to Master Alexis then no one will be harmed," a man shouted from the center of the atrium.

He held a long blade in one hand and a document in the other. He raised the document and shook it.

"This is a writ direct from Master Alexis guaranteeing your safety," the man continued. "Master Alexis wants the Station returned to its former glory. In order for that to happen, you need do nothing. Just go about your lives and let us do our jobs. When the stewards' men come, you do not join them, you do not let your husbands and sons be taken into service. Remain neutral and you remain alive."

The man raised his long blade.

"Your other choice is to fight against Master Alexis," the man said. "I'll leave you to guess how that will be received."

"How do we know you won't kill us anyway?" a man shouted from above.

"Because Master Alexis wants his people back," the man replied. "He does not want them dead or harmed. All he cares for is that Station Aelon be unified once more and the stewards returned to their proper place. This is not a revolution, this is a return!"

"We heard the Thraen is back on the Station," a woman called out. "We hate the Thraen! Why would we help that man?"

"You will not be helping DuChaer," the man responded. "You'd be helping the master." Less than agreeable faces looked down at him. "You would also be helping the mistress and young minoress. I know everyone loves the Mistress Bella and her daughter Alexis. If the stewards have their way then the mistress will be executed without a doubt and the minoress will be imprisoned or join her mother's fate."

There were gasps from many at that revelation and the man did not hesitate to capitalize on them.

"That is right! The stewards have sworn to kill off the Teirmont line! They will stop at nothing to secure their control over every aspect of this station! The monarchy will be dead on Station Aelon and only the elite will rule! No more sector wardens! No more deck bosses! They will kill everyone they see as a threat!"

The atrium erupted into harsh murmurs and grumbling, but the man knew he had them.

"You have a way with words, Chobaen," another man said.

"Thank you," the first man, Chobaen Newton, replied. "Hopefully all we will need with these passengers are words. We cannot win this war if we kill innocents. The station will turn against the master in a heartbeat."

*

Beumont, his back against his study wall, slashed out with his long blade, keeping the approaching men away for that moment. He looked about the room in horror and saw too many familiar faces mixed in with the attackers to be believed.

"This is treason!" he shouted. "I trusted you men!"

"You shouldn't have," a guard said as he stepped forward from the group. "My wife is a lowdecker, but you seemed to have forgotten that. Even after we had that conversation during yesteryear's Last Meal. I told you about how her father was ill and the Lower Decks needed more medical supplies. You said you would handle it."

The man slashed out with his own long blade, knocking Beumont's aside.

"You didn't handle shaowshit, *my lord*," the guard spat. "My father-in-law died screaming. He could have been saved by simple medicines that you probably have in your cabinets right now. But you let him die."

"I did no such thing!" Beumont replied. "I brought the matter before the meeting of stewards just as I said I would! They decided not to act, not me!"

"Oh, Jackull, Jackull, Jackull," DuChaer said from the doorway of the study. "You are full of excuses this morning, aren't you?"

"*You*," Beumont hissed. "Remove yourself from my house, this instant! I will be happy to die with honor as I fight these treasonous bastards, but I will not die before you!"

"Oh, you will not die at all," DuChaer said. "I have plans for you. You were so instrumental in my exile that I figured I would have to be in yours. Although, you won't be exiled, but imprisoned. And I will have the privilege of escorting you to your new home in the third spire of Castle Quent. It's surprisingly comfortable, yet a little cramped."

DuChaer snapped his fingers as he walked fully into the study. The men parted as an older woman and a young girl were dragged into the room, their mouths gagged and hands bound behind their backs.

"I'm afraid you can only have one person accompany you," DuChaer said. "Due to the limited space. I'll let you choose which one."

DuChaer pulled his long blade from its sheath and set the sharp edge against the young girl's throat.

"Will you take your daughter?" DuChaer asked as he moved the blade to the throat of the older woman. "Or will you take your wife?"

"You harm either of them and I will have your testicles roasted over coals," Beumont snarled. "I will not rest until your head is in my hands."

"Ooooh," DuChaer laughed. "You are a feisty steward, aren't you? So full of spit and grit!" The wicked smile on DuChaer's face left quickly and he pressed the blade harder against Beumont's wife's throat. "Choose, Jackull. Choose this second or I choose for you."

"You don't have the guts to-!" Beumont started then screamed as DuChaer whipped the blade across his wife's throat, sending a geyser of blood spurting into the room. "*Nooooooooooooooooo*!"

The young girl thrashed and cried until DuChaer backhanded her swiftly, sending her to her knees. He slammed the hilt of his bloody blade into the back of her head and she collapsed to the floor in an unconscious heap.

"Take him to the third spire," DuChaer ordered as he flicked his blade towards Beumont, sending droplets of blood splattering across the enraged and distraught man's face. "Don't harm him as we need him conscious when he is questioned."

"What about the girl?" the guard asked.

"What about her?" DuChaer responded.

"You said she would go with her father," the guard replied. "That there was room for one more."

"I did say there was room for one more," DuChaer grinned. "And I asked the man which one he would like to go with him. I never said either of them would actually be allowed to go with him, though. Did I not make that clear?" DuChaer chuckled. "Oh, dear, my mistake." He nudged the girl's body and rolled his eyes. "Do with her as you please, I could care less. Kill her, rape her, sell her to slavers on the Prime. Do all three if it makes you happy. She's a traitor's brat and her father must learn what happens to the brats of traitors."

"*You fucking bastard*!" Beumont roared as he was dragged from the room. "*I will kill you for this*!"

"Everyone says that, yet here I stand," DuChaer shrugged.

"Do you want to watch, my lord?" the guard asked as his men circled the girl.

"Oh, Helios, no!" DuChaer exclaimed. "Don't be disgusting! I am needed elsewhere. Do what you want then report to the garrison at Castle Quent. And don't take too long. We have momentum on our side and this war could be over by the end of the month, not the end of the year."

*

The passageway was dank and dark and Bella quickly felt she may have made a grand mistake, but she pushed forward until she reached the appointed meeting place.

"I honestly did not believe you would come, mistress," Stolt said, flanked by several guards. "And alone? You are either the bravest or stupidest woman I know. What's to stop me from killing you now or taking you hostage so I can end your husband's mad campaign?"

"DuChaer," Bella replied. "I will give you DuChaer."

"And why would I want that man?" Stolt grimaced. "The very thought of him makes me want to consult my physician so I know I have not contracted any disease."

"After what he did to Steward Beumont's family, DuChaer is the most wanted man on the Station," she replied. "More wanted than my husband or the Spiggots."

"The Spiggots?" Stolt exclaimed and even though the lighting was terrible in the passageway, Bella swore she saw the old steward's face pale.

"You didn't know?" Bella laughed. "Maybe I did make a mistake. I am unsure how you could not know they were behind this."

"I knew of Klipoline," Stolt admitted. "And assumed he had reached out to Alexis himself. But with the mention of the Spiggots then it all starts to make sense." Stolt waggled a finger at Bella. "Beware those two. They only have their own interests in mind, ever. At no point can you consider them allies."

"I consider no one an ally," Bella responded. "Not even my husband. The only person I trust on this station is my daughter. I come from the court of Thraen, Stolt, you forget that."

"Yes, yes, I did forget that," Stolt said. "I am getting addled in my old age. Hard to keep the lineages straight, what with all the nobility and royalty constantly interbreeding."

"I don't have time to go over family trees, Stolt," Bella snapped. "I am sure I have already been missed by now. Do you want DuChaer or not?"

"I do," Stolt nodded. "And what do you get in return for this?"

"Nothing except that vile man out of my life once and for all," Bella replied. "And you step away from the conflict, retire to your estate, and never lift a finger against the crown again."

Stolt studied her for a long while. "What are you planning, dear girl?"

"Mistress," Bella replied. "Address me with respect, Stolt, or the deal is off."

"Fine," Stolt replied. "You give me DuChaer and I will take the burden of having his blood on my hands. Not that it is a true burden, more of a heavy gift."

"Then you retire, give up your position in the meeting, and never speak ill of the crown ever again," Bella said.

"I am too old for this shaowshit anyway," Stolt said. "This was Beumont's fight, not mine. I am ready to rest, enjoy my riches, and be done with the politics and violence of the court."

"Good," Bella said, offering her hand. Stolt took it and she gripped his bony fingers between hers. "Double cross me, Stolt, and I will have your lineage wiped off this station. Not a single descendant of yours will live another week."

"Of course," Stolt said as he pryed his hand free and rubbed it. "I expect nothing less from a Thraen."

Bella caught the double meaning quickly, but chose to ignore it as she turned and made her way through the passageways and back up to the Surface.

*

The skid raced across the Surface of Station Aelon with several more following behind it. DuChaer drove in the lead, his eyes narrowed as he spied his target just ahead. He leaned over the handlebars and pushed the vehicle to its limits.

"Secure the area," DuChaer ordered when he finally brought the skid to a halt just inside the courtyard of another targeted steward's estate house. "If any of the servants give you grief, then kill them immediately. We do not have time to argue or negotiate. We slaughter the family and go. While also taking some of the more valuable possessions with us. We'd hate for looters to come by and steal anything."

His men chuckled and dismounted from their skids as well. They rushed towards the main entranceway and burst through the door.

"Well, she actually spoke true," Stolt said as he stepped into the courtyard with an entire regiment of his own men. Thirty well-armed guards quickly surrounded DuChaer. "You disappoint me, Gannot. I always thought you'd be harder to capture."

"Men!" DuChaer yelled as he looked toward the estate house.

Stolt cupped a hand to his ear and grinned. "I don't hear a response. Probably because it is hard to talk when your throat has been ripped open."

Stolt snapped his fingers and one of his men let out a long, loud whistle. Severed heads began to careen from the estate house's entranceway. They tumbled across the courtyard and several of Stolt's men stepped out of the way so the heads could roll right up to DuChaer.

"When Master Alexis hears about this, he will stop at nothing to have your guts torn from your body and sent flying out an airlock," DuChaer sneered. "While still attached to your body."

"Is that what he'd do?" Stolt asked. "What a grand idea! And here I was going to just have you beheaded. I say we go to the nearest airlock and put your plan into place."

DuChaer blanched and felt his legs weaken under him.

"I am still your son-in-law!" DuChaer shouted. "We are related, you old fool! What will your daughter think?"

"That she is finally free from a cruel monster like you!" Stolt spat. "Don't think I don't know how you have abused her and neglected her over the years! You have not produced a single heir! And I am actually grateful for that. To think I could have had grandchildren that shared your genes." Stolt spat on the ground. "The thought disgusts me. No, killing you will be easy to do."

"You wouldn't," DuChaer said. "Alexis will kill you when he—"

"Finds out? Yes, you said that," Stolt interrupted. "What you don't understand, Gannot, is that I plan on letting him watch. I may be old, but I do know a few things about showmanship still. It took some doing, but I have made it possible so not only the master gets to watch, the entire station will be viewing your death as well. It is funny that the last time there was a station wide broadcast it was an execution. Fitting."

He snapped his fingers.

"Bring him," Stolt ordered. "The port airlock will do nicely."

*

"This can't be happening," Alexis whispered as he watched the video screen in his quarters. He turned and looked over his shoulder at his wife who stood a few feet away. "Bella? Tell me this is not happening."

"I'm sorry, husband," Bella replied. "I do not know how they found him, but they did."

Alexis turned his attention back to the grainy video screen and the horrific image on it. There was no sound, only a slight hiss of static, which made the scene even worse as DuChaer was gutted and his intestines were pulled from his bloody abdomen. Men walked the guts into the airlock, setting them down in a long line before walking back and checking that DuChaer's restraints were tight as they could be to the pole that stood in the center of the airlock.

"That is where my father executed Langley," Alexis whispered. "They are treating Gannot as a traitor and not as a friend of the crown."

"This is beyond brutal," Bella said as she walked forward and rested her hand on her husband's shoulder. "The fool."

"The fool? What fool? Brother Gannot?" Alexis snapped. "How could you say such a thing?"

"No, no, not Gannot," Bella said. "Stolt. He is behind this, I can assure you. The man has gone too far. He should have stayed with his behind the scenes conniving. To show this to the Station? He's lost his old mind."

"Stolt?" Alexis asked, then narrowed his eyes and glared at the screen. "Yes, of course it is. He has always hated Brother Gannot with such a passion. Now he wants me to suffer. Well, I will not bow down to that bastard! My father always said he was the one I could trust the least on this station!"

"But what about Beumont?" Bella asked. "You hold him in the third spire. Is he not the face of the steward's revolt?"

"We both know how Stolt works," Alexis said. "He put Beumont up to it."

"And surely he must die as well," Bella said. "For the safety of the crown."

"No, no, he will be allowed to live," Alexis said, his eyes glued to the brutality on the screen. "He will live in that small cell for the rest of his life."

"But, husband, you cannot—"

Alexis held up his hand and pointed at the screen. The men had left DuChaer alone as lights started to whirl. If there had been sound, they would have heard the warning claxons blaring as the inside airlock door sealed and the outer door was opened.

Alexis turned his head at the last moment as every single organ from DuChaer's body was sucked into space. The master was green in the face as he stood and looked at his wife.

"I will keep Beumont alive so I can torment him when I feel the need," Alexis said.

He swallowed hard then walked away, headed for the main door.

"Where are you going, Alexis?" Bella called.

The master glanced over his shoulder and for the first time, Bella was scared of her husband.

"To the third spire," Alexis said. "Right now I feel that need."

Bella waited until the door had shut and sealed before she collapsed into a chair. She had expected her husband to break down, to collapse with grief. At no point had she thought he would harden and turn to dark cruelty as his way of coping with the loss of DuChaer. She knew in that instant that the small plans she had made would need to be widened considerably or she would lose it all.

CHAPTER SIX

The Spiggots sat there at the great table, Deran's feet up on the surface, so reminiscent of DuChaer that Alexis had to blink several times to realize he was not looking at his late companion. He also had to blink to keep the tears back, a common occurrence since the brutal execution only a few months prior.

"We have only five stewards left to deal with, sire," Herlen stated. "Bobdon, Claesch, Whittingson, Grouff, and Deckson."

"Chobaen has assured me he can take Bobdon and Grouff, while we may consider negotiating a peaceful end for the others," Daren said. "We already have many stewardships to fill and, I fear, too few worthy candidates. Some experienced nobility will not be a bad thing for us to deal with."

"Can we trust them not to turn on me again?" Alexis asked.

"No, sire, we can trust no one except those present in this room," Deran replied. "Myself, my father, and you, sire."

"Are you forgetting someone, Deran?" Bella asked from her seat next to Alexis.

"My apologies," Deran said. "I always consider you and his highness one and the same. I meant no disrespect."

"And the mistress takes none," Alexis said, waving his hand. "She knows that we are of the same mind. But in the future, please see her as an individual. I would not have made it through these difficult times without her."

"It is a mistake I will not make again, sire," Daren said.

"I should think not," Bella frowned. "You are new to our struggle, where I have been surviving it for the last couple of years. I would think even lowdeckers, such as yourselves, would have considered what we endured as hardships."

"We like to consider ourselves Prime men, mistress," Herlen said. "And there are hardships aplenty down on Helios, believe you me."

"But you had a choice," Bella glared. "We did not."

"No bickering, please," Alexis sighed. "I have a horrible headache and am not in the mood."

"Of course, sire," Herlen said. "I will remain quiet."

"No, no, I need to hear your report," Alexis responded. "The mistress will stay silent while I listen. We will both have our ears open so we can learn from your counsel."

"Alexis," Bella groused.

"Now hush, wife," Alexis said. "You are not helping the situation."

Bella's mouth snapped shut and she leaned back in her chair, her eyes burning with controlled fury.

"We have been at war with the stewards for near a year now," Deren stated. "And for the first time I can see the end. It will be glorious for us, sire. The spoils are ours, and all we will need do is make sure the passengers fall in line once the full balance of power has shifted."

"What of Stolt?" Alexis asked. "You did not name that man in your list of holdouts."

"Stolt is of no concern," Herlen grinned. "He has been thoroughly hobbled."

"By hobbled you mean you butchered his entire family," Bella stated. "His children, grandchildren, nieces, nephews, the whole lot, isn't that right?"

"The master wished him to feel pain and remorse like none had ever felt pain before," Deran replied. "He has felt that and so much more. The old man is broken and hides in his estate house like a withered old hermit."

"He is in his estate house?" Alexis asked as he leaned forward. "Just waiting there? I thought the man would still be on the run."

"As we thought he would be also, sire," Herlen said. "But all reports have him at his home for the past couple of months. I believe he is just waiting there to die."

"Hmmmm," Alexis said. "Maybe this is our opportunity to help him with that."

"How do you mean, sire?" Deran asked. "You want him killed? It can easily be arranged. I'll send a troop of men in and he will be dead by tomorrow evening."

"No, I do not want his end to come at the hands of strangers," Alexis said. "I believe I will accompany those men and do it myself."

The Spiggots both looked shocked and they turned to the mistress for help.

"Mistress, maybe you can dissuade the master from this course," Herlen said. "He should not leave Castle Quent. Not yet. The Station, especially the Surface, is still too dangerous."

"We need our men focused on the holdouts' soldiers, not on protecting the master," Deran added. He focused on Alexis once again and held his hands out, palms up. "I plead with you, sire, not to be rash with thoughts of personal revenge."

"Rash?" Alexis laughed. "My dearest Brother Gannot was murdered seven months ago. I have been very patient, I believe. Now the time has come for me to act, not wait. We will depart for Stolt's estate in the morning. Which sector is it again?"

"Kirke," Deran answered.

"Kirke," Alexis smiled. "Sector Kirke. I know the area well. Decent soil in Kirke. One of the few places that can actually grow produce well enough to feed most of its passengers in the Decks below." He looked at Deran and smiled. "When Stolt is gone, it shall be yours, my friend."

Bella whipped her head about and glared at her husband while Deran sat back in his chair, his feet hitting the floor with a smack, and gasped.

"You honor me, sire!" Deran exclaimed.

"Now you are being rash," Bella said as she stood up. "You should not be handing out stewardships, sectors, or estates until this war is over and won."

"Sit down, wife," Alexis said.

"I will not!" Bella growled. "I am returning to our quarters. You will find me there when you return and we can discuss this matter in private."

"The matter has been discussed," Alexis said as he rolled his eyes. "When I return to our quarters we will discuss other matters, such as our daughter's education."

"Our daughter's education...?" Bella asked. "I have no idea what you mean by that. She already has excellent tutors."

"Yes, but *station* tutors," Alexis replied. "All they do is fill her head with facts and figures. She needs a true education that only life can provide."

"What in Helios's name are you babbling about?" Bella asked. "You are not making sense, Alexis."

"If I am not making sense, it is because I have no intention to here," Alexis responded with a soft chuckle. "But it I will make sense when we discuss this matter later in our quarters. Go ahead and leave us, wife. We have much more to talk about."

Bella shook with anger, but she kept it under control as she gracefully turned and left the great hall. The three men watched her go and when the doors had closed, they returned to their business at hand.

"Stolt will die by my long blade," Alexis stated.

"You do not want him to die the same way DuChaer passed?" Deran asked. "There would be some symmetry and poetry to that end."

"No," Alexis said. "Brother Gannot's death will not be tarnished by Stolt. While the execution was horrible, it was grand and the entire station watched it happen. Stolt will get a simple death by my hand and not some spectacle. He lives alone now so he will die alone now."

Alexis stood up and clapped his hands.

"This will be wonderful! I haven't left the Castle in some time!"

The Spiggots stood as well, and both bowed to the master.

"Oh, Helios, stop that," Alexis said. "You two are my closest friends. When we are alone, we are equals, just as Brother Gannot and I were. Understood?"

"You honor us, sire," Herlen replied.

"More than you could possibly know," Deran added.

"Well, you deserve the honor." Alexis smiled. "You have delivered on every promise you have made."

*

"Master, if I may!" Deran called out from down the passageway.

Alexis, flanked by several royal guards, turned and cocked his head.

"Yes, Brother Deran?" he asked. "Is there something we forgot to discuss?"

"Well, there is one thing, sire," Deran said as he hurried up to the master. He glanced at the guards. "But it is of a private nature."

"Private nature?" Alexis smiled. "Sounds intriguing." He waved both hands at the guards. "Leave us. I'll be in Steward Spiggot's capable hands."

The guards hesitated, but only for a second, then marched down the passageway towards the royal quarters.

"What troubles you, Brother Deran?" Alexis asked.

"Oh, nothing troubles me, sire," Deran said. "I am more worried about your troubles."

"My troubles? Those are vast and many," Alexis said with a laugh. "And certainly not anything you need to take on for yourself. A master's life is one of work and burden."

"Yes, but I wanted to extend an invitation, if I might," Deran said.

He looked up and down the passageway, double-checking they were alone.

Then he placed his hand on the master's arm.

"I know how special DuChaer was to you, sire," Deran said. "He was more than just a friend and confidant. It was easy to see. Or, easy for me to see."

He stepped in a little closer.

"I would like to be that person for you now, sire," Deran said. "If you will let me."

Alexis watched the man carefully, but did not ask him to step back or to remove his hand.

"If I have been too forward, or misunderstood the signals between us, then you have my deepest apologies," Deran said. "I mean no offense, and would never besmirch your reputation."

"Besmirch my reputation?" Alexis laughed. "We have all but defeated the meeting of stewards and restored the monarchy to power. My reputation is above being besmirched, Deran."

Alexis placed his hand over Deran's and smiled.

"I believe I have a place in my life for another dear friend," Alexis said as he squeezed Deran's hand. "But let us discuss this topic another time. For now, I must tend to my family and prepare for the journey tomorrow. You understand, of course."

"Of course," Deran nodded. "And I thank you for your kindness."

"It is the least I can do, considering the kindness you have brought me." Alexis smiled. "Now go and make your preparations. The journey to Sector Kirke is a full day and a half by skid. You'll need to pack and make sure there are provisions for us and the guards."

"Yes, sire," Deran said, finally removing his hand from the master's arm. He bowed low and swept his arm out. "I am but your humble servant."

"And friend," Alexis added.

"And friend," Deran said as he stood tall. "Your most honored friend."

*

"I will not let you send my daughter down to the Prime!" Bella yelled.

"Keep your voice down, woman," Alexis replied, his own voice filled with boredom. "And it is not your decision to make. I am Master of Station Aelon and if I say the heir to the crown is to spend time on the Prime, then she is to spend time on the Prime. End of discussion."

"It is far from the end of the discussion," Bella snarled at him. "There is no discussion! If you send our daughter to the planet then I will kill you in your sleep, Alexis! That is a promise I am willing to make this very second!"

"Oh, stop with the melodrama," Alexis said. "It is not like you will be parted. I am sending you down with her."

"You are...what?" Bella gasped as she stumbled back and plopped into a chair. "You are...? What is this, Alexis? Banishment?"

"What? Banishment? Helios, no!" Alexis exclaimed. "This is for your and Alexis's safety! The Spiggots have more influence and control on Helios than they do here in the Station. I want you two to be as safe as possible while this war ends. There may only be five more stewards to contend with, but that does not mean they won't have their spies and sympathizers working to undermine my progress. With you on the planet, I can focus on establishing the crown's supreme rule once again."

"But the estate is wild down there," Bella argued. "Surely we'd be safer here."

"I do not think so," Alexis said. "I fear Stolt's men are everywhere. Except on the Prime. The man has always hated the Prime and only set foot down there a handful of times. He has no agents on the estate. Up here? Who knows how many?"

"But you are leaving to execute him," Bella said. "He won't be a threat anymore."

"He will always be a threat," Alexis sighed. "We killed his immediate family and heirs, but there are sure to be cousins and second cousins that will want to lay claim to his legacy and fortune. This war has served two purposes, Bella: one to restore me to power. and an unfortunate second of stirring a honey wasps' nest. Those honey wasps will take a long time to settle down."

"How long?" Bella asked.

"A year? Perhaps two?" Alexis mused. "Hard to say. But I promise to bring both of you home as soon as possible. And, of course, I will join you as often as I can. You know how I love the Prime."

"Then maybe you should take Alexis down there," Bella said. "I could rule as your regent. It would keep her safe and take a target off of your back."

"Don't be absurd," Alexis chuckled. "We have fought so hard these months so I can be master where I am supposed to be, not from down on the Prime with a surrogate in place. No, the decision has been made and there is no changing my mind."

Bella had a million responses, threats, and curses, but all she said was, "How long before we must leave?"

"Oh, a couple months at the soonest," Alexis said. "I need to put these last stewards down before I can be assured that my place is solid and also so when I do send for you, there will be a station for you to come back to. So, no hurry at all."

"No...no hurry at all," Bella echoed.

"We'll tell Alexis when I return," Alexis stated. "I want to do it together so it looks like we are unified on this decision, so please keep this between us until then."

"Yes, of course, husband," Bella said. "We must look unified for our daughter's sake."

"Exactly!" Alexis beamed. "For our daughter's sake!"

*

The teacup shook in his hand as he brought it to his lips. Several drops spilled from the rim and dripped down his chin, forcing him to use both hands just to steady the cup enough to get a small sip. Once his parched mouth was wetted, Stolt carefully set the teacup down on the table, ever afraid he'd drop and break it. It was the last of a set, and he didn't know what else he would drink from, since all that were left were the servants' dishes.

Although he figured those would do, since the servants had left him two weeks earlier.

Alone in his house, Stolt had been forced to fend for himself, something he hadn't had to do in many, many decades.

He leaned back in his chair and closed his eyes, which seemed to be his pastime of late, as his strength ebbed daily.

"Stolt!"

The old steward's eyes remained closed.

"Stolt!"

That did cause his eyelids to flicker, and he struggled to open them fully, having been close to falling into a deep nap.

"*Stolt*! Show yourself!"

Steward Stolt knew that voice; he knew it well, and he was more than surprised that he was hearing it on his own estate.

The man struggled to stand, and nearly toppled over once he was upright. With a crooked, defeated gait, he shuffled over to the wide window of his office and pulled the drapes aside.

"Alexis," Stolt mumbled. "Come for me, have you?"

"I have come for you, Stolt!" Alexis shouted from the courtyard.

Stolt rolled his eyes at the predictability of the man. Although he had expected his arrival weeks before. It just proved to him once again that the master's capacity for laziness and late timing was never to be underestimated.

"Stolt! Come out here, you coward!"

"I'm right here, moron," Stolt croaked as he tapped at the window. "Keep your frilly undergarments on, you flip."

The men in the courtyard, including Alexis, turned at the sound of the rapping at the window. Alexis grinned and pointed and several guards rushed towards the front of the estate house and kicked in the door.

"Oh, for Helios's sake, it was unlocked," Stolt grumbled as he turned from the window and shuffled past his desk to a mirror that hung on the wall.

He frowned at his appearance and had wished he had bathed and made himself presentable that morning instead of just wandering the rooms before tea. He did what he could with the wisps of grey hair on his head, and tugged at his tunic and robe.

"If this is how I go, then this is how I go," Stolt said to himself just before the office door burst open.

"Girard Stolt!" a guard announced as he stomped up to Stolt. "You are under arrest for treason against the crown, and for instigating a revolt and rebellion against Alexis the Second, Master of Station Aelon."

"You did not need to say the last part, fool," Stolt said. "Treason covers rebellion and revolt."

The guard looked confused for a second, but recovered quickly and motioned for the old man to be taken.

"Master Alexis has already passed sentence, which will be carried out immediately in your courtyard," the guard said.

That did surprise Stolt and he frowned.

"I am not to be taken to an airlock?" he asked.

"No, you are not," the guard said. "There will be no more executions using the airlocks on this station ever again. This has been ordered by Master Alexis in honor of the fallen hero known as Gannot DuChaer."

"The fallen hero?" Stolt gasped. "The man must be kidding. Please tell me he is kidding."

"The legacy of Gannot DuChaer is not a kidding matter," the guard replied, but Stolt could see on the sour faces of some of the guards that not all believed that to be true.

"Fine," Stolt nodded. "Then take me to Alexis. I will face the brat one last time before I die and go to see Helios."

"Your kind will never be allowed to see Helios," the guard spat. "A traitor to a master is a traitor to the Dear Parent."

"Oh, save me the dogma and let's get this over with," Stolt sighed. "I've waited long enough."

The guards marched him through the estate house and out into the courtyard where a smiling Alexis stood, flanked by the Spiggots.

"Cousin Stolt," Alexis said. "It is such a pleasure to see you again, even if our time together will be brief. And bloody."

"I hear you are looking to canonize DuChaer," Stolt said. "Good luck with that."

"Canonize? Hardly," Alexis said. "I know the High Guardian would never allow that. Nor would I seek to have it done. I merely have honored my dear friend by not allowing you the same death as he."

"I was mocking you, Alexis," Stolt said. "I did not think you were actually going to canonize the flip."

Alexis rushed forward and slapped the old man so hard that two of his teeth flew from his mouth and clattered to the paving stones of the courtyard.

"Your days of mocking me end now," Alexis growled. "It is my turn to mock you, you worthless coward. Look at you." Alexis stepped back and spread his arms. "You were once a great man, Cousin Stolt. You held power and you sat at the right hand of a master. Sure, everyone knew you had ambitions greater than your place, but that was what made you so effective. Then you went and put those ambitions to work. and now where has it gotten you?"

Alexis turned and looked at the Spiggots.

"Brother Deran? Where has it gotten Cousin Stolt?"

"Nowhere, it would seem," Deran replied.

"*Brother* Deran?" Stolt asked. "That didn't take long." Stolt clapped his hands weakly before the guards that held him slapped them back to his sides. Stolt looked nonplussed and continued. "Well done, Spiggots. You managed to worm your way into the influence of a master, finally."

"I do not know what you are inferring, Stolt," Herlen said. "We are merely here to serve the Master of Station Aelon, as is our Helios given duty."

Stolt made loud gagging noises then burst out into laughter.

"Oh, you will be serving him, alright," Stolt said, once he had calmed down. "You'll be serving him up on a platter while you feast." Stolt looked Alexis in the eye. "Know your enemies, Alexis. They may seem like friends at first."

"Yes, you would be very familiar with that ploy, wouldn't you Cousin Stolt?" Alexis sneered. "And your words have no affect on me. My father warned me about you, and now here we stand, the truth revealed. Are you ready to die, Cousin?"

"I have always been ready to die," Stolt replied. "As I have always been ready to serve this station. Mark my words, Alexis, I have always done what I have felt was right for the Station. Those two only know how to do what is right for them. They will turn on you, or at the very least, throw you under the skid as soon as their ruse is discovered. You see friends, but I see your final demise. Too bad I will not be here to witness your true fall."

"Are you quite finished?" Alexis asked, honestly bored with the old man. "Can I cut your head off now?"

One more time, Stolt was surprised. "You? You will be my executioner?" He swallowed hard and looked about. "Can I request someone else? Perhaps a man more used to wielding a blade?"

"I am an excellent bladesman!" Alexis snapped. "You know that, Stolt!"

"Oh, stop whining, child!" Stolt snapped back. "I know you can handle yourself with a blade! But you have never executed a man before!" He shook his head and sighed. "It must be in one clean motion. It is not about thrust and parry, but about strength and focus. Neither of which you possess."

"If you want my blade to be focused then perhaps angering me further is not such a grand idea." Alexis smirked. "If I am upset then I may have to hack away at your neck until that deceitful head of yours finally falls off."

"Sire, we should hurry this along so we are not forced to stay here for the night," Deran suggested. "As comfortable as this house may look, it is bad luck to sleep in a condemned man's home."

"You know nothing of bad luck," Stolt said. "But you will learn."

"Fine. Take him over there," Alexis ordered as he pointed to a low bench next to a silent and still fountain.

Murky water filled the fountain and Stolt saw his distorted image in it before he was forced to his knees, his arms jerked up behind his back, and his neck pressed to the bench. He didn't struggle, he didn't fight, only shifted his head so that as much of his neck was exposed as possible.

"My blade," Alexis said and a guard hurried to the royal skid, a full sized one that could hold several people, then hurried back with the long blade in hand.

"Your father may have had issues with rage, but he was never cruel like you, Alexis," Stolt said.

"That I can quickly argue wasn't quite the case, Cousin," Alexis replied as he held his blade up so he could see his own reflection in the metal. "He knew plenty about cruelty. As do you. It was cruelty that killed Brother Gannot. There is no other way to explain such a horrific act."

Alexis stepped up close to the bench and hefted the long blade over his head.

"Do you think I am cruel, Cousin? Do you really? If I was cruel, then I would find a much more gruesome way for you to die. When I bring down this blade it will be mercy that I show you, not cruelty."

"Say what you must to yourself so you sleep at night, Alexis," Stolt said. "I have made my peace with Helios and I am ready."

"Good." Alexis smiled. "So am I."

He brought the blade down hard and fast, but his aim was not true and he quickly learned that Stolt was right considering the difficulty of taking a man's head from his neck. Blood poured from the old man's shoulder as Alexis wrenched the blade free and lifted it once again. Stolt struggled not to cry out, but the agony was too intense and he started to whimper like a wounded animal.

"Hold him still!" Alexis barked at his guards. "You let him move! That is why I missed!"

The guards doubled their grip as Alexis tried once more. And failed. Stolt screamed as the blade dug into his spine, but did not fully sever it.

"I said hold him!" Alexis roared.

He lifted the blade and then brought it down, again and again, as he struggled to hack the old steward's head off. When Stolt's screams finally stopped, Alexis knew the man was gone, even though a couple of tendons refused to give, and still kept ahold of the head they had faithfully served for so many decades.

"Burn it," Alexis said, his the entire front covered in blood. "Burn the old wretch. Leave his scorched corpse in the courtyard for all to see who dare visit here."

"But, sire, if this is to be my new—" Daren said then stopped when he glimpsed the madness in the master's eyes. "Yes, yes, of course." He turned to the guards. "You heard the master! Burn the damned body! *Now*!"

The guards grabbed the body and dragged it to the center of the courtyard, its head bouncing and bumping along as the two tendons still refused to let go.

BOOK II

*

The night sky was bright and full, but with that slight flicker that the shield created. Bella didn't care either way as her mind was lost in the thought of having to live on Aelon Prime instead of the Station. She worried that the excuse of safety was only a veiled attempt to hide the fact she was being exiled.

She doubted Alexis was the one that had first suggested the idea and was more than confident that one or both of the Spiggots were pushing for it.

The Spiggots.

Bella was quickly figuring out that Alexis, in his grief over DuChaer, had found surrogates that would help indulge his childish whims and irresponsible ways. She knew the war was almost over, but she doubted the conflict was anywhere near done.

She leaned against the railing of the observatory and looked out at the vast expanse of land that surrounded Castle Quent. Land that had been created by ancients long dead when they were forced to escape the planet Helios. Crops of various types, pens for grendts and shaows, small dwellings for the foremen who oversaw the working of the Surface—it all seemed like it would be easy for her to adjust to a life down on Helios.

But the planet was not a place you could walk through the grass with your shoes off and raise your face to the light of the Helios star. The planet was a dreary world of Vape clouds and poisonous air. It was a hard land that could kill you in an instant—if the people didn't.

Miners and breen farmers, and the rough settlers that went with them.

Not to mention being under the constant eye of The Way. And their control. As much as the masters of all the Stations wanted to believe they were the rulers of the System, without the leave of The Way, nothing would happen. Vape would not be allowed to leave the planet, and breen would be in very short supply, since it was extremely difficult to grow on the Surfaces of the stations.

Bella did not kid herself that she was going to be anything less than a prisoner. She knew her husband did not see it that way, and because of his amazing ability for denial, couldn't even comprehend her interpretation. Yet a prisoner she would be; her walls the landscape, her cell the ceaseless boredom.

Alexis was not a cruel man, Bella knew that, but he was not a mature man. His emotions and thoughts were like those of a teenager, always about self-indulgence and never about duty. He would have been a great breen farmer, since his love for the Prime and land on the planet was even stronger than his daughter's, but Bella knew the man would never have had the patience to wait out crop fluctuations and Vape storm repairs. The life on the land that Alexis always pined for was nothing more than another of his dreams.

And Bella was terrified she was about to be lost in that dream.

She had to focus on her daughter if she planned on staying sane. Focus on raising Alexis to be the ruler she was destined to be. Bella knew the girl loved the Prime, what with all the adventure it gave to a child. The skid racing, the boiling seas, the hardcase population. Alexis reveled in the entire way of life.

Her daughter would be Bella's focus; her daughter would be her way of keeping her sense of self, her sense of royalty, her sense of purpose.

Bella gave the nightscape one last look before turning towards the stairs that led down from the observatory, past the jail cells for the more privileged prisoners, and to the royal quarters. She had never figured out why one of the old masters had decided that the third spire should be home to the observatory as well as the jail cells. Or why the royal quarters were housed so close.

It was a bit of history she wanted to look into, but knew she no longer had the time to satisfy such an unimportant whim.

She wound her way down the stairs and was surprised to see light coming from under one of the cell doors. Bella hesitated on the steps, only a couple of feet from where the door was recessed into the wall of the spire, and listened. She thought she heard praying, but wasn't sure. It could have been the mumblings of a prisoner who had long since lost his mind due to the constant confinement.

Her shoes scraped against the rough stairs as she started to leave and a soft voice called out.

"Who's there?" a man asked. "Who has come to taunt and mock me in my time of crisis?"

Bella knew that voice, but couldn't quite place it.

"Hello?" she whispered. "Who is that?"

"Mistress?"

Bella hesitated.

"Mistress? Is that you?" the man asked, his voice much closer to the door as if he had his lips pressed right up against it. "It is I, Steward, or former Steward, Jackull Beumont."

"Beumont?" Bella said. "I had assumed you were executed already, despite my husband's cruel promise."

"Not so lucky, your highness," Beumont replied. "It appears I will be held here indefinitely."

"Surely there will be a trial," Bella said. "You cannot be held without a trial now that the meeting of stewards is assembling again."

"This is war time, your highness," Beumont responded. "The rule of law does not apply and all writs are suspended, except those the master deems important to the cause of protecting the monarchy."

Bella looked down the stairway, thinking she heard voices. She listened intently, but again, no sounds were heard.

"Mistress, are you still there?"

"I am, Beumont," Bella responded. "I was distracted by a sound, but it has passed."

"All I have are sounds," Beumont sighed. "There are no windows in this cell and the only portal to the outside world is that slide hatch in the door where they give me my food."

Bella looked down at the door and saw the slide hatch he spoke of. She reached for the clasp, hesitated, then reached again and undid it. Slowly, with butterflies in her stomach, she slid the hatch open. The mistress had no idea why she did it, but the impulse was too great to resist. Two bleary eyes appeared and blinked against the low light of the stairwell.

"Do they not provide you with illumination?" Bella asked. "You act as if you haven't seen light in some time."

"I have a handful of candles," Beumont laughed dryly. "But the matches I was given are damp and spoiled. I believe they knew that when they handed them to me. Another cruel joke in this charade before I am killed."

"Have they said when you are to die?" Bella asked, crouching down so she could look the man in the eye. And what beautiful, soulful eyes they were. "I do not mean to offend you with the question, it is just that I am no longer in the loop of information here at court."

"I have been told nothing, other than to keep my mouth shut and stand in the corner when they bring my meals," Beumont said. "As if I could reach through this hatch and do any damage." His eyes disappeared, replaced by his hand, which could only reach out to the mid-forearm before becoming wedged. "See?"

"I see," Bella said as she stared at his cracked and bloody nails. "This is not right."

She clamped her hands over her mouth at the surprising utterance. She had not meant to say that out loud; she had not even known she was thinking it.

"It is not right, no," Beumont agreed. "To condemn a man to indefinite imprisonment when I have done nothing but look out for what is best for the Station. I lost my wife and daughter for this cause and every day I stay alive, stay out of Helios's grace, I dishonor their memory. If only your husband would kill me and get it over with."

He withdrew his hand and his eyes returned. They had a desperate, pleading look, but also held great nobility and strength. Bella hadn't see eyes like that in a very long time. Certainly not in her husband's face.

"I am to be imprisoned as well," Bella said. "Although a planet will be my cell, so I cannot compare my situation to yours, I'm afraid."

"You are being sent down to Helios?" Beumont asked. "Why? What have you done?"

"I have done nothing but my duties," Bella replied. "My daughter will accompany me. Alexis says it is for her protection and education, just as his time on Helios was for him."

Beumont's eyes crinkled as he started to laugh. Bella frowned and almost shut the hatch.

"No, no, I am sorry," Beumont apologized. "It is just that the Spiggots are so transparent that it is almost comical. At least DuChaer welcomed the challenge of having you around. Those two swindlers aren't even up to that. It is only a matter of time before their lack of intelligence or subtlety gets them killed."

"More war," Bella sighed. "The station cannot handle it all over again."

"This one has not ended yet," Beumont said. "Yes, many stewards have sworn allegiance to Master Alexis once again, but very few actually mean it. The Spiggots will soon be the new targets, just as DuChaer was. Then they will come for the master and he won't be so lucky to keep his title or his life as he had before."

"How do you know this?" Bella asked.

"The stewards have planned far ahead, your highness," Beumont admitted. "We knew there was the chance that the Station would be taken back by the monarchy. We also knew it would only be a matter of time before some new sycophant wormed his way into your husband's graces. He is very susceptible to flattery, isn't he?"

"He is at that," Bella said. Then a thought struck her and she felt as if the stairs had gone out from under her. She sat down hard and pressed her face to the door. "What of my daughter? What of Alexis?"

"That I cannot say," Beumont replied. "I would be lying to you if I said she would be safe. Being the only direct heir to the crown, the temptation would be far too great to resist."

"The temptation...?" Bella asked, already knowing the answer.

"To kill her," Beumont stated. "With her gone then the monarchy would be so easy to dismantle. She is beloved by the passengers, as they see a spirit in her of monarchs long since passed, and that makes her dangerous. It makes you dangerous as well."

"How do you mean?"

"The passengers adore you also," Beumont said. "They see you as a suffering mistress trapped in a marriage to a fool. And you are the mother of the first female heir. That is not something the people take lightly."

"I never really knew," Bella whispered. "I have been so busy here at court trying to keep DuChaer's claws off my husband, and now the Spiggots', that I have never taken the time to walk amongst the passengers and truly get to know them."

"And now you will not get that chance at all," Beumont said. "Unless you count the miners and farmers and other roughnecks of the Prime."

"Perhaps I should," Bella said then shook her head and moved away from the door. "And perhaps I should keep my mouth closed. I...I do not know why I have confided in you."

"Because we all need someone to confide in, mistress," Beumont said. "And I am condemned, so talking to me is safe. Soon I will be gone and only Helios will know what has transpired here."

"Only Helios..." Bella mused then started to walk away from the cell door. "Thank you for the conversation, Beumont."

"Jackull. Please, call me Jackull."

"Jackull," Bella smiled. "I thank you for opening my mind to the possibilities. I was lost for a while, but now I believe I see Helios's path for me. And for my daughter. I have you to thank for that."

"Mistress?" Beumont asked, confused. "I am not sure I have done anything of the sort."

"You have, you have," Bella said. "Fear not your future, Jackull. I believe in my heart that it is not as dark and gloomy as you suspect."

"I do hope you are right, your highness," Beumont said. "And thank you for being kind enough to speak with me. A small bit of humanity goes a long way these days."

Bella took another couple of steps then stopped. She hurried back up to the door and pushed her hand through the hatch. Beumont took her hand in his and their fingers intertwined. There was a heat and spark from the contact of skin and Bella smiled, glad in more ways than she could express.

She pulled her hand back and peered into the hatch once more.

"We are not insane," she said. "Mad people have forced us to think we are for years. But I know the truth, I can feel it. Can you?"

"Yes, your highness," Beumont said. "In the touch of your hand, I felt Helios speaking to me."

Bella gasped and held her hands to her chest.

"As have I!" she exclaimed. "This was not chance that I happened along this stairway this night. I was put here and you were put here, all so we could save this station together."

"Yes," Beumont whispered. "And perhaps save ourselves."

"And perhaps save ourselves," Bella echoed, her chest swelling with a sudden feeling of longing and energy. "I will see to it you are not killed or left here to rot, Jackull, but you must swear to me one thing."

"Mistress, I do not know if you have the—"

"Swear to me and I will worry about power," Bella stated.

"I will swear to anything you want, mistress," Beumont said.

"Swear you will help me protect my daughter and see to it that she wears the crown of Station Aelon," Bella said. "Swear to me that you will do everything you can to secure her position in history and in the glory of Helios."

"I swear it," Beumont replied instantly. "I do not know why, but I do. Helios has spoken to us, through us, and we are here to do the Dear Parent's bidding."

"Yes. Yes, we are," Bella said. "Thank you, Jackull."

"No. Thank you, mistress," Beumont responded.

"Bella."

"Mistress?"

"My name is Bella," Bella said. "Bella Herlect Teirmont, Mistress of Station Aelon and Minoress of Station Thraen. But when we are together, you will only call me Bella."

"Will we be together?" Beumont asked.

"We will," Bella stated with such certainty that there was no argument.

"Then I look forward to that time...Bella."

She did not respond as the sound of the door at the bottom of the stairs as they were thrown open echoed up the stairwell. Men began to shout and call up to the cells, their voices filled with malevolence and spite.

"Hide," Beumont hissed. "Return to the observatory before they find you speaking to me."

Bella turned and fled, racing up the stairs back to the observatory as she heard cell doors thrown open and guards shouting at the wards within.

*

Those that filled the great hall had the looks of men and women yanked from dreams and plunged into nightmares. Which, it being the middle of the night, was closer to the truth than the sleep addled brains could actually realize.

"These are the men?" Alexis asked as he took his seat at the head of the hall. "These are the last of the holdouts?"

"Yes, sire," Deran replied as he stood a couple of feet away from the stewards that had been dragged into the great hall in heavy chains. "And the ones behind them are the stewards we have kept imprisoned in the third spire."

"Traitors all," Herlen spat from the other side of the shackled men. "They deserve no mercy, sire."

"No, I suppose they do not," Alexis agreed from his seat. He looked at the men then looked past them and smiled. "Bella! Wife! There you are. I was told you were not in our quarters and I grew worried."

"I was in the observatory when I heard the commotion," Bella said as she strode to the end of the hall and joined her husband in the seat next to his.

She looked at the line of men before her then at the second line. Her eyes hesitated for a brief second on Beumont, taking in his ragged appearance and unhealthy posture. When he met her gaze she looked quickly away, for fear her face would betray the sudden feelings that he stirred. Not since she was a young woman had a man looked at her with such longing and need. She chalked it up to his desperation to be free, but down inside she knew it was the connection they had made in those few minutes of conversation.

"Are these the condemned traitors then?" Bella asked. "Have you decided on their times of execution? Is this why you have called the court together at this late, late hour?"

"I have come from Sector Kirke and must announce that Steward Stolt has met his end." Alexis grinned. "The old grendt lost his head, I am afraid."

"He went mad?" Bella asked.

"No, I cut his head off," Alexis replied, his grin widening. "And it was not an easy task, I must say. Remind me to up the wages for the executioner corps."

"Stolt is dead?" Bella asked.

"He is," Alexis said. "And as I was returning, I received word that the last stewards—Bobdon, Claesch, Whittingson, Grouff, and Deckson—the pitiful men you see before us, were captured by the royal guard, using the intelligence received by the Spiggots."

The master nodded and the Spiggots nodded in return.

"I did not want to drag this business out a second longer so have decided to pass judgment this instant on these traitorous beasts."

"Might I make a suggestion before you do, husband?" Bella asked.

"Please, my love, please suggest away," Alexis said.

"Do not kill them," she said, her face overtaken by a grin so wicked, that some in attendance made the sign of the X across themselves, and even their neighbors.

"Not kill them?" Alexis asked. "Why in Helios's name not?"

"Because then they have a chance to be martyred," Bella stated. "I have seen it all before on Station Thraen when my father removed the gatekeepers. Don't make his mistake."

"Oh, I would never stoop so low as to act like Thraen," Alexis said, completely forgetting that his wife was a Thraen. "They are frilly animals that rut and eat instead of rule."

Bella stayed silent as Alexis thought the idea through.

"Then what shall I do with them?" he wondered. "Where shall I put them? Forever in the third spire? Conscripted to work on the Lower Decks doing the most menial jobs that even the lowdeckers won't do?"

"Exile them to the lease holdings on Thraen Prime," Bella said. "Just as our beloved Brother DuChaer had been exiled."

"Sire, I would not advise—" Deran started.

"Hold on, Brother Deran," Alexis said as he held up his hand. "I think my wife is on to something here." He pursed his lips and furrowed his brow. "It has a certain amount of poetry to it, don't you think?"

The Spiggots remained quiet, their eyes flicking from master to mistress and back.

"But I do not think it safe to send them to Thraen Prime," Alexis said. "Too much opportunity for escape or help from the Thraens." Bella started to speak, as the Spiggots started to smile, but all stopped as the master continued. "No, I will exile them to the royal estate on Aelon Prime where it will be easier to keep an eye on them. Not that they will be housed inside the compound, mind you. No, they will live out with the workers, because they will be workers."

Alexis stood and held his arms out.

"Let it be decreed that these men, from this moment forward, are exiled to Aelon Prime where they will live out their lives performing hard labor in the breen fields! If they refuse to do the work expected of a field worker, then they will be sent to the mines and ordered to the bottom most level until they die. I have spoken and this is law!"

The Spiggots each glared at the mistress for a split second then looked up at the master.

"A marvelous idea, sire," Deran said.

"You are a truly inspired leader, your highness," Herlen added.

"The inspiration was all my wife's," Alexis said as he reached down and took Bella's hand, kissing the back softly before he returned it to the arm of her chair. "And the reason I acted is because she will be present on the Prime, as well. I trust her to keep these traitors in line. There will be no rest for any of them, as long as Mistress Bella is there to oversee their exile."

"No rest," Bella whispered as her eyes locked onto Beumont's.

*

Her tears were hot and heavy as they dripped down her cheeks and fell from her chin. The poor distraught girl looked up at her father, confused and hurt. He looked down at her and wiped the tears away with his thumbs, but they were instantly replaced by others.

"Why, Papa?" Minoress Alexis asked. "What did I do? Whatever it is, I'm sorry! I take it back! I'll be better! I'll be a good girl and I won't steal skids and I won't pilfer from the pantry and I promise not to—"

"Stop, my dear sweet girl," Alexis said as he crouched down in front of her. "You have done nothing wrong. This is not about punishing you, but about keeping you safe. You love the Prime! This will be a grand adventure!"

"I love the Prime with *you*," she cried. "I don't want to live down there if you are living up here!"

"It will not be forever, I promise," Alexis said.

"Any time away from you is forever, Papa! Any time!" Minoress Alexis cried as she wrapped her arms about her father's neck and sobbed into his shoulder.

"There there, sweet girl, there there," Alexis soothed. "I am only a shuttle ride away and will visit as often as I can."

"Except that would leave the Station without a regent," Bella said as she waited for the father and daughter to finish their farewell.

She glanced at the walls of the passageway outside the shuttle dock airlock and frowned. She was not a fan of traveling to the planet and was certainly not a fan of being exiled, no matter what empty words Alexis told her to the contrary.

"Who will rule when you come to visit?" Bella asked.

"Brother Spiggot," Alexis replied instantly. "Or his father. Yes, I will have Herlen be regent when I have to be away. He is older and wiser than Deran, so he will be perfect."

"I can see you have put much thought into this," Bella responded. "What could possibly go wrong with that situation?"

"Do not ruin this moment for us, wife," Alexis grumbled. "I am trying to say goodbye to my daughter."

"As I am saying goodbye to my husband," Bella countered. "Yet you do not see tears there. From either of us."

"Not because I do not have the same feelings for you as I do our daughter," Alexis said. "But we are adults and know how to handle our emotions better than children."

Bella just grinned and nodded.

"Papa?" Minoress Alexis asked as she pushed away from him and wiped her eyes. "When exactly will I see you again?"

"Oh, I cannot say for certain," Alexis replied as he stood and lifted her in the air. He twirled her once then twice and her tears became giggles. "But I think it will have to be for Last Meal at the earliest. Any sooner and I risk losing the control of the Station I have been fighting so hard to regain."

"Last Meal? That's too long!" Minoress Alexis exclaimed as her father set her down. "That is forever!"

"It is a long way off, but won't it make our love for each other that much stronger? We will hope and pray each and every day that Helios keeps us safe so when we do see each other it will be like a holy miracle."

"You sound like a silly gatekeeper," Minoress Alexis replied. She leaned in conspiratorially. "Do I have to mind the gatekeepers too?"

"You have to be respectful," Alexis nodded. "But the occasional prank or two is good for them. Keeps them on their toes."

"Toes...," Minoress Alexis mused. "That gives me an idea."

"No, it does not," Bella snapped. "You will not be bored long enough to engage in pranks and practical jokes. You will be mistress of this station one day and I plan on making sure you are fully prepared for that position. If we are to be sent to the planet, then I promise you the time will be utilized properly."

"Yikes," Alexis grinned at his daughter. "That sounds like work."

"More work than you can know, husband," Bella said. There were six chimes and she closed her eyes for a brief second then held out her hand. "Come, Alexis, time to board the shuttle."

"Will you wait and watch us go?" Minoress Alexis asked her father.

"I will stand by the porthole until you are nothing but a spot in the black sky," Alexis nodded. "Then I will picture you in my head every moment I am awake and every moment I am asleep."

"Don't do that," Minoress Alexis said. "Then you won't have room in that head to rule the Station. Just think of me when you got to bed and when you wake up. And when you ride skids. And when you eat that cake I love. And—"

"Alexis, that's enough," Bella said and the two did not know which one she was speaking to. "Time to depart."

The minoress reluctantly let herself be pulled into the airlock. The door sealed behind them and Alexis went to the porthole and watched the two board the shuttle. The outer airlock door sealed and a warning claxon blared.

"Sire, for your safety we must retreat back to the inner passageway," a guard said.

"I do not fear space," Alexis said as he remained where he stood. "I will stand here and keep a promise I just made to my daughter. Inform the engineers that I am not exiting this passageway for the other one. It will be their job to make sure the airlock doors stay sealed."

"Yes, sire," the guard bowed and hurried to a communications panel in the wall.

The claxon continued as Alexis watched the shuttle disengage from the dock and slide out of its port. The view was poor since he was looking through a small porthole in one door and identical porthole at the other end of the airlock, but he did not turn away even when he lost sight of the shuttle.

He stood there well after the claxon had quieted and the shuttle was long gone. He stood there and pictured the machine as it was propelled through space by its Vape thrusters and into the upper atmosphere of the planet below. He stood there and believed he had made the right choice for his daughter and for Station Aelon.

He stood there and cried.

ACT III

AN UNDESERVED ENDING

"The death of Alexis II is touched on in history classes throughout the System, but rarely is the horrendous act ever described in detail. Being a man of letters, and not one of the writers of the macabre or grotesque, I also will refrain from such a description. Just let it be known that I would not wish such an end on my worst enemy."

—Dr. D. Reven, Eighty-Third Archivist of The Way

"We are lifted up by Tragedy. When the path is the darkest, then one will find light."

—Book of Mirage 7:7, The Ledger

"They forgot about me. It was their undoing."

—Journals of Alexis the Third, Mistress of Station Aelon and its Primes

CHAPTER SEVEN

The outfits were lively, as were the men and women that wore them. The music was superb, a new group of musicians brought over from Station Ploerv for the occasion. The food was piled high on the long table, and the atmosphere was as merry as it could be.

Yet the master sat there, chin cupped in hand, a bored look upon his face.

"Alexis," Deran said as he finished eating what he could only describe as a cloud wrapped in deliciousness on a cracker. He reminded himself to compliment the chef after the celebration. "You look like you haven't had a bowel movement in a week. Get that wretched look off your face and enjoy yourself. This celebration is for you! It is not every day that a master lives near his forties!"

"How near his forties will never be admitted!" Herlen laughed as a woman on his lap tried to feed him berries imported directly from the hothouses of Station Haelm. "I say the man doesn't look a day older than when he took the crown!"

"*Huzzah*!" half the table cheered as they lifted their ever-full glasses. "To Master Alexis!"

"To Master Alexis!" Deran smiled. "May he be forever in our lives!"

The frown remained and it irritated Deran to no end. The master had been nothing short of a mope for weeks and even the elaborate celebration he had planned for the man wouldn't bring Alexis out of his funk.

"This will not do," Deran snapped as he casually tossed his napkin into Alexis's face. Many at the table recoiled at the act and waited for the master to retaliate, but he only sat there, chin still cupped in hand. "You will have fun if I have to beat it out of you."

The Spiggot stood and grabbed at Alexis's arm, yanking him up from his seat at the head of the table. He nearly dragged the man the length of the long table before Alexis fought back and pulled himself free.

"You forget yourself sometimes, Brother Gannot," Alexis snapped then realized his mistake. "I mean, Brother Deran."

Deran stopped and looked at the melancholy monarch as realization hit him.

"Alexis, my dear friend, how could I be so cruel and forgetful?" Deran said. "DuChaer will have been dead three years to the day next month, isn't that right?"

"Yes," Alexis said. "And this year is especially painful. I do not know why, but a great pain has swept into my heart and gripped it like a vise."

"All the more reason to enjoy the festivities!" Deran stated. "Look about you! There are nothing but friendly faces and well-wishers! When you dwell on DuChaer's execution, you dwell on a time when the faces in this hall wanted nothing but your death. These people, these *amazing* people, want only for you to live!"

The crowd cheered and more wine and liquor was poured into glasses that already overflowed with an abundance of alcohol, so that the table, the chairs, the floor were soon slick and puddled with drink that cost more than what most middledeckers made in a year. Perhaps even two years.

Deran pointed at the musicians and raised his arms, urging them to get louder, to play faster, to push the boundaries of the tastes of the day. The great hall was filled with the sound and soon the revelers that had been busy eating and drinking at the long table were all out on the floor, dancing and spinning, screaming and shouting, grinding and fondling.

Alexis found himself surrounded by celebrants and struggled to free himself, but each time he found the edge of the throng, he was shoved back into the center until, exhausted with fighting, he let go and joined in the merriment.

"That didn't take long," Herlen said as his son sat down next to him. He shoved the woman off his lap, slapped her on the ass, and pushed her away from the table. "Go dance, we have men talk to do."

The woman gave him a hurt look then lifted up her skirt and showed him her bare ass before she skipped off into the dancing, sweating crowd.

"Men talk to do?" Deran laughed at his father. "How much have you had to drink?"

"Too much," Herlen belched. "This old belly can't hold liquor like it used to."

"It's your heart and liver I'm more worried about," Deran said. "What would I do if my father fell dead before all of our plans were in place?"

"You'd run for another station and pray you are not hunted down, is what," Herlen said. He looked at the musicians and frowned. "Where in Helios did you find these butchers? Is that *Grueben's Eighteenth* they are trying to perform?"

"It's a theme on *Grueben's Eighteenth* and is supposed to sound that way," Deran stated. "It is the number one song amongst disc traders on all the stations. It was a miracle to get them to play here tonight."

"An expensive miracle," Herlen added.

"Yes, very," Deran smiled. "Good thing it is not our money being spent."

"How is the treasury doing?" Herlen grinned.

"Do we care?"

"No, we do not."

The song stopped, but before the dancers could protest, the musicians moved right into another one. It was a slower tempo song, and soon the drunken partygoers were swaying back and forth, their bodies up against each others' as they attempted some type of intoxicated group slow dance.

"What is the timeframe for the next move?" Herlen asked as he plucked a berry from the plate in front of him and rolled it about between his fingers. Ever so slowly, he pressed down, until the berry was crushed and its juice dripped to the table. "And are you certain this is the avenue we should take?"

"I am certain," Deran said as he nodded to two drunken deck bosses who stumbled by. "We take out this variable, and the Station will be only a step away from ours."

"You honestly think he will put you in the line of succession?" Herlen asked. "I know you two have made many changes to the station's charter, but that is extreme, to say the least."

"We have made it so his half-siblings are considered foreign entities under the law now, and cannot take the crown," Deran responded. "As well as any cousins he has on other stations. The treaty with the stewards three years ago nullified any claim they have to the crown, despite their bloodlines. That leaves the power in the hands of the master to appoint his successor."

"And that has been written into the charter as well?"

"So to speak."

Deran never saw the smack to the back of his head coming, and the surprise caused him to cry out loud enough that even the drunker partygoers looked his way. He laughed it off and swatted at his father, then leaned in close.

"What was that for?"

"Because you are forgetting the number one rule I have taught you," Herlen snapped. "Have everything in place before you make your move. Never give your opponent an out."

"Alexis is not my opponent," Deran replied. He received a second smack and had to restrain himself from slugging his own father. "Stop that!"

"I am not talking about Alexis, you egotistical fool," Herlen growled. "I am talking about the meeting of stewards."

"Relics, all of them," Deran replied. He watched his father closely, ready for another hit. When it didn't come, he continued. "I have all but castrated that group. Their teeth have been pulled, claws torn out, and mouths muzzled. Even if they object, they no longer have the power to do anything about it. They'll be pissing in a Vape storm."

"You never know, though," Herlen said. "Which is why I'll be taking their side, if they do object."

Deran stared at his father, his mouth wide open in surprise. Herlen picked up a berry and tossed it into his son's maw, then pushed up on his chin.

"Think it through, boy," Herlen said. "If we succeed and Alexis does appoint you as his successor, once our obstacle is out of the way, then I have no doubt the stewards will rise up and try to fight once more. I will be by their side, since I am a steward myself now, and add my voice to the opposition. If Alexis wins, then you will be next in line. If the stewards win, then I will still have a place in the meeting and I can shield you from the fallout, telling them that Alexis was obsessed with you and his perversions drove him to the decision, not anything you did."

"We play both sides at once," Deran nodded. "See, Father? That is why we make a great team." Deran sighed as he saw Alexis striding towards him. "Speaking of perversions, I know that look. I guess I will bid you goodnight."

"How you stand it, I do not know," Herlen said as he shook his head.

"We play our parts," Deran said. "Be prepared for when the news reaches the Station. I expect the obstacle to be gone within the week."

"I look forward to it," Herlen said then waved at the master. "Alexis! Having fun now?"

"Too much fun," Alexis said, his legs wobbly. "I think I sipped from the wrong drink. My head is spinning."

"Let's get you to bed," Deran said. "I'll walk you back to your quarters."

"But I'm not done with my fun," Alexis said. "You wanted me to have fun, right? I am having fun! Fun, fun, fun! I'll go to my quarters just as soon as I am ready."

"Just because you are going to your quarters does not mean the fun ends," Deran smiled at the master then glanced over at two young men grinding on each other. "It just means we move the fun to a more private setting."

"Yes," Alexis said as his eyes watched the young men with a barely concealed hunger. "More private setting."

"Goodnight, Father," Deran said over his shoulder as he steered Alexis towards the doors of the great hall.

"Goodnight, Son!" Herlen called, but knew his voice was lost as the musicians switched songs and returned to something more raucous. He glanced around the room, spied a servant girl who was busy trying to clean up some of the spilled alcohol, got to his feet and hurried over to her. "You. You are coming with me."

He pulled her by the arm towards a side door, and the small room beyond. The servant didn't protest, having been told by others that Steward Spiggot would get to her eventually, just as he had gotten to all of them.

*

The chimes were like needles in Alexis's brain and he scrunched his shoulders up as he pulled his pillow down around his ears. There was some brief relief until the pillow was yanked free and the voice of Deran did more damage than the chimes.

"Blast it!" Alexis shouted. "Why are you disturbing me?"

"Because it is late in the afternoon and we have a surprise conference with the council," Deran replied.

Alexis rolled over and carefully opened his eyes. He looked around the room and, was shocked to see so many more bodies on the floor than just the two he thought had accompanied him and Deran back to his quarters the night before. Mostly men, but with a few women, the bodies were in various poses, their eyes closed and chests rising and lowering with the sleep of the good and drunk. Not a stitch of clothing could be seen anywhere and Alexis looked up at Deran with pleading eyes.

"I'll escort them out through the servants' entrance," Deran said. "If I can get any of them to achieve consciousness. You just worry about making yourself presentable."

"I thought my schedule was clear today," Alexis said as he sat up and instantly wished he hadn't. He spun about and vomited over the side of the bed, his sick splashing onto the chest of a young woman who looked like she wasn't quite uncoupled from two men.

"It was clear," Deran said as he helped the master to his feet and through the minefield of flesh. "This was a surprise. Apparently, the meeting of stewards has issues with the reserves in the treasury. The council is now involved and wants to go over it all with you."

"With me?" Alexis asked. "Why me? I made you exchequer of the crown. You have full financial authority on Station Aelon. You handle this and let me go back to sleep." He stopped and vomited once again. "Or let me die. Yes, I would rather die right now than sleep."

"Dying nor sleeping are on the schedule anymore, sire," Deran said.

"Sire? Uh oh, this must be bad. You never call me sire anymore in private unless trouble is here. You'll get me out of this trouble, right Brother Deran? You'll do all the talking so I can just sit there and pray I don't start leaking from my ass, yes?"

"Unfortunately...no," Deran replied. "The council did not invite me and since the exchequer cannot override the council, I must abide by their wishes and stay out of the room while they speak with you."

"Oh, Dear Parent, that does not sound like a good time," Alexis replied as Deran led him into the bathroom and started the shower. "I am not in any way ready to face a bunch of old, angry faces by myself. Get me out of this, Brother. Make them postpone until tomorrow morning, at the very least."

"I have tried, Alexis," Deran said as he pushed the master into the shower. "But my powers are limited. If I was more than just exchequer I could speak to them in your stead, but alas, I am not."

The hot water rushed over Alexis's body and he sighed at the small amount of relief it gave him.

"Fine, I'll see them on my own," Alexis said. "Have my clothes set out and a large pot of tea. I may not drink it, but it will feel good to wrap my body about the warm pot."

"Your clothes will be waiting for you on your bed and your room will be cleared of guests before you wash the soap out of your eyes," Deran said. "Do not worry, Alexis, all will be fine. Just don't give them straight answers. Dodge about whatever subject they bring up and soon they'll get tired of speaking with you and adjourn."

"You promise?"

"I promise."

"Thank you, Brother," Alexis said, patting Deran's face with a wet hand. "I do not know what I would do without you."

*

The four stewards that made up the new version of the royal council sat about the end of the long table, their faces sour and bodies rigid. Alexis rolled his eyes at them as he walked into the great hall. His stomach churned at the sight of the place, an involuntary response to the smell of the previous night's festivities that still lingered in the massive room.

"They do clean up fast around here," Alexis chuckled then took his seat. "Alright, gentlemen, why am I here and being tortured at this early hour?"

"It is four in the afternoon, your highness," an old steward by the name of Cornley stated. He was pinch faced and had thick, thick glasses, making him look like eyes jammed into a balled up sock. "We have waited here for over an hour."

"Did you eat? I hope you ate, as I cannot watch you eat now. If you are hungry, you'll have to wait until after the meeting," Alexis said.

"We have eaten at the appropriate time," another steward, this one called Stampfoerd, replied. "Although we are missing tea."

"I think I could stomach some tea, but no cakes or fruit," Alexis said. "No food, just tea."

He snapped his fingers and a servant by the side of the wall hurried out of the hall.

"Can we begin before the tea is served?" Alexis asked. "Or must we wait for the steeped leaves before we start what I am sure promises to be an enchanting discussion."

A steward by the name of Lobingless cleared his throat and leaned forward. "Sire, it has been brought to our attention that the treasury reserves are at such a low level that if there were to be any sort of station emergency, Aelon would not be able to meet its financial obligations. We would default on many payments that must be made to our trade partners each and every month."

"We make payments?" Alexis laughed. "What are we? Lowdeckers renting furniture for our hovels?"

"The lease holdings on Thraen, for instance," the last steward, Schaernt, stated. "If we were to miss a payment then Master Alfonse IV will rescind our charter and retake possession of those lands. The cost to us in loss of income, as well as loss of Vape, would be catastrophic. Station Aelon would not be able to survive."

"Alfonse IV? My Helios, Thraen does switch masters like I switch undergarments," Alexis laughed. "When did my wife's third brother take the crown?"

"Just before Last Meal," Stampfoerd responded.

"Did I attend the coronation?" Alexis asked. "I don't remember attending."

"No, sire, you did not, which is why Thraen will not allow us any extensions on our payments," Stampfoerd stated. "The master was very upset since you are his brother-in-law."

"And what else do we have to deal with?" Alexis asked, as if the news of the lease holdings or his snubbing of the Thraen master made zero difference to him. Which, considering the state of his head, they did not. "What other payments must be made?"

"The tithe to The Way, is just another," Schaernt continued. "If we are late on that then all access to and from the planet will be cut off. We would need to rely on the grace of the other stations in order to receive our shipments from Aelon Prime."

"Ugh, *The Way*," Alexis snorted. "Bunch of old prunes masturbating under their robes."

Both Stewards Stampfoerd and Lobingless stood from their chairs, faces red with anger and outrage.

"Blasphemy!" Lobingless cried.

"You desecrate the holy order!" Stampfoerd added. "May Helios forgive you!"

"Sit down, sit down," Alexis said as he flapped his hands at them. "I was making a joke. I apologize if I offended your delicate sensibilities. Take your seats so we can get through this."

The stewards glared at him for some time before they sat back down. The tea arrived and they all sat silently as it was poured and plates of food were set out.

"Did I not say there was to be no food?" Alexis snarled at the servant that brought the cart to the table. "I did say that, yes? You heard me say that?"

The servant looked terrified as he glanced about the table. "Yes, sire, but I assumed you meant only for you. I brought food for the stewards, as is the custom with tea."

"*As is the custom with tea,*" Alexis mocked in a high-pitched voice. "I know what the fucking custom with tea is, you moron!"

The servant didn't have time to duck the cup that was flung at his head and he dropped to the floor instantly as blood began to pour from a cut above his eye. Another servant who stood by the wall hurried forward and helped the wounded young man from the ground. They both gathered up the food, dumped it quickly onto the cart, and exited the great hall before more violence could occur.

"Gone are the days when servants took pride in their jobs," Alexis muttered.

"Gone are the days when masters took pride in theirs," Cornley responded. "Your father would have never acted like this."

"Yes, he would have, if he'd been forced to deal with the incompetence I am forced to deal with," Alexis replied.

"Sire, can we return to the subject of the treasury?" Schaernt asked. "We all have pressing business still to attend to today, as I am sure you do as well."

The stewards exchanged looks that said they did not believe that in the least.

"Yes, yes, treasury is low, we have to make payments," Alexis said. "I understand. So...fill the treasury back up."

"It is not that simple," Schaernt responded. "In order to do that we would have to raise taxes. And therein lies the problem."

"I don't see a problem," Alexis said as he snapped his fingers again. "Bring me pen and paper and I'll write the decree now. Would a raise of five percent suffice?"

"As is in his power, the exchequer has already raised taxes on the Lower and Middle Decks by forty percent since last year," Schaernt said. "We cannot raise them higher or we'll cripple the economies of those decks. That would affect every sector on the Station."

"Not that raising them would achieve much," Lobingless added. "Most of the taxes that are collected never reach the treasury, as it is. The crown sees perhaps thirty-five percent."

"Thirty-five percent?" Alexis asked. "What percentage should the crown see?"

The stewards stared at him as if he'd suddenly spoken some new, unknown language. Finally, Steward Schaernt cleared his throat and leaned forward.

"The crown should see one hundred percent, sire," he said. "That is the purpose of taxes, to replenish the royal treasury."

"One hundred percent? What about the exchequer's take? What do you expect Brother Deran to live on? Nothing?" Alexis asked, honestly puzzled.

"No, sire, he is to live off of his many land holdings, as well as his salary as exchequer," Schaernt replied.

"Ah, I see, I think I have found the problem," Alexis said. "In lieu of a salary, I made an agreement with Brother Deran that he could take a percentage of the taxes he and his father collect. They may be taking slightly too much, as you have pointed out, so I will speak with them."

"Sire, the exchequer is not supposed to take any percentage," Schaernt said. "That is what his salary is for."

"And, like I said," Alexis snapped. "I made an agreement that he was to get a percentage instead of a salary. Was I mumbling when I said that?" Alexis stared at Schaernt. "Well? Was I?"

"I apologize, sire, I thought that was a rhetorical question," Schaernt replied.

Alexis slapped his hands on the table, causing his teacup to tip and spill. A servant hurried forward, but Alexis shoved him away as he stood up.

"Let me pose a rhetorical question, if I may," the master growled. "How would the four of you like to spend the rest of your days in the third spire? Or perhaps join your colleagues in exile on the planet? Would any of you prefer that to living free in your estate houses?"

The council remained silent.

"I thought not," Alexis said. "Then I do not want to hear another word from any of you on the subject of taxes or percentages or the Spiggots. If there is not enough money in the treasury then figure out how to fix that. That is what you are here for. Maybe you should start to kick in a higher percentage of your incomes to the crown? Otherwise, shut the Helios up, or you will find yourselves on the next shuttle down to the Prime!"

Alexis turned and stormed from the great hall, a huge, satisfied smile on his face.

*

Their skin glistened with sweat as their bodies writhed about each other. Mouths closed and opened, touching, tasting, licking. Arms entwined, legs locked, hips thrusting, Bella and Beumont went at each other as if they were love struck teenagers, with all the eagerness and energy that age afforded.

But they were not teenagers, and perhaps if they had been, they wouldn't have been so focused on their lovemaking and would have noticed the shadow that separated itself from the corner of the room.

Black as the night outside, the shadow moved towards the bed, its arms raised, a long blade ready to come down and deliver swift death.

The door burst open and the shadow, as well as the sweaty lovers, cried out in surprise and turned towards the rectangle of light of the doorway.

Silhouetted in that rectangle was a figure with a dripping short blade held in each hand. She rushed forward and with two swipes removed the head of the shadow assassin as well as the man's arms that held the long blade.

Both the arms and the head fell onto the tangled bedsheets at the feet of Bella and Beumont.

"Sweet Helios!" Beumont cried as he climbed off the mistress and switched on a light on the bedside table. "What is this madness?"

With the room lit, Bella could see who their savior was. Not one of the royal guards, since she had bribed them all to keep clear of her bedchambers. No, it was her thirteen-year-old daughter who stood there, her chest heaving with violence, her nightgown coated with blood.

"Alexis!" Bella shouted as she scrambled to wrap a sheet about her body at the same time as she leapt from the bed, her eyes filled with fear and terror for her child. "Are you hurt? Where are you bleeding?"

"It is not my blood, Mother," Minoress Alexis replied as she flicked the assassin's blood from her blades and onto the floor. "It is the blood of the two men that I killed who came to kill me in my sleep."

"Two men?" Beumont exclaimed as he looked down at the headless corpse that lay in a massive pool of its own blood. "You killed two men in your bedchambers and then another here? My Helios!"

"I killed two in my bedchamber, another in the hall, and then this one here," Minoress Alexis corrected. "The one in the hall did not bleed on me since I was able to avoid the arterial spray in my haste to reach the two of you."

Bella and Beumont both quickly realized the compromising situation they had been found in. Beumont looked about and found his trousers, then hurried to them and hastily pulled them up over his bottom half.

"Alexis, sweetheart," Bella began but stooped when her daughter held up a hand. A hand that still clutched a bloody blade.

"Don't, Mother," the minoress sighed. "Your tryst is not much of a secret. Not only does every servant and guard in this house know about it, they all laugh at the high sums you pay to bribe them for their silence. None of them would speak of this anyway, since it would mean their instant death. Father does not enjoy bad news from messengers. Or at least the Spiggots do not, which is basically the same thing these days, right?"

The mistress stared at the girl before her, unsure of who she was. This was not the daughter that worried over the fashions of the stations or what new teachings The Way had published lately. No, this was a killer and a determined soul. Bella hadn't seen someone stand with such confidence since her father. Or since Alexis the First.

The resemblance to both was more than unsettling.

"We should get you cleaned up," Bella said, reaching for her daughter, who was nearly as tall as some of the guards that protected the prime estate. "Let me take those blades from you and we'll go back to your bedchambers. You can shower while I have the servants clean up. It may be best that we all sleep in a different wing of the house for the rest of the night."

"After we talk to the fifth man," Minoress Alexis said. "He's still in my bedchambers, tied to a chair. He is missing both hands, but I believe I wrapped them well enough to stop the bleeding. He'll be groggy, but alive."

"A fifth man?" Beumont asked. "You said there were only two in your room."

"No, I said I killed two in my room and that is where this blood came from," Alexis replied. "Pay attention to detail, Beumont, it could save your life one day. Perhaps you could interrogate the man while I clean myself up?"

The minoress looked back and forth from one adult to the other, waiting for a response. When none came, she sighed again, turned, and walked from the room.

"Never mind. I'll do it myself. Just like I do everything else around here."

"Who would send these men?" Bella asked.

"Alexis," Beumont hissed. "He must know about us as well."

The minoress stopped at the threshold of the doorway, but did not turn around.

"My father did not send these men," she stated. "He would never send anyone to harm me. Say another false word about my father, or attempt any type of retribution against him due to your false beliefs, and it will be you on the floor without a head, Beumont."

The minoress stepped fully into the hall and left the two shocked lovers to themselves.

"She becomes more uncontrollable with every day," Beumont stated. "You are losing her."

"I am losing nothing, except for my mind, by being trapped on this damned planet!" Bella snapped, whirling on the man. "This proves that we must make our move soon, Jackull."

"This proves that the Spiggots are growing bolder, and no longer willing to risk your return," Beumont said. "Or the return of your daughter."

"Just a second, before you were accusing my husband of this atrocity," Bella said as she let the sheet fall and searched the room for her undergarments. They were on the floor, under the corpse that continued to leak blood. Bella turned her head away and went to her dresser to fetch fresh clothes. "Now you believe it is the Spiggots? Which is it, Jackull? My husband or the Spiggots?"

"Alexis is correct that her father would never try to harm her," Beumont admitted. "My words were rash and expressed out of shock for what just happened. Do not forget, my love, that your husband had my wife and daughter butchered. He may not be capable of harming his own daughter, but he is more than capable of committing murder."

Bella began to reply, then stopped herself and walked over to her lover. She wrapped her arms about him and pressed her face into his chest.

"Yes, of course, Jackull, I know that," Bella said. "I get so wrapped up in the royal drama of my life that I sometimes do not see the pain that still haunts you." She pulled back and looked up at him. "Forgive me?"

"Always," Beumont said as he leaned down and kissed her. "You are my heart and life now. Without you I would be stuck in that shack out on the Prime, wasting away as the other stewards do."

Bella looked about the room and shuddered. "I cannot stay here another second, Jackull. Take me out of here so we can have the place cleansed by the servants and blessed by a gatekeeper. I will not have ghosts residing in my bedchambers."

"Yes, my love. We should find the guards and have a word with them on how five men made it in here without them knowing," Beumont replied as he guided the mistress from the room.

"That is not a mystery, dearest," Bella laughed. "If I can pay them to ignore the fact that an exile lives here and shares my bed, then anyone can bribe them to gain simple entrance."

"Then you are correct that we must leave the planet," Beumont said. "The problem is how." Bella stopped and clutched Beumont's arm so hard that he winced from her grip.

"What? What is it?"

"I think I may have the solution." Bella smiled. "There was a communiqué that came across my desk last week regarding the lease holdings. It appears they are close to being in arrears. If that happens, then my brother will immediately take action and stop all Vape production on those holdings."

"And this is a good thing?" Beumont asked.

"It is, because then Station Aelon will need to send an envoy to negotiate terms," Bella smiled. "And there is no better person suited for the job than I."

"And you would take Alexis with you so she could see her uncle and cousins." Beumont smiled, but the smile quickly faded. "Yet that still leaves me here on the planet."

"Do not worry about that, love," Bella grinned. "That is purely a matter of making sure the proper donations are made to the right gatekeepers. I will get you off this planet along with myself and my daughter."

"Then what?' Beumont asked. "We live in exile on Station Thraen instead of here on Helios? It is not much of a trade."

"No, no, we will not be exiles," Bella said. "Not with the heir to Station Aelon's crown with us."

Bella did not elaborate as she took Beumont by the hand and led him towards her office so he could see the details of the communiqué and help her begin planning.

*

"I do not like it, sire," Deran said as he reread the letter before him. "Having the mistress and minoress on Aelon Prime is for their safety. If they are allowed to go to Station Thraen, then it would be like throwing them to the wolves."

"The what?" Alexis asked as he looked up from his breakfast. "What are wolves?"

"Ancient predators that once roamed the lands of Helios before the Cataclysm," Herlen said. "They hunted in packs and surrounded their prey."

"Ah," Alexis nodded. "Then you used the wrong analogy, Brother Deran. My wife and daughter are not prey to Alfonse, they are family."

"Some might argue that is one and the same when it comes to royal politics, sire," Deran said.

"I wouldn't say that," Alexis replied. "Not when it comes to my family. I love my daughter with all of my heart, Brother Deran. She is my heir and last of the Teirmont bloodline. Her safety is above politics."

"Yes, that is all true, sire," Herlen said. "But Master Alfonse may not see it that way. He could see it as an opportunity to hold the minoress hostage until we make good on our financial obligations."

"And why haven't we already done so?" Alexis asked. "Falling behind on the payments for the lease holdings is not a sign of a good exchequer, Brother Deran."

"And I apologize for the mistake, sire," Deran responded. "Unfortunately there were some issues with the Lower Decks not contributing their portion of taxes. I had apportioned treasury funds to other obligations before I found out about the slight."

"So this is Klipoline's doing, is it?" Alexis sighed and shook his head. "That man. What will we do with someone whose ego is so large? He thinks his position is above mine. It's preposterous. Send some soldiers down there to teach him a lesson and extract the back taxes."

"Sire?" Herlen asked, shocked at the proposal. "That is not the wisest course of action. Master Klipoline has always been a strong ally. I believe he just had a lapse in judgment."

"And lapses in judgment must be corrected," Alexis said. "We all know that the only way to correct a lowdecker is to smack them on the nose with a wet towel. Or, in this case, with some longslingers. We do still use longslingers, right?"

"We do, sire," Deran nodded. "They swore their allegiance to the crown once again at the end of the civil war."

"Civil war. Bah!" Alexis guffawed. "It was an irritant and nothing more."

"I wouldn't quite call it an irritant," Deran said, glancing at his father. "It was slightly more complicated than that."

"Oh, I know, but those complications are done with," Alexis said as he stabbed his fork into the pile of grendt eggs on his plate. He lifted the fork and waved it about. "Like these eggs here. The entire process of raising grendts, getting them to breed, harvesting their eggs, then transporting and storing the eggs all so I can have a delicious scramble each morning is quite complicated." He stuffed the forkful of eggs into his mouth and continued speaking. "But who cares? No one. All we care about is the results, which are light, fluffy eggs I can add a dash of salt and seasoning to."

"Right as always, sire," Deran said. "Your insights into the most complicated of matters always astound me. You make it look so simple."

The Spiggots shared a condescending look as Alexis shoveled more food into his mouth. They waited as he finished chewing and took a long drink of tea.

"Let them go," Alexis said. "It may end up being to our advantage. I'll send a letter to Bella, directly instructing her to not only negotiate the payment issue, but perhaps to strengthen some other trade ideas I have had."

"Trade ideas, sire?" Herlen asked. "You haven't spoken to us about any of this."

"What? I haven't?" Alexis wondered. "Hmmm, maybe I was just dreaming that. Well, you know what the Ledger says, 'Best to act on dreams than let them slip away'."

"I don't think that is in the Ledger, sire," Deran replied. "I am certain that is a wine merchant's slogan."

Alexis stared at the Spiggot for a good few seconds before nodding. "Yes, it is. Thank you for correcting me on that, Brother Deran. How embarrassing would that be if I'd said that in public?" He laughed heartily and eggs spewed from between his lips. "Fetch paper so I can dictate my instructions for Bella to you. I want to get this down while it is fresh in my brain."

"Yes, sire," Deran said, snapping his fingers. A servant hurried over with pen and paper. "Begin when you are ready, your highness."

*

The two siblings studied each other for a moment before arms were outstretched and smiles grew on their faces.

"My long, lost sister!" Alfonse exclaimed.

"You are a welcome sight to see," Bella replied as the two embraced warmly. "You have no idea."

"Oh, I have an idea," Alfonse laughed. "Did you not hear that Cousin DuLaern tried to have me assassinated just after Harry passed?"

"No!" Bella said, shocked. "Ephtram tried to have you killed?"

"Tried and failed miserably," Alfonse said. "The assassin was beyond inept. I cut off both his legs and he spilled everything to me, not just his blood. Would you like to see where Cousin DuLaern is now?"

"I believe we already did, your highness," Beumont said as he bowed low then stood and looked at Bella. "The body that was secured to the outside of the shuttle dock."

"That wretched corpse? Oh, my, Alfonse, you have outdone yourself," Bella said. "You wicked thing."

"I come by it naturally," Alfonse nodded. "You know how father was when he was crossed."

"I do, I do." Bella smiled then extended a hand to Beumont. "Before we go further, I would like to introduce you to my savior. May I present Steward Jackull Beumont of Sector Norbrighm."

"Yes, your reputation precedes you, steward," Alfonse replied.

"Unfortunately, your highness, I am no longer a steward," Beumont replied. "But I am honored to be called that by such a great person as yourself."

"Sister, you have told him how much we Herlects enjoy flattery, haven't you?" Alfonse laughed. "And not to worry, Steward Beumont, your title and lands will be restored once my sister returns to Station Aelon." Alfonse craned his neck and looked about. "Now, where is my niece? I must greet the heir to the Aelish crown."

"I am here, Uncle," Minoress Alexis said as she stepped from out of the entourage and gave a slight curtsey. "It is a pleasure to finally make your acquaintance."

"Dear Helios," Alfonse exclaimed. "I thought you were a servant girl what with your height and those trousers you wear. Although, I was going to question your allowing servants to wear trousers, Bella. Now I'll just question your allowing your daughter to wear them."

"I have tried, believe me, Brother," Bella sighed.

"Trousers allow me more freedom of movement, your highness," the minoress said, patting the two short blades on her belt. "Skirts can get tangled and also be grabbed and used against me. As can a nightgown, as

I found out the hard way. Luckily, my skill was greater than the men that came to kill me. I sleep without clothing now, just to be safe."

Alfonse stared at the girl, his mouth wide open.

"She speaks her mind like father did," Bella said. "And fights like my father-in-law. Many may question the choice of a woman taking the crown, but I have no doubts on that front."

"Nor do I, sire," Beumont added. "And I pray for the souls of those that do."

"I wish you two would stop talking as if I'm not standing here," Minoress Alexis said.

"Oh, get used to it, Niece," Alfonse said when he found his voice. "Until you wear the crown, it is as if you are not here. I spent my entire life realizing that." He stepped forward and took her by the arms. "My, she is a beauty, though. Those Teirmonts are a handsome lot. And with those legs I should say that wearing trousers will soon be all the fashion amongst the women of Station Thraen once they get a look at you!"

Bella looked about. "Are we to stand here outside the shuttle airlock or will we be invited in properly, Brother?"

"You can keep your cheek to yourself, Sister," Alfonse said, smirking. "And no, we are not to stand here outside the airlock." He extended his arm and Minoress Alexis took it happily. "Allow me to escort you to our great hall where the most scrumptious feast awaits. I have spared no expense for you arrival. Food, drink, entertainment, it will all be there to welcome you the Thraenish way. Oh, oh, and acrobats! I found the most incredible troop on one of our Middle Decks! Wait until you see what these people can do with their bodies! Makes me want to get into the gym more often, I can tell you."

"Will there be marksmen?" Minoress Alexis asked. "Longslingers? Father would have longslingers perform at times."

"No, unfortunately, we do not have any of the famed longslingers here on Station Thraen," Alfonse frowned. "That is solely a privilege of Aelon. But I have heard you are quite the shot with those, those...what are they called?"

"Particle barbs," the minoress answered.

"Yes! Particle Barbs! What an inventive name!" Alfonse laughed. "I believe we may have a longsling about with those particle barbs. A gift from your grandfather to my father. It collects dust on a shelf in one of the libraries. I will have it cleaned and brought to the celebration. Maybe, if your mother allows, you can give us Thraens a demonstration?"

"I would be honored, sire," the minoress replied.

"Oh, stop. Call me Uncle Alfonse, please. We are family, you tall child, you. I will not stand for formality with family."

"Should I tell her the nickname I gave you when we were younger, Brother?" Bella laughed.

"Do that and you'll join that corpse outside the airlock!" Alfonse guffawed.

Beumont looked alarmed, but Bella patted his arm. "He's joking, my love. It's part of how we speak to each other here in the Thraen court. This is no longer stuffy, reserved Station Aelon we are on. Here we tempt fate and test life."

"As long as it gets us to our goal, my dear, then I will not be alarmed by anything," Beumont replied as the party made their way down the passageway towards the great hall.

*

Alexis sat at the long table, his eyes filled with fear and shock as he looked from one member of the council to the next.

"I do not understand," he said. "How can you remain neutral through all of this? The station is threatened! It is your duty to support your master in defending it!"

"Except that the Station is not under attack, sire," Steward Lobingless said. "Your rule as master is what is being threatened. The mistress's terms clearly state that those that stay out of the fight will not be harmed or judged as traitors. The entire meeting of stewards, as well as the meeting of passengers, has voted. This is not a fight we feel we must join."

"That is ludicrous!" Alexis snapped. "I am the master! You fight for me!"

"Yet the one coming to oppose you is none other than your daughter, a person that you yourself made heir to the crown," Steward Stampfoerd said. "What are we to do? Fight for you against the legitimate heir? And what if she wins? Then we will be traitors and your wife will not hesitate in having us all killed!"

"My wife holds no power," Alexis grumbled. "She is playing my daughter like a puppet."

"That may be true," Steward Schaernt replied. "But you are wrong about her not holding power. She has a thousand Thraen mercenaries at her disposal. That is quite a lot of power, sire."

"See! There! You must join with me to defend Station Aelon!" Alexis shouted, his voice high and desperate. "Thraen soldiers are going to be setting foot on this station! It is your sworn duty to protect Station Aelon against any and all foreign aggression!"

"Except they are not foreign soldiers, sire," Stampfoerd responded as he struggled to keep the smile off his face. "They are mercenaries being paid for by Mistress Bella. Private contractors who are not beholden to any crown and only loyal to the person paying for them. We have no obligation to fight against them for your purposes."

"How in Helios's name is she able to afford such an expense?" Alexis asked. "I doubt even we have enough in our treasury to pay for a thousand mercenaries."

"No, sire, we do not," Schaernt said. "As you are well aware. It would be my guess that the Spiggots are not the only persons with their hands dipping into the taxes. My sources say that Mistress Bella has been skimming for some time now. That is the money she is using to fund this shift in leadership."

"Shift in leadership?" Alexis frowned. "Is that what you are calling it?"

"It is what the meetings voted to call it," Schaernt replied. "It isn't quite a coup, nor is it an invasion. Calling it a shift in leadership will make it easier during the transition."

"The transition?" Alexis asked.

Then he realized he was simply parroting everything that was being said and the meeting with the council served no purpose, other than to humiliate him in the eyes of the stewards present.

Alexis stood and had to focus hard to keep himself from swaying.

"You are useless to me," Alexis said. "I hereby disband the council and institute emergency rule. The meetings no longer have power. I advise you retire to your estates and hide there like cowards while I deal with this situation."

"And how will you deal with it, sire?" Schaernt asked. "By fighting and killing your own daughter? That is what will have to be done if you take up arms against Mistress Bella and her forces."

"It is none of your business now what I do!" Alexis shouted. "So get out! Get out of this hall!"

The four men stood quickly and gladly removed themselves from the master's presence. Even after the doors to the hall had slammed closed, Alexis stayed standing, his mind reeling and confused from all the information.

"Sire?" Deran asked as he came in from one of the side doors. "I saw the council leave. Have we secured their support?"

"No, Brother Deran, we have not secured their support," Alexis replied. "You said we would, but you were wrong. Now we must figure out a way to fight back against Bella without the meeting of stewards."

"The royal guard will fight for you, Alexis," Deran said as he walked to the master's side and placed his hands on the man's shoulders. "It is for the best that the stewards stay out of this anyway. We would never be able to trust a thing they say or do."

"I don't want their damned trust! I want their soldiers and resources!" Alexis shouted as he shook off Deran's hands. "Without that we will be overrun in days. Do you hear me, Brother? Days!"

"Yes, I hear you," Deran said. "Then, I am unsure of what we are to do, sire."

"We run," Herlen said as he joined them in the great hall. "We run to the very lowest regions of this station and hope we find mercy with the only person that has benefitted from Master Alexis's reign more than us."

"We run? Like cowards?" Deran asked.

"No, we run like survivors," Herlen said, shifting his focus from his son to the master. "Sire, we must go now. It is said that Mistress Bella has already launched a shuttle from Station Thraen and is on her way here. It will be a full day before she arrives with her forces. We need to use that time to descend to the Lower Decks."

"The Lower Decks," Alexis repeated, back to parroting what was said to him. "Yes, the Lower Decks. Klipoline will help me. He owes me everything. We return to my quarters and pack then we descend into the bowels of the Station."

"There is no time to pack, sire," Herlen said. "I have gathered enough provisions and credits to get us where we need to go, but we must leave now. To stay would be to invite others to have a go at us. There are many that would capture us in hopes of a reward being paid by Mistress Bella. From this moment on we trust no one except for the three of us, sire. No one."

"No one," Alexis echoed. "No one can be trusted."

Chapter Eight

The master's plate was piled with food, but it was obvious, as the three men looked about, that the rest of the court of the Lower Decks was not so well nourished.

"You want me to support you in fighting off Mistress Bella and a thousand Thraenish mercenaries, not to mention the heir you made to your crown, yet you offer absolutely nothing in return?" Master Klipoline laughed as pieces of grendt flesh dribbled from his lips and back onto the pile of food in front of him. "That is the deal you bring before me? Are you three completely bonkers? Are you sniffing Vape now, Alexis, is that it?"

"Master Alexis is not sniffing Vape," Herlen said. "He is asking for your support just as he supported you when he gave you your title."

"He gave me nothing," Klipoline replied. He set the grendt leg down and leaned back in his chair. While he was close to Alexis's age, he had not kept himself fit by any stretch of the imagination. The man was grossly obese and his clothes showed many stains as evidence of his love of eating. "I gave him the men he needed to fight off the stewards. That is why I have my title. And now that I do, and it is legally binding no matter what master is in place, I have zero desire to stick my neck out for a man that has nearly run this station into the ground. You can forget any help from me, gentlemen. Your days are numbered and I would like you to leave."

"Master Klipoline," Deran started in his most charming voice. A voice that stopped quickly as a half eaten grendt leg was tossed in his face.

"Shut it, you damned conman," Klipoline said. "Every word out of your mouth is a lie and there isn't an ounce of truth in your soul. I know that, the stewards know that, and the entire station knows that. You are probably more reviled in Aelon than Master Alexis!"

"Reviled? I'm reviled?" Alexis asked.

"It speaks!" Klipoline laughed. "I thought you only moved your mouth when a Spiggot had a hand up your ass!"

"I can speak on my own," Alexis said weakly. "I am the Master of Station Aelon."

"Yeah, you keep telling yourself that," Klipoline replied.

"And it is mistress," Alexis stated.

Klipoline looked from the Spiggots to Alexis and back.

"I am sorry, but what is he babbling about?" Klipoline asked.

"I am...not sure," Deran said. "Master? How do you mean it is mistress?"

"He said his title was legally binding no matter what master was in place," Alexis said. "But if Bella wins, then my daughter will take the crown and a mistress is in place. You will want to read the charter carefully, Klipoline. I believe it states that you are granted your title by the current master, not mistress. A technicality, but one that my wife will not hesitate to argue."

All present stared at the man as if a shaow had walked into the hall and begun to tap dance on all four hooves.

"He is right on that point," Herlen said. "The charter is very specific in its wording. You may not have a title if a mistress takes the crown."

"Your technicalities mean nothing to me," Klipoline responded. "They will have to pry this mastership from my dead, cold fingers."

"That would be quite a task considering how fat those fingers are," Alexis snorted. "You'd need a saw to cut them off first."

"Alexis, please," Deran hissed. "You are not helping."

"No, I am not," Alexis said as he stood. "And neither is this blob. Let us leave the shaow to his feeding trough and go find more hospitable environs."

"I'll ignore the insults, even though I should have your balls cut off and fed to you," Klipoline said. "Mainly because I know you will not find more hospitable environs on this station. My advice to you is to commandeer a shuttle and get your asses down on the Prime. I have heard you know your way about the Prime better than any master before you, Alexis. That is your only advantage. Especially since your diplomacy leaves something to be desired."

"Thank you for your advice, Master Klipoline, but I have another destination in mind," Alexis said. "I wish you all the luck in the Station."

"Luck? For what?" Klipoline asked.

"For surviving your next heart attack, you fat fuck," Alexis spat as he looked to the shocked Spiggots. "Come, friends, we have an appointment to keep."

The two quickly stood and followed the master out of the hall and into the passageway that led to the lift. Both Spiggots stayed quiet as they continually looked over their shoulders, ready for the attack after the insults Alexis had thrown at the Master of the Lower Decks. Not until they reached the lift, and were safely on board, did they relax enough to speak again.

"What in Helios's name were you thinking?" Deran nearly shouted when the lift doors had closed and they knew they were ascending. "He would have been within his rights to kill you right there!"

"I am Master of Station Aelon," Alexis said. "And a Teirmont. I would have had his head in my hands before a single one of his guards made a move."

"While you are an excellent bladesman, sire," Herlen said. "You are woefully out of practice. Lowdeckers are never to be trifled with. They are a vicious lot and do not play by the rules, as we gentlemen do."

"Well, none of it matters, because what is said is said, and we are now leaving these stinking Lower Decks," Alexis replied, completely unaffected by the warning Herlen gave. "I believe our next stop will be much more successful."

"And where exactly is our next stop, sire?" Deran asked.

"Middle Deck Twenty," Alexis said. "Are you not married to a Wyaerrn? We will sway the longslingers to our cause, Brother Deran. Or, at least, you shall sway them. I'll just sit back and let you do your magic."

The Spiggots shared a look of fear that the master did not catch, as he was too absorbed in his own smugness to notice anything resembling reality.

*

"How is it that he still roams free?" Bella snapped as she stood in the great hall, her eyes on the master's chair at the far end. "This is a Station, Beumont. It is not a vast system! There is nowhere for him to run! I did not gather my brother's men so I could play hide and seek with my flip of a husband!"

"We believe he is in the Lower Decks, Bella," Beumont said. "So please calm down. We must move carefully and cautiously, or we risk losing the support of the passengers. Right now public opinion is fully on your side. If we send Thraens storming through the Station, then we risk losing that public opinion. We will not only have a master to track down, but an uprising to deal with. Is that what you want?"

"I want my husband deposed and my daughter in his place so I can rule as regent of this station," Bella replied. "That is why we are here. If some of the passengers get their feelings hurt and feathers ruffled, then that is the price to pay." She looked away from her lover and over to her daughter as the young minoress walked along the side of the great hall, her fingers tracing along the murals and tapestries. "Don't you agree, Alexis? A mistress must make tough choices and cannot always please everyone, yes?"

"Whatever you think, Mother," Minoress Alexis responded as she stopped in front of a tapestry that depicted an especially violent and bloody point in station history. "If you are to be regent, then it is your decision to make. All I ask is that my father's life is spared in order for me to take the crown."

"That is not wise," Beumont whispered. "Having one monarch still alive while another rules is a dangerous game."

"Being born a royal is a dangerous game, lover," Bella said. "A fact you cannot relate to, as you were born a passenger."

Beumont kept his tongue and bowed his head, not wanting to anger the mistress further.

"Alexis, if you are to be mistress of this station then the decisions will be yours to make," Bella said as she walked over to her daughter. "As regent I can only give advice."

"You just said that you wanted to be regent so you can rule," Minoress Alexis responded. "You would not be ruling if the decisions are mine to make. I have already said I will defer to you until I am of age to fully take the crown on my own."

The minoress bowed low and swept her hand in front of her.

"The station is yours, my lady. May your rule be wise and just."

"Oh, stop it," Bella said as she gave a playful smack to the back of her daughter's lowered head. "Do not make fun of me, Alexis. This undertaking is not easy for me."

"I know, Mother," Minoress Alexis said as she straightened and moved in to hug her mother. "I am just worried about Father. I do not want him killed. That would break my heart. Please, promise me you will not kill him."

"I promise, Alexis," Bella said. "On my soul and in Helios's name, I promise."

Beumont looked on at the two women, quite content with the fact he had made no such promise.

*

The second the lift doors opened, Alexis and the Spiggots found themselves in the clutches of a very angry mob. The three men were dragged down the passageway and out into the deck atrium where dozens more passengers waited for them. To Alexis's horror, rotted fruit, vegetables, and other refuse rained down on them, and he was fairly sure soiled diapers were part of the mix as they were made to stand alone in the center of the atrium.

"Master Alexis!" a voice boomed from above. "I never would have thought your ego would drive you to show your face here, of all places!"

Alexis peered up at the atrium levels and squinted into the light, unable to see who called to him.

"I am sorry, but you have me at a disadvantage," Alexis said. "To whom am I speaking?" His use of the word "whom" was quickly mocked amongst those that glared at him, but Alexis ignored their jibes and kept searching for the source of the voice. "It is polite to show yourself when addressing royalty, you know."

A large man appeared at the railing of the level just above Alexis and the Spiggots.

"I am the grandnephew of Gornish Wyaerrn," the man stated. "I am the deck boss of Middle Deck Twenty and you are trespassing on a level that does not want you, sire."

The word "sire" was spat about and mocked just as vehemently as the word "whom."

"Quiet!" the man yelled. "My name is Torlin Tweyyrn, but you can call me sir."

The passengers of Middle Deck Twenty erupted into laughter.

"I will call you loyal subject if you grant us asylum on your Deck," Alexis said.

The crowd went silent and all looked to Torlin.

"Asylum? Are you completely daft? Why in Helios's name would I grant you asylum?"

"Because I am the rightful Master of Station Aelon, and it is your duty to do so," Alexis said.

"Sire, perhaps we should talk before you continue," Deran said. "I think you may be overplaying your hand here."

"Quiet, Brother," Alexis said. "I have this fully under control."

"But, Alexis, there are certain facts you need—"

"I said quiet, Deran," Alexis snapped.

"Trouble?" Torlin smirked. "Is the demon there whispering lies into your ears as he has whispered them in ours for years now?"

"Demon?" Alexis asked as he looked about. "I see no demon here."

"He stands at your shoulder," Torlin said as he pointed down. "The one called Deran Spiggot. He has wronged this Deck to no end!"

Alexis turned slowly and regarded his dearest friend.

"Deran? Is this true? How have you wronged them? I thought you were married into the Wyaerrn family and these were your people."

"We were never his people," Torlin said. "Because he never treated us as such. This entire Deck, every single passenger, was nothing but one giant mark in his con game. Did he tell you he married one of Gornish Wyaerrn's daughters? Is that the tale he told?"

"Yes, and that is why you all supported me during the steward uprising," Alexis said. "You kept the longslingers from entering the fight so that I might retake my crown."

"Kept the longslingers...?" Torlin spat. "That is what was said? No wonder we did not hear word one from the monarchy once you were back in power. You thought we had volunteered our neutrality! Care to tell the master the truth, Deran?"

Alexis looked at the Spiggot with deep worry and fear on his face.

"I am confused," is all Alexis could say.

"There may have been some slight exaggeration as to my betrothal," Deran said. "I never actually exchanged vows with the woman."

"No, but he knocked her up right good," Torlin said. "Then instead of marrying her, as he promised, he stole her inheritance and abandoned the woman and child."

"Then...then, why did you support me during the civil war?" Alexis asked, stunned.

"We didn't support you, idiot!" Torlin shouted and the entire atrium burst into laughter. "We had sworn an oath to your father to never turn against the crown and always be there when called! You never called, dumbass!"

"I...never...called," Alexis said. "But...but..."

"But, but, but," Torlin mocked. "If you had called upon the longslingers then we would have taken up arms against the stewards in a heartbeat. The war would have been over in days, not months. None of the puffed up nobility can stand against the power of our particle barbs!"

The atrium exploded into cheers.

"All I had to do was call on them?" Alexis asked as he looked at Deran. "That is why you said you would handle it all? You kept them away from me, Brother. You...used me."

"I didn't, sire," Deran pleaded. "These are all lies they tell. I knew we shouldn't have come here. It is because I had a falling out with my wife... well, that part may not have been a lie since we never formally married. But I didn't abandon them. I visit the child when I can. Give him sweets and toys. I just may have let it spill about my feelings for you. She was none too happy."

"Your feelings for me...? Oh, Brother Deran, what did you do? You know we cannot be accepted by the passengers as we are. It is against the Ledger, The Way, and Helios to love another man. You were lucky she did not tell everyone and have you executed."

"What do you think is going to happen now?" Torlin asked. "We just let you go? No, I do not think so. Your dear Brother Deran will not live to see another day, Master Alexis. He won't even live to see another hour!"

"Father, get Alexis out of here," Deran whispered. "Hurry. Take him and go. Let them do what they want to me. As soon as they begin then they will be distracted enough to let you slip away."

"Son, I will not leave you to be butchered," Herlen said. "What kind of father would I be?"

"A loving and caring one," Deran replied. "Alexis must live! He is the rightful Master of Station Aelon and he must survive this!"

Alexis stood there and said nothing as the two Spiggots argued back and forth. The atrium spun about him and he felt as if he was going to faint when rough hands grabbed his arms and yanked him backwards.

"No!" Deran yelled as he lunged for the master. "Let him go! It is me you want, not Alexis!"

Alexis began to thrash like a wild man and the hands let go instantly. He turned and drew his long blade, his eyes like a feral animal's.

"Take mine as well," Deran said as he pressed a second long blade into Alexis's free hand. "You fight for your life. Hide yourself until the rotation gives you a shuttle window down to the planet. There you will be safe. Father made arrangements some time ago, just in case."

"Just in case? You knew this all might happen?" Alexis asked as he swung a blade out, keeping the crowd at bay.

"I knew something could happen," Deran replied. "Was not my preparedness part of why you fell for me?"

"It was because you were kind to me," Alexis said quietly. "When no one else would be."

"I know where we can stay until the rotation is in our favor," Herlen said. "It won't be comfortable, but it will be safe and close to the shuttle dock. We'll take one of the cargo shuttles down and then get you to your estate on Aelon Prime."

"Yes," Alexis nodded. "They will be loyal to me there. I grew up on the Prime."

His voice sounded far away as if he was no longer present in the chaos of the atrium. Even his blades started to sag, but he lifted them quickly as the crowd tried to come for him again.

"Fight on!" Deran said as he rushed headlong into the crowd, fists flying. "Fight on!"

"We go now," Herlen urged as he shoved Alexis forward towards the passageway that led back to the lift. "Keep those blades swinging, sire! Do not let up!"

Alexis let the blades fly in a wild and clumsy manner, but it was enough to get them free of the crowd. A couple of men tried to pursue them, but the look in Alexis's eyes kept them several feet back and they lost interest as soon as the screams from the atrium reached their ears.

"Fight on. Fight on. Fight on," Alexis mumbled as Herlen got him into the lift. "Fight on. Fight on. Fight on."

Deran's screams turned to shrieks of agony and even when the lift doors closed and it began to ascend, Alexis could still hear his dear, dear friend's cries in his head.

*

The Burdened.

That was who greeted Alexis and Herlen as the crate they stowed away on was opened to the light of The Way Prime.

"I will not hesitate to fight you all!" Alexis cried out as he lunged forward with his long blade.

"Stop that, boy," a familiar voice said. "No one is here to hurt you. Quite the contrary. I am here to escort you to Aelon Prime and see to your safety and comfort."

Alexis blinked into the light several times before his eyes focused on the one who spoke to him.

"Auntie?" he asked in a small voice.

"Oh, for Helios's sake, act like a man and call me Gatekeeper Teirmont," Melinda Teirmont said. "Your auntie died a long time ago, you silly boy."

"It is good to see you, gatekeeper," Alexis said as he studied his aunt.

Other than the robes, and the obvious aging, she looked almost the same as when Alexis had last seen her. The thought of the Taking, and how that was the night he met DuChaer, brought on a wave of melancholy that was so evident on his face he might as well have been wearing a sign to announce it.

"No moping," Melinda said. "You are alive and you are safe. The hard part is done. Now, you can live out the rest of your life in retirement and comfort on the Prime."

"They won't let me live," Alexis said.

"They will if they want a willing mistress to mold," Melinda said. "Your daughter has been very vocal about you not coming to any harm. That girl does love her Papa."

Alexis met his aunt's eyes at that statement and smiled.

"I love her too," Alexis said then suddenly remembered the man that stood next to him. "Forgive me, Gatekeeper Teirmont, but this is—"

"I am well acquainted with who Herlen Spiggot is," Melinda interrupted. "As is every foreman of every Vape mine on this planet."

"I'm sorry?" Alexis asked.

"Nothing to concern yourself with, sire," Herlen said. "The gatekeeper and I met once before. It is good to see you again."

"Well, I applaud your optimism there, Spiggot," Melinda said. "We'll see how long it holds out."

"I have no illusions as to my fate," Herlen said.

"Good," Melinda nodded. "That will makes things go much easier for all."

"Will someone care to tell me what that means?" Alexis said.

"No," Melinda stated bluntly. "There will be time for that once we reach the Prime. Our cutter awaits, Master Alexis."

"Cutter? I assumed we'd be stealing passage on a barge heading back to pick up a load of breen," Alexis said.

"Is that how you want to travel?" Melinda asked.

"No, it most certainly is not," Alexis admitted. "But it was what I prepared myself for."

"Then be glad that is not how you will travel," Melinda said. "You are riding aboard the royal cutter and will be staying on the royal estate. It has all been sanctioned and arranged by the High Guardian himself."

"The High Guardian is involved?" Alexis asked. "But why? He would not get involved when the stewards rose against me."

"This circumstance is...different," Melinda replied. "Let us say that there are enough confusing factors involved that it took a little divine intervention to sort it all out."

For some reason, the thought of the High Guardian being involved in his life was more troubling than the thought of traveling on a breen barge had been. Even more troubling than having to hide in a crate for the journey from station to planet. But Alexis could not figure out why it troubled him. His mind was spent and exhausted. All he cared to do was slip into a comfortable bed and sleep until it all went away.

"I can see we are losing you," Melinda said as she took her nephew by the arm and led him away from the shuttle dock and towards the marina. "Let's get you suited up before you fall asleep. As there are quite a few stewards that have still not signed off on the High Guardian's plan, you will have to go in through the back entrance of the estate, which does mean some walking in the open air."

"I love to walk in the open air," Alexis said. "I miss my environmental suit. It has been such a long time since I was on the planet. I welcome all of the experiences it brings."

"Good for you, Alexis," Melinda said. "That attitude will get you far down here."

*

The grey light filtered in through the blinds of his quarters and Alexis had to remind himself where he was when his eyes finally opened and he looked about.

The Prime.

He knew the room, the light, the smell, everything like it was an extension of himself. He would have been elated if it hadn't been for the reason he was there. That reality came crashing down fast and it took all of his strength to get out of bed, wash himself in the water basin, get dressed, and place his hand on the door.

The master was not sure if he had strength enough left to open the door, but that problem was solved as there came a brief knock and the door slid open before him.

"Oh, you are up," Melinda said, dressed in casual attire instead of her gatekeeper robes. "Don't stare, Alexis. gatekeepers get to dress down too, you know. It can't all be robes and incense twenty-four hours a day."

"But I thought that was how it worked," Alexis said.

"Just as masters were supposed to keep their crowns until they died?" Melinda asked as she looked past the man and into the room. "Are you going to invite me in?"

"Oh, I was ready to come out now," Alexis said. "That nap did me some good and I figured it was time to get back to the business at hand."

"That nap was a three day sleep, nephew," Melinda said. "I had the physicians come in twice a day to check to make sure you hadn't died."

"Three days?" Alexis asked, stunned. "I don't believe it."

"Believe it, nephew," Melinda said, pushing the master back into his room so she could shut the door. She switched on the light and pointed at the bed. "Sit, Alexis. We must talk."

"Am I to be executed?" Alexis asked. "I dreamed I was executed."

"You did?" Melinda asked. "And what was your demise?"

"I would rather not say," Alexis replied as he sat down on the bed. "Just tell me what it is you need to tell me."

"I'll be blunt since I do love you," Melinda said. "You are being deposed. There is the official decree out in the main room that I am supposed to read to you. Once it has been read, then you will be stripped of your crown and it will go to your daughter."

"Masters once actually had crowns," Alexis said. "Did you know that? I wish I had one now that I could take off and give to my daughter. Then there would be a physical connection between us."

"That would be nice, but a real crown would make a master look too much like a king, and we can't have that, can we?" Melinda said. "Now hush your mouth and listen. This is not easy for me to say."

Alexis nodded and waited.

"In order for this transition between monarchs to happen there was a stipulation put in place by your daughter and supported by the High Guardian."

"A stipulation? What kind of stipulation?" Alexis asked.

"That is what I am getting at," Melinda grumbled. "Helios, you are still such a child. Ruling a station did not mature you one bit."

"I guess that is why I am being deposed," Alexis said, a sly grin on his face.

"Cheeky bastard," Melinda said and smiled with him. "Now shut up. The stipulation that your daughter has ordered is that she will not take the crown unless you agree to the deposition."

"So I could still be master if I don't agree?" Alexis asked.

"Is that what you plan on doing?" Melinda responded. "Because if you refuse to agree, then Station Aelon will be plunged into chaos, and control of the monarchy will be assumed by the High Guardian himself."

"Ah, so that is why this has his support," Alexis said. "He actually thinks I will fight and then he gets, not only The Way Prime, but Station Aelon."

"And Aelon Prime," Melinda said. "Yes, the High Guardian is an ambitious son of a bitch."

"Auntie!" Alexis exclaimed. "You blaspheme the High Guardian!"

"And you blaspheme Helios whenever you enjoy cock instead of twat," Melinda shrugged. "We all sin. We all deal with our sins when we die."

"I have no intention of fighting the deposition," Alexis stated. "I fully agree, and will allow my daughter to take the crown as Mistress of Station Aelon and Aelon Prime without any conflict or regret. That is my last act as master."

Melinda studied her nephew for a minute, making the man very uncomfortable. That was quite an achievement since comfort was not something he was familiar with of late.

"Maybe I was wrong about you, Alexis," Melinda finally said. "Maybe you have matured."

"No, I haven't," Alexis replied. "I just love my daughter with all of my heart."

"If that is the case then it is time you came out of your bedchambers and faced the world," Melinda said. "I am to read the official proclamation, then you will give your assent and all will be done."

"Then what?" Alexis asked.

"Then you live here in exile until you die," Melinda said as she twirled her finger in the air. "Yay."

Alexis smiled at his aunt and stood back up.

"Lead the way, gatekeeper," Alexis said. "I am ready to give my crown away."

*

The room was silent as Melinda finished reading the proclamation of the deposition of Alexis the Second, Master of Station Aelon and Aelon Prime.

Alexis looked about at the expectant faces and gulped, knowing they were waiting for him to speak. Melinda wasn't the only gatekeeper present and Alexis averted his eyes from the judging gazes of the holy men and women. The Burdened were present, as were the Aelish royal guards. Servants were spaced about the walls, and the only person there that Alexis could consider on his side of things was Herlen, but he sat in a chair with his shoulders hunched and head in his hands, as he refused to meet Alexis's eye.

"Alexis?" Melinda prodded. "Now is when you do your part."

"Right, yes, of course," Alexis said as he stood up from his chair and cleared his throat. "With sound mind and of my own choosing, I accept the terms of the deposition and give up my title as Master of Station Aelon. From this moment forward, may it be known that my daughter, Alexis the Third, will be master, uh, I mean, Mistress of Station Aelon and Aelon Prime. I do this willingly, and wish her nothing but the greatest of luck as she has a long road ahead of her."

"Well, said," Melinda nodded, then turned her attention to Herlen and frowned. "And now we can move on to the next order of business."

She looked at the Burdened and they swooped down upon the old Spiggot and yanked him to his feet.

"Hey, now!" Alexis shouted as he rushed forward, but was shoved back quickly by two of the Burdened. "What are you doing with him?"

"It was another term of the deposition," Herlen said weakly. "Once you gave up your crown, I was to be executed for my crimes against the crown and station. Normally, due to my age, I would be imprisoned in the third spire until I died, but since my son has already been killed by the mob in Middle Deck Twenty, they needed my death to be the symbol of justice."

"The symbol of justice? What justice? Who ordered this?" Alexis demanded.

"Regent Beumont," Melinda said. "This is non-negotiable, Alexis. Not that you can negotiate anything ever again, but so you know that any protest you make will only harm your future, not save this man's life."

"Do not jeopardize yourself for me, Alexis," Herlen said then chuckled. "Alexis. I can call you that without worry now. You are a man like me and nothing more. And therein will you find your fate, because men like you and me don't get glorious ends. We get nothing but tragedy."

The Burdened escorted Herlen from the room and Alexis looked at his aunt.

"What is the method?" Alexis asked. "How are they going to kill him? Please tell me there's at least some mercy in his end. Can you tell me that, gatekeeper?"

"I cannot," Melinda replied. "The order was for the man to suffer as so many suffered under him and his son." Melinda swallowed and looked away from her nephew. "He is to be stripped naked and shoved outside the house. The Vape will cause his skin to burn and peel and his insides will boil then burst from his orifices. The man will suffer for several minutes and die in the worst agony possible."

"No, no, no," Alexis said as she shook his head back and forth. "He was good to me. He was always kind to me."

"He tried to have your daughter killed, Alexis," Melinda said. "While his son gave the actual order, he was party to the plot. He does not deserve your pity."

"He what...?" Alexis asked and stumbled back to his chair. His ass fell into the cushion hard and the sound of a spring breaking echoed through the room. "I am sure that is a lie. There is no way that either of the Spiggots would dare to have Alexis harmed. They knew how I loved her."

"If Alexis died, then who was in line to succeed you?" Melinda asked.

"No," Alexis replied, his head still shaking.

"Answer my question," Melinda ordered. "Part of your new life is to face truths you refused to see before. So tell me, who was in line to succeed you."

"No," Alexis continued. "No. No. No."

"Dammit, boy, tell me!" Melinda shouted.

"Deran Spiggot!" Alexis shouted back. "I had made it so he would succeed me!"

"And how long do you think they would have let you live once your daughter was out of the way?" Melinda asked. "There would have been a period of mourning for the loss of a minoress, then you would have had some tragic accident. The Spiggots would have ruled Station Aelon within maybe six months of Alexis being killed."

"They..." was all he could say.

"Yes," Melinda nodded. "*They.*"

Then the screams began.

Even through the airlocks and muted by the winds outside, everyone across the house could hear as Herlen Spiggot met his fate.

Alexis closed his eyes tight and wanted to cover his ears, but he knew he needed to hear the man's agony. Despite his aunt's accusations, Alexis believed he owed the man his life and so much more. If just for the memory of what he shared with Deran, he owed the man the dignity of listening to his last, dying sounds.

The screams went on and on, and even the hardened men of the Burdened marveled at how long the man lasted outside in the poisonous atmosphere. Men half his age would have already collapsed and given up to the Vape, letting it cook them from the inside out. But Hereln Spiggot fought and fought until, at last, his vocal cords disintegrated and his screams were cut short.

Later, when Alexis finally had the courage to ask, he was told that Herlen lived another five minutes before dying, his body twisting in on itself as his flesh and tissues softened and became nothing but soup.

*

"So this is it?" Alexis said once all the other gatekeepers had departed, taking the Burdened with them, and the servants had been sent away for the night. "This is what a deposed master does with his life? Sits here and drink liquor with his old aunt?"

"Who are you calling old?" Melinda smiled over her fifth glass of honey wasp liquor. "I will have you know I'm still one of the most sought after gatekeepers during the Taking. Not that this body can carry a child any longer. No, that cutter has sailed, my friend. But the young ones learn a thing or two from me, that's for sure."

"I can tell you what I don't want to do for the rest of my exile," Alexis said.

"Hmmm? And what's that?"

"I don't want to hear you talk about being part of the Taking ever again," Alexis said as he drained his own glass and reached for the decanter. He looked at his aunt and shook it and she nodded, so he filled her glass first before filling his own and settling back into his seat. "I think you forget that when I last saw you it was naked in a pile of gatekeeper bodies. That was an image that I struggled to scrub from my brain for years."

"Don't knock it until you have tried it, my boy," Melinda said as she raised her glass high. "Looking forward to the Taking is what gets me through life most days. Being a gatekeeper was not my first choice, you know."

"No, I suppose it was not," Alexis nodded.

He sighed and looked about the room, a room he knew so very well.

"Strange to be home," he said.

"Home? Well, I suppose it is, isn't it," Melinda replied. "You were so happy here. A shame you couldn't have ruled from the Prime. Maybe things would have been different."

"But this is where I met Gannot," Alexis admitted. "And he may not have been the best influence on me."

"Ha! Now that is something I never expected to come out of your mouth," Melinda said.

"I have matured in just the last few hours," Alexis shrugged.

"Or the weight of an entire station has been lifted from your shoulders and you are free to take the blinders off that you've kept so tight over your eyes," Melinda responded.

"Ugh, now you sound like a gatekeeper," Alexis laughed. "I almost prefer my crude aunt. Where did she go?"

"She's right here, just a little buried under years of piety and drinking honey wasp liquor and gelberry wine."

"At least you can drink," Alexis said.

"And I'll drink to that," Melinda replied as she raised her glass once more. Liquor sloshed up over the edge and she sighed. "Oh, dear, I suppose that means it is time to retire."

"Hold on," Alexis said. "Speaking of retirement, have you ever heard from Corbin?"

"That old coot? I'm sorry, Alexis, but he passed away years ago," Melinda said as she set her glass down and struggled to stand up. Alexis got to his own unsteady feet and helped her from her seat. "Thank you."

"How did he die? Do you know?" Alexis asked.

"Neglect," Melinda frowned. "When they found him he was only a bag of bones lying in his wheelchair. He had been dead a long time. Looked like he ran out of food or something."

"But he was supposed to be taken care of for life," Alexis said. "That was in my father's will."

"There are a lot of things written down that do not end up happening, Alexis," Melinda said. "Trust me, I have firsthand experience with that. Oh, speaking of…" She reached into her pocket and brought out a small envelope. "This is for you."

Alexis recognized the handwriting instantly and he had to sit down quickly before the strength in his legs gave out.

"I'll leave you to that," Melinda said as she stumbled her way across the room towards her quarters. "Tomorrow we'll have breakfast together then I must return to The Way. I don't know how they have managed without me this long."

Alexis waited for his aunt to leave before he tore open the envelope and withdrew the letter inside. His eyes filled with tears as he gazed upon the carefully printed script that covered the page.

A sob caught in his throat as he read out loud, wanting to give his daughter's words life.

*

"Dear Papa,

First, let me say how much I love you. When you read this letter, and if any part of it makes you angry or sad, please return to the first line so you know where my heart always lies. You are my everything, and I can't express how hard it is to write this. Mother said I shouldn't, that it would just be torture, but I couldn't let you think I wanted this to happen.

I didn't.

I'm thirteen, Papa, I'm not ready.

Mother and Beumont say I was born ready, that I am the leader Station Aelon needs.

I just nod. What can I say? That Station Aelon has a leader in you? No. I can't say that. Because no one thinks you are a leader.

Except me, Papa. You have shown me everything that is important in life.

When I am with you, I know I am safe. That is important.

When we are on the Prime, you teach me how to farm and how to race skids faster than anyone else. That is important.

You showed me that my grip was awkward on my blade, but you didn't correct me; you let me find out how to fix it myself and now my grip is better than yours! Oh, and while I was gone I started using two blades, Papa! Two! One of the guards said my left hand is scarier than my right!

I miss you.

I miss you so much, Papa, that sometimes, when I know Mother and Beumont can't hear me, I get under my covers and talk to you. I know I'm not talking to you, but it feels like I am. I tell you of my day and what adventures I had (even if I didn't have any) then I say prayers with you and I go to sleep. It's easier to sleep knowing we've talked. Even if we haven't talked.

But that doesn't matter, does it? That we don't really talk? I don't think it matters because you are in my heart and I know, with my whole soul, that I am in yours. We are Teirmonts, Papa. Connected through blood and destiny. When I see myself in the mirror, I see generations of masters that came before me and I feel so proud to be a part of it.

Then I realize I am the first mistress, and I get scared.

I'm so scared, Papa.

You won't be here to keep me safe, or to race skids, or to talk about the siggy worm blight. You won't be here to attend my coronation or give me advice when the meeting of stewards wants me to sign something I don't want to sign. Which they will, Papa. Mother has already said we are to follow the easy path for now, and do as the meeting wishes until I come into my full power and no longer need a regent.

And did you know that the regent will be Beumont? Not Mother. I heard them yelling this morning before I wrote this. Mother feels betrayed.

She doesn't know what betrayal is.

Betrayal is when you find out you are only loved for your title. Betrayal is realizing you are a pawn in other people's games. Betrayal is knowing that your own father is being exiled so you can sit with a crown that others want to control.

Betrayal is Mother and I will never forgive her for it.

But, at least I know you are safe. That was one thing I would not let them sway me from—your safety. Beumont insists that two monarchs alive at once is dangerous for the crown and for the Station. He says that if you decide you no longer want to be in exile, that you could contest the deposition. He is afraid of you, Papa.

Mother wants you dead because of her guilt. She knows that she has been a bad wife. She has not loved you and accepted you like she should have. I'm not stupid, though, and I know of the problems you two have. She loves another man and you, well, don't love women. Or can't? I don't know. I always wanted to talk to you about it, but I was afraid. If I am ever allowed to leave the Station again and go down to the Prime then we will talk about it.

That is important. For me to know who you are inside. I don't care what the meeting of stewards say, or what the passengers say, or even what Mother and Beumont say, what is inside you is worth knowing.

Because you are my Papa and always will be. They can take your crown and give it to me. They can take the Station and control it for their own greed.

They can take the Prime from me while they keep you down there in exile. They can take my freedom by not allowing me the full powers of my title.

They can do all of that, take all of that, but they can never take my Papa away.

In my heart and soul is where you live. In my heart and soul.

Not on the Prime, but in my heart and soul.

My heart and soul.

When that day comes, the day I don't want to ever hear about or have spoken to me, you will live on in my heart and soul.

They think they have taken you from me, but they haven't. They have given you to me forever.

I love you so much, Papa. I don't really know what kind of master you were, but I know what kind of father you were. A loving, caring, joyful father. You were everything a daughter could hope for.

I love you, I love you, I love you.

Please remember that. Take that with you to eternity.

I love you.

Your forever daughter and keeper of your love,

Alexis the Third, First Mistress of Station Aelon and Aelon Prime, and girl who loves her Papa more than anything"

*

The letter crumpled in Alexis's grip as his grief overwhelmed him and he brought his legs up into the chair and against his chest. His tears barely flowed since he had shed most of them while reading the letter, making it damp and heavy with salty water, but his sobs and cries were loud and full-throated.

The man did not care when guards came to check on him. He did not care when his aunt was brought from her room to try to comfort him. He did not care when they all helped him to his feet and walked him to his quarters. He did not care when a physician was called, because he could not stop shaking.

He did care when they tried to pry the letter from his fingers.

Alexis fought hard. He punched and kicked. He bit and clawed. It took a half dozen guards to hold him down so the physician could sedate him. But even then, he refused to let go of the letter. As his mind drifted into artificial sleep, he vowed he would never let the letter go. It would always be with him.

Just like the love of his daughter. Just like her heart and soul.

Chapter Nine

Plink, plink, plink.

The vase was filled with small, smooth pieces of decorative glass. The color of the glass ranged from bright blue to smoky grey. They were the colors of the planet Helios.

One by one, Alexis plucked pieces of glass from the vase and flung them at the pile of gelberry wine bottles stacked just inside the door to his bedchambers. He tried to count the huge pile once, but he kept getting distracted and could never finish. So he flung glass at the bottles instead.

To Alexis, it was the most productive thing to be done.

Months and months had gone by and no one came to the prime estate to visit him. When his aunt left, she had told him to expect dignitaries from The Way and other stations. They would come and make small talk, but in the end, they'd want something from him. She could not say what, but she was very sure they would never leave him in peace.

The thought had paralyzed him with fear and he had holed up in his bedchambers since.

Not that it mattered; no one came.

No gatekeepers or messengers from the High Guardian. No dignitaries or envoys from other stations or their primes. No visitors from Station Aelon that came to the Prime to check on breen production methods or the lease holdings. Not even the foremen from the breen fields, who had to know that he was a fount of information when it came to agriculture and cultivation techniques.

Of all of those, the last snub hurt the most.

The thought of retiring on the Prime and being the breen farmer he had always wanted to be was the only spark that had kept him from taking his life. Yet, as the months progressed and he lay in solitude except for the servants that brought him his meager meals and his essential wine, Alexis began to wonder if he hadn't been forgotten.

There were no communications, no letters, nothing. It was as if he had been tucked away in a dark hole in the System, left to rot in his own stench and drunkenness.

Plink, plink, plink.

He threw the pieces of glass until the vase was empty and he was left with nothing else to do. He needed to piss, but barely felt like getting up. In his master days, he could have pissed in his bed and a dozen servants would have taken care of it for him.

But on the Prime, he was yelled at for such behavior.

Although, they did call him "my lord," which he enjoyed. It took everyone on the estate a while to figure out how he should be addressed, since he was no longer master and had been stripped of all titles. Even the token "Steward of Quent" was removed from him.

He sat there for a few minutes before he found the resolve to get out of bed and stumble his way to the bathroom. The floor around the toilet was worse off after his visit, but at least the bedsheets didn't get soiled.

The mirror in the bathroom was less than clean and he grabbed a hand towel that was even dirtier than the mirror to give it a perfunctory wipe. The grime smeared enough that he could see his haggard face. It was not a pleasant sight.

"Look at you," Alexis said to himself. "Pitiful, pitiful you."

He half expected the semi-familiar face to reply back, but it didn't. Which, for the sake of his sanity, was probably a good thing.

"What will you do?"

He titled his head one way and then the other.

His hair had thinned and his cheeks were sunken and drawn. The beard on his face was long, scraggly, and peppered with patches of white. His nose was red and webbed with spider veins. He didn't even want to see what his tongue looked like, since the feel of it alone made him shiver.

"You are a mess, my lord. An ugly, scary mess," he told himself. "Perhaps we should do something about that."

Alexis turned around and looked at his shower. He wasn't surprised to see it mostly full of wine bottles.

After a couple of minutes clearing the debris, he stripped off his sweat stained clothes and switched on the faucets, his eyes watching and waiting for the tendrils of steam to begin swirling up to the ceiling. Once the water was hot, he stepped in and nearly screamed as the boiling water seared his skin.

But he tolerated the pain and set about scrubbing himself down until his skin was pink and closer to healthy looking than it was before. It didn't take long to find clean clothes once he was done showering and dried off. He had a closet full of tunics and trousers he hadn't bothered to change into.

Freshly clean and dressed, Alexis held his hand on the doorknob of his bedchambers and stood there. With one turn, he would be able to step back into a world he hadn't seen in so long. He glanced about at the four walls of his bedchamber and sighed. It was hard to believe he hadn't set foot outside the room since the night he had arrived.

"My lord!" a servant girl cried out when she found him walking towards her in the hallway. "Are you hurt? Do you need--" She stopped and looked at his hair and clothes. "Oh, you have showered and dressed. Uh...would you care for some dinner?"

"Dinner?" Alexis asked. "What time is it?"

"It is close to seven in the evening, my lord," the servant replied. "I can tell the kitchen that you are hungry, if you'd like. I am sure the cook would be more than happy to prepare whatever you desire."

Alexis smiled at the girl and thought about what would sound good to a stomach that had been basically on nothing but a liquid diet.

"Is there any pie?" he asked. "I would love a slice of pie and perhaps a glass of juice."

"I am certain there is pie, my lord," the servant replied. "Any specific type?"

"No, just pie," Alexis said. "And have it brought to the east library, will you? I want to look outside, and maybe read a book while I eat."

"Yes, my lord." The servant nodded and hurried off.

Alexis, of course, knew the estate house like the back of his hand. He wound his way through the hallways until he found the room he was looking for. It wasn't nearly as big as he had remembered it, but then he was only a child the last time he'd decided to visit the east library.

"Where are the books?" he asked out loud when he saw the empty shelves. "Not a single one left?"

He walked the length of the room to the set of wide windows that were obscured by thick breen drapes. The lack of reading material did not especially bother him since he had chosen the room for the view it afforded out onto the estate. All other rooms had their views blocked by various estate structures, but the east library's view was unobstructed.

He stared out at the evening landscape and wished he had roused himself a couple of hours earlier so he had more light to admire the estate lands.

"My lord?" a different servant girl asked as she carried a tray into the library. "I was told to bring you this. I am sorry, but we are out of juice. The chef prepared a pot of tea for you, though. I hope that is acceptable."

"Quite," Alexis replied. "Tea is better than juice with pie, anyway. I do not know why I asked for juice. Probably because that is what I drank with dessert when I lived here as a child."

The servant girl stood there in the middle of the room with the tray in her hands and waited. Alexis raised his eyebrows then smiled.

"Forgive me," he said. "Set it on that side table there. I'll get to it shortly."

"Yes, my lord," she said and hurriedly set it down. "Is there anything else I can get you, my lord?"

"No, that will be all," Alexis replied. "Thank you."

The servant turned and walked briskly towards the door.

"Hold up, please," Alexis said.

"My lord?"

"The books. Where are they?"

"Oh...well, I was told they were removed for safekeeping."

"Safekeeping?" Alexis frowned. "Safekeeping from what?"

"I cannot say, my lord. That is all I was told."

"Are all the books gone from the other two libraries as well?" Alexis asked as a slice of fear crept into his belly. "Or were the books from here moved to those rooms?"

"I...I do not know, my lord," the servant responded and Alexis could see her hands shaking.

"Who told you they were removed for safekeeping?" Alexis asked.

"Helbley, my lord. The lead guard. He told all the servants a couple of weeks ago that anything of value would need to be removed for saf—"

"Safekeeping, yes you said that," Alexis nodded. 'Thank you for your help. You may go."

The girl rushed from the library, leaving Alexis alone with empty shelves and a slice of pie. And tea.

He walked to the tray and poured a cup then realized he hadn't been given any sweetener or shaow milk. He preferred his tea with milk and sweetener.

Alexis thought about calling for the servant girl, but decided that a visit to the kitchen was a better idea. When he made it across the house and into the sparse kitchen, Alexis was surprised by the lack of smells that usually emanated from the room. He had always loved coming into the kitchen as a boy and smelling the roasting meat and the bread that was in the oven.

But the kitchen he walked into looked as if it hadn't been properly used in some time. Most of the counters had a coating of dust on them and the massive stove that could be used to feed a garrison of soldiers only showed two burners that looked like they'd been used recently.

"Hello?" Alexis called out, but his voice only echoed off the metal cabinets and equipment. There was no response even after a second call.

Alexis tried not to worry, tried not to let that sliver of fear in his belly grow. He walked to the pantry and found a large bag of sweetener. It took him a minute to hunt down a small dish, and a few more minutes to clean up the spilled granules after he tried to pour the sweetener directly from the bag into the dish. The shaow milk was easy since he just grabbed a glass bottle from the large walk-in cooler and tucked it under his arm.

Then he stopped.

The walk-in cooler was barely stocked. There were a line of milk bottles, some butter, a few vegetables and perhaps a couple of pounds of meat. But that was it.

"Must be late with the supply cutter," Alexis said, knowing how Vape storms and unfriendly seas disrupted life on the Prime at the drop of a hat. "There will be more soon."

But that sliver of fear would not be still.

Alexis shook his head and hurried from the vacant kitchen. He worked his way through the house until he was back at the library. Setting the milk and sweetener down on the tray, Alexis turned and regarded the empty shelves once more. He walked to a set of them and ran his finger along the surface, sure he would find a thick coating of dust.

Yet there was barely any dust, which told him that the books had been removed recently. But why? The servant girl's explanation didn't make sense unless someone expected the estate to be damaged soon. Perhaps a Vape storm was coming? One that was expected to hit the estate in the near future?

Alexis forgot about the tea, and the sweetener and milk he had fetched, and hurried out of the library to find someone that knew what was going on. His feet led him to the guards' barracks and he pushed the door open without bothering to knock.

It was empty.

The long rows of cots on each side of the barracks had been stripped of sheets and the mattresses were rolled and bound, left at the end of the cots to wait for the next occupant to free them.

"Helios," Alexis growled, his fear turning to anger. "Where is everyone?"

He walked the length of the barracks to a single door at the far end. This time he did knock, as he heard voices coming from the other side.

"Yeah?" someone called out. "What?"

"It is Alexis Teirmont," Alexis announced. "Open up at once."

There was the sound of shifting furniture and the scraping of chair legs on the floor. Then nothing. Alexis listened and knocked once more.

"Hello? Open up, please!" he shouted.

Still nothing.

Alexis tried the knob, but it was locked, so he turned to the room for a solution. In the corner to his left was a large push broom with stiff breen bristles and, luckily, a metal handle, not the polybreen he had expected it to have.

"That will do," he said as he took the broom, flipped it about, and slammed the handle end down on the doorknob, again and again, until it broke free.

Alexis shoved the door open with the broom head and then cautiously peered inside.

Empty.

Whoever had called out to him had fled the room quickly. But why?

And that was the question of the evening: why?

Why was any of it all happening?

He saw another door across the room and hurried to it, hoping maybe he would catch someone on the other side of that. But all he found was an empty back hallway.

"Hello?" he yelled and, as he expected, there was no reply.

Alexis, his Teirmont anger starting to get the best of him, stomped down the hallway until he came to another door. He flung that one open and found himself in the small guardroom that was by the main entry hall to the estate house. Still no one there.

"Hello?" Alexis yelled as he walked from the room and into the main entry hall. "*Hello*?"

The first servant girl he had encountered came running towards him after a couple of minutes.

"My lord? Do you need something? Is everything alright?" she asked.

"No, everything is damn well not alright!" Alexis barked. "Where in the Helios is the rest of the staff, and why did the guards flee from me when I went to speak with them?"

"Well, my lord, the rest of the staff has retired for the evening," the servant girl said. "It is only myself and Verlot that are up to assist you."

"Shaowshit!" Alexis snapped as he closed on the girl and grabbed her by the arm. "Let me show you something!"

He dragged her along through the house until they reached the kitchen.

"Do you see what I see?" he asked, finally letting go of her arm. "Do you?"

"I see a kitchen, my lord," the girl replied.

"As do I," Alexis sneered. "A kitchen that is poorly stocked and hasn't been used to feed more than a couple of people in some time. Now, are you honestly going to tell me that the staff has retired for the night? Or are you willing to admit to a former master that you and that other servant girl..."

"Verlot."

"Verlot, yes, her," Alexis nodded. "Will you please be honest and admit to me that you two are all that is left of the staff. Except for the coward guards that refused to face me."

The girl stood there and Alexis saw mortal fear on her face.

"Tell me your name," he said, his voice calming down. "I am sorry for yelling and being upset. Tell me your name, girl."

"Kamda, my lord," the girl whispered.

"Kamda, I am not going to hurt you and I will not let anyone hurt you if you tell me the truth," Alexis soothed. "You have my word on that. I just need to know what is really going on around here."

"I...I do not know, my lord," Kamda replied. "That is the honest truth. Velot and I were brought down from the Station only a few days ago. This is how the house was when we arrived. We were told to serve you when you called and if you asked any questions we were not to give any details other than what the instructions stated."

"Instructions?" Alexis asked. "What instructions?"

Kamda blanched at the question as she realized she had said too much.

"Never mind," Alexis said. "I doubt the instructions will provide any more answers than you can give. But answer me this, Kamda, what were you told would happen to you if you did not do exactly as you were instructed? Did they threaten your family back on the Station?"

"I have no family, my lord," Kamda replied. "I was orphaned young. I had been working a food cart in the Lower Decks when men came to see me. They said I could be moved up in the Station if I agreed to work here on the Prime first. It was an opportunity lowdeckers rarely see so I said yes. When I got here I met Velot and the two guards."

"Two guards? That is all that is left?" Alexis asked. "Where are they now?"

"I don't know," Kamda said. "We aren't allowed to be around them. Part of the instructions were that we had no contact with the guards after our introductions and that we only focus on you, my lord. I hope I have done a good enough job that you will recommend me for service on the Station."

"You'll never see the Station," Alexis said.

Kamda blanched and took several steps away from the former master.

"No, no, I do not mean you won't see the Station because I am going to harm you," Alexis sighed. "I mean it because the people that brought you here have no desire to let you leave. That is why they went to the Lower Decks to find orphan girls."

"But they promised, my lord," Kamda said. "They had me sign a contract."

"Did you read the contract?" Alexis asked.

Kamda hesitated. "No, my lord."

"Can you read, Kamda dear?"

"No, my lord."

"Then you have no idea what you signed," Alexis said and sighed again. "And probably better that you don't." He rubbed his face with his hands and turned from the girl. "I am going back to my quarters. Please wake me in the morning as soon as it is light. I plan on seeing the land again before..."

He didn't bother to finish his sentence as he walked out of the kitchen, leaving Kamda alone to stand there, her hands wringing the short apron she wore as part of her uniform.

*

The scrim grass barely touched the skid as Alexis pushed it full throttle across the plains. He avoided the breen fields since he did not want any of the workers to know he was outside the estate, which meant he had to add several hours onto his trip, but it was worth it for the safety of anonymity.

The sky above him was unusually bright and Alexis worried that he wouldn't make it to his destination before the impending Vape storm hit. Being out in the open in a storm that looked to be a bad one would not have been a good idea for a man who was only protected by an old environmental suit.

He came quickly to the edge of a small cliff and swung the skid about so he could look down on the valley below. There, in the center, stood the cabin. He had never been there, but he had made sure he knew its exact location when it was first mentioned to him so many, many years before.

Alexis ignored all the safety rules of skid driving and aimed the vehicle for the edge of the cliff. He gunned it and took a deep breath as he plummeted over the side. It took all of his strength and experience to pull up on the handlebars at the right moment so the skid didn't crash nose first into the approaching ground. Alexis felt the tail end bump on a pile of rocks, but other than that, it was if he was a teenager again tempting Helios.

He stopped several feet from the old cabin and stared at it, amazed that it hadn't been destroyed by the elements. He didn't have to wonder if the small structure still had its seal intact as he could see holes in the roof and one of the windows lying on the ground, having fallen out of its sill.

Alexis sighed, powered down the skid, and stepped onto the land, his boots sinking into the mucky ground. He had to step carefully to keep from getting stuck and he cursed at the sucking mud that tried to hold him in place. It was if the Prime didn't want him going forward; as if it was warning him that the cabin held nothing for him and he should just get back onto his skid and leave.

Yet one glance up at the sky told him he would never make it back to the estate before the Vape storm hit.

After a frustrating struggle, Alexis finally reached the door and gave it a hard push. The whole door, including the frame collapsed inward and Alexis shook his head as he looked at the sorry state of the cabin and then back up at the foreboding sky. Since the door was collapsed anyway, creating a rather wide opening, Alexis decided it was worth the effort to slog back to the skid and drive it right inside the cabin. He couldn't afford having his only way home damaged.

Once inside, he stepped from the skid, struggled to lift the door and frame back in place then moved the skid in front of it to keep it upright and secure against the winds that had already started to pick up. Once he felt sure the skid would keep the door in place, and weather out, Alexis turned to look at the cabin he had travelled to.

"This is where you went to retire?" Alexis asked. "This one room shack with an open bathroom in the corner?"

He looked at the cracked toilet in disgust. Besides that, there was a small sink, a stove that looked like it was built for camping, not for living, and a rotted cot. No chairs, no table, no shelves of any kind. Alexis knew the man wanted to be left alone, but he didn't think he wanted to live the rest of his life like a vagrant.

Then he saw the buckled floorboard by the edge of the cot.

Alexis walked over, shoved the cot out of the way, and pulled at the floorboard until it gave way. Underneath was a small keypad and Alexis racked his brain for an idea as to what the code would be. He worked through what he knew of the man and then cautiously reached down and pressed the star symbol six times.

There was an audible click and the floor beneath him started to slide away. Alexis scrambled to the edge of the cabin as he watched a hatch open and a ladder appear.

"How in Helios's name did he get down there in a wheelchair?" Alexis wondered.

A rumble overhead got his attention and he moved to the hatch, placed a foot on the ladder to test its soundness then descended into the darkness below. Once down at the bottom, he switched on his helmet lights and looked about the small space. The hatch closed above him, but he had expected it to and didn't give it a second thought as he studied the bunker he found himself in.

Another cot, but also a chair and a table, filled the space. Metal cabinets lined the walls and Alexis opened them one by one to find ample supplies of food packets, water bottles, and various other sundries. Vape canisters of different sizes filled one cabinet, while weapons filled another. The bunker was more what Alexis had expected to see when he had first entered the cabin above.

"Take the man from the Royal Guard, but never take the Royal Guard from the man," Alexis said. "Still, I don't know how you lived this way, Corbin."

A muffled rumble and then several loud bangs told Alexis that the Vape storm he had predicted had arrived. He hunted about the space for a light switch, but didn't find one and settled on using a Vape lantern from one of the cabinets. He lit the lantern and set it on his table.

A small beep from the wristband on his suit got his attention and he panicked for a minute when he realized how low the suit's oxygen levels were. The air scrubbers should have been sufficient to keep him safe, but the suit was old and he had no idea how long it had been since it was last serviced.

He thought of going back up top and trying to race the storm with the skid, but then he realized he'd found his answer already in one of the cabinets. He went to it and pulled out the five tanks of oxygen it housed. Three were empty, but two were completely full and he sighed with relief as he sat down on the cot and connected the first tank to his suit.

"You think I'd let you die down here, you silly flip of a boy?" Corbin said from the chair, his arms folded in front of him on the table. "You think I'd be so careless as that? I didn't spend my final years on the Prime training your sorry ass to let you suffocate and die in this hole."

Alexis's mouth went dry and he struggled to swallow as he looked at the man who sat there before him.

"You're not real," he said finally. "You are long dead."

"Yes, that is true," Corbin replied as he looked at his body. "But, yet, here I am. It's a fucking miracle."

"What are you then?" Alexis asked. "How am I seeing you?"

Corbin tapped his temple then pointed at the former master.

"Boy, I have always been in your head," Corbin replied. "Moreso than your father's voice ever was."

"So I'm hallucinating?"

"I don't give a shaowshit what you're doing," Corbin shrugged. "This is your problem, not mine."

The familiar obstinacy made Alexis smile and he relaxed into the cot, even as the cabin above rattled and shook from the Vape storm.

"It's going to be a bad one," Corbin said. "Good thing you found your way down here."

"Yes, it is," Alexis agreed.

"You scared, boy?"

"Do I look scared, old man?"

"No, surprisingly, you don't," Corbin nodded. "You look more at home than you have in months."

"How would you know?"

Corbin tapped his temple again.

"Don't be stupid, boy. I'm you and you know it."

"Stop calling me boy," Alexis insisted.

"I will when you stop seeing yourself that way," Corbin replied.

"Is that how I see myself?"

"Isn't it?"

"No riddles, asshole," Alexis grinned. "Tell it to me straight since you are me anyway. I don't need to spar with my own mind."

"Yet you spent decades neglecting it," Corbin shrugged. "And now you want it to behave? Silly flip."

"Don't call me that either," Alexis snapped. "I am not a flip!"

"Sweet Helios, Alexis, you have such a capacity for denial that I wonder if you ever experienced reality once in your life."

"I did down here," Alexis replied. "On the Prime. This land was the only reality I ever knew."

"That's far from the truth," Corbin countered. "The only reality you have ever known is written in that letter you keep in your pocket." Corbin spread his arms wide. "This is shaowshit. Always has been and always will be." He tapped his temple for a third time. "And we know we can't trust what's up here. That leaves that letter and the words from a scared and heartbroken girl."

"She'll be fine," Alexis said.

"That I can't argue with," Corbin nodded. "Of all the Teirmonts I've known, she is the only one that will ever be fine."

"What does that mean? My father was just fine as well."

Corbin laughed heartily and slapped his hands on the table.

"Your father? Your father had a rage in him that was far from fine. He also had an ego that kept him from enjoying his last days of life. The man left you a legacy of conflict and strife. No to mention that he never dealt with Stolt, leaving that mess for you to clean up as well."

Corbin crossed his arms and leaned back in his chair. The storm raged above and he briefly glanced at the hatch. Alexis followed his gaze and frowned.

"Don't worry," Corbin said. "It will hold. You know I wouldn't have built this place any other way."

"I know," Alexis nodded. "It's just been a long while since I was in a Vape storm."

"Let me break it down for you," Corbin smiled. "There will be a massive amount of thunder, some very scary, and potentially dangerous lightning, and then a poisonous rain that would eat through your flesh in a heartbeat if you were exposed to it. But you aren't. You are safely tucked away down here. And having a nice chat with an old friend."

"A nice chat with an old friend?" Alexis laughed. "Now I know you are part of my brain. Corbin would never say anything like that."

"But he would call you a flip," Corbin responded. "And you'd be pissed at that. Why?"

"Because I'm not," Alexis protested.

"But you are," Corbin countered. "Maybe your objection is to the derogatory nature of the word and not the actual definition."

Alexis didn't reply.

"Brother Gannot is proof enough," Corbin continued. "Have you ever stopped loving that man?"

"No," Alexis said quietly.

"Even when you were with Brother Spiggot?"

"Even then," Alexis admitted. "Nothing could replace my Gannot."

"No, nothing can," Corbin nodded. "So just finally admit to yourself who you are."

"I cannot do that," Alexis said as he shook his head. "A master cannot be that kind of person."

"But you are no longer a master now, are you?" Corbin grinned. "Take these final moments and be honest with yourself, Alexis. Don't die in denial. That is no way for a master to go."

"You just said I was no longer a master," Alexis replied.

"And you said you were," Corbin said. "Which version of yourself do you want to be?"

"The one that lives," Alexis said.

"That is not in the cards, I'm afraid," Corbin stated. "We both know that."

"No, we..." Alexis began then stopped, knowing he was only lying to himself, figuratively and literally. "Yes, you are right. I won't be living much longer, will I?"

"My guess?" Corbin said as the sounds of something crashing above caused him to look up once again. "They'll kill you as soon as you get back to the estate house. Or soon after. Depends on his time frame."

"Beumont," Alexis said.

"Beumont," Corbin agreed.

"You think he will come all the way down to the Prime to do it himself?"

"I think he has been planning it for some time. You looked at the rotational schedule before you left. Station Aelon has the window. Odds are he was on a shuttle and coming your way before your skid hit the scrim grass."

"He can't just kill me," Alexis said. "That would go against the orders of my daughter. There was an agreement in place that was ordained by the High Guardian."

"Accidents happen," Corbin shrugged. "Especially during a Vape storm. A chance bit of lightning coupled with an understaffed estate is a recipe for trouble."

"And all the books and valuables have already been removed," Alexis nodded. "You think they'll kill me and burn the estate down?"

"It's how I would do it. And I'm speaking as Corbin, not as you. The only way for you to die is to make it look like it truly was an accident.

Two guards and two servants will perish as well, perhaps more depending on Beumont's mood, so there are no witnesses. But those servants are orphans with no family to wonder at their deaths. And guards die all the time. That is their job."

"I could just not go back," Alexis suggested. "Stay here and wait them out."

"You could, but then you'd die like a coward and not a master. Up to you."

"Or I could try to contact my aunt and have her come to my aid."

Corbin laughed. "Melinda died only a couple of weeks after you arrived here. Heart attack. They told you, but you forgot all about it once you hit your fourteenth or fifteenth bottle of wine."

"Oh, right," Alexis sighed. "Thank you for reminding me. That truth had been nagging back there for some time."

"My pleasure."

Alexis leaned against the wall, his legs tucked up against him as he sat on the cot and stared at the image of his old tutor and protector. The two watched each other, knowing words weren't needed, but both still willing to play the game.

"I go back and it's suicide," Alexis said finally.

"But it would be on your terms, not his," Corbin smiled. "You'd know it was coming. You can walk into that house with your head held high and a smirk on your face. Be the Alexis of old, who didn't have a care in the world. Sure, he was a moron, but he did know how to be happy."

"I don't know," Alexis said. "It is all too much for me right now."

"Then sleep on it, boy," Corbin smirked and Alexis wasn't quite sure if he was looking at the old man or at himself. "Curl up in that cot and rest while the storm blows over. Your death will still be there waiting for you in the morning. No need to decide right now."

Alexis yawned and nodded. He didn't have to say anything more to convince himself of what he needed to do. He stretched out on the cot and placed his hands behind his helmeted head.

"I hate sleeping in a suit," he muttered as he started to drift off.

Corbin didn't respond and Alexis lazily rolled his head in the direction of the table. The old man was gone, all that was there was an empty chair.

He sighed and closed his eyes.

*

It took some work, but Alexis was able to get the debris off his skid and start the vehicle up without too much trouble. He had to follow a winding path up out of the valley, which gave him more time to consider his fate.

By the time he had gotten to the plains, and raced his skid back to the estate house, he knew exactly what had to be done.

He barely let the vehicle come to a stop as he jumped off, his eyes catching sight of the large skid that hovered in place before him. Guards started to jump down from the skid as Alexis ran towards the airlock and hurried inside the house.

"Beumont!" Alexis yelled as he tore off his helmet and stormed through the airlock and into the main entrance hall. "I know you are here!"

"Alexis?" Beumont said as he came around a corner, still dressed in his environmental suit. "I was worried when I arrived and couldn't find you."

"You don't have to do this, Beumont," Alexis said as he stared at the man. "You can get back on that skid out there and leave me in peace. Don't even bother sending supplies anymore. Helios, you can take the servants with you. I'll make do. I grew up on the Prime, I know how to live down here."

"That's the problem, Alexis," Beumont frowned. "I can't let you live down here. As long as there are two living monarchs of Station Aelon, there will always be uncertainty as to your daughter's rule."

"And uncertainty as to your role as regent," Alexis smiled. "How is Bella handling that change? I'll bet there was a little bit of yelling and shouting when she found out. Does she still allow you into her bed?"

"Bella's bed has never concerned you before and shouldn't concern you now, Alexis," Beumont replied. "And she handled the news of my regency like a true royal—with dignity and grace."

Alexis shook his head. "I'm guessing you have zero plans on killing me with the same considerations, do you?"

"No, Alexis, I do not," Beumont said. "I plan on killing you with the consideration you showed my family when you had them butchered."

Alexis smiled then dashed for the small guardroom to the side. He reached just inside the door and pulled out a long blade he'd set there before his excursion out on the land.

"Well, if you plan on cutting me up, you'll have to work for it," Alexis grinned.

"I don't plan on cutting you up," Beumont said as he snapped his fingers. Guards came at Alexis from all directions, but he didn't put up a fight. "You were expecting all of this, weren't you? Who tipped you off?"

Alexis was held so firmly by the guards that he couldn't even shrug.

"An old friend gave me a heads up," Alexis smiled.

"You don't have any friends, Alexis, so just tell me who it was."

"It doesn't matter," Alexis said. "Just get on with it. Do I need to kneel so you have a better angle at my neck?"

"At your neck?" Beumont laughed. "No, Alexis, you will not receive such a dignified end. I have a better idea in store."

He snapped his fingers once more and the guards slammed Alexis to the ground and stripped him of his environmental suit. Alexis, his face and belly pressed to the floor, didn't struggle until Beumont crouched in front of him and wiggled a Vape canister before his eyes.

"Do you know what happens to the human body if Vape gets inside it?" Beumont smiled. "It combusts from the inside. Organs boil and blood burns. Such a horrible, horrible way to go."

"Just kill me, Beumont! Be a man and kill me! You don't need to torture me to death!"

"Torture? No, I have zero intention of torturing you," Beumont replied as he nodded to the guards that held Alexis's legs. They yanked down his trousers and undergarment, leaving his ass bare and exposed. "I am going to insert this nozzle into your anus and turn it all the way up. That's an execution, not torture. A very painful and grotesque execution, yes, but one you so willingly deserve."

Tears spilled from Alexis's eyes, but he did not respond. His time engaging the man was done.

"Nothing to say?" Beumont laughed. "There's a first."

He stood up and was lost from Alexis's sight. The former master braced himself, but was far from prepared for the pain as the Vape canister nozzle was jammed up inside him. He screamed once then clamped his mouth shut.

"No need to be stoic, Alexis," Beumont said. "Scream all you like. In fact, I would prefer it if you did."

There was a slight hiss and Alexis didn't even have time to brace himself for the pain. He writhed on the ground as he felt the burning inside build and build until he swore he was on fire. Which, in a chemical sense, he was, just internally and not externally.

Alexis Teirmont, former Master of Station Aelon, lasted all of three seconds before he began to wail and scream so loud that some of the guards let go of his flopping body to cover their ears.

Beumont stood over the dying man and then turned. He held out his hand and his helmet was handed to him.

"Once he is dead I want this entire house torched," Beumont said. "Arrange the bodies of the servants next to Alexis so it looks like they tried to escape the fire. There is to be no evidence that we were here."

"Yes, my lord," several of the guards said. They quickly stepped away from Alexis's body as smoke started pouring from the dying man's ears and nostrils.

Alexis's body stopped flopping and writhing, as muscle connections were burned away, but his screams continued. Beumont sighed at the sounds.

"Now I can rest easy at night," he said as he placed his helmet onto his suit and clasped the seal tight.

He opened the airlock and closed the door behind him, surprised that he could actually still hear Alexis's screams. The outer door opened and he motioned for the guards present to mount up on the large skid. Some gave him strange looks since it was the only vehicle they had brought and their comrades would be stranded when they left, but none argued.

"Are we to leave, my lord?" the pilot asked as Beumont stepped next to the man.

"We are," Beumont said. "Another skid will be along soon to handle the guards that are cleaning up. No need to wait."

The pilot didn't bother to ask what that meant as he turned the skid around and aimed it for the coast and the dock where the royal cutter waited. He certainly didn't bother to ask why there was a Burdened cutter tied to the dock when they arrived there.

"That isn't there," Beumont said to the pilot. "Do I need to explain further?"

"No, my lord," the pilot nodded. "It is not my place to question The Way's intentions."

"Good man," Beumont smiled as he jumped off the skid and walked the length of the dock to the cutter.

As the regent stepped onto the cutter, and into the protective dome, he was never happier to be able to strip off an environmental suit than he was at that moment. He left the suit piled on the floor for one of the servants to deal with as he walked over to an empty couch, sat down and waited for a drink to be handed to him.

"Will I be dining with the High Guardian tonight?" he asked, as an attendant moved from the side of the dome with a notebook in hand.

"Yes, my lord," the attendant replied. "He has confirmed and is looking forward to it. He also has sent his gratitude for the generous breen allotment that Station Aelon donated to The Way. He has arranged for some special entertainment while you two dine."

Beumont nodded as he sipped at his drink. "That sounds delightful," he replied. "But I doubt it will top the day's entertainment. In fact, I doubt anything ever again will top today's entertainment. Kind of makes me sad in a way."

"My lord?" the attendant asked, confused.

"Never mind," Beumont said, waving his free hand at the man. "Go do whatever it is you do and leave me to my thoughts. I don't want to be disturbed until we arrive at The Way Prime."

"Yes, my lord," the attendant said as he bowed and stepped away.

Beumont sipped at his drink again and looked out at the seas that were still upset by the Vape storm that had passed the night before. The man sneered at the view, glad that he never had to see them again. When he returned to Station Aelon, he planned to appoint someone to handle all aspects of Aelon Prime, freeing him to deal with his plans on the Station.

And, oh, how many plans he had.

About the Author

Jake is the author of the bestselling *Z-Burbia* series set in Asheville, NC, the *Apex Trilogy (DEAD MECH, The Americans, Metal and Ash*) and the *Mega* series for Severed Press, as well as the YA zombie novel, *Little Dead Man* and the Teen horror novel, *Intentional Haunting*, the *ScareScapes* series, and *the Reign of Four* series for Permuted Press.

Find Jake at jakebible.com. Join him on Twitter @jakebible and find him on Facebook.